Alpha Mine

by

Brenda Sparks

Alpha Mine

COPYRIGHT © 2013 by Brenda Sparks

Cover Art by *Rae Monet, Inc. Design*

The Wild Rose Press, Inc.
PO Box 708
Adams Basin, NY 14410-0708
Visit us at www.thewildrosepress.com

Publishing History
First Black Rose Edition, 2013
Print ISBN 978-1-62830-116-8
Digital ISBN 978-1-62830-117-5

Published in the United States of America

"So tell me, young one, is Kat short for something or did your parents just have a fascination with felines?"

"It's short for Katrina. But everyone calls me Kat."

She began to gather the playing cards from the table, but Stephan stilled her shaking hands by covering them with his own. Something akin to an electric current passed between them. Katrina gazed at Stephan, drinking him in, dangerous, magnificent, and so very beautiful.

"Where are my manners?" she asked, her voice quivering. "Would you like a drink?"

"You read my mind," he replied as he rose, pulling her toward him. "I am a little parched, actually."

Their eyes locked and Kat once again fell into his dark gaze. Her mind detached, as if she watched herself from above.

The feel of his mouth registered on her lips, while the smell of sandalwood engulfed her. His lips feathered kisses down her jaw, coming to a rest where her shoulder met her throat. She swooned. His arms closed around her like a set of steel bands, pulling her up against his firm body. Kat moaned when his tongue flicked out to taste her sensitive skin. He inhaled deeply against her neck causing goose bumps to pimple her flesh.

"Honeysuckle," he murmured, his lips brushing against her flesh. His fangs lengthened, scraping the skin where her pulse beat, sending her heart racing. He cupped her bottom in one hand and tightened his arm around her waist. Her body stiffened only a little as he pulled her tighter against him, lifting her off her feet.

Acknowledgments

First and foremost, I want to recognize the readers,
who mean so much to me!
My deep appreciation goes out to my good friends
and beta readers Barbara, Elizabeth, Susan, Naomi, and
Debra. Their insights and feedback have been
invaluable to me.
Love and appreciation goes out to my family,
who gave me the kind of support I needed
while writing this book.
And last but most certainly not least,
I owe my sincere gratitude to my fabulous editor,
Callie Lynn Wolfe, cover artist, Rae Monet,
and the wonderful staff at The Wild Rose Press, Inc.
for helping me share the Alphas with the world.

Chapter 1

Seven years earlier…

He stood stone still, wrapped in the darkness of the
shadows. His crossed arms rested on the black T-shirt
that stretched across his broad chest. Stunningly
handsome with his chiseled features and platinum hair
that shimmered down to his waist, he made most
women, and even some men, sway like the pitch of the
sea.

The music from the club pounded in his sensitive
ears. One day he would learn to control the noise, but
he was young, and had yet to hone that skill. No matter.
It was not the music that brought him here this night.
He came to this place for only one reason, to find a
beautiful, delicious woman.

His gaze slid over the humans gyrating on the
dance floor. They looked like fish flopping on the
shore, gasping for air, awaiting death to overtake them.
He smiled at the thought. They may not be gasping for
air, but at least one of them waited for death—she just
didn't know it yet. His eyes slid over the horde, coming
to rest on a buxom blonde. At least five-foot-ten by his
estimate, she stood taller than most of the dancing mass
around her. Her hair flowed around her shoulders,
swaying in time with the music, but the *way* she moved
attracted his attention most. Unlike the others on the

floor, she was lithe, more graceful than the rest. Her every move fluid and smooth like fine cognac. She was…

The one.

He glided across the floor, the humans parting to give him room as if they could sense his inner predator and wanted to be sure they were not his main course. Moving with the grace of his kind, he approached the blonde, smoothly dancing his way in front of her. He caught her with his eyes, and her face went blank as he placed his hands on her hips. With him leading, they moved their bodies in perfect synchronicity to the beat. He maneuvered them smoothly through the crowd toward the exit as his two *compadres* flanked her rear, all four swaying to the rhythm of the music.

Once outside, he moved the party into the dark shadows of the alley behind the club. When they were deep enough to ensure they would not be disturbed, he released his enthrall. The leggy blonde blinked twice and shook her head, as if trying to sweep the cobwebs from her attic. She looked around in disbelief. "Where am…"

Cutting off her obvious question, he held up his hand. "You don't need to finish that question. Everyone always says the same thing." He addressed the other two with him. "Humans are so predictable."

"I want to go back into the club." She began to move down the alley on shaking legs.

He shook his head, tossing his platinum hair around his shoulders. "I'm afraid I can't let you do that, pet."

He heard her heart race, knew her blood flooded with adrenaline as she looked around and assessed her situation. Panic twisted the pretty features of her face when she noted the three muscular males surrounding her.

"Why not?" she asked, her voice shaky with fear.

"Because my friends and I aren't done with you yet. It would be a shame for our transaction not to be completed."

"Transaction?" She paused. "Do you want money? I don't have much, but I'll give you all I have." She tried once more to back away, stepping up against one of his men. The body behind her was solid, walling her in. She looked over her shoulder to see an evil grin spread across his thick face.

"You'll give us all you have." When his man spoke, his fangs were visible, white and long. She must have noticed, because she blanched when he continued. "But it's not money we are after."

The three of them descended as one, bringing her down to rest on her back, uncaring that the hard asphalt would bite into her skin. Being the leader, he blanketed her with his body and sunk his fangs deep into her throat while his friends each sank their teeth into her wrists. She screamed in pain, flailing her legs wildly in an attempt to dislodge him, but the effort was for naught. She was no match for the three slaughterers.

They devoured the woman with such voracity they spilled as much of her blood as they drank. A puddle of dark red began to ooze past the woman's feet, feet that stilled as her eyes rolled back into her head. He heard her heartbeat flutter, recognized the end neared.

The thrill of the kill almost kept him from sensing the vampire behind them. He tore his fangs away from her delicate neck and looked at the large male coming toward them. Muscular, he moved with a confidence that bespoke of years of training in the art of combat.

He knew a moment of panic, as the warrior pulled a blade from its sheath in a graceful slide and descended on the trio, just before his world went dark.

****

Present day...

The penthouse kitchen was warm and welcoming, if not well used. Dark cherry cabinets descended from the ceiling. The black appliances matched the marble countertops which reflected the images of the people within. Tonight, the kitchen was abuzz with a flurry of activity.

Katrina Spencer glanced around the marble table. Her gaze landed on her best friend, Marcus Botticelli. Originally from Italy, he'd lived in the States so long he now called the U.S. home. His dark eyes and chestnut-brown hair complimented the form of his handsome face. His was a warrior's face, one that could have been sculpted by the Gods for the battlefield. He wore a confident look that gave him a commanding presence.

Her eyes darted from her best friend to her co-workers, Dana and Cathy. They all sat in various stages of undress. A deck of cards, chips, and articles of clothing lay scattered about. Participating in their weekly strip-poker tournament, the group would most likely end the evening with at least a couple of people naked in one of the bedrooms.

The poker game always took place on Wednesdays because the girls didn't work that night. The women danced together in an adult show, named Desire, which played five days a week at the club Marcus owned called Reapers. Performing that often kept them in

4

fantastic shape. Shapes which Marcus claimed to appreciate without shame.

"Ha, I've got a full house. Ante up, Kitty Kat." Marcus threw his cards down on the table and grinned.

Kat removed her bra, throwing it on the table before narrowing her eyes as she spoke. "I think you're cheating. You've won almost every hand tonight. There's no way you are that lucky."

"What can I say? Lady Luck is with me tonight." Marcus lifted her black lace bra off the table, put it on his head so that the cups covered his ears like a set of earmuffs, and sang the theme from the movie Weird Science. Kat, her friend Cathy, and Cathy's sometimes girlfriend, Dana, all chuckled as they watched Marcus wiggle his body in his chair, dancing to the song he sang.

"Ohemgee, he's hysterical," said Cathy, between giggles. Cathy had been fairly fortunate herself and sat completely dressed, except for her missing shirt. "How did you ever get to meet this guy, Kat?"

Katrina glanced at Marcus and smiled. "It's a long story."

"Basically, I rescued her," Marcus supplied, reaching for the cards.

"You did more than just rescue me, Marcus." Kat turned her attention to the two women at the table, noting the looks of rapt attention on their faces. They wanted details, but there were only so many Katrina could share and keep Marcus' secret safe. She promised her friend years ago she would never reveal what she knew about vampires, let alone that he was one. "I was attacked in an alley by three men. Marcus heard the commotion and came to save the day."

"It was nothing." Marcus gave an insouciant shrug as he started shuffling the deck.

Dana sighed. "Like a knight in shining armor."

Marcus snorted and began to deal.

In more ways than one. Kat took the card Marcus dealt reviewing it as she continued her story. "After he nursed me back to health, he offered me a job at his club."

Cathy picked up her cards from the table, and perused them. "I bid five." She tossed a chip into the middle of the table and looked at Kat. "How did you end up living here?" she asked, gesturing around the large home.

"I'm in." Marcus tossed a chip down. "Once I found out about the hovel where she lived and the sleazy club she was dancing in, I couldn't let her remain there."

"I call." Kat sent an appreciative smile his way and tossed in her bid. "He offered to let me stay here with him. Even gave me the master suite."

"I knew there was a reason I liked this guy," Dana jerked her thumb a couple of times toward the handsome male at the table. "I'll take two."

Marcus handed Dana two cards to replace the ones she discarded. "Anyone else want any?"

"No," Cathy and Kat replied in unison.

"Then let's see 'em," Marcus requested, laying his hand down on the table.

"You win, *again*." Katrina could not keep the incredulousness from her tone. She and the three other women each removed an article of clothing.

"Looks like it is definitely my lucky night," Marcus remarked, doing his version of a seated happy dance.

"You still have my bra on your head." Katrina laughed.

He cupped the bra over his ears with both hands. "It keeps my ears warm," he quipped before starting into another round of singing the theme song from the movie Weird Science.

Dana giggled. "My deal, give me those cards Marcus, if you can stop your magnificent singing and dancing long enough."

Marcus looked at the woman with a sly smile. "If you like my singing and dancing, wait until you see what I'll do later for an encore, baby." Marcus winked and slid her the deck.

Katrina watched in awe as Dana began to shuffle. Having worked in the casinos in Vegas, this was a skill her friend possessed on a grand scale. She sorted, flipped, and assembled a deck like no one else. She had her hands cupped ready to flip the two piles together when a figure appeared in the archway to the kitchen, drawing her attention.

Kat gazed at the man. His menacing, large frame filled the entryway to the kitchen. Hard sapphire eyes stared at them. His shoulder length hair, the color of dark chocolate, was tied back exposing the hard line of his jaw and perfectly chiseled features of his face with its scruffy five o'clock shadow. The black sweater he wore tucked into leather pants that were settled low on his hips, hugged his sculpted chest. A pair of shitkicker boots and a leather jacket finished his ensemble. The look on his face said he could kill you as easily as he could say hello, and Kat wondered just which of the two he would do to them.

The distraction caused Dana to forget what she was doing. The cards went up like firecrackers on the Fourth of July, flying over the table and onto the floor.

"Looks like the game just changed to Fifty-Two Pick Up," joked Marcus.

"Mind if I join the game?" the stranger asked, his deep voice bouncing off the walls of the kitchen. Marcus whipped his head around and looked over his shoulder at the voice.

"Stephan," he exclaimed, surprise evident in his voice. "I didn't know you were in town."

"I can see you weren't expecting me." Stephan surveyed the scene with his steely gaze, nodding toward the group, a look of disdain on his face. "Good evening…ladies."

Kat watched the large male pin Marcus with a poignant stare while he crossed the kitchen in three large strides. Her gaze flicked between the two handsome men, watching as they seemed to be communicating silently to each other. Having reached their table, Stephan stooped down to help Dana pick up the cards from the floor.

"Here you go, my dear." Stephan handed the cards to Dana who was dressed in only her white silky bra and matching panties. She blushed as she took them.

"Well, Marcus." Stephan straightened to his full height. "Are you going to sit there with that brassiere on your head all night, or are you going to introduce me to your friends?"

Marcus yanked the lace bra from his head. "Yes, of course. Ladies, this is Stephan von Haas. He is my…friend. He owns this place."

A look of comprehension crossed Kat's face. She

knew all about Stephan, had heard many stories from Marcus when alcohol loosened his tongue—stories about battles, feeding and sexual exploits with his sire. She finally had a face to put with the name, and boy what a face, with his strong jaw and deep blue eyes framed by two stray wisps of hair that had escaped the thong. Just looking at his strong handsome face made Kat think of long nights under silk sheets. And his voice—his voice dripped sexuality, sending a surge of heat through her blood.

As if hearing her thoughts, Stephan leaned down to whisper in her ear, "And just who might you be?" She turned her face toward his. Their mouths were mere centimeters from each other, so close they breathed the same air. "I'm..." *What's my name again? Oh yeah.* Her brain kicked back into gear. "Kat."

Stephan smiled—the smile every bit as sexy as the rest of him. "You look more like a kitten to me, young one."

Stephan held Kat's gaze. It felt as if she'd fallen into his eyes.

"I'm Cathy and this is my, um...friend, Dana," chimed in Cathy, as she gestured her thumb between herself and Dana.

Stephan held Kat's eyes fast. Without breaking their connection, he said formally, "It's nice to meet you ladies."

Marcus broke in, clearly growing uncomfortable with the situation. "I think we're gonna have to call it a night. Cathy and Dana, thanks for coming over, but I'm going to have to ask you to leave."

Kat blinked, pulling her gaze away from Stephan's intense stare to watch Marcus stand. He ushered the two women toward the door while they hastily donned the clothing they'd lost in the game. The women's breathy protests could be heard as they made their way down the hall.

Stephan slid into the empty chair beside Kat with a gracefulness she could appreciate from such a large body. "So tell me young one, is Kat short for something or did your parents just have a fascination with felines?"

"It's short for Katrina. But everyone calls me Kat." Nervously she began to gather the playing cards from the table, but Stephan stilled her shaking hands by covering them with his own. Something akin to an electric current passed between them. The sensation crept from her hands up her arms to course throughout her body. Katrina gazed at Stephan, drinking him in. If a jaguar could wear leather, he might be mistaken for Stephan's brother. Dangerous, magnificent, and so very beautiful.

"Where are my manners?" she asked, her voice quivering. "Would you like a drink?"

"You read my mind," he replied as he rose, pulling her toward him. "I am a little parched, actually. "

Their eyes locked and Kat once again fell into his dark gaze. Her mind detached as if she watched herself from above, like an out of body experience. She watched him lean into her. Their lips touched and she allowed the sensation to take her.

The feel of his mouth registered on her lips, while the masculine smell of sandalwood engulfed her. His lips feathered kisses down her jaw, coming to a rest where her shoulder met her throat. She swooned in his arms. They closed around her like a set of steel bands, pulling her against his firm body. Kat moaned when his tongue flicked out to taste her sensitive skin. He inhaled deeply against her neck causing goose bumps to pimple her skin.

"Honeysuckle," he murmured, his lips brushing against her flesh.

His fangs lengthened, scraping the skin where her pulse beat, sending her heart racing. He cupped her round bottom in one hand and tightened his arm around her waist. Her body stiffened only a little as he pulled her tighter against him, lifting her off her feet. Her bare breasts pressed against his chest, the material of his sweater rasping against her tender flesh.

This will not hurt, young one. You will feel nothing, he whispered to her mind placing her fully under his enthrallment. Kat's momentary anxiety suddenly left, replaced by absolute acquiescence.

Chapter 2

As he walked the dancers to the door, Marcus replayed the recent events in his mind. Stephan's intense stare, wholly focused on Katrina, was unsettling. He reminded Marcus of a lion stalking its prey.

He had known Stephan a long time, since Stephan converted him over two hundred and fifty years ago. They'd spent centuries together, become close friends. But there were times, like tonight, when Stephan seemed distant. More aloof mentor than pal.

Marcus hoped it was simply because they'd not seen one another in decades. Hopefully, they would quickly fall back into a familiar ease, because Stephan was a powerful vampire and Marcus greatly preferred the at-ease version of his sire. When Stephan became disapproving and sullen, as he seemed to be this night, he could be difficult to deal with.

His appearance at the penthouse had been a complete surprise. Marcus hadn't sensed Stephan's presence when he arrived, and that could only mean one thing—Stephan had purposely blocked him.

Being sired by Stephan created a special connection. They could always sense each other. They shared a mindlink, a kind of mental telepathy that allowed the two of them to communicate without saying a word out loud. In spite of all that, Marcus had not realized Stephan had come to town, let alone was in the penthouse.

Marcus tested the mindlink as he approached the door with his escorts. *So what have you been up to lately, Stephan?* His thought sounded weak, even in his head.

Stephan's irritation at the interruption came across their link. *I'd ask you the same thing, Marcus, but I think I already know the answer to that. I allowed you the use of my penthouse, and you turn it into a house of ill repute? I know this town has changed much since I've been gone. It has quite a reputation now, but I would have expected better from you.*

Marcus flinched as his sire snapped a mental barrier down, blocking any further communication. Stephan's contempt regarding what he had walked in on this evening was obvious through their link. Marcus knew he did not wholly approve of modern human women. To him, modern woman wore too little and cursed too much. They did have their purpose though, especially when Stephan had a hunger that needed to be sated.

The thought made his heart clench. Marcus fought to remain calm; though his insides felt like they were twisting so hard they would shoot from his mouth at any minute.

"You'll have to come back soon so we can finish our game," Marcus said, forcing a friendly grin, after he opened the door for the two women.

"Maybe your friend could play next time. I wouldn't mind seeing him lose a hand or two." Cathy winked at her boss.

"Hey what about me?" complained Dana, placing

her fisted hands on her hips in feigned pique.

Cathy threw a friendly arm around Dana's shoulders. "Perhaps we could make a Stephan sandwich."

"Um…yummy. You always have the best ideas, Cathy."

"Sounds like a plan," Marcus said, forcing the lighthearted comment as he ushered them out the door. "I'll see you at the club tomorrow night. Goodnight, ladies."

Not waiting for their reply, he closed the door and locked it with his mind, then headed toward the kitchen. A sense of foreboding overtook him, and he put on a burst of preternatural speed. He got to the kitchen in time to see his sire lift Kat off the ground.

"Stop!" he commanded, with wide, panic-stricken eyes.

Stephan raised his head slightly, pinned Marcus with his intense stare. "Go away," he muttered. His lips peeled back over his fangs before he lowered his mouth back to Kat's throat, ready to pierce her creamy skin.

"No, stop! I beg you, please."

Stephan raised his head fully, but retained his grip upon Katrina. "Why? Is she yours?"

"No. Not exactly. Look, I'll explain. Please release her and we'll talk…in private."

Stephan took a deep breath. His fangs receded before he gently placed Kat on the ground and released her from his enthrall.

When she swayed slightly, Marcus took control, grasping her gently by the arm. "Kat, excuse us please. You have something to do in the bedroom." He gave her mind a gentle mental push to emphasize his command.

"I think there is something I need to do in my bedroom," Kat parroted. "If you'll excuse me, I'll see you both in the morning."

She stood on her tip toes and kissed Marcus on his cheek, earning the vampire a questioning look from his sire.

As she exited the kitchen, the leggy blonde grabbed her clothing off the table. She sashayed from the room while Stephan and Marcus were treated to the sight of her walking away clothed only in the boyleg panties that hugged her thin hips.

"That is something a male could really sink his teeth into," Marcus murmured as he watched her disappear from view. He scrubbed his hand down his face and turned his attention back to Stephan.

"I was thinking that very thing until you came in here demanding I not drink from her. Explain yourself, boy."

Marcus barely hid the flinch that threatened to hunch his shoulders. *Boy.* That was not a word Stephan usually used when referring to him. This was not going to be a fun night. He better explain. After Marcus gestured toward the table with a sweeping motion of his hand, he drew up a chair and straddled it, nodding for Stephan to sit across from him.

"It's...complicated," Marcus started on a sigh. "Kat is a friend. We have an understanding. She doesn't want to be a donor."

"Since when did you start giving humans a choice in the matter?" Stephan asked incredulously.

"Since I was able to start getting blood from ways other than the vein. In fact, I have some bagged blood in the refrigerator. Would you like some?"

Stephan waved off the offer. "Not now, finish telling me about this Kat. Why do you care if she doesn't want to donate? I would have wiped her memory. She wouldn't have remembered any of it."

"I realize that, but I promised her I'd keep her safe. She was attacked several years ago. When she recovered, I swore a vow that I would never allow harm to come to her again—that I would protect her from our kind. I keep my promises."

Stephan's eyes widened, realization dawned on his face. "You promised her you'd keep her safe from *our kind*? Does that mean she knows about our breed?"

Being an honorable male, Marcus could not help but admit the truth, albeit reluctantly. "Yes, she is aware that vampires exist, and she knows that I am one."

"How did she take that information?"

"She attacked me."

Stephan barked out a laugh. "I would have liked to have seen that."

"It was bad." Marcus shook his head, trying to keep the memories from settling in. It didn't work. "I had arranged for a special dinner complete with candles on the table, champagne-soaked caviar, and lobster marinated in the finest Cognac. I made sure everything was perfect. It started off great. Over dessert I grabbed her hands, told her I wanted to take our relationship further, then confessed I was a vampire."

"Why in the hell would you do that?"

"Because I didn't want to start our relationship off with a secret between us." Marcus folded his arms on the back of his chair.

"So you told her you were of the same breed as those who had attacked her?"

Marcus nodded his head. "Kat freaked out and took off for the door. Of course, I couldn't let her leave, not as upset as she was, so I raced to the door in a blur to block her from leaving. That only made things worse.

"She thought I was going to hold her against her will and feed off her, so she attacked me." Marcus rubbed his face at the memory. Kat scratched his face, and punched his chest. Her kicks landed hard on his shins. He had allowed Kat's blows, for he knew she needed to vent her pent up anger toward his kind.

He really couldn't blame her for her reaction to his confession. He knew all too well that some vampires were monsters, and he had spent his entire vampiric life trying to rid the evil from the world.

"I had to restrain her to keep her from hurting herself, which only made her anxiety and panic increase. I wrapped myself around her body, taking her down onto the couch. I held on to her until she was physically exhausted and unable to struggle any longer."

Stephan shifted in his chair. "I take it eventually she calmed down enough to listen to you."

"I reminded her of our friendship and that her feelings ran as deep for me as mine did for her. Ultimately, I calmed her down and made her understand that even the vampire world has good and evil."

Stephan steepled his fingers, rested his elbows on the table as he gave Marcus an assessing stare. "You care for her, don't you?"

Marcus could sense his sire riffling through his

mind. "I do, but we are just friends."

"But you have slept together. I can see it in your mind."

"Yes," Marcus readily admitted, knowing his sire could take the information from his mind with or without his consent. "We are occasional bed partners, but not lovers. Our relationship is…complicated, but it works for us. Over the past seven years we tried to become a couple, but it never seemed quite right, so our relationship grew into a strong friendship instead."

Marcus had proven he could be trusted with her life and Kat gave him the love and companionship he so desperately wanted. Now content for the first time in centuries, he wanted Kat with him forever. Of course he knew forever would not come to be.

Humans were like beautiful butterflies, flying with delicate gossamer wings, full of beauty and color. But their lives were short, gone forever in the blink of an immortal eye. Marcus only hoped he could help Kat reach a ripe old age. He hated the thought of her flying away one day, but had resigned himself to the fact that day would eventually come. Until that time, he had vowed to do everything within his power to keep her safe, protected, and loved.

And that included making sure no one ever drank from her again.

"So drinking from her is off limits," Stephan mused, easing back in his chair and crossing his thick arms over his chest. "I will respect that because of your promise to her. Are there any other promises I should know about?"

Stephan arched a dark eyebrow and smirked.

"If you are talking about sex, no. She is free

to…um…see who she pleases. I have no claims on her. She can bring anyone here she wants to share her bed."

"Bring anyone here," his sire repeated. "You mean she's living here?"

Stephan's calm demeanor was replaced by a suspicious look on his face.

"Yes." Marcus shifted uncomfortably in his seat.

Stephan leaned forward, bunched his hands into fists on the table. "Let me get this straight. I'm gone for a few decades and come back to find that you have a human female living with you. A beautiful woman, who you do not drink from. Not only is she off limits to you, but you have promised that none of our kind will drink from her either. And to top it off, she knows about the vampire breed. Do I have this right?"

"That about sums it up." Marcus braced for the reaction he knew would come.

Anger lit Stephan's eyes. "Have you lost your mind?" he bellowed. "Marcus, I realize I have not been here to guide you, but you were under my tutelage for over two hundred years. You know that keeping knowledge of our existence from humans is vital to the survival of our breed, and yet you have a pet human living with you who knows about us."

"We can trust her. She would never betray us!" Marcus banged his fist on the table to emphasize his point. "I trust her with my life."

"You certainly have." Stephan leaned back in his chair and took a deep breath. His voice was softer when next he spoke, but Marcus could feel the tension radiating from Stephan's body. "I hope she lives up to that trust."

"She will," Marcus said with conviction as he went

to the refrigerator and withdrew two bags of blood. Casually switching the subject, Marcus shook the bags of blood and said, "O negative, your favorite. Want some?"

Stephan nodded and leaned back in his chair watching Marcus thoughtfully. "I will capitulate to your arrangement with the human for now. But I will observe the woman, watching for any sign of betrayal. If I find any threat, she can be taken care of easily enough."

Marcus stilled, knowing Stephan did not make threats, he made promises. He turned to pin his mentor with a hard stare. "Kat is not a threat, Stephan. You will see. We can trust her."

The vampires stared at one another in an old-fashioned game of bet-you'll-blink-before-I-do. Both of them statue still, the air thickened between them. It was Stephan who broke the strained silence.

"I believe you said something about a drink."

Marcus took the hint. The subject of Kat was closed—for now.

Emptying the bags into two glasses and adding some whisky, he handed one to Stephan and inquired about Stephan's time in Europe. The two males drank their fill as Stephan shared his European exploits. With their hunger sated, they headed off to rest when dawn approached.

Marcus pushed a button on the remote, sending the special UV shades down over the windows. "What are you doing?" Stephan asked, his feet stilling on the stairs that led to his bedroom.

"Drawing the blinds," Marcus explained. "They are made from special protectant material that will keep the sun from the room."

"Only in Vegas," Stephan murmured, shaking his head. "There have been so many changes to this town."

Marcus smiled mischievously. "You have no idea."

Chapter 3

Stephan put on his cotton pajama bottoms and lay between the smooth sheets on his bed, surrounded by the smell of honeysuckle. Obviously, Katrina had stayed in this bedroom. He found the redecorated master suite to be a grand room. The black lacquer king size bed boasted an ornately carved headrest adorned with silver accents. Covered with a white down comforter over yellow silk sheets, it was flanked on either side by identical lacquer nightstands. Across from the bed sat a matching chest of drawers that Stephan discovered contained a large plasma TV which rose out of the smooth shiny chest with the touch of a button. Marcus had offered the room to him out of respect, partially because it was customary for a younger vampire to offer his sire the best room in the house and because this was *his* place after all. Of course, that meant Kat now slept in Marcus' room, as his was the only other bedroom in the penthouse.

And for some unfathomable reason, that bothered him. Stephan crossed his hands behind his head and settled into the bed ready for a long rest. When his eyes closed, his thoughts turned to the past, in an attempt to block the woman from his mind.

Centuries ago, Stephan and his comrade, Demetri Romanoff, two of the oldest living vampires known to their kind, had become aware of the traitorous plan of a rogue vampire with designs on world domination. They formed the Alpha Council to stop Eldrich and his group of rogues called the Miscreants.

At that time, the Council, with Stephan as their leader, consisted of fifty powerful warriors, who were stationed throughout the world to fight against each of the numerous factions of the Miscreants. As the Alphas took down the Miscreant fighters in each country, Eldrich disappeared, and the world had become more stable. Team by team, the Council membership dwindled. Some left to start families; others were recruited by the policing agency for their kind. Now the Council only numbered seven. Referred to as simply the Alphas, they were the Special Forces for the vampire breed, and they dealt with those who became too violent, abusive, or demented to remain in civilized society.

Stephan smiled at the memory of when he brought Marcus to the Alphas. The young vampire learned to fight well, impressing the other members of the team. During a fight, he was somber, all business, someone Stephan could count on to follow orders. In stark contrast, during his down time Marcus blew off steam by acting outlandish and indulging his inner desires. Yes, Marcus might be what Vegas would call a playboy, but he could always be counted on. He'd proven that over the years.

A soft knock on the door pulled Stephan from his reverie. Perturbed by the interruption, a soft sigh escaped his pursed lips. His preternatural senses told him who was beyond the door. "Come in," he spit out between clenched teeth.

Marcus opened the door. "Excuse me, Stephan, but

Kat has a headache. I need to get her pills from the medicine cabinet in the bathroom."

"It's a bit early for her to have a hangover, isn't it?"

"It's not a hangover." Marcus' clipped tone matched the insulted look on his face. "She has a migraine. It's a particularly bad one. She's in my bathroom vomiting as we speak."

Stephan knew pain, especially the kind that made you ill to your stomach. But the woman needn't suffer. He could do something to help.

Marcus grabbed the medicine from the cabinet and headed out of the room, Stephan on his heels. At the base of the stairs, they parted like the Red Sea, Marcus heading for the kitchen probably to retrieve a glass of water for Kat and Stephan heading for Marcus' bedroom.

Without knocking, Stephan opened the bedroom door and treaded purposely across the space to the bathroom. Kat lay whimpering, curled in the fetal position on the marble floor beside the toilet, wrapped only in a shiny robe. He could feel the waves of pain radiating from her. "I can help you," Stephan stated in his deep baritone voice as he scooped her up in his arms.

"Only if you don't talk so loud, please." Kat covered her ears with her hands.

Stephan softly placed her on Marcus' black leather Viking bed. She moaned and tucked back in on herself.

Stephan sat crossed legged on the bed and whispered, "Put your head in my lap." He cradled her head in his hands, helping Kat turn over, and guided her head onto his legs. Her robe fell to one side when she turned, exposing a long, lean leg.

Stephan rubbed his hands together, channeling his healing energy, then placed two fingers on each of Kat's temples. He began to rub tiny circles.

"That feels nice," she whispered, closing her eyes.

"Just relax," Stephan instructed as the pain left her head through his fingers. He absorbed the stabbing ache into his body. It traveled up his arms, over his shoulders, and lodged in his own head, drumming a harsh beat. The warrior visualized the pain being destroyed and leaving his body through the top of his head.

Marcus entered the room and immediately stilled in the doorway. Noting the look of wonder on his face, Stephan asked, "What is it?"

Kat moaned softly, a combination of exasperation and relief. The sound drew the warrior's attention.

"She looks like an angel laying there in her white robe, with the golden light from your hands bathing her face and blonde hair," Marcus whispered, awe quieting his voice.

Stephan smiled. *You sound like a woman. Going a bit soft in your old age?*

Marcus scoffed. *Hardly.*

Stephan refocused on the woman lying in his lap. "How do you feel now?" The Alpha leader eased his ministrations.

"Um, better. Much better, thanks to you," Kat answered sleepily, looking at him from beneath her hooded eyes.

His heart raced from the look of gratitude in her eyes. Her face softened, the pain obviously easing. He couldn't disagree with Marcus' declaration that she looked angelic lying on the bed. It was enough to make him want to kiss her. Run his tongue over her pulse, taste her smooth skin once more.

Desire warred with his self-restraint. Touching her had driven the logic from his mind. His inner beast roared in frustration. She was temptation incarnate. Her blood and body called to him, but he'd promised Marcus.

Dammit, what was it about this woman that drew him to her?

"Good, then I'll be going." He got up to leave, gently placing Kat's head on a pillow before he gave into the temptation she presented.

Kat flinched as soon as their contact was broken. "It's back," she cried. "The pain is coming back." She reached for Stephan, and he sensed her pain start to subside when her fingers touched his arm. "Never mind. It's getting better again."

Katrina's hand fell to the bed. Seconds later her face contorted in pain. He pushed into her mind to discover what was happening. Her head thumped in time with her pulse. Through the pain, her muddy mind struggled to process what was happening. Her hand snaked out to touch his arm.

"It's you," she whispered, clutching his arm once more. "When I touch you the pain goes away. Don't leave me!"

The glass of water Marcus had been holding slipped from his hand. Using his preternatural speed and agility he caught it before it hit the floor. Marcus' concern for his female friend showed on his face.

As Stephan stared down at her delicate hand on his arm, the sound of Marcus' voice came over their mindlink. *I have seen you do many things over the years. I've seen you heal before, but never have I seen your mere touch take pain away. That is amazing!*

Stephan looked pensively over Kat, debating about what to do. She obviously needed him, and his honor would have him do no less than help her. But he was tired, more so now that his strength had waned from use of his ability to heal.

Decision made, he scooped her into his arms, saying simply, "You'll sleep with me tonight."

Marcus' eyebrows shot up. "Don't you think…" The rest of the protest died in his throat, cut off by a sharp look from Stephan.

Marcus moved to one side so the two could exit the room. *Stephan don't you think she should remain here for tonight?*

Their eyes locked. *No. My decision is made.*

The younger vampire knew there would be no arguing. Stephan was used to being in charge, in control. He was older, stronger than Marcus. And Marcus was not powerful enough to stop him from doing what he wanted, so the younger vampire did the only thing he could. He watched as Stephan left the room with Kat.

Take care of her, Stephan.

As if he needed that advice. Why else was he taking her to his room?

Her weight was no more consequential to him than that of a small child. Stephan carried her up the stairs and placed her on the bed under the yellow satiny sheets. When his hands left her, a painful look twisted the pretty features of Kat's face and a whimper escaped her pouty lips.

Stephan crawled in beside her, bone tired. Katrina reached for his hand, holding it tightly, as if she was drowning and he was her life preserver. When she placed her other hand on his arm, the tension in her body eased. Obviously wanting more relief, she rolled over his arm onto her side, spooning against his chest.

Stephan sensed her pain ebbing the more she touched him. He swept her legs back so they were against his and placed one of his muscular thighs over her limbs. Next, he took his free arm and draped it around her waist, effectively hugging her tight against him. She relaxed into him.

"The pain's gone. Thank you," she murmured as she burrowed against him, wrapping her arms around his.

He placed his chin on top of her head, and breathed in her honeysuckle scent, taking it deep into his lungs. It wrapped around his body in a warm embrace. For the first time in his long life, he felt content, truly content.

He wondered about the woman in his arms. He'd healed others before, but he couldn't remember a time when someone felt better by simply touching him. He'd sensed something different about this woman the first time their eyes met. As his lids drifted shut, he silently vowed to discover what it was.

****

Kat awoke that afternoon feeling the after migraine fuzzies, but at least she was pain free. She squeezed the muscles around her eyes, trying to force the blurriness from her vision. Desperately needing to get a drink to dispel the cotton in her mouth, she attempted to rise from the bed. To her surprise, Kat found herself unable to move.

"Where do you think you are going?" asked a dark voice from behind her.

All her senses came back online. She could feel the hard muscular body wrapped around hers. Stephan must have remained all day with his arms and leg wrapped protectively around her. Kat turned to face the healer. Embarrassment made her press her head to his chest. The rich masculine sandalwood scent, that was uniquely his own, dispelled her awkwardness. After a deep breath, she pushed back slightly and studied his features.

He was every woman's fantasy. When she looked into his sapphire eyes, her stomach knotted and heat pooled low between her thighs. Drawn to him, her reaction, animalistic and primal, concerned her for she knew what he was.

She placed one hand on his cheek, marveling at his features. "You look so normal. Human," she mused.

Stephan's eyes darkened. "You should never make the mistake of pretending that I'm human. I am a vampire, Kat, not a man."

"I know what you are, and I don't care," she replied, moving her hand down to settle over his heart. "It's not what you are, but who you are that matters to me. You are the man who took away my pain. You are the man who helped me last night. You didn't have to help me, but you did. You are a good man, and I'm not scared of you," Kat announced with all the bravado she could muster.

Without warning, she found herself rolled onto her back. Stephan loomed over her, his hands planted on either side of her head. He bared his fangs, a low growl rumbled in his chest. Kat looked him in the eye. Her heart raced, though she wasn't sure whether from fear or excitement.

"I am not a man, not any more. You should fear me, run while you can, before I give into my..." He paused, his eyes darkened to the color of pitch. "I am a thing of nightmares."

"More like fantasies," Kat muttered and kissed him.

He pulled back breaking their kiss, his eyes wide with shock. Then he descended on her. The soft satin of her robe shifted across her chest, the silky material gliding over her nipples when he lowered his weight onto her. Her lips parted in invitation. Their tongues dove back and forward between their mouths in a dance as old as time.

The taste of his kiss consumed her. He pushed all thoughts from her mind. Only he remained. The ripple of his corded muscles as he moved. The sensation of his body pressing her into the mattress.

He trailed kisses down her neck until his lips rested over the pulse beating a steady rhythm in her vein. His teeth scraped sinuously along her neck. Her hands kneaded his flesh. The muscles of his back tightened beneath her fingers. Her nails dug into his skin, her passion threatening to consume her.

His lips left her throat. She only had a second to look into his dark eyes before he leapt from the bed.

"Get out," he commanded harshly.

Kat looked up at him, confused, frozen in place. *What the hell?*

"Get out, now!" he repeated, pointing to the door. It opened, untouched by any hands.

Katrina's eyes darted from the door back to the

male standing over her. The look on his face, a mixture of pain and anger, terrified her. What had she done to deserve this cruel treatment?

A warning growl from his throat pushed her into action. Grabbing her neck with one hand and holding her robe closed with the other, she ran out the door, her robe streaming behind her.

Chapter 4

Stephan crossed to the door with two angry strides and slammed it shut behind the fleeing female before returning to sit on the bed. He covered his face with his hands, disappointed in himself. What was it about this woman? Being near her drove all rational thoughts from his head, leaving only her.

He could still hear her blood calling its siren song to him. His hunger beat at him, his fangs, fully lengthened, pressed against his tongue. Taking blood from a donor could be an intimate act, capable of bringing pleasure to both the donor and drinker. For many vampires, often intercourse and drinking from the vein were done in unison. He'd wanted to take her as he sank his fangs into her creamy neck, absorb her very essence into himself, surrounding himself with her heat inside and out.

Luckily for both of them, he'd quickly come to his senses and left his bed before he could act on his instincts. Then he had growled, actually growled at her like an animal. Now she was probably terrified of him, and really he supposed she should be. Her lush body, the rush of her blood under her skin, her delicate features and wonderful scent all called to him, and he was only so strong.

There was only one thing to do with temptation like that—avoid it.

That was close, he thought as he headed to the bath for a cold shower. *Too close. I almost broke my promise to Marcus.*

And his honor would never allow that.

****

Stephan and Marcus sat across from each other at the marble table in the kitchen, drinking their first meal of the night. Human food, while tasting wonderful as it slid over their tongues, did not sustain them physically. They needed to have blood to survive.

They preferred to begin their evenings consuming the blood their bodies demanded for sustenance. Once their bodies were sated, they could then satisfy their hunger with more palatable items. Marcus was particularly fond of sweets, while Stephan preferred fine foods such as lobster and caviar. Unfortunately, one of the physical changes that occurred when they became vampires was their stomachs shrunk, so while they enjoyed human food, they could only eat very little in one sitting.

"Where is Katrina?" Stephan asked, downing the last of his drink.

"I don't know." Marcus shrugged his thick shoulders. "I guess she went out."

Stephan took in his friend with a long pensive stare. As the Alpha leader, he was secretive by nature and had worked very hard over the years to protect his breed from being discovered by humans. It made him uncomfortable that a human he didn't know well knew not only that Marcus was a vampire, but also knew he was one as well.

He was all too aware of what could happen if vampires were known to exist, and it wasn't pretty.

Many years ago just after what became known as the Spanish Inquisition, a human had learned of the existence of Vampires. That human spoke to other mortals about the breed. Fear and superstition spread through the village like a plague. The humans had formed a hunting society bent on destroying the vampires.

Stephan and his kind were hunted while they slept during the day and the population of vampires in Germany was almost completely wiped out. He and only a few others escaped the slaughter. Having lived through one genocide, Stephan vowed that year to do anything to prevent such a tragedy from happening again. And he intended to keep that oath.

"If you don't know where she is, how do you know she isn't betraying us, Marcus?"

An incredulous look crossed Marcus' face. "Because she would never betray *me*," he announced with absolute certainty, downing the last of his crimson drink before placing the empty glass on the table a little harder than necessary.

"It doesn't take much for a human to betray a trust, especially one so callow. They don't have the same code of honor we do."

"Stephan, I think you have what humans call trust issues." Marcus chuckled.

"This isn't a laughing matter. You were not alive when the Germans hunted our breed almost to extinction. It was terrible, so much senseless loss." Stephan shook his head sadly. "I will do whatever it takes to make sure such an event never happens again."

Marcus stilled under Stephan's watchful gaze. The Alpha leader saw anger flash in his friend's eyes.

"I'm positive Kat would never betray us," Marcus proclaimed. "She's probably out shopping or something."

"I hope you're..." The sound of the front door to the penthouse opening interrupted Stephan's reply. Kat entered the kitchen with a swish of her hips.

"Hi," she greeted the pair with a smile.

"Where have you been?" demanded Stephan.

"What's it to you?" she snapped, the smile disappearing from her beautiful face.

Not used to such insolence, especially from a mortal—a female at that, Stephan crossed his arms across his broad chest, leaned back in his chair and affected an intimidating look.

"I asked you where you have been?" he repeated slowly, enunciating each syllable.

"And I asked you, what's it to you?" Kat said, equaling Stephan's tone and slow enunciation.

Marcus stood, grabbed Stephan's cup, and took it along with his to the sink to rinse them out. "Hey now you two, I think you guys need to break and go to your corners. Ding. Ding. This round is over."

Kat took in a deep cleansing breath and let it back out slowly before speaking. "If you must know, I was at the Divine Mercy Shelter."

"Why?" questioned Stephan, his voice heavy with confusion.

"Because I volunteer there."

The Alpha leaned forward slightly in his chair, still suspicious. "What do you do at this shelter?"

"I usually work the soup line."

"Why do you go to such a place?"

"Because I'm looking for a date," Katrina replied

sarcastically. Marcus' deep laugh echoed in the kitchen as he rejoined Stephan at the table.

"Seriously, why do you go to such a place?" Stephan asked with sincere curiosity.

Before responding, Kat crossed to the refrigerator and poured a glass of water. "I guess I go there because it makes me feel like I'm giving something back. I like to help people." Katrina looked pointedly at Marcus. "I remember a time I needed the help of a stranger. Now I can give a little help, so I give it. It's like Karma."

See, sent Marcus across their mindlink. *I told you she can be trusted. She wasn't out betraying us. She was out helping people less fortunate.*

Stephan's eyes flicked to Marcus. *Today. But what about tomorrow or the day after that? She'll have to earn my trust as she has earned yours, Marcus.*

Oh she'll earn it. Just give her a chance.

Stephan eyed the lissome blonde from the corner of his eye. *I'll be watching her closely.*

I just bet you will. A wry grin raised the corners of Marcus' mouth.

Stephan turned his attention fully on the woman in the room and found her watching the two of them carefully with a strange look on her face. His curiosity made him push into her mind to glean what she was thinking. He found she could see that something transpired between them, but she had no idea what. Her eyes darted between the two men briefly before coming to rest on Stephan.

He diverted his gaze but stayed a quiet shadow in her mind, listened to her thoughts as she reviewed his features. His straight nose and strong jaw line made the heat of desire flood her body, tighten her belly. She loved his eyes, felt like they drew her in when he looked at her, the deep blue color calling to her like the sea calls its captain.

Stephan turned to look at Katrina with a grin on his lips. The flush on her cheeks betrayed her thoughts. She shook her head. "I need to get ready for work," she said giving herself an excuse to leave the room and his scrutinizing gaze.

Stephan watched her leave the kitchen, appreciating the delicious view of her backside.

"I see you are already watching her closely." Marcus chuckled.

Stephan raked a hand through his hair. "She is something worth watching, my old friend. I don't think I'll mind watching her one bit."

Chapter 5

It had been a week since Stephan had told her to get out of his room, and Kat had done what she could to avoid him. Most days she made sure to get up by noon, so she could leave the penthouse before he awoke. On the few occasions she'd run into him, they had been cordial enough to each other; there were even times Kat thought he might be flirting.

Tonight, however, was not one of those times.

Earlier in the evening she and Marcus had been in her dance studio. The studio was small, but boasted floor to ceiling mirrors along one wall with a *barre* attached so Kat could practice her ballet and dance routines. The floor was made of oak, polished to perfection.

She and Marcus had a standing agreement; Marcus taught her self-defense lessons in exchange for her giving him dance lessons. This night they had been dancing the tango when Stephan entered.

Stephan stood in the doorway, watching as the two of them moved seductively around the room, their images reflecting in the mirrors. As Marcus twirled her in his arms, Kat only had eyes for Stephan. She watched his eyes follow her around the room.

Katrina felt his stare rake over her while she glided along in her stilettos. Her skin tingled, as if tiny champagne bubbles danced along her flesh. Stephan's solicitude was palpable. She licked her suddenly dry lips, practically tasting the hunger she saw in his deep blue eyes.

When the music came to an end, Marcus dipped Kat and planted a kiss squarely on her lips in a dramatic finish. Stephan, clearly displeased, grunted his dissension, turned on his heels and stormed from the room. When he later passed Kat in the hall, he walked by without acknowledging her in the slightest.

Enough mixed signals from Stephan! One day he'd flirt with her, the next he'd ignore her. Tonight's indifference was the final straw.

Determination constricted the muscles of her face, drawing her brows tightly together. If Stephan didn't want to play nice, that suited her. She might be attracted to him, who wouldn't be with his handsome face and stunning eyes, but she certainly didn't have to act on that attraction. In fact, she could be just as aloof and uncaring as Stephan seemed to be.

Kat stormed into the kitchen wearing a pair of skinny jeans which hugged her curves and accentuated her long legs. Her hot pink T-shirt stretched tight, emphasized her ample bosom. Carefully avoiding Stephan's gaze, she lifted an apple from its basket on the counter and began to slice and core it without uttering a word of acknowledgement.

"Take it easy there, Kitty Kat. Any harder and you'll cut through the counter top," Marcus commented, obviously taking note of the unnecessary force she used on the apple.

"I won't cut through the counter top," she curtly replied through tight lips, her shoulders tightened with tension as she autopsied the apple. She spread peanut butter on each slice, gathered them into a plastic container, and after snapping on the lid, turned to leave.

Kat gracefully crossed the kitchen and gave Marcus a kiss on the cheek. "I'm off to work. I'll see you after the show. Goodbye."

She sauntered out of the kitchen without so much as a glance in Stephan's direction, leaving the two men sitting in silence. She felt two sets of eyes follow her as she left the penthouse.

Neither of them flinched as the door slammed behind Katrina.

Stephan looked at Marcus and raised his eyebrows. "Your human seems to be in a bit of a snit tonight."

"It may have something to do with the fact that you told her to get out after kissing her."

"She told you about that, did she?" Stephan's brow lifted questioningly.

"Yeah, she did. And I have to say, I understand why she might be a little angry. What the hell were you thinking?" Marcus demanded, leaning his forearms on the table.

"That happened a week ago. She should be over it by now." Stephan folded his arms defiantly over his chest. "Besides, I don't have to explain myself to you."

Marcus gave an insouciant shrug. "Very well, but you might want to explain yourself to Kat. She thinks you hate her."

Stephan didn't hate her. In fact, he found her exciting, fun, and very sexy, but that was no one's business but his own. "Why would I want to do that?"

"Because I can tell you are interested in her...and she is interested in you."

Stephan raked a hand over his face. "I may be

interested, but I don't think she is. She's barely said three sentences to me in the past week."

Marcus shook his head back and forth slowly. "You don't know anything about human women, do you? She is interested, that is the whole reason she hasn't said anything to you. She's pissed, and she is letting you know it. She's waiting for you to make the next move."

Stephan wondered if his friend's rumination might have validity. "Perhaps," the elder vampire admitted reluctantly. "Perhaps."

Stephan glanced down at the table, took another swig and finished his blood as he mulled over Marcus' revelation. He had noticed Katrina looking wantonly at him, caught her sneaking side glances when she thought he wasn't looking. He could hear her heartbeat race when he looked at her.

But he had also noticed how she'd shown signs of perturbation, seen her hands fisted at her side when he spoke. There was no doubt Marcus was correct about her being upset, and he had to admit she had good cause to be. He'd been running hot and cold. And perhaps it was time to turn up the heat and let things get steamy.

****

Under Cathy's watchful stare, Kat threw her purse into her locker so hard it ricocheted off the back and tumbled down to the floor, spilling its contents. Kat knelt down to retrieve the items as her friend quickly bent down to help her. "What's wrong with you tonight, Kat?"

"Don't even ask."

"Why? What's wrong? Please tell me. Maybe it

would help to get if off that huge chest of yours." Cathy handed her the compact from the floor.

"Well…" Kat paused staring down at the heap on the floor. "It's Stephan."

"You mean Marcus' hot friend, the man who came in the other night when we were playing poker?"

"Yeah, that's him. He's a total jerk." Kat fiercely stuffed the last of the items in her purse like a child throwing a tantrum while putting away her toys.

"Why? What happened?"

Kat relayed the story of their first kiss, leaving out the part about Stephan easing her migraine. Cathy rolled her eyes in disgust when Kat mentioned the part about Stephan yelling at her to get out.

"That's terrible!" Cathy said with disdain.

"I know. It's just that for a few minutes, I thought there could be something between us." Kat's eyes clouded with unshed tears as she stared ahead sightlessly. "Like maybe we had feelings for each other."

She shook her head, sending her blonde curls bouncing over her shoulders as she spun the lock on her locker. "But screw it. In fact, for the past week, he's been running hot then cold. One minute he's smiling at me or looking like he'd love to kiss me and the next he's ignoring me."

"Just another example of a man being a jerk." Cathy leaned up against her locker with her arms crossed over her chest. "You know what they say; all the good ones are either taken or gay."

"Yeah well he's neither taken nor gay, so I guess Stephan must not be a good one." Cathy giggled as Kat sighed.

The women sauntered down the white, florescent-lit hallway to the dressing room and grabbed their costumes from the garment rack. They slipped into the leather and lace creations with perfunctory ease before sitting down at their makeup stations to apply color to their faces.

"You going to be able to get over this guy?" Cathy attached fake eye lashes on her eyelids with a crinkled nose from the smell of the adhesive.

"What do you mean?" Kat asked with a tone of annoyance.

"It's obvious you have it bad for him."

"What are you talking about? I don't even like Stephan." Kat barked the denial out a little rougher than she meant to.

"Yeah, right. I can tell that by the look you get in your eye every time you say his name."

"I don't get a look."

A sardonic grin graced Cathy's face when she looked at Kat from her mirror. "Oh you get a look, trust me."

Kat blew out a dismissive raspberry from between her painted ruby lips. When she finished slathering the pancake makeup on her angry face, she rounded on her friend. "Shut up, you don't know what you are talking about."

"Actually, we've been friends for many years." Cathy lowered her voice. "I know you, girl. I'm telling you, you have it bad for this guy."

The stage manager poked his head in the door just when Kat opened her mouth to deny her friend's observation. "Five minutes ladies, let's go," he called, opening the door wide so the stampede of scantily clad dancers could exit. Kat and Cathy were the last to leave.

"Think about what I said," Cathy suggested, giving Kat's arm a little squeeze.

Kat walked silently to the stage, where she intended to dance off her frustration. Her mind raced through the past week, replaying her interactions with Stephan. She was sure he found her attractive, had seen the lust in his heated stare. Hadn't she? He could be so cold and aloof at times. Was she misreading him?

Back and forth she wavered like a girl picking petals from a daisy. He likes me, he likes me not, he likes me, he likes me not, he…

Blissfully, she arrived on stage and took her mark, waiting for the curtain to open. She pushed all other thoughts aside to concentrate on the routine she would begin when the curtain parted and welcomed the reprieve from the thoughts of the sexy blue-eyed vampire.

Chapter 6

Gage looked down on his mate, Andrea, with loving eyes. She was his one true love, his heartmate. He'd known their souls were one the first time he'd tasted her blood and it made his world spin. She belonged to him, made solely for him and he'd protect her fiercely.

Tonight he awoke as he did most every evening, naked, wrapped in his lover's arms, and hungry. Lazily he fingered Andrea's brunette locks that lay pooled on her pillow.

They had been together for centuries, for they were what others of their kinds referred to as ancients, vampires who had been alive for more than five centuries. As the years went by, as was the way for vampires, their powers had increased so much so that the two of them together were near invincible.

Gage brushed a stray lock of hair from her eyes. "Hard to believe you are only one hundred years younger than me," he mused, looking down into her young face.

He was proud of the many powers she had developed during her life time. Like him, she enthralled other's to do her bidding, she read minds, and commanded people and items with her mind. But there was one thing he did that she still could not— dematerialize. Unfortunately, his Andrea had never learned how.

Without leaving their bed, Gage turned on the stereo. Marilyn Manson blared through the speakers. Andrea had developed a particular fascination with his type of music, though Gage could not understand the appeal. But if his heartmate liked that kind of music, then he'd gladly provided what she wanted. Gage issued a mental command for Andrea to wake from her induced sleep. "An-dray-ah," he called in a soft sing-songy voice.

His mate stretched her arms above her head, and Gage captured them in one of his large hands. His other hand lightly traced a line down her soft throat, over her collar bone, and finally down to her breast. He cupped the weight of it in his palm as his lips found the other breast, already puckering up to greet him. As he suckled, he slipped his hand under the covers finding the juncture of her thighs wet and ready for him. "Good evening, my love," he said as he blanketed her with his body. "Did you sleep well?"

It was a rhetorical question because Gage knew she had slept deeply, he made sure of it. As he did every morning he'd issued a mental command, sending Andrea to sleep until he alone would awaken her. It was one of the things he insisted on; needing to ensure his mate would be well rested and cared for.

Having lived through much in his long life, Gage was a powerful male who held onto the old ways. He had been the lord of his castle, literally, and expected all the rights and privileges afforded to one such as him. He was the decision maker and his word law. He expected everyone in his household to obey, even his mate. Some might think him high-handed, but he did what was necessary to assure those under his domain were safe.

"You know I slept well." Andrea smiled up at him and moved her hips seductively under his heavy erection. Beneath her thick lashes her eyes darkened when her gaze roamed over his face and down his neck. "But I am rather hungry."

He slid one hand behind her head, bringing her mouth to where his shoulder met his neck. "Take, my mate. Take from me," he commanded.

Gage felt the warmth of her breath whisper over his skin when her mouth closed over his flesh and her fangs sank deep. His shaft jumped in response to each draw of her mouth. He closed his eyes, savoring the erotic sensation. It would have been so easy to give into the temptation to stay in bed with his heartmate, but they had things that needed attention.

After Andrea licked the small wounds on his neck closed, Gage pushed down his own hunger and slowly removed himself from their bed, offering her his hand.

"Come, my dear. We have much to do tonight. We have many arrangements to make for our gathering."

Andrea placed her hand in his, allowing him to escort her to the bathroom. In no time, Gage sat behind his mate in a steaming tub of hot water, enjoying the feel of her naked body touching his.

He soaped a washcloth as he spoke. "Are you looking forward to Halloween, my dear?"

"You know I am. Auguste Roux has agreed to be our chef for the evening."

"The world famous French chef?" A moan escaped from his mate's lips while he worked the cloth over her body.

Andrea nodded her head and leaned back against him. "I wanted to make this year extra special, since it is the tenth year of our little gathering."

"Auguste will be perfect. Being a vampire, he will know how to prepare the food in such a way that our guests will have no trouble digesting it." She opened her thighs for him when he headed south with the soapy cloth.

"I rented a room at that hotel on the strip for the ball Friday night to kick off the festivities." Gage kissed the top of her head and she continued. "And Saturday evening will begin at our home, where Auguste and his staff will serve the finest delicacies from around the world."

Gage grabbed the soap and lathered the washcloth before beginning to cleanse his own body. "I'm sure the drinks and food will be as plentiful as the sand in the desert, but of course, all the guests will save room for the final course of the evening."

Gage licked his lips in anticipation, knowing the evening would culminate in a trip to the Red Rock Canyon for the night's entertainment. Waiting for the vampires would be a group of humans, specially selected by him and his mate. They would release the humans into the canyon while Gage's guests were told to wait patiently, because the couple wanted to afford their guests an opportunity to indulge their baser predatory nature to track their meal rather than just have it handed to them.

"I am so looking forward to our event." Gage could not keep the excitement from his voice as he stood, offering a hand to his mate.

After handing her from the tub, he gave her a

towel, seeing to her needs before his own.

"Thank you," Andrea said, taking the towel. "If only hunting clubs hadn't been banned by the Vampire Enforcement Squad."

Gage hissed his disapproval at the mention of the agency. Gage and his friends were part of a small group of vampires in the world that did not recognize the Vampire Enforcement Squad, or as it was otherwise known, VES, as having the right to police the breed. He believed in the freedom to be what he was and allow his basic instincts to rule his behavior rather than the VES. And because VES agents were stationed throughout the world, including Vegas, Gage needed to be very careful with his gathering.

"We definitely do not want VES to crash our little get together. And keeping it a secret from the agency is no small feat. Even though we kept the guest list small, we need so many humans."

Andrea flashed him a brilliant smile as she worked the towel over her lush body. "Humans are like potato chips, darling. You can't eat just one. And we must make sure all our guests get their fill."

"I agree, but when many humans go missing, VES comes snooping." Gage wrapped his towel around his waist.

"Which is why we have gathered them throughout most of the year and waited until Halloween to have our party." Andrea twisted her hair up into a bun, holding it there with a well-placed clip.

As they dressed, Gage contemplated why he always held his gathering during a weekend near Halloween. First, Halloween was celebrated all week long in Vegas, so no matter which day of the week

Halloween fell on, there were still people in costumes come the weekend. And second, during Halloween, no one looked twice at a vampire walking the streets with his fangs showing and blood on his clothes, so if they returned from the canyon a little messy from the night's event, no one noticed. His fangs lengthened from his gums at the thought in anticipation.

As Andrea and Gage made their way through their home, they walked down the halls, greeting each guard by name. Not taking any chances, Gage had a security force watching his home every night to keep unwanted agents out and the humans they had collected in.

They descended the circular staircase leading from the second floor to the foyer. Their large home was decorated in a medieval motif—their favorite period in history, the one they enjoyed living in most. At the bottom of the stairs stood a suit of armor holding a coat of arms flag in one hand and a sword lifted above its helmet in the other. As they entered the foyer, a commotion could be heard from the back of the house, drawing the couple.

"I have another for you," an average size male called out to them when they entered the kitchen.

The hunter stood before the couple, holding a flailing human by her arm. "I picked her up in the alley off Henderson."

Andrea walked over to the woman and took her chin firmly in her hand, forcing the woman to look at her. "Thank you, Wade. She looks decent enough. "

"She's clean, Andrea."

His mate shot the man a harsh look as he mispronounced her name. Her ire rolled over Gage. "My name is An-*dray*-ah. Not An-dree-ah."

How dare he! Anger heated Gage's blood like molten lava at the hunter's disrespect.

"My apologies, Miss An-dray-ah." Wade had the decency to look properly chastened. "I tasted her blood myself to test the cleanliness," the hunter offered to make amends.

Andrea gave an approving look. "Good, you never know with ladies of the night. Even though we can't catch any human diseases, there's no reason to eat infected food." This remark caused the woman to thrash harder. Andrea turned her attention back to the woman. "Be still. There is no way you can get away from us."

Gage came up behind Andrea. "My love, why don't you introduce her to her roommates while I reward Wade's hard work. I'll join you in a minute so we can play with our new friend."

He watched the anticipatory smile light his mate's face as she took the woman from her kidnapper and marched her down the basement stairs. It was almost enough to quell his anger at the hunter's mispronunciation of Andrea's name. Almost.

"Here you go." Gage struggled to keep the anger from his face when he handed Wade a handful of bills. "You'll find your usual fee is there."

"Thank you, sir." The hunter wisely chose not to count the money before he pushed it into the pocket of his jeans.

As Wade turned to leave, Gage pinned him against the wall by his neck, his feet dangled off the ground. "And Wade, if you ever call my heartmate by the incorrect name again, I will punish you. She gets very angry when someone mispronounces her name. And when she's angry, I'm angry. Got it?"

The male nodded as best he could with the limited movement Gage's hand allowed. He slowly lowered the man to the floor. Releasing his neck, he smoothed the wrinkles from the man's shirt. "Now I trust you can see yourself out. I have a new plaything waiting below."

"Of-of course, sir," Wade stuttered, rubbing his throat.

Gage took the stairs to the basement two at a time and greeted the set of burly male guards located on each side of the door. He hungrily licked his lips in anticipation, while one of them unlocked, then swung the door open for him.

"Thank you, Trace," he called over his shoulder as he walked through the door.

"Enjoy your meal," the guard returned.

An evil chuckle burst through his lips. "You know I will."

Chapter 7

It had been several weeks since Stephan returned and things were beginning to become somewhat normal, as normal as living with a human could be, he reasoned. He and Katrina had been getting along, and Marcus seemed to be happy that his sire and his human were cordial. The three of them did things together like going to shows and having what Marcus referred to as Wednesday Night Game Night.

Tonight the three of them sat together on the overstuffed black leather couch in the living room watching TV on the seventy inch plasma that hung on the wall. On either side of the TV, a series of ceiling to floor length windows gave them a beautiful view of the strip. Each window had specially made dark burgundy drapes which, combined with the roll down UV shades, kept out the sun's rays, making it safe for the vampires to roam around the home during daylight hours. Tonight the blinds were opened wide, which allowed a view of the glittery lights of the city outside that rivaled the images on the TV screen.

He rather liked the improvements the younger vampire had made to his home, the new appliances, special shades, modern furniture, and TVs. Marcus kept the penthouse modern and up-to-date, and he appreciated it. It was beginning to feel like home, even with the human staying within.

Marcus turned toward Stephan and Kat, TV remote in hand. A bump of his finger clicked off the TV, and Marcus laid the remote on the coffee table. "What do you want to play tonight you two? Poker? Pictionary?" A gleam lightened Marcus' brown eyes, and he wagged his brows. "Naked Pictionary? Oh wait, I know, how about Naked Twister?"

Kat hit Marcus playfully on his chest and giggled while Stephan groaned. The image in his mind of Kat and him twisted together, their bodies naked, was enough to cause his member to harden. In fact, it did, prompting him to readjust himself after he grabbed a nearby throw pillow to cover his lap.

"Oh, I know," Kat said between giggles. "How about Charades?"

Marcus gave her a wide smile. "Yeah, that sounds like fun. The person who guesses correctly is the next to go."

"I'll go first," Kat volunteered. Stephan breathed a sigh of relief to have some space between him and Kat. He needed to get his body under control, and that was impossible with her sitting so close, touching him. He didn't want to acknowledge it, but his body wasn't his own when Kat was near. She elicited responses in him that would take a lesser male to his knees. It took every ounce of his carefully honed self-control to be close to her every night and not take her in his arms to drink from her while they made sweet love.

Marcus poured himself a drink. "Anybody want one?" he asked, lifting the bottle of brandy.

"Not right now," Stephan replied while their roommate shook her head.

Kat stood in front of the black onyx coffee table, an

excited look on her face. She held her hands as if she were praying, and then opened them outward.

"Book?" Marcus guessed.

"Right, it's the name of a book," Kat said.

Stephan smiled and crossed his arms over the pillow in his lap. "It's been a long while since I have played this game, but thought you were supposed to be silent."

"Kat and silence are two things that never go together like a bathtub and a hairdryer." Marcus quipped, and Kat shot him a look.

"Okay, from now on I won't talk," Kat promised as she lifted two fingers in the air.

"Two words," stated Stephan.

Kat nodded while Marcus said, "I'm surprised you know the title of a book, even if it is just two words."

She gave him a one finger salute, flipping him off. Stephan laughed a deep bass sound that rumbled through his chest. He rather enjoyed her tenacity.

"I thought you said it's two words, not one," teased Marcus.

Kat mimed eating, then got down on all fours. Blood rushed through Stephan's veins as his treacherous mind pictured him behind Kat, pumping into her. The image made his shaft push against the button on the waist of his jeans. Stephan repositioned himself again behind the pillow, swallowing the lump in his throat.

"I have no idea what you are doing, but I got to tell you, baby, it's working for me," Marcus said. Stephan shot him a warning sideways glance, which he missed.

"Is it Old McDonald's Farm?" guessed Marcus.

"That would be three words, Marcus, not two. I

thought you could count," Stephan remarked, shifting on the couch to ease the growing pressure of his pants. "And it's a book not a song."

Kat shook her head, laughing at Stephan's wisecrack. The sound warmed his heart.

She stood on her tip toes and stretched her arms over her head, clasping her hands together as if they were bound, which sent Stephan's mind up to the bedroom with an image of his naked body hovering over Kat while he restrained her arms above her head on the bed. Stephan swallowed a moan and thought he might just be the first person to ever be killed by Charades.

"Is it diving?" guessed Stephan desperately wanting to end Kat's turn before he exploded.

Kat shook her head. She smiled as if an idea popped into her head and grabbed both of her breasts in her hands, pushing them together, sending another rush of heat through Stephan's body.

"The Rack!" Marcus shouted suddenly realizing the title of the book. Kat nodded.

"Thank god," Stephan muttered too quietly for Kat to hear, but Marcus' preternatural hearing must have caught it easily for he smiled.

"My turn." Marcus bounded up from the couch. "Hey Kat, what was that bit you did in the beginning with the eating and then crawling on the floor?"

"That was Rack of Lamb," Kat answered, shrugging her shoulders and returned to the couch. "And then I pretended to be strung out on a rack."

Stephan shook his head and smiled. He expected Kat to plop down in Marcus' spot on the couch, but instead she returned to her previous spot beside him.

Their legs touched as she sunk into the butter soft leather, sending the equivalent of electric current racing through his bloodstream. Her honeysuckle smell surrounded him, wrapping around him like a boa constrictor, making it hard to breathe.

Stephan placed his arm on the back of the couch behind her head, trying to appear relaxed while his entire body tingled with prickly heat. He turned his attention fully on Marcus and away from the impulse to hook his arm around Katrina's shoulders and pull her to him for a kiss.

Marcus mimed movie, then held up three fingers sending them off in round two. Marcus touched his eyes.

"Eyes," guessed Stephan. Marcus nodded and put his arms straight out from his shoulders.

"Letter T?" guessed Kat.

"Yeah, that's it, Eyes T. I loved that movie," The jest earned a friendly swat from Kat on his thigh.

Marcus shook his arms bringing their attention back to him. He opened his arms out to the side.

"Wide?" guessed Kat correctly.

Marcus nodded his head and clapped his hands together, one on top of the other.

"Wide Clapping?" Kat speculated, leaning forward in her excitement.

"Closed?...Shut?" guessed Stephan.

Kat jumped up as she and Stephan simultaneously shouted, "Eyes Wide Shut!"

Stephan could sense Kat's arousal, the change in her pheromones. Without conscious thought, he gently pushed into her mind to find out what had caused her sudden change. He immediately saw the image of the three of them in bed, and his erection jumped in approval.

A shadow in her mind, he watched an image from the erotic movie come into Kat's mind. The image quickly morphed into her with both Marcus and him, all of them naked, acting out the scene.

When Kat sat down quickly, her heady scent surrounded him. He heard her heart pound in her chest, very much aware of the places his body touched Kat's as she sat beside him on the couch. The mental image of the three of them would not stop playing in his head.

When he turned to look at Kat, her tongue peeked out to wet her lips. A groan pushed from his throat at the sensual sight. He could think of several intimate places he would like her tongue to explore.

"That was a tie, who's turn is it?" asked Marcus as he made his way back to the couch.

Stephan shifted uncomfortably on the couch trying to adjust himself to ease his growing discomfort. "Kat can go. I need a break. You two play without me," he bit out through clenched teeth, his self-control slipping as the beast within wanted to mate. He stood then and quickly walked up the stairs with the pillow still in his hands.

Kat heard the door to Stephan's bedroom slam shut. Her eyes darted to Marcus. "I wonder what that was about."

He gave her a weak smile. "He's been so moody since coming back here." Marcus lifted his glass and downed the rest of the amber liquid from inside.

"Sometimes, I don't think he likes me," Kat said. "I feel like I make him uncomfortable. Maybe I should find my own place."

"Don't be silly. I told you, you will always be welcomed here."

"By you. But now that Stephan's back—"

Marcus spoke over her, interrupting her sentence "Stephan doesn't want you to go either."

Kat raised one corner of her lips, giving her friend a disbelieving smirk. "How do you know that?"

"I can read him. I've known him a long time. You leaving is not what he wants, trust me."

Katrina crossed her arms over her chest. "What does he want?"

Marcus looked into his empty glass, then his brown eyes met hers. "I need a refill. The night is still young, Kitty Kat. You want to go downstairs to the casino and see if we can lose some money?" he asked, changing the subject.

Since he'd done so by mentioning one of Katrina's favorite past times, she decided to go with it and smiled. "You paying?"

"Yeah. My treat. I'll go get my stash of cash, and we'll get out of here."

While Kat sat on the couch waiting for Marcus to return, her thoughts drifted to the vampire upstairs. She admitted to herself she liked him. A lot. But did he have any feelings for her?

As she had sat sandwiched between the two males, their thighs touching, she was all too aware of the two powerful, gorgeous bodies that flanked her. She and Stephan had been flirting for weeks, but neither of them seemed to have the courage to take things to the next level by admitting their attraction. And though she had no idea why, Marcus had barely shown her any affection since Stephan returned. She supposed Marcus kept his distance out of respect for his sire, but all she knew for sure was the pair of them left her feeling unsatisfied and achy.

Marcus told her Stephan wanted her to stick around, but did he truly want her to stay or was he tolerating her because of Marcus? She decided to make it her mission to find out if the sexy vampire had any feelings for her.

As she and Marcus exited the penthouse, she committed herself to one mission—find out if Stephan liked her. She just hoped it wouldn't prove to be mission impossible.

Chapter 8

Andrea awoke to the music of another one of her favorite bands, Smashmouth. She stretched her arms over her head and turned to look at the male she loved. Gage lay beside her, propped on his elbow. Love and lust darkened his eyes.

"Good evening, darling," she said in a sultry whisper. Gage responded by capturing her lips in a fierce kiss. Their tongues danced back and forth, and the heat from their kiss rushed through Andrea's blood. Her stomach cinched as her excitement rose, but she pushed her desire aside ruthlessly. She had something she needed to talk about, and if she didn't pull back now, talking would be the last thing they would end up doing.

Andrea broke their kiss, pulling her head back to lick her kiss swollen lips. Gage tracked the movement of her pink tongue as it darted across her full lips.

"Gage, I have a surprise for you."

"What is it, my dear?" His voice sounded thick with lust.

Andrea's smile reached her eyes. "I'm with child. We're going to have a baby."

"It cannot be. Are you sure?" Gage whispered, disbelief suffocating his voice.

"Yes, I'm sure. I've been to the doctor, and he confirmed it. I'm six weeks along."

"I-I can't believe it. This is such a miracle!" he gushed, squeezing her tightly against him. He laid his cheek on top of her head. "After three hundred years, we are blessed with a child! We have waited so long, I had lost all hope."

Andrea thought about all the times they'd discussed having a family. How sad they were when each year passed with no baby. Now they were finally going to have a little one to love and cherish. Gage raised his head, his eyes held a joyful twinkle. "Is it a boy or a girl?"

"Yes." Andrea nodded her head and laughed.

"Of course, it's too early to know. I can't believe I am finally going to be a father!" Gage squeezed her tighter still, obviously forgetting his own strength so lost in his happiness.

"Um Gage, you're squishing the baby." His chest muffled Andrea's voice.

Gage immediately released her. "I'm sorry. I lost my head." He ran the back of his hand down her cheek in a soft caress. "I have never been happier in my entire life. Thank you!"

Andrea leaned up and gave him a small kiss. "I'm happy too, my love."

Gage hopped out of bed and began getting dressed. "I know, let's celebrate. We'll go to dinner, and I'll get tickets to your favorite show." His fingers deftly worked the buttons of his shirt as he spoke. "You know, the one at Reaper's."

"Desire?" Andrea supplied the name of the show, propping herself up on her elbows to ogle her lover as he dressed. Corded muscles played under his pale skin, his blond hair caressed his forehead when he bent to don his trousers. Andrea appreciated the way his clothes hugged his toned body, and she sighed in appreciation.

"That's the one. Here, let me help you up." He scooped his mate into his arms.

Andrea giggled. "I'm pregnant, not ill. I can get out of bed all by myself."

"Make no mistake, my dear, I will be over-protective of you every minute until our baby is born healthy."

As she dressed in a little black number with a rhinestone belt, she looked at her profile in the ornately carved full-length mirror which stood in the corner of their bedroom. Soon her belly would no longer be flat, but swollen with their child. She could sense her child's presence within her, knew it was strong for now.

Unfortunately, vampire pregnancies were a difficult thing. Miscarriages were common. If the baby carried to term, sometimes both the baby and mother died in childbirth. This baby was a miracle and a curse at the same time. She protectively covered her stomach with both hands. She would do whatever it took to see this child born, even if it meant giving up her life.

Their eyes met in the mirror.

You won't have to give up your life. Gage's voice sounded heavy with emotion in her mind. *I'll protect you and our baby fiercely! I promise you, my love, we'll have our miracle.*

He crossed the room, coming behind his mate and encircled her in his arms. She settled back against him with a sigh. *I know you will keep us safe. I have complete faith in you.*

****

Katrina joined Marcus and Stephan on the terrace. It overlooked the strip, giving the trio a beautiful view of the neon forest before them. They watched the cars crawl by, the brake lights blinking like lights on a Christmas tree. The city was alive, the pulse of the strip keeping time with the blinking lights.

Stephan took a drink of his actual Bloody Mary and admired the view, but not the city. He only had eyes for Kat this evening. The short, black miniskirt she wore made of glossy vinyl that reflected the neon from the strip created a psychedelic pattern of swirls and lines as her hips swished back and forth when she meandered around the terrace. A red silk shirt and black stiletto heels completed her ensemble and sent need slamming hard into Stephan. He couldn't take his eyes off of her, which he hoped was most likely the reaction she had hoped to elicit from him.

Marcus voiced what Stephan did not. "Wow Kat, you look amazing!" Marcus swept her into his arms and gave her a kiss on the cheek. A growl of warning escaped from Stephan's throat.

Back off Marcus, she's mine. He sent his mental warning directly through their mindlink, immediately wishing he had censored it.

She's mine? Where had that come from? She wasn't his. They hadn't even gone out on a date. Sure they had been living together for weeks, but that didn't count. Staying in separate rooms, they were nothing more than roommates, but the way he felt tonight made Stephan determined to change that. Those two little words, she's mine, changed everything. His brain finally registered what his body had been trying to tell him since the first night they met, he wanted her. He wanted her near, wanted to be inside of her body and mind. Standing on the terrace, he knew he had to have her.

And he would.

The kind of male used to having what he wanted, he didn't let anyone or anything get in his way. Being a warrior, he knew how to fight for what he desired. The only problem was he couldn't fight to have Kat; he would have to win her, and tonight was as good a night to start as any.

"If you two will excuse me, I need to make a phone call." Marcus slipped silently off the balcony leaving the couple alone, closing the sliding glass door with a snick behind him.

"Marcus is correct, you do look wonderful." Stephan stepped closer to Katrina and tucked a stray golden curl behind her ear. He felt her shiver under his touch.

"Thank you." Kat smiled up at him. "You look pretty good yourself."

Stephan swept his long arm down his smoke gray dress shirt and matching designer slacks. "Thank you. I'm glad you like what you see."

"Very much!" She murmured low as if she hoped he wouldn't hear. Of course with his preternatural hearing, Stephan easily caught what she said.

He leaned into her, barely a breath's space between them, to capture her eyes with his dark sensual gaze. "I'd like to take you out sometime."

Kat swallowed hard, and in a breathy voice she replied, "I'd like that."

"How about tonight?"

"I have to go to work." Kat stared up at him with

doe eyes. He wanted to get lost in those eyes forever and forget about the real world for a while, but she had to go soon.

Stephan quickly looked at his watch then back into Kat's eyes. He could hear her heart beat faster and smiled, showing a hint of fang that he knew she found sexy. "Will you allow me to drive you to work?"

He would love to take her to work, for many reasons, not just because it would allow them a little more time together, but because a male wanted to do things for his female, protect her, care for her.

When she agreed, his heart soared in triumph, knowing he was on his way to making her his.

Chapter 9

Katrina donned her leather and lace costume and completed her make up routine in record time. As she sat at her makeup station humming to herself, Dana asked, "What's with you tonight? You're glowing."

Kat smiled. "I just feel really good, like everything is right with the world."

Cathy slid her a suspicious glance. "It's Stephan isn't it? Something happen?"

Dana sat straighter in her chair and placed her brush on her makeup station. "Oh tell! I want to hear all about tall, dark, and handsome."

Kat laughed. "There's nothing to tell, he just brought me to work."

"Must have been quite a ride, you are on cloud nine," Cathy commented, applying an overly generous amount of rouge to her cheeks.

"It was an ordinary ride." Katrina gave a carefree shrug before giving her friend a mischievous look. "But he did ask me out."

"Ooooooh! That explains the humming. Where are you going?"

"He said it was a surprise, but we're going tomorrow night."

Before they could question her further, the stage manager did his stage call, and they scampered onto the stage. They stood frozen in their beginning positions,

Kat front and center, as the curtain parted. The music started, and the women began their seductive dance. Kat felt particularly light on her feet. She had to struggle to keep her mind on the choreography and not on Stephan. As she danced, she imagined him in the audience and danced only for him.

****

On the arm of her mate, Andrea entered Reapers, noting the decor. The club, designed to showcase the show, discreetly housed a large bar in the back manned by four bartenders doing flips and tricks with the liquor bottles. The floor had three levels, the top two of which supported a series of tables and chairs positioned in half moon shapes toward the stage. The bottom level contained high backed semicircular private VIP booths where couples could sit on padded benches and view the show in virtual privacy corralled by tables with long white tableclothes. Big burly bouncers, most of whom her senses told her were vampires, patrolled along the walls, waiting to step in when needed.

At the front of the room, the spotlighted stage stood front and center with its blood-red curtains pulled back and the club's beautiful dancers on display. The women cascaded in threes down a set of stairs onto the stage, swaying their hips, their red stiletto thigh-high boots clicking with each unified step. Their dance elicited from the customers exactly what was promised by the name of the show, desire. It filled the room, settling over Andrea as they made their way to a private booth.

The dancers twirled and swept their bodies in suggestive ways while the stage lights glistened off the shiny leather costumes, accenting their best assets. Each dancer wore a fire engine red smile designed to illicit thoughts of steamy wanton nights.

As Andrea and Gage watched the show, the mood of the crowd mixed with the swaying and gyrating hips on the stage in a titillating combination. The blonde in the middle looked particularly beautiful. Her hair glistening in the bright lights, she moved with a grace that drew the eye. Andrea could feel Gage's lust rise as his gaze followed the woman.

Feeling practically naughty, Andrea moved her hand under the table onto Gage's thigh. She squeezed as she leaned into him. "See the one in the middle with the long blonde hair and the large chest?"

"Yes," Gage rasped as Andrea's long fingers began making their way up his thigh.

"Isn't she pretty?" She brushed her finger tips over the bulge in his pants.

"Yes." Apparently that was the most complicated statement he could make with her fingers dancing over his pants.

"I want you to think of us with her as I do this." She moved her hand up to the fastenings on his slacks. With nimble fingers, she undid the hook and slid down the zipper, freeing his erection from the offensive material. She took him into her hand and stroked him with one long caress from the bottom to the tip, causing him to suck a deep breath.

"Do you like that?" she asked, knowing the answer before the question even left her lips.

"Yes," he breathed.

"Can you say anything besides, yes?" She stroked him harder as his eyes tracked the sultry movements of the blonde on stage.

"Not. Right. Now."

Andrea smiled.

****

Marcus sat outside his club, waiting in Stephan's sleek silver Mercedes-Benz SL 65 AMG Roadster with the top down. Looking exhausted, Kat sank into the ash-gray leather passenger seat, letting it cradle her tired muscles.

"You ready to go home?" asked Marcus, trying not to notice how long her legs looked peeking out from under the black mini she had changed into. He turned the key and brought all twelve cylinders to life, starting their short trip home.

"Yeah. I'm tired." Kat laid her head back, a sigh escaping her lips before she closed her eyes. The wind whipped her hair behind her in golden waves when they pulled away from a stop light.

"Marcus, can I ask you about Stephan?"

Marcus tightened his grip on the leather wrapped steering wheel. "Yes." His voice was as even as the expression on his face.

"I have to know. Does Stephan really like me or is he just attracted to me sexually?"

"That is a complicated question for a vampire. Our desire is different from humans. It's not just sexual, or bloodlust or companionship. Our hunger can be a combination."

"So how does Stephan hunger for me?" she asked, turning to look at him.

"Honestly, I don't know for sure. He has blocked me from his mind. I can tell you that physical changes come over him when you enter the room. His muscles tense, his testosterone increases, pupils dilate. I've never seen him react to a woman the way he reacts to you."

"Oh."

"In fact, in the two hundred and fifty years I have known him, he has never been so cranky. I think that's because of you too."

"Thanks a lot!" Kat shot him a perturbed look, and Marcus smiled.

"That's not a bad thing. I think you have gotten under his skin, and he doesn't know how to react. It's making him edgy."

"Huh, that makes two of us."

"Yeah. I know. If you two don't hook up soon, I'm going to have to move out. I can't take much more of your moods." Marcus laughed as he pulled the car into valet parking.

They rode the elevator in companionable silence up to the penthouse. Before the doors opened, Kat turned to Marcus and gave him an affable hug.

"Not that I'm complaining, but what's this for?" he asked, wrapping his arms around her back.

"For being such a good friend."

Marcus stifled a moan. It felt good to have Kat in his arms. He loved the way she felt against him, and he knew that if she and Stephan became a couple, he was going to lose the ability to be close with her.

Most vampires didn't share their mates with another, and Stephan was definitely the possessive type. This might be the last time they ever got to hug, and he wasn't going to let it slip by. He rested his chin on the top of her head, absorbing the scent and feel of her, memorizing it for all time.

A pang of regret tightened his chest. Kat would not

have an easy time if she became involved with Stephan. He was not a gentle man, but a warrior long ago hardened by battle. However, Marcus knew he would not stand in their way. They each deserved happiness. He only hoped they might find it in each other's arms, without Kat getting hurt in the process.

He hugged her close, refusing to let her go even when the elevator door opened to reveal Stephan standing with his arms crossed over his thick chest. As his gaze drifted over the friends, his expression changed from one of welcome to a glaring sneer that left no question about whose arms Kat belonged in.

Chapter 10

Kat entered the living room dressed in black skinny jeans that accentuated her long legs, and her eyes immediately found the tall vampires in the middle of the room. Stephan stood next to Marcus rolling up his sleeves. He wore dark blue jeans and a fitted white oxford tucked neatly into his pants, emphasizing how his body created a Vee from his broad shoulders to his narrow waist. Yummy. Damn, she'd never seen anyone rock an oxford like him.

His eyes locked on her. Was he watching her hips? She gave them a little more swish than normal just in case as she crossed the room in her bright green T-shirt with the swirling design across the bosom. Her hair flowed down her back in smooth waves with each step. His gaze roamed over her then locked on her eyes. She felt as if she was falling into his dark, hungry gaze.

"Ready to go, Kitten?" he inquired, snapping her from her daze.

Kat brushed her sweaty palms down the thighs of her jeans. Her heart raced, aflutter with the anticipation and excitement of this evening's events.

"I guess I'm ready." She smiled up at him. "You still haven't told me what we are doing."

"I know. It's a surprise, for me to know and you to find out," he answered, cryptically, with a wink.

The phone rang, making Kat jump. Marcus picked

up the receiver and murmured, "thanks" into the phone. "Your ride is here," he called to the couple. "Have fun."

"Shall we go?" Stephan asked and formally offered his arm to Kat. She slipped her arm in his, feeling the tight muscles and sinew through his shirt. Wearing what looked like a forced smile, Marcus waved the pair off, bidding them goodnight.

Once downstairs, the parking attendant opened the limousine door for the couple. Kat crawled into the vehicle, giving Stephan a nice view of her derrière. Realizing what she had done, she peeked over her shoulder and smiled sheepishly at him.

Returning her grin, Stephan chuckled. "Nice view, Kitten."

Stephan slid in beside her, tucking her under his arm. Kat watched out the window as they left the strip, and headed toward the airport.

"Are we going to the airport?" Kat asked with raised brows.

"Yes, that is where our journey begins this evening."

"Journey?" Curiosity widened her eyes. "Where are we going?"

"You'll see, my little kitten." A sexy smile spread across Stephan's face. "I've planned a little adventure."

A surprise. She loved surprises.

They arrived at the airport in record time. A moss green EC-130 helicopter awaited them. Inside, theater seating, covered in the finest leather, welcomed her. The spacious interior gave them freedom of movement, while the wrap around windows, allowed for an unobstructed view.

Once they settled in the soft leather seats of the

aircraft, they donned their headsets.

"Ready to go?" cut in the pilot over the headset.

Kat nodded, looking up into Stephan's eyes.

"We're ready." His deep voice rang through the intercom system causing a shiver down Kat's back.

"We're off," said the pilot as the rotors spun to life. Small swirls of dust danced like mini tornadoes on the tarmac outside. Stephan reached up and hit a button on the ceiling of the craft, creating a private channel on which she and her date could speak.

Once in the air, he gestured out the window. Kat turned sideways to glance where he pointed. Stephan leaned his body against her back as he tapped on the glass. "Look, you don't want to miss that view."

It was difficult to concentrate with him pressed against her, but somehow she managed, and it was definitely worth the struggle. The view of the Vegas strip mesmerized her. She'd seen an aerial shot of the strip at night on TV, but it didn't compare to the buffet of colors that fed her vision tonight. Below them an ocean of gold flowed where red, orange and pink neon creatures flitted about the blue and green neon coral.

As they flew, Stephan continued to describe points of interest. They flew over the Hoover Dam admiring the architecture and its grand scale. Lake Mead seemed smooth like blown sugar as they went by, the boats tucked neatly into its harbor for the night. With the hum of the rotor blades in the background, they listened to music in their headphones, lovely music. And she wondered if Stephan had specially chosen it for its romantic quality.

They arrived at the Grand Canyon and followed the Colorado River as it snaked through until they came to a cascading waterfall. The helicopter descended into the canyon past the rust colored waves on the rocky walls. They touched down beside the base of the falls, where the falling water met the still river causing a white wake that crashed with a purring sound. Kat watched as the full moon's reflection shimmered and shook in the ripples of the water.

Once the rotors settled to a stop, Stephan handed Kat out of the helicopter, then grabbed a blue cooler and quilt from their hiding place in the chopper. He tucked her under his arm and escorted her to the falls. It felt natural, tucked up against his side. The smell of his cologne wafted on the breeze. She couldn't help herself. She took a deep breath and knew she'd remember that delicious woodsy scent for the rest of her life.

When the sound of whirling rotors caught Kat's attention, she turned and watched the helicopter ascend. Her long blonde hair whipped around her in the wash from the blades. She looked back at Stephan whose own hair was tied neatly back in a leather thong at his neck. As she worked to gather her whipping hair Kat asked, "Where is the helicopter going? It's not leaving us here, is it?"

Stephan looked down at Kat, a mischievous smirk on his face. "Why so worried, Kitten? Are you afraid to be alone with me?"

"I don't know. You are a big bad vampire after all. Should I be afraid of you?" she teased.

Suddenly serious, Stephan replied, "No, Katrina, you never have to worry. I would never hurt you. Never!"

Kat watched as a flash of emotion crossed Stephan's face. Could he have been hurt by what she said? She was only kidding. She knew she would be safe with him.

"I feel safe with you, Stephan."

She knew him through Marcus, knew he was honorable, knew he would never hurt her, at least not physically.

But emotionally was another issue.

Being here with him, alone, made Kat's heart race, not from fear, but from the strength of emotions running through her. She could fall hard for this man. And therefore, he could break her heart.

"I hope you mean that. I would hate to think you were regretting coming out with me. The thought that you might be afraid to be with me is inordinate."

The sincerity in his voice stilled her feet. She looked up into his handsome face, easily reading his concern. "I'm not afraid to be with you," she assured him, putting all the sincerity she could behind the statement.

He paused for a moment, his eyes searching her face as if he could see into her mind. Her breath hitched as she fell into the sapphire depths of his intense gaze and then the moment was broken by him giving her shoulders a squeeze before releasing her to fling the quilt onto the floor of the canyon. The fluffy white quilt was a stark contrast, in both color and texture, to the hard, red canyon floor.

Kat sat on the soft quilt listening to the sound of the rushing water, watching as Stephan withdrew the items from the cooler. He removed the contents one by one and laid each carefully on the quilt before Kat.

It looked amazing. He'd brought all her favorite foods. For the appetizer, Stephan produced a nutty

Manchego cheese with crisp apples. He followed that by a loaf of French bread with a bruschetta made of diced tomatoes with onion and basil. A vinaigrette-based potato salad and cold sliced ham with a fruit glaze comprised the main course.

Katrina licked her lips and wondered how he knew just what she liked most. She didn't miss the knowing smile that graced Stephan's face. It was as if he had read her mind.

The food tasted delicious. As Stephan fed her, Kat chewed each bite slowly, savoring the exquisite taste. The conversation remained light while they ate, Stephan alternating between feeding her and himself.

Sated, Katrina leaned back on her arms. "I'm stuffed. I can't eat any more," she said as Stephan tried to feed her another bite of the glazed ham.

He dusted off his hand. "Want to walk off our dinner? We could explore the canyon," he offered, rising to his full height beside her.

"That sounds lovely." She allowed him to take her hand in his. The warmth from his large hand encircled her delicate appendage as they walked.

They strolled along the shore of the Colorado, hand in hand. Katrina took in her surroundings. The walls of the canyon rose around them, the jagged rock face casting shadows under the moonlight. The aromatic smell of shale and limestone mixed with the river to create a primal, outdoorsy scent that surrounded them as they wandered.

The soft scuffling sound brought them to a stop when they came upon a tan and black coyote with her three pups. Stephan squeezed her hand in a friendly gesture, as she watched the three pups nuzzle into their mother. A smile graced Katrina's face when she heard one of the pups sing out, his cry high pitched and long, almost joyful.

Stephan stepped up behind Kat, his arm tightening around her waist, as he rested his chin on her shoulder to watch. She couldn't ignore the fact that her back pressed firmly against his perfect, muscular body. The scents of dark sandalwood and honeysuckle mingled, surrounding her while they watched the coyotes. The feel of him mixed with his unique scent in a heady combination that made white-hot desire course through her veins. Kat sighed, her body screaming with the need to turn in his arms and feel his lips on hers.

His lips brushed her ear as he whispered, "They are beautiful, aren't they?"

"They are so cute," she replied, careful to keep her voice low. "Why is that one crying?"

"They're singing. Coyotes love to sing. They sing to each other, at the moon, to show emotions." The feel of his hot breath ghosting over her sensitive ear sent a tremor through her body.

"Oh look," she practically squealed.

The couple watched as the pups began to wrestle. On shaky legs they stumbled over one another, nipping each other's ears and paws. Stephan laughed, the sound stirring something within her chest that caused her heart to flutter. Katrina tilted her head, looking up at him. "I love the way you laugh," she said on a sigh. He didn't do that nearly enough.

The look on his face softened, making butterflies dance in her stomach. She pulled her eyes away from his and gazed on the coyotes as a flush heated her cheeks.

The mother coyote ended the match when she noticed they had an audience. With a quick nip she brought the wrestling to a halt and led the pups into an opening in the canyon wall.

They stood for a minute longer, Stephan still holding Kat. She loved being in his arms. Being held by him seemed so right, and she was in no rush to let the moment pass. Unfortunately, as moments in time do, it moved on too quickly.

Slowly Stephan's arms fell from around her. "Shall we?" he invited, gesturing back toward the area from which they came.

As they approached the quilt, Kat stopped and cocked her head to one side. She could hear a soft melody drift along the wind. "Do you hear that?"

"Hear what?" Stephan held a straight face.

"Either I'm losing my mind or I hear classical music."

Stephan smiled wide, flashing his perfect white teeth. "You aren't losing your mind. I thought you might like some music this evening."

"I don't see any radio. What, are you a magician? How did you get music out here?"

Stephan looked at her with the Cheshire cat smile. "I may have a few tricks up my sleeve." He offered her his hand. "Would you care for a dance?"

Kat smiled as she placed one hand in his and rested her other hand on his muscular chest. "I'd love to."

He held her close, making her very aware of how her soft curves fit perfectly against the hard plane of his body. He tightened his grip around her waist, sending a wave of pleasure zinging through her body. The masculine smell of his cologne encircled her in the scent of dark amber with a hint of vanilla. They swayed gracefully to the music as Stephan twirled her around the canyon floor in the moonlight like a professional.

"You are an excellent dancer," Katrina commented while he dipped her.

"Thank you. I learned to dance as a young man. I grew up expected to attend balls so I had to learn all the modern dances. I guess the notion was so ingrained that I have continued to learn the newest dances of today." He spun her under his arm before bringing her back up against his body once more. "I find dancing is one way to fit into human society."

He kept his arm about her waist and grasped her hand in a gentle embrace. He gazed deeply into her blue-gray eyes while they danced. He moved with a grace only one of his kind could possess, taking her breath from her lungs. Each sway fluid, each step sure. He was poetry in motion. A perfect partner.

The moonlight cast a silvery glow over the canyon. Stephan moved with an elegance no human could ever hope to match, but Katrina was determined to try. She loved the feel of his muscular arms around her, guiding her over the ground. It felt like dancing on a cloud.

As the piece came to an end, the couple stopped. Stephan took her chin between his finger and thumb and gently brought his lips to meet hers in a tender kiss. His kiss, feather light, made her stomach knot when he touched his lips to hers.

Kat's arms encircled his back, and she pressed her body into his. Her fingers roamed, tracing each muscle, sending little sparks of want through her. Stephan moaned softly against her lips as if need coursed through his body in response to her touch.

He lifted her green T-shirt and splayed one of his large hands against her stomach feeling his way up to cup the weight of her breast in his hand. He rubbed his thumb across her nipple, making the pink bud harden against her lace bra. He deepened his kiss, squeezing her body closer to his.

She melded into him as she ran her hands up his thick biceps, bringing them to rest on his shoulders. She swept her fingers lightly over his chest, opening his shirt so she could touch his bared skin and taut muscles.

He lightly kissed along her jaw, trailed down her neck. His tongue flicked out, tasting her creamy skin. His lips parted, teeth raked her delicate skin. A shiver went through her and her fingers flexed around his biceps, anchoring her as the sensations he created threatened to carry her away.

His muscles flexed under the pads of her fingers. He went stone still. She felt him inhale deeply, his lips closing to hover just above her skin.

He straightened, pulling back to create space between them. "What is your favorite flower, Kitten?"

Kat blinked, not sure she had heard him correctly, still lost in the erotic sensation of Stephan's lips on her neck. "What did you say?"

"I asked what your favorite flower is."

Kat blinked up at him in surprise. "Uh…tulips, I guess."

"I'll be right back," he said and disappeared before her eyes, a wisp of smoke was all that remained behind.

Kat looked around, unsure what had happened. One minute Stephan was there, the next there was only a little black smoke. He had disappeared like a Vegas magician.

"Stephan," she called out, turning a tight circle. "Stephan, where are you? If this is a trick, ha ha ha. Very funny. You can come out now."

Katrina looked around for any sign of him. Finding none, she wandered back to the blanket, hoping either Stephan or the helicopter would return soon. Trying to push away the growing feeling of abandonment, she sat down on the soft quilt, listened to the gentle music, and watched the waterfall.

Panic threatened to rise as she looked around her. She tried to focus on the gentle, comforting sound of the water, the delicate melody of the music, but found it impossible. Her mind kept returning to the fact that she was alone, a city girl surrounded by unpredictable nature.

Just when she decided to get up to pace off her growing anxiety, she felt Stephan's presence behind her. She turned to look at him. He stood over her, a commanding presence bathed in the light of the moon. The incredible sight eased the panic. He handed her one perfect white tulip.

"Where did you get this?" her voice full of wonder.

"Do you like it?"

"I love it," she said, twirling the delicate flower between her fingers. "It's perfect, but where did you go?"

He knelt next to her on the quilt. "I went to get you the best tulip I could find."

"You disappeared," she said, the look on her face making it more of a question than a statement.

"Yes."

"How can you do that?" She had never seen anything like that.

Stephan gave a shrug of his broad shoulders. "It's something most vampires learn to do as their powers grow. Surely Marcus has dematerialized for you."

"No, I've never seen him do that. In fact, I don't think he knows how."

"He can't?"

"I've never seen him, if he can."

"Huh." The perplexed look on his face made her wonder what he thought. "I'm sorry if I scared you. I just assumed you had seen Marcus dematerialize. I did not intend to frighten you, Kitten. I was only gone five minutes."

His hand reached out and cupped her cheek. Kat's gaze raked Stephan from his boots to his head. The heat from the desire coursing through her veins burnt the last of her fear away. She sighed and smiled. "It's okay. Now that you are back, everything is fine."

His features softened as if he believed her and was much relieved. It was cute to think that he had been concerned about how she saw him. His eyes darkened with lust as he stared down at her. Scared definitely wasn't the emotion she was feeling now.

She felt wanton. Sensuous. Alluring.

He moved. At first, she thought he would kiss her, then he turned. From the cooler, he pulled a bottle of Cristal champagne along with two glasses and a bowl of strawberries. He sat behind Kat, cradling her against his chest as he poured the champagne. After handing her a fluted glass, he said, "I really am sorry, Kitten. I would not have vanished like that without explanation if I had known you hadn't seen that before."

Kat snuggled into his welcoming body, allowing his heat to warm her. "Tell me about what you did.

84

What's it like?"

His warm breath blew against her ear as he spoke. "Basically you will your body to dissipate while your consciousness streams toward a destination."

"Can you go anywhere?"

Stephan offered Kat a strawberry which she took a bite of when he held it to her mouth.

"Only to places I've been before. You have to know where you are going. You can't just imagine a place and then go there."

"So where did you go to get the tulip?"

"A little shop I know of in Virginia."

"Virginia? As in the state? But you were only gone a few minutes!" Kat could not keep the incredulousness from her voice as she halted Stephan from placing another berry in her mouth.

"It's an almost instantaneous process. I just have to picture a destination, and I'm there." Stephan pushed Kat off his chest. "Here, sit up for a minute, and watch." With that, Stephan appeared on the opposite side of the river waving at Kat.

"Oh my…that is amazing." Faster than the blink of her eye, Stephan returned to his place behind her and picked up another strawberry.

"It is convenient." Stephan shrugged, then held the berry to her lips.

She chewed and swallowed the proffered fruit. "I bet it is. Think of all the money and time you'd save by getting from place to place like that."

"It's not always possible to get to places like that. If you are going to dematerialize you have to be careful. We can't do it where humans are likely to see. We can't do it to new places we've never been before. And it is considered rude to do it into someone's home."

Kat leisurely ran her finger around the top of her champagne glass. "So you mean that if you were to appear at someone's house, you wouldn't materialize inside?"

"No, I would arrive on their doorstep and ring the bell just like any civilized person." Stephan took a sip of his champagne.

"Huh." Katrina's unfocused gaze stared across the Colorado as she considered the information Stephan shared.

"I'd like to propose a toast." Stephan effectively changed the subject as he raised his glass. "To the beauty of this majestic place, and the woman whose beauty far surpasses the nature surrounding her."

Warmth spread throughout her body, though whether from his words or the champagne, she couldn't be sure. They clinked their glasses together, and Kat smiled around the rim while he drank.

As the evening hours wore on, they spoke of their lives. Stephan shared how he'd come into his wealth by investing in art galleries and real estate throughout the world. They discussed Kat's passion for dance and desire for a family. The moon provided soft light while they talked about their past and present, carefully avoiding any talk of the future and their place in it.

The couple had just finished off the bottle of Cristal when Kat yawned discreetly behind her hand. As if on cue, she heard the hum of the rotors from the helicopter when it crested the top of the canyon on its way to retrieve them.

Snuggled safely against Stephan in the aircraft, Kat carefully cradled the delicate tulip in her lap, closed her eyes, and smiled. *This could be the start of something beautiful,* she thought as she let the gentle swaying of the helicopter lull her to sleep, taking her to dreams of Stephan.

Chapter 11

Katrina sat on the black leather couch looking at the now wilted tulip in the crystal vase on the coffee table. It had been five days since Stephan gave it to her, five wonderful days. She and Stephan had painted the town neon red, each night a different adventure.

They'd gone indoor skydiving. Of course, Stephan had taken all of ninety seconds to acquire the skill. While he did tricks and turns in the wind tunnel, Kat needed the steadying hands of an employee just to stay horizontal over the huge fan. But she had such fun; she did not care how much better her date had been than her.

Stephan took her dancing at the hottest club in town. It amazed Kat that no matter which club they went to, Stephan seemed to know the bouncer by name, and they easily passed through the velvet ropes. No matter how crowded, no one forbid them entrance.

They dined in the finest restaurants located high above the strip. Sometimes they ate Mediterranean cuisine, other times it was Parisian, but always it was a wonderful experience. The portions were gourmet small, but with six to eight courses, neither Kat nor Stephan left hungry. Each time, Kat marveled at the view from the sky high restaurants, the neon vista never a let-down. Looking down on the strip reminded her of being in the helicopter and the memory of which made butterflies flutter in her stomach each time she remembered their first date.

They'd even gone on a tour through the desert on an ATV. As they explored the desert, Stephan pointed out the wildlife that scurried around in the night. The guide brought a small UV light which caused the scorpions to glow blue-green and yellow like walking desert jewels. Katrina reveled at the sensation of him in her arms as she sat behind him on the ATV. Her arms wrapped around his waist, her soft breasts pressing into his back as they rode. She especially had enjoyed how his abs felt when she traced the outline of his corrugated stomach with her fingers while they bounced along the terrain.

Kat was having the time of her young life. Stephan was like no man she'd ever known. Though incredibly good looking, with a body to die for, that wasn't what drew Kat to him. It was the way he looked at her, the way he treated her. His power was so strong even Kat could feel it fill a room, but yet with her he was gentle, so careful with her it was as if she was as delicate as the tulip she sat looking at.

She knew the flower had outlived its time, but she couldn't bear to throw it out, not yet. Somehow, it would be like throwing a part of Stephan away.

"When are you gonna throw that thing out, Kitty Kat?" Marcus asked when he plopped down in the leather recliner.

"I don't know. I know it's past its prime, but I'm not ready to get rid of it yet."

"It's got to go sometime. You want me to get rid of it for you?" he offered and leaned forward as if he intended to pluck it from the table.

"No!" she replied a bit too emphatically, panic raising her voice.

"Leave her alone, Marcus. She'll get rid of it when she's good and ready." Stephan's deep voice resonated throughout the room. While he crossed to where Kat sat, she couldn't help but smile up at him, for just the sight of him made her heart race with joy.

"Close your eyes, Kitten. I have a surprise for you." He joined her on the couch waiting for her to comply before placing something in her lap. "All right, open your eyes."

Kat looked down and squealed. "What is it?" Her eyes went wide with excitement.

"Open it and see." Stephan smiled, exposing his perfectly straight teeth.

Kat lifted the rectangular box, examining it from all sides. "I have no idea what it could be."

"Open it already," teased Marcus from his chair with a knowing smile.

Kat carefully took the box in her long fingers, pulled the pink ribbon away and opened it. Awaiting her inside were two tickets. She pulled them from the box, reading the scrolling print.

"Two tickets to the ballet! Ooooh, Swan Lake!" Kat threw her arms about Stephan's neck and squeezed tight. His arms wrapped around her, encasing her in his steel embrace. His lips brushed her ears when he spoke, "Do you like them, Kitten?"

"Oh yes! Thank you! Thank you!" Kat leapt into Stephan's lap. "When is the show?"

"Tomorrow night," he answered, shifting her slightly so he cradled her in his strong arms.

"Oh no, I have to work tomorrow," she said,

looking at Marcus with a downtrodden face. She poked her lower lip out in a pout.

"I think the boss will let you have the night off." Marcus winked and smirked at Katrina. "Actually it's already arranged."

"You're the bestest boss ever." With one graceful leap, she was in Marcus' lap, hugging him around the neck. Stephan growled possessively behind her back, making Marcus shift uncomfortably in the recliner.

"Down tiger, I'm not trying to steal your girl." Marcus shifted Kat off his lap, gently pushing her back in Stephan's direction.

"Watch yourself, Marcus," Stephan warned in jest. "You are getting dangerously close to being insubordinate."

Marcus put both hands up in mock surrender. Katrina's heart grew as she looked down on Stephan's handsome face. She had noticed the tension growing between the two and wondered if she might be the cause. But she believed their friendship could withstand the growing feelings between Stephan and her. It was a delicate situation that the three of them would work through in time. They had to, because Kat wasn't willing to give either of them up.

Kat sat beside Stephan, and he pulled her back onto his lap.

"I have another surprise for you, sweetheart." He pulled another box from behind his back. Identical to the previous one, Kat opened it quickly with excited fingers. A gasp escaped her lips when she looked within.

"Oh Stephan," she breathed as she fingered the contents. "It's beautiful!"

"Here let me put it on." Stephan pulled the blood-red ruby necklace from the black velvet box and fastened it around her neck. A square of diamonds outlined the biggest princess cut ruby she'd ever seen. Set in platinum, it hung on a polished platinum chain.

"How does it look?" Kat fingered the necklace and waited for the reply.

Stephan looked from the necklace into her eyes. "Beautiful. Not as beautiful as you, but still, on you it's beautiful."

Her heart pounded in her chest at the compliment. Kat rose with a smile on her face that lit the corners of her eyes, determined to admire her present in a mirror. Stephan followed as she made her way into the bathroom. She pet the necklace, admired its reflection.

"Oh Stephan, I can't accept this," she whispered, meeting his eyes in the mirror.

"Do you not like it?" His voice dripped with concern.

Kat turned to face him. She stood so close, the warmth of his body surrounding her. "Oh no, I love it, but it's too expensive. I can't accept something like this."

Stephan leaned his hands on the counter, walling her in, and bent forward so their lips brushed as he spoke. "I don't want to hear another word regarding money. I bought it for you as a gift. It doesn't matter what it cost, it is but a small token of my feelings for you."

Kat's heart raced like she ran a marathon. The heat from his body engulfed her in a heady combination with his masculine, sandalwood scent. She inhaled deeply, her breasts pushed against his chest.

He swallowed a moan and kissed her. They wrapped their arms around each other, their bodies melding together as one. Pressed so close to him, it was impossible to miss the hard evidence of his mounting desire.

Stephan lifted her, placing her bottom on the edge of the counter and stepped between her thighs as he worked her shirt over her head. Katrina's fingers nimbly unbuttoned his shirt, then pushed it off his broad shoulders, allowing it to fall to the floor. She traced the lines of his muscles with her fingers, careful to find each one as she went lower down his chest to trail over his abs. She loved the way he felt, firm, masculine. She wanted to know what the rest of him looked like, felt like, especially within her.

Their eyes met. Flames of desire blazed in his dark blue depths. He looked like he wanted to devour her. Heat pooled low in her core at the realization. Her breath sawed from her lungs in perfect rhythm with his.

A knock at the door arrested the moment like a cold shower.

"Hey, Stephan, phone for you," called Marcus.

"Not now!" Stephan bit out his voice, echoing in the marble bath. He lowered his head once again to capture Kat's lips, and she was bathed in sensual sensation.

Marcus' voice lowered an octave as he said ominously, "It's Nicholai. He says it's very important. I think you better take this."

Stephan groaned and withdrew from Kat, pushing away from the counter. He scraped a large hand down his face. "I'm sorry, Kat, I better take this."

****

93

Gage climbed the stairs leaving the stench of the basement behind. He was looking forward to the hunt, but he would admit he'd be glad to have it over with so he could get the humans out of his home. He strolled into the pristine, white kitchen and rinsed the filth from his hands.

Andrea looked up at him from the table when he entered. "Everything go okay?"

"No actually. One died."

"Oh no, not the big burly blond I hope. I was looking forward to having him for myself."

Of course she was. The lady always did prefer blonds. Luckily for him. He shook his head. "No, not him, a female…Brownie."

"Oh Gage, I'm sorry. I know how you enjoyed her." Andrea took a sip of her coffee. Gage watched a look of utter contentment take her face. She liked her coffee like she liked her men, strong and rich.

Gage shrugged his shoulders, a carefree gesture that said he would not be shedding any tears over the loss. "We'll need to get another human now or we won't have enough for the hunt."

Trace entered, carrying the day's paper and presented it to Andrea, like a good little guard. His heartmate immediately sorted through to find her favorite section—Arts and Leisure.

"Oooooh, look Gage. The Peterhof Ballet Company is coming to town. I haven't been to the ballet in so long. I'd love to go."

Gage walked over and kissed her on the forehead. "Then go you shall, my dear. I'll call and get us tickets." He sat down, acknowledging the guard. "Trace, bring me the phone."

"I know just the dress I'll wear, the green gown that is low cut in the front." Andrea's eyes lit with excitement.

"You know, Andrea darling, I think a vampire owns that ballet company. If memory serves, I believe Nicholai Peterhof is the owner."

"If that's the case, then we must invite him to the hunt. He could stay in town until Halloween and come to our party. It would be quite rude not to invite him."

Gage pondered the idea. It would be advantageous to have one as regal and well-connected as Nicholai Peterhof at their party. It would elevate their standing within vampiric society, for Nicholai was Russian royalty.

He gave a short nod of his head. "Let's do it. After we watch the ballet, we will go and speak with Nicholai, invite him to the hunt."

"Oh Gage, that's a wonderful idea. Thank you!"

Trace handed Gage the black cordless phone. "Do you have any further need of me this evening, sir?"

Gage waved his hand dismissively. "Not at this time. You can go."

Thinking twice, Gage called the guard back to him with a gesture of his hand. "Wait a moment, Trace. If we invite Peterhof, we'll need more humans. I want you to take Alvero and go get two more humans for the hunt."

Andrea reached across the table, laying her hand over his. "Is getting two at the same time safe, my darling? They might draw attention to themselves."

Gage considered Andrea's observation before continuing. "Be sure you get them from different states," he instructed. "We do not need to draw attention, especially from the Vampire Enforcement Squad. The last thing we need is for VES agents to start poking around here. Do you understand?"

Trace gave a curt nod of his shaven head. "Of course, sir. You can count on us, Mr. Lucio. We will be discreet."

"You better. That's why I hired you. You're the best."

Trace bowed his head in respect, then left to retrieve his partner for the evening. The sound of Andrea's stomach growling drew his attention.

"Have you eaten this evening? You need to keep your strength up, you know."

"Not yet." She gave him a sly look. "I thought you might like to watch."

Gage smiled an evil grin and cocked his eyebrows. Fates above, how he liked to watch his female feed. "Did you now? I know just the human. Her blood smells particularly sweet."

Andrea rubbed her stomach, gracing him with a smile. "The baby will like that."

Gage rose and offered his hand to Andrea. He escorted her up the stairs to their bedroom. "Wait here. I'll be right back."

When Gage appeared back in the doorway holding a woman with a mass of fiery red hair by her arm, he found Andrea waiting patiently on the bed. She leaned back on her hands, crossing her legs at the ankles, and gave the woman a perusal with her heated stare.

"My dear, I'd like to introduce Red. Red, this is the mistress of the house. You will please her or you will die."

****

Stephan and Marcus sat facing each other in the living room. With a punch of a button, Stephan hung up the phone and turned toward his friend.

"What did Nicholai want?" Marcus asked.

"He wanted to tell me about some rumors he had heard. Apparently, the word overseas is that there is a hunt club in town."

Marcus shook the shocked look from his face. "Here in Vegas? No way! I'd have known about something like that."

"As I said, it's just a rumor. But that is why Nicholai is bringing his ballet company here. He wanted a cover so he could come into town and poke around."

"I can't believe he'll find anything. I think I'd have noticed if a bunch of humans disappeared."

"I haven't noticed anything unusual since I've been here either, but Nicholai seems concerned."

"Is that why you bought tickets to his show?"

"No." Stephan shook his head. "I got them because I knew Katrina would like to go to the ballet. But now I'm glad I bought them. I will see Nicholai after the show and invite him back here to discuss the rumors. It will give us a chance to talk to him together."

"I just can't believe there would be a hunt club here in Vegas." Marcus raked his hand down his face.

Stephan rubbed his stubbled chin thoughtfully. "I know. It is hard to believe that one of our kind could put something like that together right under your nose."

"I can only hope he is wrong…Please let him be wrong," Marcus said quietly as Kat strolled into the living room with her purse on her shoulder.

"I'm going out," she announced. " I'll see you boys

later."

Over his dead body. Not if there was a hunt club in the city. Stephan stood and crossed the room to meet her. "Where are you going?"

"I need to get a dress for tomorrow night. I'll be back in a little while."

"I'll go with you, Kitten." It was a demand, not a suggestion.

"You can't. I want it to be a surprise. You know what they say. It's bad luck for a boyfriend to see his girlfriend in her dress before the ballet," Kat bantered, smiling up at him with a wry grin.

Stephan sighed his frustration, and rested a hand on her shoulder. "Don't be silly. There is no such saying."

"I'm serious, Stephan." Kat lifted her chin defiantly. "I don't want you to see the dress before tomorrow."

An idea struck him. *Brilliant*. "Then let me bring the store here to you. I'll arrange for a variety of garments to be brought here."

"No," she said between clenched teeth, putting her fisted hands on her hips in pique. "You'll still get to see the dress."

Stephan balled his fists by his side, his temper rising. If there was even the slightest possibility someone was running a hunt club in the city, he had no intention of allowing Kat out on the streets of Vegas alone. She was being unreasonable. There was no reason he should not escort her or see the dress.

Marcus, obviously reading Stephan's concern, stood. "Come on, Kat. I'll take you shopping. I know just the place."

He could always count on Marcus. He shot him a

grateful grin.

Kat looked suspiciously between the two males. "Something is up."

Putting on his best poker face, Marcus looked innocently at Kat. "Can't a guy take his best girl shopping? Now come on, let's go. You don't have much time before you have to leave for work."

Kat let a sigh of acquiesce blow between her lips. "All right. Let's go, Marcus."

Stephan watched the subtle sway of her hips as she strolled toward him. He was struck by her beauty. Her hair flowed down her back in smooth waves that drew his attention. How he longed to run his fingers through those golden locks. Her sensual lips, straight nose, and beautiful blue-gray eyes all begged to be kissed, and he was more than ready to oblige. But what struck him as the most beautiful thing about her was her personality. She could be sassy one minute, charming the next, and he loved every sweet and sour moment with her.

Kat rose up on her tiptoes and kissed him goodbye. Wrapping his arms about her, he deepened the kiss, his tongue darting between her lips to thoroughly explore her mouth. He broke their kiss to feather light kisses down her neck, his mouth coming to rest over her beating pulse.

Need slammed into him hard, a hunger only his kind could have. His fangs lengthened, as his body craved that which was but a bite away. He could hear the siren call of her blood, begging him to take what he needed to survive.

His lips parted, his fangs raking her delicate skin. Just a little pressure would break that skin, allowing her sweet liquid to his mouth. The temptation built. The need to taste her pushed at his restraint. Never had he been so tempted.

Remember your vow, Stephan.

Hearing Marcus in his mind gave him the power to push his need aside. He called on the discipline he'd so carefully honed over his long life, stilling his hands and lips. The warrior took a deep breath, willing his fangs back to their normal length. His body shook slightly from the effort as he put her away from him.

"You'd better go," he suggested, barely containing his desire.

She nodded, reaching up to cover her lips with her fingers as if she could still feel his kiss. Silently, he watched Katrina head out the door with Marcus. She turned when the doors to the elevator opened. "Bye," she whispered.

"I will see you later."

The elevator doors closed, taking them from his sight. His chest tightened at the thought that Katrina might be in danger. If there was a hunt club in Vegas, as their fellow Alpha, Nicholai, feared, then no human was safe. Until they knew for certain, he would do everything possible to keep her protected.

He sent a message to Marcus using their mind link. *Take care of her, my friend. And bring her back to me safe and sound.*

Marcus gave the mental equivalent of a nod. *You know I will. I'd protect her with my life.*

Chapter 12

The next evening, Marcus watched Stephan straighten the cuffs on his white tuxedo shirt, before affixing diamond studded cufflinks to each sleeve. "So, did you get a limo for tonight or are you taking the Mercedes?"

"I thought the occasion called for a limousine."

Marcus nodded his approval. "Good choice. Every woman likes to ride in a..." Marcus stopped short, his breath caught in his throat as his gaze swept to the stairs.

Kat descended, dressed in a gown made of golden silk which clung to her lean body in all the right places. Her designer shoes were satin high heels that ruffled on one side with a sparkly jewel detail. The ruby necklace from Stephan completed the elegant outfit, drawing attention to the ample cleavage exposed by her gown. She wore her hair up in a golden chignon with tiny wisps framing her face.

Marcus stilled, not a breath did he take while he watched her glide gracefully down the stairs. Beside him, Stephan sucked in a breath of his own as they both watched Kat's gown trail behind her when she stepped off the stairs.

"I have never seen anything so beautiful in all my six hundred plus years," his sire murmured, watching her move elegantly toward them.

Stephan took her hands in his. "Words cannot describe how beautiful you look."

Kat smiled a wide grin that reached the sparkle in her eyes. "You don't look so bad yourself."

The Alpha leader quirked one dark brow. "Hardly the compliment I was going for, but it will have to do."

The questioning look on Katrina's sweet face made Marcus push into her mind to glean the cause. He found her thinking how funny it was Stephan would care about a compliment when surely he knew how gorgeous he looked. She couldn't understand why, with the confidence and power he exuded, he would question her attraction to him. She found him unbelievably attractive, in his custom tailored black tux slacks and crisp pleated shirt with the black neck tie that hung straight to emphasize his flat stomach.

T-M-I. Did NOT need to know that. Marcus pulled from her mind, regretting his curiosity, and turned this attention on Stephan.

He knew his sire well. Knew what the look of awe and wonderment on his face meant. It was the look of a man who could get lost in the human woman standing before him. A man who wanted to know everything about her, like her favorite color or perfume, or even the color of her toothbrush. Stephan looked at her as if she had curled herself around his heart to become a part of him. And that was something Marcus could relate to.

A sad smile came to his face. His emotions churned in his gut, a mixture of happiness and sorrow. Happiness that Kat and Stephan seemed to be in love. Sadness because when they finally admitted it to one another, Marcus would be relegated to the third wheel, the odd man out. He knew Stephan would not tolerate another male near his woman, even if that other man had been her friend long before Stephan came into the picture.

Marcus cleared his throat. "I hate to break up this beautiful moment," his voice leaden with sarcasm, "but don't you think you should be going?" He tapped the watch on his wrist. "The curtain goes up in fifteen."

"He's right." Stephan dropped Kat's hands. "We should be leaving."

Stephan held her coat as she slipped her arms in, then he shrugged on his black jacket. Marcus watched the Alpha lay his hand on the small of her back and escort her out of the door without so much as a goodbye or see-you-later. Alone, Marcus' heavy sigh was the only sound in the quiet home.

****

They arrived at the theater as the curtain was being drawn and quietly made their way to their assigned green velvet chairs. Kat's gaze swept the room, taking in the grandeur of the theater from the hunter green drapery that hung along the walls to the ornate crown molding framing the domed ceiling. She looked around at the men, outfitted in dark evening attire and the elegant women dressed in gowns of silk and chiffon. Katrina felt utterly regal sitting among them.

She quietly gasped as the ballerinas entered the stage. A smug grin of male satisfaction graced Stephan's face when he looked at her, obviously having heard the intake of breath. He looked so self-assured and confident. Sexy. Kat quickly looked back at the stage when her cheeks flushed.

The dancers wore white fluffy tutus with white feathers that circled their heads like halos. They pranced gracefully on their toes. The arms of the ballerinas fluttered elegantly while the *premier danseur*, dressed in white and gold, twirled the prima ballerina in his strong arms as she stood on point.

Never had Kat seen anything more graceful. Swan Lake was her favorite ballet, and that alone would have made the evening enjoyable, but the joy she felt while she watched them perform it expertly made her heart soar.

As the ballet continued, Kat observed the sorcerer, von Rothbart, capture the Princess Odette and turn her into a swan by day. Completely engrossed, her fists tightened in her lap. She wept softly when Prince Siegfried became smitten with Odette and vowed to save her.

Katrina sat mesmerized by the charming performers and felt a little bereft when the curtain lowered on Act Two for intermission. Stephan gently wiped the tear that ran down her cheek with the pad of his thumb.

"I'm sorry. I don't mean to cry, it's just so beautiful. I've never seen a group of dancers so graceful before."

Stephan leaned over, warm air from his mouth brushed her ear as he whispered, "I think you would look beautiful dancing the part of Odette." She blushed. "These particular performers look so graceful because most of them aren't ordinary dancers. They are like Marcus and me."

"You mean they are…" Kat hesitated, knowing she shouldn't say the word vampire out loud in public.

"Yes, and so is the owner, Nicholai Peterhof."

"Well that explains a lot." Kat smiled. "I think I

better go to the powder room and freshen up before the intermission is over. Excuse me, please."

Stephan rose with Kat. Her backside brushed against him as she passed between his body and the row in front of them, causing a rush of exquisite heat to flood her body. He made an audible inhale at the unintentional touch. She looked back over her shoulder, found his eyes had darkened with lust briefly before he shook his head ruefully as she made her way down the aisle.

Kat stood in the elegant power room, touching up her makeup, when a sultry brunette, dressed in a low-cut green gown, moved beside her to wash her hands. Katrina suddenly flinched as cold water hit her arm from the faucet in front of the brunette.

"Oh, I'm sorry. Here." The woman handed Kat a paper towel.

"That's okay. It only got my arm. No harm done." Kat glanced at the woman, and the hairs on the nape of her neck rose. Something about those reddish-brown eyes were not right. They looked afire, intense…*evil,* Kat realized. Her stomach knotted.

Kat fought the urge to recoil in fear, took the offered towel and wiped her arm dry, watching the woman leave the restroom. Wanting to give the brunette plenty of time to return to her seat so Kat wouldn't have to run into her in the theater, Kat waited several minutes before she herself left.

When she returned to her seat beside Stephan, his body immediately coiled tight in full protection mode, as if ready to pounce. He glanced around them, eyes roaming the crowd seemingly in search of the danger.

He leaned over to whisper in her ear. "I can smell

your fear. What happened?"

"Nothing," she hissed. Her hands clenched the handbag in her lap.

"Come on, Kitten," he coaxed, covering her hands with his. His thumb rubbed soothingly across the back of one hand as he continued. "Please tell me what scared you so much."

Kat reluctantly relayed the story of the woman from the bathroom, toying nervously with her purse while she spoke. "It's not like she did anything. It was just those eyes."

Her voice trailed off as the curtain rose on Act Three. Stephan placed his arm around her shoulders and drew her close. She nestled into the comfort of his strong body, allowing his warmth to surround her, melt her tension so her attention focused once again on the drama onstage.

Kat wanted to cheer at the end of Act Four when the swans drove Von Rothbart and Odile into the water to drown. Then once again she found herself softly weeping as she watched the spirits of Prince Siegfried and Odette ascend into the heavens above Swan Lake, their spirits united in death. Stephan gently wiped the tears from her cheeks with the pocket square from his tux. His hand rested a moment on her cheek.

"So sad," Katrina murmured as the curtain came down on the final act. "So romantic, but so sad that they had to die to be together."

Stephan forced a smile. "Come, Katrina," he said, rising as he extended his hand to her. "I have someone I'd like you to meet."

"Who?" Katrina placed her hand in his and rose to her feet.

"Nicholai Peterhof."

"The Nicholai Peterhof! As in the owner of the ballet company?" she asked incredulously, her eyes wide.

Stephan nodded his head. "Yes, that Nicholai Peterhof."

Chapter 13

Stephan led Kat by the hand down the row and contemplated Katrina's tears. He knew a flash of impotency.

Kat was an amazing woman who should not have to ever shed a tear. It tore at his heart to see her cry, especially knowing he could do nothing to stop it. He cared for her—the delicate, soft, fragile woman walking next to him.

When they arrived in the aisle, he wiped another tear. The room spun around them when he looked down into her watery gaze. And it hit him. He did more than care for her, he loved her. *Loved. Her.* The realization staggered him, arresting his hand half down her cheek as he went to wipe another tear away. He tucked the awareness away for closer examination later.

Stephan laced his fingers with hers, and they made their way through the audience to the back stage door, then through the sea of white tulle and feathers milling around the stage, steering her around the lead dancers. Stephan wanted to be the Prince Siegfried to her Princess Odette. He smiled as he thought about how they could be like the couple in Swan Lake, spirits united in death. If he converted her, through her mortal death, they could live forever, loving each other.

But she wouldn't want that, would she? Surely if she wanted to become a vampire she would have asked

Marcus to convert her. With a soft sigh, he resigned himself to the fact he might just have to accept what little time her mortal life had left. He knew he would love her until the day she died—he just hoped that he could convince her to make that a very long time.

What might come would come, for tonight, he would concentrate on taking her sadness by giving her something besides the ballet to think about. He rapped his knuckles on the door marked *Authorized Personnel Only,* and a deep voice bade them entry.

Kat seemed to notice Nicholai immediately. How could she not, Stephan supposed. His presence filled the room. At six-foot-five, he stood a head taller than the couple with whom he spoke.

Stephan slipped into Katrina's mind like a shadow on a moonlit night, silent and still to find her thinking about another male. His date found Nicholai attractive. Her eyes roamed over the yellow dress shirt he wore, which was unbuttoned half way down his muscular chest, exposing the trail of fine hair that drew her eye downward. Stephan fought to suppress his inner beast which struggled to rise to the surface at the threat Nicholai presented.

His possessiveness grew as he remained quietly in her mind listening to her thoughts. She found Nicholai's dark hair attractive, slicked back as it was from the chiseled features of his face. She thought his amber eyes were lit with a passion for life.

He is the kind of man who makes a woman go weak at the knees, thought Kat, *but he's not my Stephan.*

The threatening growl was stopped in his throat, suppressed by the smug smile that graced Stephan's face as he give Katrina's shoulders a quick squeeze, happy in the knowledge that she preferred him to Nicholai. His inner beast settled at the realization. The tension in his shoulders eased slightly.

They stepped into the room, and the couple turned to face them. Kat froze beside him. Katrina's muscles tensed beneath his arm, and his gaze quickly fell to her. He watched her, easily discerning her growing discomfort. Stephan's hand moved to the nape of her neck, messaging it gently.

Nicholai stepped around the couple, extended his hand to Katrina in welcome. He brought her hand to his lips as he bowed at the waist, placing a kiss on the delicate skin on the back of her hand. "It is a pleasure to meet you, Miss Spencer. Stephan has told me much about you." His R's rolled off his tongue in his rich Russian accent. He rose, holding her gaze with his fiery eyes.

Kat giggled nervously. "It's a pleasure to meet you too."

"Allow me to introduce my companions. This is Gage and Andrea Lucio. Gage, Andrea, this is Stephan von Haas and Katrina Spencer."

Stephan glanced at the couple, noticing how Gage's eyes narrowed slightly. The male watched Stephan carefully, observing the protective way he rubbed his date's nape.

Gage extended his hand to Stephan. "It's nice to meet you…" He looked to Kat. "Both."

Kat shifted uncomfortably under his gaze.

"Yes, it's nice to meet you," Andrea chimed in. Her voice slid over Stephan's skin like an oily black mass, making him uncomfortable. There was something off about this couple, but he couldn't put his finger on it.

"You seem familiar, have we met before?" Gage eyed Kat with an intensity that did nothing to alleviate her tension.

"I-I don't believe so. I think I would have remembered."

"Huh, I would swear we have met somewhere before," he said, a look of careful consideration crossed his face briefly before his features lightened. "Perhaps I'm thinking of someone else."

Gage turned to his mate. "Andrea, my dear, I think we should be going." His gazed flicked to Nicholai. "Nicholai, I look forward to seeing you again soon."

Andrea crossed the room to join Gage. He encircled her waist with his arm. "Come, my dear."

"We didn't mean to run you off," Stephan volunteered.

Gage waved a dismissive hand. "We were just leaving when you knocked. It was nice to meet you both." After one more concerning glance at Kat, he swept his mate out the door, murmuring in her ear, "I swear I know that woman from somewhere."

Stephan pinned Nicholai with an inquisitive look, one eyebrow raised. "That was interesting."

Kat took a deep breath and whispered, "That was the woman from the bathroom."

Stephan's instincts all fired at once. Powerful emotions threatened to overcome him. Protect her. See to her safety.

The woman obviously made Kat as uncomfortable as she'd made him. And her mate was not much better. Stephan was glad they left before Kat mentioned who the female was. He would have been sorely tempted to allow his instincts to take over if she were still in the room. He did not keep the concern from his face when he looked from Kat to Nicholai.

Now it was Nicholai's turn to look inquisitive, but not wanting to explain, Stephan distracted him by saying, "What did he mean when he said he looked forward to seeing you again?"

"He invited me to his home for a meal. He claimed Andrea is a big fan of the ballet and wanted a chance to speak to me, at length, about the company."

"You sound as if you don't believe him." Stephan observed, astutely deciphering Nicholai's tone.

"I'm not sure," Nicholai mused. "I cannot say precisely why, but I have a feeling there is more to the story than just wanting a friendly dinner."

"Perhaps we should meet later and discuss your concerns in depth. Would you like to come to my penthouse for a drink?"

"I'd be honored," Nicholai replied, placing one hand over his heart. "Will Marcus be there? I haven't seen him in years."

"More like several decades, my old friend."

Nicholai shot a look to Kat. "She knows we're...?" Nicholai left the question hanging in the air.

"Yes, she knows we're vampires."

"She's right here." Kat placed her hands on her hips. "If you are going to talk about me as if I'm not here, perhaps I should leave."

Stephan pulled her into his arms. "I'm sorry, my dear. We didn't mean to be rude."

Watching the two hold each other in a lover's embrace, a warm grin lit Nicholai's face. "Ah, 'the world is full of beauty when the heart is full of love.'"

He brushed a hand over his blue-black hair.

"That's a quote from W.L. Smith, isn't it?" asked Stephan, raising his head with a smile on his lips.

"You are correct, my friend. It is nice to see you so happy."

"I am that." Stephan looked back down into Kat's gray-blue eyes. "So very happy." He squeezed her tightly to his chest.

"Shall we sit?" offered Nicholai, moving toward the brown couch that lay against one wall in the room.

"I'm afraid we need to get back home. Cinderella here might turn into a pumpkin." Kat hit the solid wall of his chest in protest. "Will you be able to come to the penthouse tomorrow night?"

"I'll be there with…How does the saying go…chimes on?"

Kat giggled. "Close. I believe you were looking for bells. Be there with bells on."

"Ah yes, well either way, I'll be there tinkling."

Kat and Stephan were still chuckling when they left Nicholai and headed for home.

Marcus greeted them at the door. "How was it, Kitty Kat?"

"It was the most graceful, beautiful, sad, romantic thing I have ever seen," she gushed.

"Could you think of any more words to describe it?" Marcus teased.

"Oh yes, gorgeous, majestic, dramatic…"

"Okay, okay, I get the point." Marcus raised his hands out in a consolatory gesture.

Kat pirouetted, her gown flaring out slightly as she twirled into Stephan's open arms. He rested his chin on her head. "I'm glad you enjoyed the ballet."

Kat laid her head against his chest. "I loved it. I truly loved it. Oh Stephan, thank you so much for taking me. I'm so happy."

Stephan pulled back slightly and looked down onto her glowing face. "I'd do anything to make you happy, Kitten. Just name it. And I'll do it."

Kat kissed him, a kiss that said all she didn't. He felt her pour her love, her happiness, her very soul into that kiss. Telling him she belonged to him. She broke the kiss when a yawn threatened to overtake her. Stephan easily sensed her growing fatigue.

"You look sleepy, Kitten."

Kat stretched, and lifted her arms above her head. Looking at him through heavy-lidded eyes, she said, "I guess I am."

Katrina glanced down at the watch on Stephan's wrist. Her eyes widened slightly. "I hadn't realized how late it was. I guess I'll go to bed. Goodnight."

"Goodnight." Stephan gave her another quick kiss.

"Goodnight," echoed Marcus, as she pulled out of Stephan's arms.

Stephan watched Kat bend down to remove her shoes. Holding them by the heels in one hand, she sauntered down the hall toward Marcus' room. Jealousy slashed through him in a fiery blaze. He couldn't abide the idea of Kat lying next to another male while she slept. He wanted her in his bed, embraced in his arms all day. He wanted his to be the first face she saw when she awoke.

"I'll sleep on the couch from now on," Marcus offered, obviously reading Stephan's emotions. The Alpha's tone, soft with emotion he knew not to voice, told Stephan that Marcus struggled to come to grips with the changes his relationship with Kat would bring.

Stephan simply nodded. He knew he could trust Marcus. Marcus was an honorable male. He would not touch Katrina now that they were together.

Logically he understood he should give Marcus permission to keep sleeping in his comfortable bed with Kat, but he couldn't. He'd come to think of Kat as his, and he couldn't tolerate another male sleeping in the same room as her.

He recognized the possessiveness he felt toward Katrina came from his love for her. The woman had somehow weaved her way into his heart, wrapped around it so tightly that now it would not beat without her.

The desire to claim her washed over his body, tightening it. He wanted her desperately. Wanted her in his bed. Wanted to show her he cared about her. Wanted her…body and soul.

Soon, he vowed to himself, soon he would claim her body, making her truly his.

Chapter 14

Nicholai sat across from his hosts in a wing backed chair, watching as Andrea returned with a tray of hot hors d'oeuvres. Their tempting smell did not cover the lingering odor that plagued Nicholai's senses. A faint scent of stale, dirty human wafted to his nose, making him wonder where the scent emanated from. Though he could smell several humans, none had been seen anywhere during the tour of the home his hosts had taken him on.

"So Mr. Peterhof, tell us how you came to own a ballet company," Andrea said, smiling as she settled back onto the sofa beside Gage.

"Call me Nicholai, please. Mr. Peterhof is too formal." The warrior flashed her a warm smile before continuing on to tell his story. "When the Soviet Union collapsed, the economic crisis brought about financial hardships to the ballet companies. Without the state budget to back them, they looked to private investors. I happened to be fortunate enough to be in the right place at the right time and bought one of the companies from Mother Russia."

Andrea leaned toward Nicholai, seemingly hanging on every word he spoke in his heavy accent. "That's fascinating. I've always loved the ballet. I think the ballet is the most beautiful form of dance. Don't you?"

"Da, I would have to agree, Mrs. Lucio." He swept

his blue-black hair to the side of his face with a shake of his head.

"Andrea, please." She affected a shy look, and a blush took her cheeks.

Nicholai reached for one of the cracker hors d'oeuvres. "I have always enjoyed the ballet, so when the opportunity came along for me to purchase a company, I could not resist."

"I would love to dance the ballet, to be a prima ballerina."

In a show of obvious male possessiveness, Gage pulled Andrea back under his arm. "I afraid you won't be dancing the ballet anytime soon, my dear, at least not until the baby is born."

"You are with child?" Nicholai asked. His face wore an expression of surprise that widened his eyes.

"Yes." Gage beamed. "We just found out."

"My congratulations to you both."

"Thank you. We are very happy about the blessed event." Andrea placed a protective hand over her slightly rounded stomach.

The expectant father covered his mate's hand with his own. "Speaking of events, Nicholai, we are having a party next weekend on the twenty-ninth. We would love for you to attend."

"What kind of party, if I might be so bold as to ask?" Nicholai kept his voice steady, careful to not sound suspicious. His mind worked quickly. His thoughts turned to the rumors he had heard about the hunt. Perhaps this couple played some part in the illegal activity. It could prove useful to infiltrate their party, if only to make other connections should they be proven to be innocent of any wrong doing.

Andrea winked at Gage, the movement noted by Nicholai's watchful gaze. "Oh, the kind with yummy food and drink. It's a two day event starting with a ball on Friday."

Gage swallowed the food in his mouth. "You should come. I think you will like it."

"It is kind of you to invite me. Perhaps I will be able to attend."

"We would be honored if you would come," Andrea chimed in.

"Then I shall put it on my calendar."

His suspicions growing, Nicholai kept his voice light and even as he cautiously inquired, "Where will the events be?"

"The ball will be Friday at nine p.m. in the Lancelot room of the Camelot Hotel. The next evening's events will start here in our home after dusk."

The Alpha nodded his head once in acknowledgment. "Thank you for the invitation. I shall be there."

"Excuse the intrusion," a large male vampire said, entering the room. "Dinner is ready."

They made their way into the dining room, and Nicholai's mind processed the home, noting each entry point, each closed door, every guard. This was a couple with something to hide. He was sure of it.

During the meal, Nicholai carefully probed the couple for more information, trying to discern if they might be involved in the hunt club. After all, they had not come right out and referred to their party as a hunt, but Nicholai couldn't shake the feeling of evil that surrounded him in their home. His preternatural senses were firing, telling him something was amiss. He just needed time to figure out what.

After they finished their meal, he spent a little more time with his hosts making small talk, then Nicholai made his excuses and left, determination quickening his stride as he made his way to his rental car. He headed for Stephan's penthouse, for he needed to talk things through with his fellow Alphas, share what little information he had been able to amass from his hosts.

As the saying goes, he thought sliding behind the wheel, *three heads are better than one.*

Chapter 15

Marcus and Kat stood in the penthouse gym facing each other on the blue padded mat. Marcus had pushed all the equipment to the walls and raised the platform on the treadmill so they would have room to spar. Stephan rested his weight against the wall which had three full-length mirrors. He stood with one ankle crossed over the other, his thick arms folded across his chest. He'd been overseeing these sparring sessions for weeks, the protective side of him not entirely comfortable with Kat fending off Marcus.

Stephan knew Marcus himself felt equally uneasy, as well he should, because the vampire he sired wasn't sure what Stephan would do if Katrina accidentally got hurt. And to be honest, Stephan wasn't exactly sure either.

Under Stephan's narrowed gaze, the session continued. Marcus grabbed Kat from behind in a Full Nelson with both of his arms encircling her under her armpits, his hands secured at her neck.

"Okay, Kat. Do you remember how to get out of this one?"

"Well…I could let my body go limp." Kat did just that, letting her arms reach up against both sides of her head as her knees went weak, and she dropped. Marcus, obviously expecting the move, tightened his grip, keeping her firmly in his hold. Stephan straightened in protest when Marcus held Kat suspended from her arms and neck.

"Good try," Marcus said while Kat straightened once again to bear her own body weight. "But what if your attacker didn't drop you? What else could you do?"

"Well, then I could do this…" Kat threw her head back into Marcus' nose. The room filled with the sound of crunching bone as his nose broke. Blood flowed down, coating the back of Kat's head, turning her golden locks crimson. Stephan smiled, a feeling of pride washing over him.

Marcus grabbed his nose and slid the bones back into place.

"Very good move, Kat," Stephan said with little concern since he knew Marcus would heal from the small wound quickly thanks to the vampiric blood running through his veins.

"Thank you." Kat smiled at Marcus. Stephan handed Katrina a towel which she took with a thanks and wiped the blood from her blonde strands.

"Are you ready to do a little hand to hand combat now?" Marcus asked after stuffing two wads of cotton up his nostrils to stay the bleeding.

"Don't you think I should be asking you that?" Kat smirked. "You seem to be the one who could use a break."

Marcus smiled, looking pointedly at Stephan. "You are right, Kitty Kat. I *am* always the one who gets hurt during our sessions."

"As well you should be." Stephan smiled his approval.

"If I didn't let you use full force, Kat, how would

you learn? You need to get used to using appropriate force, and since I heal quickly, there is no reason not to let you injure me," Marcus said as he donned pads while Kat pulled on her boxing gloves.

Marcus had told him that he wanted to keep the sessions as real as possible so he went after Kat with as much force as he dared. The purpose of the sessions was to teach her how to defend herself in the event she was ever attacked again, and it was hard to do that if Marcus didn't at least use the equivalent of human strength and speed when attacking Kat.

Marcus placed his padded hands up in a fighting stance, and Katrina's punches flew. She threw upper cuts, followed by a series of left and right punches into the pads. Marcus easily blocked each blow. After a few minutes, Marcus straightened dropping his guard. "That's great, now let's try some kicks."

Kat took a deep breath and wiped the perspiration from her brow. She began a succession of kicks, each one easily blocked by Marcus.

Stephan watched, smiling. "That's my girl. You're doing great! Kick his ass." Kat looked at him and smiled, clearly enjoying the compliment while letting her guard down.

Marcus took advantage of Kat's momentary distraction and grabbed her from behind pinning her arms to her side as he lifted her off of her feet. Her instincts took over, and she struggled against his hold. She threw her head back once again, contacting with his nose. Marcus dropped Kat as his head snapped back, his face contorted in pain. She landed in a heap on the blue mat. Stephan chortled, his laughter echoing throughout the gym.

"Way to go, Kitten! That was impressive." Stephan felt a flurry of pride, his chest expanding with satisfaction at the sight of his woman besting his friend. He was instantly beside her to help her to her feet.

As Marcus wiped the blood from his nose with his forearm, the doorbell rang.

"That will be Nicholai," Stephan said and easily drew Katrina to her feet, dusting off her behind. "Marcus, go get cleaned up while I let Nicholai in. We'll meet you in the library."

"Can I offer you a drink?" Stephan asked, as he led his friend to the library.

"That would be appreciated. I will take vodka if you have any."

Stephan sent Marcus a mental command, asking him to bring in drinks when he joined them in the library.

The library was a semi-circular room with built-in bookcases lining the curved walls. Stephan kept a thick, ornately carved desk in the center of the room. Two matching chairs with hand-carved arms and claw-foot legs sat flanking a matching small claw-footed table with a glass top.

"Marcus will be joining us soon. Please sit down." Stephan informed his fellow Alpha, gesturing to one of the matching burgundy print upholstered chairs. Marcus entered the room carrying a vodka tonic in one hand and a scotch on the rocks in the other.

Nicholai crossed one ankle over his knee and accepted the glass from Marcus. "Thank you." He did a double take. "Shit, you look awful, Marcus. What happened to you?"

Marcus wiped the blood from his nose and sat in

the chair opposite from Nicholai. "I was sparring."

"With Kat," Stephan offered with a genuine smile that reached the corners of his eyes.

Nicholai laughed. "A human female did that to you?"

"Yeah, she did this. Don't worry your pretty little head about it. I'll be fine."

"I am sure you will, comrade. I trust Miss Katrina is unharmed?"

"Kat is just fine. Marcus was the only one who took a beating." Stephan beamed, bringing a heavy hand to rest on Marcus' shoulder.

Nicholai grinned wide, showing his teeth. "I have always thought the beautiful ones were the most dangerous."

"You can say that again," Marcus said, straightening his nose one final time as the bones knit back together. He pulled the cotton from his nose.

Stephan eased into his chair behind the massive desk. "So Nicholai, have you seen the couple that was in your office after the ballet performance?"

"I just came from there. I think they may be a place to start looking for clues about the hunt club." Nicholai took a sip of his drink.

"What makes you think that?'

"Nothing was out of the ordinary when they took me on a tour of the home, but there was a smell, like stale human and a strong sense of dread and fear, the stench of which permeated the house. There is something not right in that house. I do not know if it will turn out to be the hunt club, but definitely something is not right."

Stephan nodded in understanding and took a swig

of his scotch. "I think we should do some recon on the house. Watch it for a few days and see if we notice anything suspicious happening."

"I can do that," Marcus volunteered. "The only thing is that someone will need to pick up Kat after work."

"That is not a problem. I'll get her," Stephan volunteered a little too quickly, bringing a smirk to Marcus' face.

After taking another gulp of his scotch, he inquired, "If Nicholai shows you where the house is located, can you dematerialize there or will you need to borrow the car?"

Marcus dropped his gaze to his shoes. "I can't dematerialize yet, I'll need the car. I'll take the Hummer."

Stephan smiled, a sinful idea popped into his mind like a firecracker. "If I'm picking up Kat, I'll need the Hummer. You can take the Mercedes."

The three warriors discussed their plan in detail, agreeing that Marcus would watch the home from a mountain located nearby and report his findings back to Stephan. By the time the evening turned into early morning, they'd worked out a plan, decided which part each of them would play, as well as established a timeline. When the pink hues of dawn threatened to take the sky, the Alphas made their way downstairs.

After escorting Nicholai to the door, the males bid each other goodbye, grasping forearms in the way of the warrior. Kat strolled up as Nicholai was leaving. "Goodbye, Mr. Peterhof."

Nicholai stepped past Stephan and Marcus, and bowing over Kat's hand, he placed a kiss squarely on the back. "Please call me Nicholai, Ms. Spencer."

"Only if you call me Kat."

"A rose by any other name," Nicholai mused as he straightened to his full height, still holding her hand in his much larger one. "Kat it is then. Goodnight, sweet Kat." He turned on his heels and once outside the door dematerialized, leaving only a wisp of smoke behind.

"Does he do that a lot?" asked Kat, looking up at Stephan.

"Do what? Dematerialize?" Stephan tucked her under his arm.

"No, quote poetry. Both times I've met him he has quoted poetry."

Stephan pondered the observation as they made their way to the kitchen to join Marcus. "Yes actually. He does quote poems often. I hadn't really noticed until you mentioned it."

"A man with a heart of a poet. How romantic, especially for someone so young."

Marcus snickered. "Young? Nicholai is older than I am."

"Really?" Katrina could not keep the disbelief from her voice. "He looks like he's around my age."

Stephan shrugged deftly changing the subject to bring Katrina's thoughts back to him. "Want something to eat? I'm thinking about having some ice cream."

"Sure, that sounds good."

"I'll get the bowls," volunteered Marcus.

Stephan grabbed the ice cream and toppings while Marcus placed the bowls on the table. The three sat and created their sundaes. Marcus took the spray can of whipped topping and shook it ominously with a smirk on his face. He lifted one eyebrow, eyeing Kat, mischief darkening his eyes.

"I think I owe you for earlier," he threatened.

"No. You wouldn't dare." Kat furrowed her brows. "Stephan, stop him."

The Alpha leader raised his hands in mock surrender. "This is between you and Marcus. You wounded his pride, now he wants retribution."

Marcus shook the can aiming it toward Katrina and looked for approval from Stephan. A quick nod of his head and Marcus gave a squirt of topping on her nose. Stephan's gut tightened when Katrina's lips parted to inhale an indignant gasp of air and her tiny pink tongue darted out to lick at the cream.

Stephan reached one long finger and scooped the whipped cream from her nose. Kat quickly grabbed Stephan's hand before he could retract it. Bringing his finger to her mouth, she drew it in, sucking the white goodness from the end of his finger. Stephan closed his eyes, a soft moan escaped his lips. Without thinking, he reached out with his thoughts to gently stroke her face. Her eyes widened in shock. "What was that?" Kat placed her hand on her cheek.

His lips smirked as he purposely shifted his thoughts to give the impression of him trailing his fingers up her thigh. "What was what?" he asked with mock innocence.

"You know darn well what I mean. I can feel you touching me. How are you doing that?"

"You mean this?" Without touching her physically, he teased her nipple into a hard pink point that could be seen through the blue T-shirt she wore.

She gasped. "Stop that."

"What? Don't you like it?" A smile of male

satisfaction crossed his lips.

She smiled at him "I think if you keep this up, I won't be able to think straight."

Marcus cleared his throat. "Why don't you two get a room?"

"That won't be necessary because Stephan is going to stop now before things get out of hand. Aren't you, Stephan?"

"If you wish." He touched her other breast, mentally taking the heavy weight of it in his hand as he gave her a crooked smile. "Are you sure that's what you wish?"

A blush reddened her cheeks. "I…I…" She took a steadying breath and let it out very slowly. "I think we need to get back to eating our ice cream before it melts."

Chapter 16

Trace and Alvero put on their clothes as the woman lay sleeping on the bed, naked from their earlier escapades. After having their way with her, Trace had compelled her to sleep. The guard raked his hand down his face. "We still need another human."

"I know just the one," Alvero volunteered. "I was in a bar several months ago and a waitress there was rather interested in me. I bet if we go there, she'll come willingly."

"Sounds easy." Trace pulled on his sweater as he spoke. "How do you know she won't be missed when she's gone?"

"I'll probe her mind once we are there." Alvero shrugged into his black leather jacket and threw Trace his duster.

"Fine, let's go. We're burning moonlight." Trace grabbed the keys to the van and glanced over his shoulder at the sleeping woman on the bed, satisfied his compulsion would keep her unconscious while they hunted.

The two males locked the door to their cheap hotel room and jumped into the dark van that waited for them in the parking lot. It was a basic delivery van with two bucket seats in the front and no windows in the back, the perfect vehicle for what they had planned. The tires screeched as they rode off toward their next target.

Jasmine Newfield sat in the back of Bunker's taking a smoke break. Her long black hair was done up in a tight ponytail. She wore a skin tight uniform of hot pants and a T-shirt with the Bunker's logo plastered on it. A dirty mini apron hung from her waist, just large enough for her to put her order pad and pack of cigarettes in the pockets. Her pretty, Asian features drew tight as she took a long drag from her cigarette, hoping to inhale away the events of the evening.

Two frat boys had come into the bar and ordered a pitcher of beer along with some wings. Her coworker, Betty, brought their order, and they gave her a hard time, wanting her to sit with them. When one of the men touched her inappropriately, Jasmine noticed and went over to the table. A confrontation ensued which ended with the other waitress dumping the sauce for the wings on one of the men and the other man dumping the pitcher of beer back on her coworker. Jasmine escaped relatively unharmed, though some of the sauce splashed on her apron, but Betty had to go home to change. Now they were one server short for the dinner rush.

Tonight she was definitely going to earn her two week vacation that was scheduled to begin tomorrow. She took one last drag from her smoke before stomping out the butt with the heel of her sneaker and heading back inside.

"Hey, Jasmine," said her boss and owner of the place, Kelly Bunker. "Two men just sat down at table thirteen. Will you please take their order?"

"Yeah, sure," she mumbled out between pursed

lips. Kelly was okay to work for, but she could be a bit of a slave driver.

On her way to the table, Jasmine lamented about how table thirteen would have belonged to her beer-covered coworker and she wouldn't be working the table if those frat boys hadn't been such jerks earlier. The last thing her tired feet needed were extra tables to handle. She plastered a fake smile on her face.

"Good evening, gentleman. Can I bring you a drink?" Jasmine looked at the men. They reminded her of muscle men. Beautifully handsome, both were broad in the shoulders with large arms and thick necks. It was obvious they worked out, and Jasmine couldn't help but wonder if they had any brains to go with their brawn. She swallowed her lust and waited for them to reply.

The bigger of the two spoke first. "I was in here several weeks ago and there was a woman with blonde hair, about five feet tall, who was waitressing. Is she here tonight?"

"You mean Betty. She was here earlier, but she had to leave." Jasmine refrained from adding the reason for Betty's departure—the beer bath.

"Oh, that's too bad. I hoped to see her." The man shot Jasmine a sexy smile, flashing his perfect white teeth.

"So what can I get you guys to drink?"

His buddy looked at Jasmine, capturing her eyes in his gaze. "We'll have two beers. Anything American you have on tap."

Jasmine nodded slowly. Mesmerized by his gaze, her brain went fuzzy. She felt a tingling sensation in her mind as information about her life passed through. She lived alone, no family in the area. Not even a pet to keep her company. Vacation starts tomorrow. The tingling eased. Her vision blurred momentarily before coming back in focus. "Two beers...coming...right...up," she murmured slowly, swaying slightly.

"She's perfect," said the larger man who was now wearing an evil grin. His chair creaked under his weight as he leaned back to leer at her.

Her flesh crawled. She couldn't get away from these two fast enough. She felt the weight of their stares when she made her way to the bar. Unfortunately, it only took a few minutes for the bar tender to fill the beer steins, then she headed back to table thirteen.

One of the men looked up at Jasmine as she placed the mugs on the table. "So what time do you get off work tonight, honey?"

"That's the oldest line in the book, buddy. Sorry I don't go out with customers."

"Don't be that way. Let me make introductions. My name is Trace. And this is Alvero."

"If you're looking for company, try the bar down on 4th Street."

"I don't want to go to another bar," the one who called himself Trace countered, palming his beer. "I happen to like this place just fine."

"Suit yourself, but I'm not on the menu." Jasmine pulled her order pad and pencil from her apron. "Do you guys know what you want to order?"

"We'll have a pizza, extra pepperoni and mushrooms," Alvero answered quickly.

"Got it." Jasmine wrote down the order. "Anything else?"

"No, just the pizza," Alvero replied.

"And you," Trace muttered under his breath.

Jasmine's eyes blurred as she stared at their order on her pad. The strange tingling came back. Off at nine. The image of her car. She shook her head trying to vibrate her brain into lucidity. Everything cleared and she turned crossing the bar to place the order with the cook.

The creepy men ate slowly, killing the hours until it was almost time for Jasmine to get off work. At eight thirty they left money for their meal and a small tip on the table. Bastards. Luckily things were still hopping, so she easily put them out of her mind once they left.

Having finally made it to quitting time, Jasmine took off her apron, slipped her tips into the back pocket of her shorts, and pushed open the back door of the bar, heading toward her car. She climbed into her rusty nineteen eighty Chevy Citation and kept her fingers crossed hoping it would start as she turned the key in the ignition. After three tries, the engine finally turned over and she was off. She planned on stopping by the video store and picking up a romantic comedy to watch, hoping it would make her forget about the shift she just completed. Suddenly, an urgent need to just go home struck her, the kind of do-not-pass-go-do-not-collect-$200 type of need.

She paid no notice to the cars around her, just wove her way through the streets. Her only thought was to get to her house, though for the life of her she could not remember why she needed to get home so badly.

After turning into her drive and shutting down the engine, she sat for a moment in the quiet car. She felt hazy like she'd driven home in a fog bank, and didn't remember the drive, only the unending need to get there quickly. She shook her head trying to clear away the fuzzies and stepped from the vehicle.

Suddenly, a set of steel bands clamed over her mouth and around her waist simultaneously. For a moment she stilled, not comprehending what happened, then she realized a hand and a very strong arm engulfed her. She kicked and flailed like a wild animal caught in a trap.

Her struggles seemed to barely register to the person holding her. As he pulled her back toward the waiting van, the man leaned down and bit out beside her ear, "Stop fighting. It's useless."

She recognized that voice. This was one of the men from the restaurant. Trace? Was that his name?

The back doors to a black van opened of their own volition. Trace threw Jasmine unceremoniously into the back causing her to hit her head on the metal wheel well. The cold metal floor made her shiver as she lay holding the back of her head with both hands. She could feel the knot rising. It throbbed in time to her beating pulse, bringing tears to her eyes. She began to cry as much from the pain in her head as the fear of being taken.

"Who...are...you?" she sobbed out. "W-why are you...d-doing this? W-where...are you taking m-me?"

Alvero looked back at her from the driver's seat. "Shut up. No questions," he barked as the van tilted from Trace's weight when he entered the passenger's seat.

Jasmine whimpered on the metal floor in the van. She tried to get her bearings as they drove, but with the limited view out the windshield, she could not tell where they were.

Fear gripped her chest as her bare legs absorbed the chill from the metallic floor. Her fear coupled with her sobs took the breath from her lungs, making it hard to breathe. She drew her knees up and wrapped her arms around her legs, making herself as tiny as possible. Her mind raced in time with the speeding van.

The two men were absolutely silent while they drove. No radio played, no sounds came to her other than her own sobs. There were no sounds of other cars, she realized. No hope of being discovered.

Dread settled in her heart. Where were they going? What would happen to her once they arrived? One thing she did know was that she wasn't sure she wanted her questions answered, for those answers were sure to be bad. That thought brought another round of tears streaking down her cheeks.

Arriving at their destination, Alvero backed the van up to the old rundown hotel room they'd rented the previous evening. He put the vehicle in park and stilled, his hands resting on the steering wheel.

Alvero turned in his seat, glanced at their victim and pushed into Jasmine's mind. He silenced her cries before he immobilized her limbs, but left her conscious.

With their victim completely under his control, Trace moved silently from the van and walked around the back to open the doors. He pulled Jasmine from the vehicle, cradling her in his arms, so if anyone noticed them, they would think her asleep.

"Got her?" Alvero asked as he joined his fellow guard at the back of the van.

"Of course." The larger male shot him an incredulous look.

They opened the door to the room and walked in.

The room smelled of stale smoke. The worn, dirty carpet contained the same brown and orange color as the stained bedspread. It was the kind of place that had seen its share of drug deals and prostitution. The kind of place people minded their own business, hoping to keep others from discovering their own misdeeds.

Trace dropped Jasmine onto the unoccupied bed. She lay sprawled, still unable to move because he maintained his mental control. Only her eyes were free to move. They darted around the room, wide with fright.

"We should get going. Let's grab the woman from last night and get them both to Gage," Alvero said.

A malicious grin crossed Trace's face. "I have a better idea. We have a few hours before we have to leave. Let's stay here for a little longer and have some fun. We've been working hard, we deserve a bonus."

Alvero glanced at his watch. "I don't know if we have time. Besides, Gage won't be happy if we bring him damaged goods."

"Then let's not damage the goods. We'll just sample the goods before we deliver them. We have time. It's early yet."

Alvero looked pensive, his gaze darting between the two women as he considered what Trace suggested. "Well, that one was fun last night," he said gesturing with his thumb toward the naked woman still asleep in the bed.

An evil leer took Trace's face as he watched a single tear escape down Jasmine's cheek. "That's what I'm talking about. Which one do you want?"

Chapter 17

Marcus gradually slowed the Mercedes and pulled over to the shoulder of the highway. Bringing the vehicle to a stop, he grabbed his high power binoculars and silently exited the car. He started down the road at a brisk jog, since he'd parked two miles away from Gage's home—far enough his car would not be seen from the house.

Marcus hung in the shadow of the mountain as he made his way toward the Lucio compound. He came to a stop just south of the homestead and stared up at the large rock wall that awaited him. The mountain side loomed before him, stealing the moon from his view. He needed to find a place where he could lay unseen as he watched the large compound.

Damn I wish I could dematerialize, he thought when his eyes located a potential opening high up in the rock face.

Marcus slid his hands along the mountain until he located a place that offered the small slits and ledges he needed to scale the rock. His fingers found purchase in tiny fissures, and he began his perilous climb toward the small cave he would be calling home for the evening.

Half way to his goal, the fingers on his left hand came loose as he prepared to push up to the next ledge. Suspended from only three fingers, his body bounced hard into the rock. His breath sawed from his lungs, his heart beat a furious pace when he looked down and realized he hung more than one hundred feet in the air. He bobbed along the rocks. They bit into his skin with each impact.

When his body stilled, he looked up and discovered a small ledge above and to his left. With a mighty heave, the fingers of his left hand found the ledge, and he pulled himself up. He held himself still, taking a moment to take a deep stealing breath. Marcus let it out slowly to center himself before continuing his climb.

By the time he reached the cave he sought, his muscles screamed in protest. His skin itched from the healing cuts as he shimmied into his hidey hole.

He pulled himself into the crevice. Tight and confining, it required him to lie on his stomach. The cold, damp space combined with the hardness of the stone made an uncomfortable berth. Marcus brought the binoculars to his eyes and looked across at the compound.

The Lucio home backed up to the adjacent mountain, at least two acres of grass surrounded the place—the only green within a ten mile radius. The large house contained two stories with roll down shutters to keep out the sun and a heavy oak door painted red at its front. All the windows were extra-large, no doubt built to allow for a wide view of the surrounding countryside.

Looking through the binoculars, Marcus observed a set of four men, all dressed in identical black uniforms, casing the perimeter of the house. He watched them walk the sides of the home like hornets buzzing around their hive. They were precise, their paths did not cross, but clearly were designed so no area was left untraversed. They were guards. He knew a patrol when he saw one.

Marcus trained his binoculars on a large window located on the second floor. His eyes widened as the scene played out before him. A male and female lay naked on a bed while another woman, dressed in sheer lingerie, stood beside the bed watching the activity. The male was motioning for the standing brunette to join them on the bed, and she willingly obliged. She slipped down along side of the other female, and lifted the woman's red hair to her nose. The male pushed the red head down on her back and blanketed her with his body. As he began working his hips against the young woman, the brunette bent her head to one side and sank her fangs into the woman's vein. A pained look came upon the young woman's face, but she didn't call out or seem to be distressed.

Marcus lowered the binoculars in revulsion and sighed. Some vampires really disgusted him. He would definitely not be looking in that window again anytime soon.

Marcus noticed movement out of the corner of his eye. He watched a black van pull up by the side of the house. Bringing the binoculars back to his eyes, he saw a tall, brawny man exit the van dressed in the same black attire as the patrol around the house. A second male jumped from the vehicle and joined the first at the back of the van.

The two carefully looked around as if to assure no one was watching. In tandem, they opened the doors and removed what appeared to be two females from the back of the van. The two men casually flung the lifeless women over their shoulders like sacks of oats. They loped around to the front of the home, pausing briefly to talk to the guard posted by the front door. He opened the door and the two bodies were taken into the house.

That was suspicious.

Marcus continued to watch throughout the evening. He wasn't sure whether the females from the van were alive or dead. They did not move when they were carried in and he had a sick feeling in the pit of his stomach that the two women he'd seen were in trouble. If they were alive, were they a snack or would something more nefarious be their fate? The Alpha closed his eyes in disgust and shook his head, fighting his instinct to charge into the home to demand their release. He'd be outnumbered by those guards. It would be wiser to wait until he could bring back-up and execute a rescue plan.

There were those of his breed who could be quite cruel, using their enhanced strength and power to degrade others. He'd witnessed much in the two hundred years he'd been on the earth. He had seen much senseless bloodshed, watched as people were tortured simply because they were weaker.

It still amazed him how those with power, be they human or vampire, could become such monsters, taking what they wanted when they wanted without thought or conscience. The inhumanity, the immorality sickened him.

Marcus kept his vigil until two hours before dawn. Then, when nothing more of interest happened, he carefully descended the mountain and made his way back to the Mercedes. He slid behind the steering wheel and tossed the binoculars onto the empty seat beside him.

He scrubbed a tired hand down his face, drawing the skin taunt. The images of the home played in his mind like a never ending reel of a horror flick. He started the engine, it purred to life as he gave it gas and cranked the wheel. With a quick U-turn, he headed home.

He drove back to the penthouse, pondering the fate of the women from the van, wondering if they would live to see another day, hating the feeling of impotency that came with the knowledge there was nothing he could do for them at this time.

Chapter 18

Kat pulled on her white jeans and tucked her navy shirt into the waistband. It had been a long night. Having just completed her third show of the evening, she felt bone-sore tired. She hung her costume on the garment rack then headed for the exit.

As she walked down the hallway with the florescent light reflecting harshly off the linoleum floor, her thoughts turned to the dark vampire waiting for her at home, sending her heartbeat into a canter. She knew she'd fallen in love with Stephan, but she wasn't sure exactly how he felt about her. When he looked at her, she could see what she believed to be love in his eyes, but he never actually said the words. She decided to interrogate Marcus tonight when he came to escort her home from work about Stephan's possible feelings for her. She thought about how to broach the subject as she opened the door and stepped into the alley behind Reaper's.

Stephan waited, leaning against the hood of Marcus' black H3 with his arms crossed against his broad chest. His dark chestnut hair shimmered in the reflection from the light above the door. He wore a crisp white oxford shirt unbuttoned just enough to draw Kat's gaze down toward his narrow waist where a pair of black jeans hugged his hips and accentuated his muscular thighs—as well as his other assets. Her eyes returned to his handsome face, and he flashed his sexy smile. The man was walking sex and her heart went into a full gallop at the sight of him.

"Ready to go, Kitten?" he asked, straightening to his full height.

"Where's Marcus?"

"I sent him on a little errand. He won't be back for a while, so I'm to escort you tonight." Stephan made his way around the H3 and opened the passenger door. He held the door for her as she heaved herself into the Hummer, helped by a push on her *derrière*.

After reaching over her to buckle her seatbelt, he walked back around the vehicle with a sexy swagger Kat appreciated. Stephan jumped into the driver's seat, and brought the engine to life.

"I have a confession to make," he said, glancing sideways at Kat before he pulled out of the alley. "I purposely sent Marcus away tonight, so I could have some time alone with you."

Kat didn't mind hearing that particular news. "Why's that?"

"Oh, I don't know, maybe because you are a beautiful, sexy woman and because I have a surprise for you." He ran his fingers through his hair, pulling it away from his handsome face.

"What kind of surprise?"

"You'll see." He lifted one eye brow as he glanced at her.

Kat watched the streets whiz by. One. Two. Ten. They definitely weren't headed home.

"Um, Stephan, you missed the turn for the penthouse. It was back there." Katrina turned in her seat and pointed behind them.

"I know," he replied cryptically, as he switched lanes and gunned the engine.

"Where are we going?"

"Don't you trust me?"

"Of course I do."

"Then just sit back and enjoy the ride." Stephan flashed his fangs in a naughty smile. He reached over and gave her hand a quick squeeze as they rode in companionable silence.

The man beside her, so dark and mysterious, certainly knew how to keep a secret but then so too did Marcus. Maybe it was a vampire thing. Kat glanced down on the large hand resting on her leg and followed the thick arm up to the strong profile of the man beside her. His hard jawline complimented his straight nose. His eyelashes brushed a dark crescent over his cheek with each blink.

Heat coursed through Katrina's blood, sending warmth to her cheeks. Just looking at this man did things to her. Having his hand on her pushed her lust higher, wound her body tighter. Sometimes, like now, just sitting close in a confined space was too much.

She needed air, needed space to cool her burning desire. Katrina pulled her gaze away from Stephan and found the button for the window. With a touch, it slid the window down sending a cool breeze over her skin.

Kat's curiosity rose when she noticed they headed toward the outskirts of the city. "Hey, Stephan, you never answered my question. Where are we going?"

"You'll see. We'll be there soon." He squeezed her knee, sending a feeling of warmth and comfort through her body.

Able to breathe again, Kat visibly relaxed and

settled into the seat. She wasn't sure if it was the easy tone in his voice or his soothing touch, but she trusted him. She watched the empty highway stretched out for miles before them.

"How far out are we going?" Kat noted the digital time on the dash. "We only have a few hours before sunrise."

"We should be fine. Though I'm glad you are concerned about my safety." Stephan shot her a heart melting grin. "We should be back before dawn."

"This car won't provide much protection from the sun."

"The H3 wasn't my first choice, but we need it to traverse the terrain."

Ah, a clue. "Terrain? What kind of terrain?"

"This terrain. We're here." Stephan brought the vehicle to a halt.

Katrina's head snapped around. She'd been so wrapped up in their conversation she hadn't noticed her surroundings. "This is Red Rock Canyon. I've hiked here before."

"Not with me." Stephan exited the H3 and circled the car coming to rest outside Kat's door. "Come on." Stephan held open the passenger door and offered a hand to Kat.

Kat looked down at her tennis shoes. "We aren't going far, I hope. I'm not exactly dressed for hiking."

"You're dressed perfectly." Stephan raked her body with his heated gaze, obviously admiring how her shirt and jeans hugged her every contour. "Let's go."

The canyon was beautiful at night. The moon cast a silvery glow on the rocks playing off the red and white stones. It created shadows that seemed to move with them as they walked. If she was by herself, Katrina might have been somewhat afraid, but with Stephan by her side she did not fear a thing.

He grabbed her hand and led her toward an opening in the rock formation. They bent over at the waist to pass through. It was a tight squeeze and they were forced to go forward one in front of the other. Just as the walls seemed to be closing in on Katrina, they squeezed through a slit in the rock, popping out into an opening where she could stand next to him.

Katrina wiggled her fingers in front of her face, unable to see them in the pitch of the cave. "It's awful dark. Did you bring a flashlight?"

Stephan cursed under his breath. "No, I didn't think about it. Honestly, I forgot you would not be able to see." Stephan thought for a moment. "There is a way you could see. If you drank a little of my blood, it would enhance your vision."

Kat turned, reached for Stephan in the darkness to thread her fingers in the material of his shirt. "Did I just hear you right? Drink your blood?"

Stephan gathered her protectively in his arms. "I'm an ancient. My blood can enhance your senses. If you drink a little, you would be able to see just fine, and I could show you why I brought you here."

Her face turned up toward his, though she could not see his handsome face. "So if I take just a little of your blood I'd have superhuman sight."

"Among other things." She felt him shrug.

"Such as," she prompted.

"All your senses would increase, hearing, sight, smell...touch." He ran his finger along her arm.

"And I'd only need a little?" Curiosity to see why

Stephan brought her there tempted her, but she was reluctant to drink blood. She'd never tasted blood before, and it wasn't something she particularly wanted to do.

"Yes, just a little will do."

Stephan held her patiently awaiting her answer. His arms tightened around her as he waited. She weighed the decision carefully, then took a deep breath before she spoke.

"Okay, I guess." Kat said, albeit reluctantly, when her curiosity won out. Stephan took something out of his pocket.

"What's that?" Kat asked.

"The knife I always carry."

Kat chuckled. "That's handy."

"It is a special knife, made of the finest steel and coated with titanium, the one metal that is toxic to vampires. The titanium will keep me from healing too quickly, giving you a chance to drink."

"I'm not sure about this." She swallowed.

"I'll do a shallow cut. It will keep the blood from flowing too freely. You need only take a little." He nicked his wrist and placed it to her lips before she could protest further.

Kat gingerly licked at the wound. When her tongue touched his wrist she felt a jolt flow between their bodies. A shiver slid down her back, making her tremble.

His blood tasted coppery, but the smell enticed her. It smelled of musk and spice, very male. She closed her lips around the wound and took a tiny sip. With the small swallow, she felt different, stronger. More alive. It was utterly addicting.

She sensed his intense gaze on her as she closed her eyes, relishing each draw. A low rumble sounded from his chest. She felt him start to pull his wrist away, but Kat grabbed his forearm with both hands, not ready to stop drinking. She moaned against his skin, sending a tremor coursing through him.

"That's enough, Katrina. Stop now," Stephan commanded, his voice low as he gently pried his wrist out of her hands. He licked the wound closed. "I can taste you on my skin. Delicious."

He framed her face with his hands and stepped into her. She wrapped her arms around his waist, pulling him tightly against her. He kissed her soundly and their bodies melted together, hers soft and pliant against his larger frame. He deepened the kiss, his tongue darting between her lips. Their tongues swirled between their mouths, their breaths came harder. The world tunneled down to him. He overwhelmed her, his kiss claimed her. Lost in the sensation of lust and desire he created, only when Stephan pulled back slowly did Kat remember where they were.

She opened her eyes, and stared into the blue depths of his. He gently turned her to face away from him, wrapping his hard arms around her.

"What do you see?" His voice sounded thick with lust.

Kat's breath caught in her throat when she looked around. She could see perfectly, like having infrared vision, only in color.

"Breathe, Kitten," Stephan whispered in her ear.

Kat obediently took in a deep breath, and tasted the rock and minerals of the cavern. The musky smell of damp earth filled her nostrils as she scanned the cave.

Stalactites hung like chandeliers from the ceiling sparkling from the water that dripped from them. The water collected in a pool, lining the bottom of the cavern. Kat could see clearly to the bottom of the grotto where stalagmites pushed their way up. The drops of water caused ripples on the surface that made the stalagmites look as if they swayed to music.

"It's…" Kat struggled to find the appropriate word to complete her sentence. "Beautiful...no gorgeous…no stunning…" She turned in Stephan's arms to look up at him with awe in her eyes, and whispered, "There's no perfect word to describe it."

"I feel the same way about you, Kitten." He hugged her to him, placing his chin on the top of her head. "If you like this, you should see the view from up there." Stephan pointed to a small ledge some twenty feet above them.

"How can you get up there?"

A sexy smile played on his handsome face as his arms tighten around her like steel beams. Stephan's body coiled then the next moment they flew through the air toward the ledge. Stephan put her down gently on the thin shelf. Kat clung to him, digging her nails into his biceps.

"I've got you. You can relax." Stephan ran a comforting hand softly down her back. "Look down." Kat shook her head, squeezing her eyes tightly closed.

"Look at me, Kat," he commanded gently, waiting until she finally complied before continuing. "I promise I won't let anything happen to you. Look down; see what it looks like from up here. Trust me. I've got you, Kitten."

The absolute truth of that statement hit Katrina like

an arrow to the heart. There were many ways to take those four simple words. *I've got you, Kitten.* The words replayed in her mind, giving her courage to trust the man holding her with her safety.

Kat carefully glanced down and the view quickly made her forget her fear of heights. As pretty as the view of the pond was from the floor of the cave, it was ten times as beautiful from up above. From this vantage point she could see the individual colors created in the bottom of the pond by the various minerals in the rocks. Yellows, reds, whites, and blues. They swirled around the stalagmites creating a mesmerizing pattern.

"Oh Stephan," Kat whispered.

"If I live another six hundred years, I'll always remember the sound of my name on your lips this night."

"It's beautiful, isn't it?" Kat breathed.

"Beautiful is exactly what I was thinking." Stephan tightened his arms, kissing her on her cheek.

He feathered kisses down her neck, brushing her shirt to the side so he could continue the trail along her shoulder. He moved them back, pinning her to the wall with his body. Her arms wrapped around his neck, fingers tangling his silky hair.

He laid a trail of kisses back to her lips. Her lips parted in an invitation he gladly accepted. Their tongues danced like lovers, lips pressed firmly together in a bruising embrace. Their scent mingled to become as one, a perfect mix of honeysuckle and spice. It was intoxicating, the combination of fragrance and touch. When their bodies began to sway, Stephan broke their kiss.

Kat raised her hand to her kiss-swollen lips,

breathing hard, and whispered, "Whoa, I've never been kissed like that. I felt everything, even your heartbeat."

"It's my blood. It improved your sense of touch." Stephan ran his fingers through her hair.

"Did it ever," Kat rasped, still trying to catch her breath.

"I think I need a cold shower. Want to go for a dip?"

"What? I don't have a bathing suit."

Stephan smiled. "We don't need suits."

"Is it safe?" She glanced down at the grotto.

"Yes I've been in there lots of times. I promise, it will feel good."

Kat shook her head in disbelief, sending her locks tumbling over her shoulders. "Why not?"

In the blink of her eye, she found herself on the cave floor with Stephan working at her clothes. She allowed him to undress her, enjoying the feel of his fingers as they brushed her sensitive skin. After doing away with his own clothes, Stephan picked her up in his strong arms and headed for the pool. The cool water lapped at her bottom as he held her just above the surface.

"It's cold," she squealed, kicking her legs.

Stephan tightened his grip. "It's not cold. Your skin is just more sensitive than usual." A mischievous grin lit his face and with a flash of movement he withdrew his support, letting her fall into the tranquil pool.

Kat's head broke the surface, treading water.

"I can't believe you did that." She splashed him sending the cool water down his body. He watched as her appreciative gaze followed the water sluicing down his body. The evidence of his arousal thickened in response to her heated gaze. Kat gasped at his size.

Kat was not innocent. She'd seen many of her fellow dancers naked as well as the few lovers she'd had, but never had she seen such an amazing looking body as the one she watched in the cave. Even Marcus' toned form could not compare.

Every muscle was defined by hard lines, this man didn't have a six pack; he had eight perfectly defined abdominals. The water lapped at his groin, drawing her eye to the long, thick erection that promised an erotic night.

"How dare you splash me!" Stephan said, mock outrage raising his voice. "I think you deserve to be punished for that, you naughty girl."

The heat in his eyes told her it was time to run, though whether to run to him or from him, now that was the question. She swam away from Stephan on her back. His grin exposed his fangs as he dove in after her. A small squeak escaped Kat's throat before she plunged into the water to swim away. Kat surfaced and turned a circle, scanning for her pursuer.

The hair on her neck stood at attention. She sensed him near, but she couldn't see him. Katrina started to drop back under the water when she felt a large hand snake its way up her leg. She kicked wildly, but was stilled by his strong arms. He pulled her under the water to meet him.

Stephan glided her lean body down his own until he found her kiss-swollen lips. He kissed her fiercely, causing small bubbles to float to the surface. He wrapped his thick arms around her and kicked them to the surface using his strong legs, never breaking their kiss.

Kat's eyes widened in amazement. Heat flared through her body, pooled low in her core. Her body went up in flames, fire licked along her skin. Her fingers clutched at his back as she arched her hips toward him in a silent plea for relief. She wrapped her legs around his waist and allowed him to move them to the side of the pool where he set her onto the edge.

He spread her thighs wide and drank in the view. "You are so beautiful," he rasped just before he sank down to explore her with his mouth. He took one long lick to find her most sensitive spot and began circling the nub with sure strokes. Her overly sensitive skin helped her to reach the precipice of orgasm quickly. It built fast, and with one more flick of his tongue, he took her over the edge.

She moaned in ecstasy when he rose above her, his muscles bunching as he stood up sending water running over his chest down and down his most manly parts. Katrina's tongue flicked over her lips at the sight as her eyes tracked the droplets on their sinuous ride down his body. Her hand reached out to trace the water path with two fingers.

He leaned his head back and moaned when she wrapped one of her hands around his shaft. Katrina ran her fingers along the length of him, sending tiny tremors through his body. He watched her eyelids droop wantonly with desire. Her hand tightened around him, her enhanced sense of touch enjoying the feel of soft velvet over steel. She stroked from tip to base, her pace quickening as the minutes passed.

By the look on his face, she could tell she drove him mad with her touches. Her soft fingers continued to work their magic. She reveled in the knowledge that she affected him as much as he affected her. She loved the way his body tightened under her touch.

"Katrina, if you don't stop that, I won't last much longer."

She looked up at him from under the light crescent of her lashes, a wily grin spreading across her face. "We wouldn't want that now, would we?"

She boldly positioned him at her entrance. In one smooth thrust, he slid into her wet heat. She gasped, the sensation so intense she thought she might explode. She trembled as she opened herself to his masterful strokes.

His hands grabbed her calves, wrapped her legs around his waist. The water sloshed around his powerful thighs as he worked his hips. He slid his hands down her legs to grab her hips, bringng them over the edge of the pool. He lifted them slightly allowing him to angle in deeply, hitting the internal sweet spot that sent a lightning bolt of lust through her body. Her climax built in time to his increasing thrusts, and once again the delicious sensation coiled inside her, driving her up and up. The coil shattered inside her, and she called out his name when her body fragmented.

Gasping and moaning, she writhed through the intense pleasure washing over her. He built the delicious pressure while he thrust into her again and again, holding her hips exactly where he wanted. Their flesh pounded together as he brought her pleasure. Soft keening sounds left her throat, becoming louder when the pressure within built once more. The luscious sounds of her excitement quickened his pace until they tumbled together to their release.

Panting from exhaustion, Kat slowly opened her

eyes to find Stephan looking down at her with a smile of male satisfaction on his striking face.

"What?" she asked, taking her legs from his waist. It shifted the pressure inside her sensitive core. His shaft jumped in response, but he did not withdraw. Unable to move, her legs hung limply over the side of the pool. The cool water a shock to her heated skin.

"I was just thinking," he replied coyly and bent at the waist to settle his weight on his forearms.

"About what?"

"How amazing you are." Stephan tucked her hair behind her ear.

"You were the one who was amazing," she admitted propping herself up on her elbows. "I have never felt like that before."

"It was my blood. Did I mention in addition to heightening senses, it happens to be an aphrodisiac?"

Kat's eyes widened, then she relaxed and laid back on the ground. "I don't think that was it. I think it was you."

One side of Stephan's mouth raised in a smile. "We could test that theory by trying this again tomorrow after the effects from my blood have worn off."

"Sounds like a plan to me." A grin took Katrina's face.

Chapter 19

Stephan stood in his penthouse, cradling Kat in his strong arms. She'd fallen asleep on the ride back home. Not wanting to wake her, Stephan had simply picked her up and carried her. He mentally unlocked and opened the door.

Marcus greeted them with a nod when they walked through the door.

"I have a lot to tell you," Marcus said in a whispered voice.

Quietly Stephan replied, "Let me put her to bed, then I want you to brief me on what you found tonight." Kat snuggled into Stephan as he spoke.

Stephan could feel Marcus watching him carry Kat up the stairs to the master suite. He was probably giving him a knowing smirk behind his back. They would speak about the sleeping arrangements later, but first he had to see to the needs of the woman in his arms.

Stephan placed Kat gently on his bed and tucked the covers up under her chin. His chest swelled with love for her. She looked so desirable in his bed. He knew she was exactly where she was meant to be. It felt right looking down at her as she slept soundly wrapped in his sheets. For the first time in his long life he felt complete, whole, and it was because she had come into his life.

He brushed a blonde curl from her face, gently

tucked the errant strand back behind her ear and smiled, sighing as he wondered how long their relationship could last. There was so much against them. Her mortality. His vampirism. *It will be difficult*, a smile graced his lips, *but then anything worth having is worth fighting for.* And one thing Stephan was very proficient at was fighting.

"Sleep tight, Kitten," he whispered bending over to place a light kiss on her forehead.

He left the room, but paused in the doorway to turn and take one more look at her over his shoulder. Reluctance kept his feet from moving forward, his body refused to leave her presence. In that moment, he realized she had become everything to him. His entire life had changed.

He'd never been so protective of anyone before. The closest he had ever come was the protective nature he felt toward Marcus, like that of an older brother. But with Kat he definitely didn't feel brotherly, far from it. He experienced a deep connection to the woman lying in his bed, one he wouldn't deny any longer.

Duty pushed in on him. Council business called. He needed to know what Marcus had discovered. If there was a hunt club in this city no human was safe, not even Kat. Only his driving need to protect her pushed him from the room.

Stephan joined Marcus in the library and sat behind his desk. "Let's call Nicholai to come over, so he too can hear what you found." Stephan punched the numbers into the phone and hit the speaker button.

"Hello." Nicholai's booming voice filled the library.

"Hi, Nicholai, it's Stephan and Marcus. I've got

you on speaker phone. Marcus was just going to tell me about what he found out tonight, and I thought you would also like to hear it."

"Yes, I would. Thank you for calling."

"Would you like to come over to discuss it?"

"I cannot come tonight. There has been a problem with some of our scenery, and I need to stay here to help out the company. The show must go on, you know.

"But I can take a quick break. Can Marcus share his information over the phone?"

"Of course. Okay, Marcus, tell us what you found out tonight." Stephan sat back and crossed his thick arms across his chest.

Marcus relayed what he witnessed from his cramped crevice in the rock, carefully describing the two bodies he saw removed from the van.

Stephan leaned forward onto his desk, steepling his fingers. "So you aren't sure if they were alive?"

"That's correct. They were limp and the way the guards carried them, I could not see if their eyes were opened or shut. And they were too far away to tell if they were breathing or not."

Nicholai interjected, "Something is definitely not right. Between what I sensed in the house and what Marcus saw tonight, something is very wrong."

"I agree," said Stephan. "But we need more information. We don't have enough to be sure exactly what they are up to. Do you think one of us should go out and watch the compound again tomorrow night?"

Marcus leaned forward. "I think we need more than eyes on the place. We need ears. We need to hear what is going on *in* that house."

A thoughtful look crossed Stephan's face. "That's

a great idea, exactly what we need. We need to have ears inside."

From the speaker phone the two males heard, "I know someone in VES who can probably hook me up with a…what is the word? Insect?"

"You mean a bug?" laughed Marcus.

"Da, that is it, a bug. Andrea wanted me to get the autographs of my prima ballerina and *premier danseur*. I can go to the home under the pretense of dropping off the autographs and plant the bug."

"That might just work," said Stephan smiling with satisfaction across his desk at Marcus.

"It has to work," commented Marcus. "If Gage Lucio is the one doing the hunt club, we have to prove it so we can stop him before the hunt."

"Da. If Gage is behind the club, he will most likely be doing the hunt during the party he invited me to."

"That would make sense," concurred Stephan. Marcus nodded his head in agreement.

"All right then, we are all set," said Nicholai. "I will go to my contact at the Vampire Enforcement Squad and get the bug, then hide it in the house. I will call you when I am done and let you know how it went."

"Just do me a favor, Nicholai," Stephan said. "Don't tell VES why you need the device. It's too early to bring them into this. We aren't even sure there is a hunt club."

"Personally, I think if we find out there is a hunt club, we Alphas should take care of things, not VES." Marcus earned a nod of acquiescence from Stephan at the suggestion.

"I will be careful. I will find a way to get the

device without involving the VES. Perhaps I will tell them I need the device to listen in on a cheating lover." Nicholai's deep chuckle cracked over the speaker.

Marcus laughed. "Not sure that will work. Maybe you should tell them that you need the device for research. You could say you're thinking about buying some and would like to try them out before you invest in any."

"Hmm," said Nicholai thoughtfully. "That might work. I will come up with something."

"We have a plan, so I think we are done for tonight." Stephan clapped his hands together once before rubbing them back and forth in satisfaction. "Thank you, Nicholai. Good luck planting the device. Goodbye and safe travels."

"Safe travels, my friends," the Russian said, his thick accent purring the Rs.

With a punch of the button, Stephan cut the phone connection and looked up at Marcus. He appreciated the way the Alphas always worked so well together. He supposed centuries of fighting together could do that. There was a special bond they shared that went beyond simple friendship. A small smile lit Stephan's face as he fondly remembered good times with the warriors he had come to think of as his friends.

Stephan leaned back in his chair. "The Alphas have definitely been through a lot. A lot of fights, conflicts, empires, and…fun."

"Yes, we've had some very good times over the centuries." Propping his elbow on the arm of his chair, Marcus leaned his head onto his hand. "And some not so good times."

After several moments of reflective silence,

Marcus spoke, bringing both of them out of their thoughts. "Soooooo," said Marcus in a sing-song voice. "I noticed when you took Kat to bed, you went to your room. Does that mean…"

"It means that from now on you are welcome to go back to sleeping in your room."

Marcus flashed a knowing grin and rose to leave. He dipped his head once toward Stephan.

"As you wish…sire," he said formally before giving Stephan a wink and leaving him alone in the room.

Stephan padded silently out of the room behind Marcus. Making his way down the hall to his room, his thoughts turned from the violence of his past to the soft, docile woman who was his present.

Once in his suite, he reverently disrobed Kat, his only intention to make her comfortable as they slept. After silently removing his own clothes, he slipped into the bed beside her. He laid one arm across her stomach enjoying the gentle lift with each breath. He closed his eyes, allowing her warmth to surround him as he drifted off to sleep.

Chapter 20

Kat's eyes fluttered as she emerged from her dream state. She'd been dreaming about Stephan making love to her in a cave. It had been a sensuous fantasy, in vivid life-like Technicolor.

As the sleepy haze cleared from her mind, slowly she realized she was not recalling a dream but instead a beautiful reality. She and Stephan had made love and it had been the most amazing experience of her life. Never before had she experienced anything with such intensity and feeling.

Stephan said it was his blood, but she knew better. They experienced a real connection between them, like two halves of the same whole coming together. The earth moved, her heart beat in time with his. Perhaps the blood enhanced the experience, but their connection was none the less real.

She turned her head and gazed at the chiseled features on the face lying beside her. Kat stirred slightly, wiggling her toes, testing her body.

Stephan's eyes snapped open and locked with hers immediately. He seemed instantly ready for action, no sleepy fog for him. His sensual smile exposed his straight white teeth and extended canines, which Kat found sexy.

"Good evening, Kitten," he said, his deep voice sending a bullet of desire shooting through her body straight to her core.

"Good evening," she replied back dreamily, more breath than voice.

"I believe we were planning on doing a little experiment this evening. Weren't we?"

A shiver of anticipation traveled through her. Kat smiled coyly, lowered her eyes, and did her best southern accent. "Why my good sir, whatever are you talking about?"

"If my memory is correct, and it always is, I believe you were going to convince me that I am just as—what was the word you used—*amazing* tonight as I was last night." Stephan propped himself up on one elbow and trailed one of his long fingers down the valley between her breasts.

Kat ran her tongue over her suddenly dry lips, moistening them, the motion tracked by his eyes. "Oh. Well I guess the least I could do—in the name of science—would be to find out if sex with you is just as amazing tonight without your blood affecting me." She smiled at him as he bent to capture her lips.

"Ah, the sacrifices we all must make in the name of science," he whispered just before his lips descended on hers in a hot and hungry kiss.

He slid his hand through the valley between her breasts, blazing a fiery trail down her stomach to the juncture between her legs. She parted her thighs slightly allowing his fingers to find her dewy with need. He drew tiny circles over her swollen nub, and a moan escaped her lips, vibrating against his own as they kissed.

Stephan drew back to watch the expression of ecstasy on her face. Her eyes closed, her top teeth biting into her lower lip as he continued his sinuous ministrations.

Small mewling sounds escaped her throat as Stephan gently slid two fingers in and out of her sex while his thumb continued to circle her sensitive pearl. Pressure within boiled up hard and fast. She thrust her hips shamelessly against his hand in wild abandonment, demanding release. A release he happily gave. Calling out his name, she fell over the edge.

Kat lay panting, looking at Stephan as he blanketed her body with his own. With a skilled thrust, he entered her, causing her to arch against him, her breasts meeting his chest. Kat snaked her arms around his neck. She threaded her fingers in his hair and brought his head down to lock their lips in a deep kiss.

Stephan slowly built the pressure between them as he increased the speed of his thrusting hips. He slipped his hand beneath her bottom, raising it so he could penetrate her deeper. With one long, hard stroke he rammed fully into her. The invasion caused her to stiffen slightly from the feeling of him filling her so, but when he began to piston in and out of her, her body relaxed, adjusted to accommodate his girth.

Katrina ran her hands down his back, holding onto his solid form to keep herself secured to this plane as he sent her body soaring higher. Her hands tightened over his muscles that flexed with each sure stroke.

She matched him stroke for stroke. Her nails bit deliciously into his buttocks, spurring him on. His hips pistoned faster into her moist heat.

Stephan bent his head and captured her lips to once again savor the sweet taste before he suckled at her breasts, pulling on her pink taut nipples. They puckered, thrusting out as he swirled his tongue over them. He took his time, making sure each had equally lavish attention.

He kissed a trail up her body, running his tongue over her neck. Teeth grazed ever so lightly over the sensitive skin, making her writhe beneath him.

She felt him nip at her flesh. His body started to quake under the pads of her fingers as they traced the taught muscles on his back. The sound of her beating heart filled her ears. It pounded in her chest, pushing her breasts against his body. He moaned against her neck, the sound almost animalistic.

Sensing a change in her lover, Kat stilled beneath him. She felt the slight sting of his teeth against her neck. It both excited and terrified her, the two emotions warring within her. She knew she was safe with Stephan, but her phobia was still strong from her attack. No one had bitten her since the night of the attack. Could she allow such a thing now? Would the sensation of Stephan's teeth sinking into her flesh be any different from the way those other fangs felt?

Her fear surrounded them, breaking the moment in a way nothing else could have. Stephan's mouth closed against her skin. He murmured a string of vicious oaths and groaned against her neck, burying his face in the spot where her neck and shoulder met.

Stephan pushed himself up on his forearms, rising above her to look at her with sad eyes. "I can smell your fear. I'd never hurt you, Kitten," he said softly.

"I know. I trust you," she whispered, believing she truly felt that way. She knew in her heart she could trust the man with her. She just wasn't ready to have him bite her. And really, how unreasonable was that? There were plenty of people who didn't want their lovers to bite. She wasn't into that BDSM stuff.

She looked at him, letting her trust show in her eyes. It was enough to ease the features on his face. He allowed her to pull him toward her when she encircled his neck with her arms. Kat wrapped her legs around his back as her mouth wrapped around his tongue.

She was the first to move, rocking her hips, joining them fully once more. Stephan kissed away the last of her trepidation, building her lust into a burning inferno that consumed her body with a scorching heat.

Fingers clenched in her hair, holding her still while he took her mouth, kissing her soundly until she felt him jerk. Swell inside her. He quickened their pace and brought Kat her release once more, this time her inner muscles milked his own release while she called out his name. He threw back his head and let out a triumphant cry. Together they tumbled into ecstasy.

Kat cradled Stephan in her arms, hugging him to her bosom. The rich, musky scent that was a combination of sandalwood and sex surrounded her, and she found herself smiling, happier now than at any other time in her life. She felt wanted, loved…cherished.

"I love you," she breathed, forgetting Stephan had preternatural hearing.

"I love you too, Kitten." Stephan rose on his forearms to look down on her. A smile came to his face. "I have an idea. It's early yet, and you have some time before work. Let's go over to the Florencia hotel. I want to ride the gondolas with you. After the ride, we could get something to eat."

"I'd love that!" Her face lit up in anticipation.

"But first I have to know," he said, looking down at her.

A confused look furrowed her brows. "Know what?" she asked.

"How was the experiment?" Stephan asked separating their bodies so they could dress and get ready for their date.

Amazing. Stupendous.

"So, so," Katrina replied, fighting to keep the smile from her face.

Stephan froze. The look of concern and shock on his face forced the laughter from her lips. His face softened, then he pounced, pinning her to the bed for a punishing tickle.

****

Nicholai rang the bell and waited for the door to open. He fumbled with the listening devices hidden in the pockets of his brown slacks. His contact at VES offered not one but two of the small round devices to Nicholai, and he readily accepted both.

The guard who'd been introduced to him as Trace opened the door wide and motioned him inside. "Please come in, Mr. Peterhof."

"I have come to see Andrea. Is she in?"

"Yes. Have a seat in the living room. I'll get Mrs. Lucio for you." The guard motioned for Nicholai to enter the room with a grand sweep of his arm. After watching Nicholai sit down on the couch, Trace turned on his heels, leaving the room to fetch the mistress of the house.

Moments later Andrea walked through the room wearing a dark purple pants suit. Nicholai didn't know much about fashion, but he was sure the outfit was designer and very expensive.

"Good evening, Nicholai," she greeted as he stood to kiss the back of her hand. "It is a pleasure to see you again." Her toothy smile was blinding. "To what do I owe the pleasure of your company?"

"I promised you some autographs, I believe. I had the chance to acquire them." He handed her two eight by ten photographs of his dancers, each of which had been signed by the pictured performer.

Andrea's eyes raked the photos. "Oh," she squealed in delight. "I love them! Thank you so much, Nicholai." Andrea turned her gaze back to him. Her assessing stare said she appreciated what she saw.

The warrior scanned the room, trying to determine where to put the listening device. Deciding most owners did not have many conversations in their formal living room, he needed an excuse to move throughout the rest of the house. Nicholai turned toward his hostess. "Excuse me, I need to use the facilities."

"Of course. Go down the hall, it's the third door on the right."

"Thank you, Andrea." He slipped her a sensual smile and made his way out of the living room. He heard an audible sigh escape her lips, sensed her admiring gaze on his back as his strides ate up the floor.

Nicholai stood in the small bathroom leaning on his hands as they rested on the granite vanity. He stared vacantly at his reflection in the mirror and tried to decide where would be the best place in the house to put the listening device. They were small enough to go anywhere, so he wondered just where the couple would most likely talk about a subject like a hunt club. He had considered the hallway, but thought better of it when he realized any conversations there would be brief as people used it to walk from one place to another. He considered the living room again, but decided it was too formal, not a place the couple was likely to spend much time.

Nicholai decided to place one device upstairs and one downstairs to allow for the best coverage. After a number of considerations, he finally determined one should go in the kitchen. He imagined long conversations would take place at the kitchen table over a meal.

He raked his hand down his face. One down, now where to place the other one. He tried to imagine where he would want to talk with a heartmate, if he had one. An image of himself lying in bed talking at length with a lover came to mind, so he decided the master bedroom would be the second place.

Now, he just had to figure out how to get into those rooms. He washed his hands, as if he had used the facilities and opened the door, stopping short when he almost collided with Andrea.

Nicholai flashed her his sexiest smile, the one that made most women melt in his arms. He looked down at the mistress of the house. She gazed back at him with passion sparkling in her eyes and smiled, offering him a drink.

"You read my mind, I'd love a drink."

"How about some coffee?"

"That would be perfect," he purred. "Can I help you get it?"

"No, you go back to the living room. I'll take care of it."

He watched her saunter down the hallway, then he

turned and followed her rather than doing as she had instructed.

Andrea was preparing the coffee maker, pouring water into the top, when Nicholai came up behind her on silent feet. "I can help with that," he offered, causing her to jump.

"No, no you go sit down. I'll just be a minute. I've got this."

"Do not be silly. You are with child. The least I can do is help make some coffee." He moved closer and took the ground gourmet coffee from her hands, purposely sliding his own hand over the top of hers as he grabbed it.

Andrea turned her back and made her way to the kitchen table, giving him the opportunity he needed. He quickly reached into his pocket, withdrew one of the tiny devices, and slipped it under the counter.

His fingers fumbled with the device, turned it over and stuck it against the underside of the counter. He risked a glance over his shoulder to assure his hostess was oblivious to his devious behavior.

A groan of frustration nearly escape his throat. Before he could set the device, Andrea turned around. He quickly leaned against the countertop, effectively hiding the hand with the bug.

"Where do you keep your coffee cups?" he asked, hoping to distract her so he could set the bug.

"In the cabinet to the right of your head."

He reached with his free hand to take two mugs from the cabinet while his other hand firmly pushed the bug into place.

Hoping the device would stick, he slowly withdrew his hand, carefully lifting one finger away from the counter at a time. Relief flooded him when the device did indeed stay put rather than falling into his waiting hand. The sound of the coffee pot gurgling brought his attention to the counter. The aroma of the Columbian brew filled the kitchen.

"Cream and sugar?" he asked.

"I take my coffee black."

"As do I."

"Something we have in common." Andrea smiled.

He poured two cups and brought them over to the table. After handing one to Andrea, he slid into the empty chair across from her and blew across his cup.

As they talked about nothing in particular over their coffee, Nicholai's mind continually tried to come up with a plausible excuse to get upstairs into the master suite. He couldn't use the bathroom excuse again, although after drinking the coffee, he was beginning to wish he had actually used the facility earlier.

Desperate to find an excuse, his mind threw out some wacky ideas. He could say he was tired and needed a nap. He could claim he wanted to see if the upstairs was as clean as the downstairs. He could make a run for it, hoping no one would catch him before he could plant the thing.

Yeah, definitely not good ideas, he chastised himself. *Come on, you are smarter than this.*

Finally his mind came through, giving him a plausible idea. Knowing she'd designed and decorated the house herself, he decided to play on Andrea's pride.

"You know, the last time I was here, you gave me the fifty cent tour. Could I get the full two dollar tour? Your home is beautiful, and I'm in the process of renovating mine. I'd love to see your rooms, especially the master bath, and get some ideas for what I might want to do in my own home." He waited, hoping she wouldn't think the excuse odd.

Andrea beamed. "Sure, I'd love to show you the rooms upstairs. I'm sure you'll get some wonderful ideas."

He exhaled a relieved sigh and followed her as she led the way up the stairs. She gave him the full tour, all the guest rooms as well as the library.

In the library, Nicholai hesitated, second guessing his master bedroom choice.

This could also be a good place for a device, he thought, suddenly wishing he had three of the devices instead of only two. Indecision gripped him. Andrea made the decision for him by hustling him from the room toward the master suite before he could plant the device.

"I saved the best room for last. Right this way." Andrea licked her lips, glancing over her shoulder to rake Nicholai with her stare, her desire for him palpable. She looked at him like a lioness would her dinner. Nicholai could swear he actually heard her growl as she opened the double doors to her suite.

She ushered him into the room and crossed to her bath. As she went into the bathroom, he spotted the perfect place for the second device—the bookcase built into the wall beside the bathroom door.

Using his incredible speed, he whipped one of the books from the shelf, placed the listening device against the back of the case and put the book back in place. He sent a silent prayer up to the heavens for the speed and grace his vampiric abilities gave him as he made his way to the bathroom.

Nicholai joined his hostess in the bath, carefully looking around and asking enough questions to seem truly interested. Andrea proudly shared the details of her home with him, moving closer until their bodies brushed against each other. Nicholai's eyes widened, instantly realizing it had been a bad idea to get Andrea to bring him to her room.

He feigned interest in the Jacuzzi tub, and leaned over for a closer look hoping to put some space between him and the female. Andrea came up behind him, leaned against him as she touched the faucets to point out the brand.

Nicholai straightened. She obviously needed a stronger hint, putting space between them wasn't enough.

He knew he was in trouble as Andrea leaned into him once again and suggested, "Why don't we try out the bath...together?"

"Excuse me?" Nicholai turned toward the door, eyeing the exit. "What about your mate?"

"Gage? He knows I appreciate a handsome man. Especially one who moves like you do. The way your muscles ripple under your clothes when you move—it's driven me wild since I met you. I'm betting you are the kind of man who would know how to satisfy a woman. And personally, I wouldn't mind finding out whether or not I am correct in that opinion." Andrea lunged, desire in her eyes.

****

Stephan sat in his living room, the plasma showed some team Marcus apparently loved, but the game didn't interest him. His attention rested on the picture he fingered.

When he and Kat had ridden in the gondola, a ride attendant took their picture. Kat begged him to buy the souvenir and now he was glad he had. He ran a finger along her face, marveling at how beautiful she looked. Her smile lit her eyes, making them sparkle. Her face, so young and creamy smooth. He could almost feel the softness of her skin as his imagination took over.

Lost in his mind's eye, he barely registered Marcus whooping beside him in the leather recliner when the phone rang. It took two rings for him to notice, and by then Marcus had already reached for the phone and brought it to his ear.

"Hello," he said, turning down the TV. "Great. Okay. I'll go check right now. Hold on." Marcus placed his fingers over the mouth piece and addressed Stephan. "It's Nikko. He planted the bugs. I'm going to go see if we're up and running."

Stephan strolled behind Marcus into his room. The Alpha leader took notice of the changes that had been made to the bedroom. Along one wall stood a long table holding two PC's each with large monitors and earphones.

Marcus sat at the table and brought the machines online. They whirled to life, both screens containing a series of wavy green lines. Marcus lifted each set of ear phones and gave them a listen. He smiled, obviously liking what he heard. He turned and looked at Stephan. "The computers are set up to record 24/7. I'll be able to review everything the devices pick up," Marcus explained, pointing to the lines on the monitors. "The lines become wavier as people talk, letting me know which ear phones I should be listening to."

Marcus put the phone back up to his ear. "We're up and running, man." Marcus paused. "Yeah, both."

Stephan stood behind Marcus, and an extended silence filled the room while Marcus intently listened to Nicholai.

"No way!" said Marcus and stifled a laugh. "I can't believe she did that. How did you get out of there?"

Another long silence ensued, during which Marcus covered the phone receiver with one hand and snickered quietly.

Suddenly, Marcus straightened and shook his head, a disgusted look on his face. "Man, well go take a shower and scrub yourself down, then try to get some sleep. We'll call you if we hear anything. Later."

With a punch of a button, Marcus clicked off the phone and looked at Stephan. "You aren't going to believe this!"

Stephan listened intently while Marcus relayed the story of what had happened between Nicholai and Andrea. A smirk brought one corner of Marcus' mouth up as he spoke. "Okay, so Nikko was planting the bugs and the first one went off without a hitch. But the second one was a problem.

"He put the thing in the master bedroom. Apparently, he convinced Lucio's wife that he was renovating his place and wanted decorating ideas. Specifically he needed bathroom ideas."

Marcus shifted his weight to his other foot as he continued. "When Nicholai turned to exit the master bathroom, Andrea leaped, throwing herself against him. He tried to back away from her, but the tub caught his knees making him fall off balance." Marcus' chuckle broke his explanation.

"And this is funny why?" Stephan shot his friend a sardonic look.

"His butt landed on one of the faucets, breaking it off causing the pressurized water to spew out. Of course, with his ass in the way, the water only had one place to go, up his butt. And that caused Nicholai to lurch up, knocking Andrea back."

Marcus' deep laughter echoed in his room. He took a deep breath and continued. "Picture this, the water, now flowing freely, coated the marble floor. Andrea lost her footing and screamed. Wanting to protect her and the baby, Nicholai grabbed ahold of her as she was falling, but he too slipped on the wet floor."

Stephan crossed his arms over his chest and shook his head, picturing the bathroom scene. He chuckled.

"Wait." Marcus wagged his brows up and down. "It gets better. To protect her, he twisted their bodies so Andrea would land on top of him instead of the hard marble floor. The two of them landed on the floor with the water from the faucet raining down on them from above.

"Drenched by the newly made water fountain, Andrea leaned down trying to kiss Nicholai. He said he flipped them over so he rested on top of Andrea, pinning her to the floor to avoid the kiss. Of course, it was precisely at that moment one of the guards burst into the room, having heard all of the commotion, and misinterpreted what Nicholai was doing. The guard pulled him off of her and threw him out of the house."

Stephan shook his head slowly, before running a hand through his hair. "I can't believe Lucio's wife threw herself at him, especially when the female is pregnant."

"Apparently the baby isn't affecting her libido." A wry look lifted one corner of Marcus' mouth.

Stephan was still wearing a no-freaking-way look on his face when he glanced down at his watch. "It's time to go pick up Kat. I'll be back in a few."

"I can pick her up if you'd like," offered Marcus.

"That's okay. I don't mind picking her up."

"I bet you don't," bantered Marcus with a grin before wishing him safe travels as he turned back to the monitors and donned the ear phones with a tired sigh.

He was in for a long night, and any other time Stephan would be willing to help, but not tonight.

Katrina was waiting.

Chapter 21

Stephan walked into Marcus' room and crossed to the listening station where Marcus sat wearing a set of earphones. He clamped his hand down onto Marcus' shoulder. "Well, my friend, anything yet? It's been three days." Stephan voice sounded hopeful, even to him.

"No." Marcus looked up at him and slid the earphones to his neck. "Still nothing."

"Damn. I've got a bit of a problem. I need your help."

Marcus lifted one eyebrow questioningly and waited for him to continue.

"I have something special planned for Kat tonight. Could you arrange for her to have tonight off?"

Marcus hesitated. "I guess so, but the manager won't be too happy. I'll make some calls and see if I can find someone to fill in for Kat."

"Thank you, Marcus. I owe you one." Stephan turned to leave, ready to begin his evening.

"Mind sharing why I'm going to piss off my manager, *again*?"

Stephan smiled. "I have something special planned. That's all I'm going to tell you. It's a surprise, and I know how Kat can pry information out of you."

Marcus gave a snort of derision. "Me? How about you? You are putty in her little hands. I've never seen you so…sweet and gentle before."

Stephan's brows narrowed and he shot Marcus his best you-better-watch-your-step look. "I can still kick your butt."

Marcus chuckled, and shook his head, raising his hands in surrender. "I know. I know. Didn't mean to imply you aren't still a big badass. I just happen to think it is nice that you have a female you care about."

"Uh-huh." It was time to change the direction of this conversation. "So about Kat getting this evening off, do you think it can be arranged?"

"Yeah. You know," Marcus bantered with a smile, "Kat has been taking a lot of time off since meeting you. I think you are a bad influence on her work ethic."

"Can I help it if she would rather spend time with me, than at your smoky old club?"

"Excuse me, smoky old club?" Marcus feigned insult by placing one hand over his heart. "I'll have you know Reapers is one of the better clubs on the strip."

"That may be, but if I have my way, soon Kat will not be working there anymore."

"What do you mean?" Marcus crossed his arms across his chest, leaning back in the chair.

"I love her, Marcus." Marcus' eyes widened in disbelief. "I'm hoping that soon I'll be able to convince her to come live with me in Germany."

"I never thought I'd see the day when you would settle down."

A genuine smile took Stephan's face. "There is something special about Kat."

"Is she your heartmate?"

"I don't know. I haven't drunk from her." Marcus started to speak, but Stephan cut him off holding up one hand. "You asked me not to drink from her, remember?" The younger vampire nodded as Stephan continued uninterrupted. "So I haven't yet. I'm waiting until just the right moment, then I'll ask her permission."

And he had to admit he was nervous about that, which wasn't an emotion the warrior was used to feeling. He decided in that moment that within the week he would ask her to be his evermore, ask her to spend eternity with him as his heartmate. He'd come to believe she must be his mate, the other half of his soul, but he had to make sure by taking a sip of her blood. He would only need a small sip of her sweet blood to know whether or not she was his true heartmate. Surely she could now trust him enough to allow him the pleasure of drawing from her vein.

Wouldn't she?

****

Excitement and anticipation bubbled in her veins like champagne as the elevator rose. Kat couldn't wait to discover what Stephan had planned for this evening. When he'd informed her that he'd arranged for her to have the night off and that a special surprise waited, her mind raced with the possibilities.

Nervously, she ran her hands over the blue, sleeveless, A-line gown, brushing imaginary wrinkles from the boat neck and accenting ties at the waist. She glanced at Stephan and could not help but admire how great he looked tonight. Dressed in a dark blue, silk shirt and a suit that matched the gown perfectly, his eyes seemed like deep pools of sapphire blue. His dark hair, pulled back in a leather thong, allowed for an unobstructed view of his handsome face. She'd never seen a more beautiful man. As if reading her mind, he looked at her and winked.

Her stomach did a little flop when the elevator came to a quick stop on the forty-first floor.

Stephan offered his arm and gave her the sexy smile that melted her bones. "Shall we?"

They stepped out into a cavernous room. Filled with tables covered in burgundy linen clothes and padded chairs to match, the room bespoke of elegance. From the crystal chandeliers to the gilded molding, the restaurant glistened and shined. Kat's eyes swept the room, taking it all in, and she noted the place seemed empty.

Her eyes met Stephan's gaze. "Are they closed?"

His smile widened. "Not exactly. I rented the place for tonight. We will be the only customers."

Kat couldn't begin to imagine how much that must have cost.

A pretty blonde, wearing an evening gown, came up to them. "Good evening, Mr. von Haas."

"Hello, Missy. I presume our table is ready."

The hostess blushed and gave Stephan a coy look which made Kat's blood boil. "Of course. We do aim to please." She batted her eyes flirtatiously.

The woman led them to a table next to a fireplace, and Stephan held the padded leather chair for Kat while she sat. He pulled a chair from across the small table around next to her and sat down. The hostess quickly moved the elegant place setting in front of him, taking the opportunity to brush up against his arms while she rearranged the dinnerware.

While Kat noticed the way the blonde shamelessly flirted with him, Stephan, much to his credit, did not respond. His attention wholly focused on Kat. His eyes never left her when he ordered their drinks.

"I hope you don't mind, but I took the liberty of ordering for you as well. When I booked the restaurant, they wanted to know what we'd like to eat."

Kat thought back to their first date, remembering how Stephan seemed to know all her favorite dishes. She trusted him to make similar choices tonight. "I'm sure you chose well. How could anything be bad in a place like this?"

Missy arrived posthaste, like she couldn't stand to be away from Stephan for two minutes. Kat knew the feeling.

"Water for the lady. And for the gentleman, Earl Grey tea." She placed the drinks in front of them, her eyes never leaving Kat's date. "Is there anything else you need? Anything at all?"

The insinuation was clear in the tone of her voice, and Kat had had enough. "Yes, you can leave."

Missy left in a huff, but Kat didn't care. Her palpable jealousy hung in the air like a thick fog between Stephan and her. When she glanced at her lover, he wore a smug look.

"What?" he asked, shrugging his shoulders and a smile tugged at his lips.

Katrina's eyes bore into the back of the woman's head as she sauntered away.

When Kat didn't reply, he once again asked, "What is it, Kitten? If you don't talk to me, I can't fix whatever is wrong."

Kat took a deep breath and blew it out through her pursed lips. "I can't believe you let her flirt with you right in front of me."

Kat felt the sensation of a hand sliding down her face. It came to rest under her chin. Her eyes locked with his, and the twinkle told her he'd created the sensation.

"*Schatz*, it is you I love." The sincerity in his eyes was plain to see. "I can't believe you feel threatened by her."

Katrina brushed her fingers under her chin as if to push his imaginary hand away. "You have to admit, she made it quite clear she wants you."

"But *I* could care less. I only want you." He took her hand in his. "I would never be unfaithful to you. I love you. *You*, Kat, no other."

Kat looked deeply into his eyes and believed him. She saw his love for her reflected in the depth of his deep blues. She wanted to believe him, needed to believe him. She'd fallen deeply in love with the man sitting beside her. He was quickly becoming her whole world. She wanted to be his. His only one.

"You are my one and only, *mein schatz,*" he assured her, as if he'd somehow gleaned her thoughts.

She softened toward him, her belief in his love replacing her resentfulness and jealousy. She replayed his words in her mind. *You are my one and only,* mein schatz.

"Wait, what did you call me? Shats, Shots?"

"*Schatz*," Stephan supplied. "The literal translation is treasure. *Mein schatz* translates roughly as my dear or my darling. It's a term of endearment in German."

The tension left her shoulders and a genuine smile graced her face. "I'm sorry. I guess I was just a little jealous."

Stephan chuckled, the sound played over her skin

like velvet. She loved when he laughed. Always the serious warrior, she liked when he loosened up.

"The way you looked at that woman…the saying 'if looks could kill' was obviously coined by someone who had seen the look you just gave." He leaned in, his warm breath flowed over her ear when he whispered, "Though I must admit, I rather like it when you are possessive. It makes me all tingly inside."

A tremor raced through her body as her mind flooded with images of things they'd done that made her tingly. Stephan was pure sin all wrapped up in a beautiful package. He did things to her body with just a look. Her mind raced with all the things they might do later.

Luckily two waiters arrived with their meal, providing Kat with the distraction she needed. The meal passed quickly, with pleasant conversation and tasty gourmet dishes. By the time dessert arrived, Kat relaxed and forgot all about Missy.

A bucket of chilled champagne and two etched, fluted glasses were brought to their table by a waiter. After filling their stemware, he asked, "Is there anything else I can bring you this evening?"

Stephan waved him off. "We have everything we need. Miss Spencer and I wish to be left alone for now. I'll let you know if there is anything we require."

Kat took a sip. It tickled going down, and she giggled. When a small bit of champagne escaped, Stephan took her chin gently in his hand, tipped her head up, and captured her lips. His lips brushed against hers in tender kiss. Once. Twice. The kiss became more insistent; her tongue explored the heat of his mouth. His kiss tasted of champagne and spice, a heady mix. Her world tilted on its axes as he lifted her into his arms without breaking their kiss and placed her on his lap.

His fingers threaded in her updo, pulled the strands free from the clip. A clinking sound vaguely registered, and she realized the barrette had fallen to his plate. She paid it little attention when her mouth captured his moan. Their tongues waltzed between their lips in perfect synchronicity.

She broke the kiss, nibbled along his chiseled jaw, to his ear. His arms tightened around her when she bit the lobe, then soothed it with a swipe of her tongue. Her breath glided over his flesh, eliciting another moan. His breathing increased in time with hers. Her heart raced, belly tightened. She reveled in the knowledge she did this to him. Made him hunger for her as she did for him. Made him love her.

"Katrina," his voice sounded low, heavy with lust, "as much as I love this, I think we should stop. If you keep doing that, I'm liable to lay you across this table and take you here and now."

She nipped his neck, then laid a kiss over the slight mark. "And that would be bad because…"

He growled, actually growled and it was the sexiest sound she'd ever heard. Her core clenched, moist heat rushed low.

When next he spoke, it was between clenched teeth. "Because, as much as I want you, there is still one surprise I have yet to show you this evening."

Her head snapped up, eyes wide when she looked at Stephan. "What is it?" she asked, barely containing her excitement.

He chuckled. "Always ready for a surprise, aren't you?"

"You know I am." Kat laughed. "Now tell me."

"Do you remember I mentioned that I own several art galleries?"

"Yes."

"Well, I arranged for a private showing, just for us."

"Really? Where?"

"In the gallery downstairs. Shall we go?"

Kat warred with the decision. To see the showing, she'd have to leave his lap, and she happened to be very comfortable and content right where she sat.

"There is something special, just for you waiting down there," Stephan teased with a sly grin.

"What is it?"

"You'll have to go down to find out."

Kat rolled her eyes, weighing her decision. Stephan's surprises were always wonderful. What in the world could be waiting for her downstairs? She decided to find out.

Kat jumped off his lap and took him by the hand. "Come on. What are we waiting for?"

The ride down in the elevator seemed to take forever, and Kat was determined to pass the time by finding out more about Stephan.

"Stephan, you mentioned that you not only own a gallery in New York, but also one in Germany. Just how many galleries do you own?"

"Several," Stephan answered nonchalantly. "In addition to those two, I also own one in France, another in England, and three or four in other countries around the world."

That must be where he gets his money. "Is art profitable?"

"The galleries hold their own. But I have other investments as well. I own some real estate and have been fortunate in the stock market. Living over six hundred years lets a man learn a few tricks and pick up some tips along the way, and I'm not just talking about making money." Stephan winked and cupped her bottom, giving it a quick squeeze.

Kat supposed after six hundred years a man would learn quite a lot of tricks, and she had enjoyed every one of the tricks he shared so far with her.

When the doors opened, the soft strains of classical music filled the air. Moving into the gallery, Kat found it spacious, made more so by the fact that once again they were the only two in the room. A large, open design, the pieces were arranged along the walls with white up lighting that gave the faces in the portraits an ethereal glow. Kat stood awestruck, impressed by the artistic compositions.

Stephan slipped silently behind her and circled one arm around her waist. "What do you think, Kitten?" He raised his glass of champagne toward the canvas in front of them.

"It's perfect." Kat smiled.

"I'm so glad you like it."

"You arranged this for me?"

"I happen to know the artist."

"They are beautiful. They seem so real, but yet too real, too beautiful. There is something different I just can't place my finger on."

Stephan smiled and bent his head. He lips brushed her ear when he whispered. "It's the fangs."

Kat leaned closer for a better look. She could see the tips of two fangs just peeking out from the upper lip of the person in the portrait. "Ahhh, you're right." Quickly her eyes darted to the next portrait and the one beside that, realizing that each had a small set of fangs showing.

"So the artist paints vampires?" Kat whispered, not sure if they could be overheard. Surely there had to be some staff for such a large gallery.

"No need to be quiet. We are quite alone," Stephan assured her, straightening. "Most of his subjects are actually humans. He just adds the fangs. Appropriate to debut his work just before Halloween, don't you think?"

"Very clever."

Stephan maneuvered her around the room, pointing out the composition and contrasts in the paintings. Kat had an appreciative eye but did not know much about art. Stephan made the perfect teacher—patient and enlightening. He never caused her to feel uninformed for asking questions about the pieces, and she appreciated that.

"Now this next one is my absolute favorite." Stephan moved her to the next portrait. Kat covered her mouth with one hand.

"It's me." She reached toward the picture with her other hand. Her heart beat hard in her chest from excitement.

Stephan grabbed her extended hand, enveloping it in his much larger one. "Yes, it is you. I hope you don't mind, but I sent Lars your picture and commissioned the portrait for you."

Joy spread warmth through her body. "It's beautiful, almost unearthly."

Stephan nodded. "It is a beautiful painting, but it's

nothing compared to the real you. You are so much more than that portrait." He gave her a quick kiss. "Tell me, do you really like it?"

"Oh yes," she all but squealed. "I love it!"

"Good." A small smile took Stephan's face as he nodded his approval. "Lars will be happy to hear you admire his interpretation of your likeness."

"Admire? I more than admire it. I am bewitched. I can't take my eyes off of it."

Kat plucked his glass from his hand and took a sip, her eyes never leaving the portrait. It mesmerized her, seemed to stare into her soul. She could lose herself in the painting if not for the handsome man standing next to her who anchored her to the world.

Her heart, full and heavy with love and adoration, sang for him. Stephan was everything she'd ever wanted. Smart. Strong. Sexy. She knew she could rely on him to keep her safe. She heard the love in his voice when he spoke to her, knew she could trust him with her heart. If only that trust didn't come with a set of fangs.

Thanks to Marcus, Kat knew enough about vampires to know Stephan would eventually want to drink from her. Since the attack, she'd had a real phobia about anyone taking from her vein. A full blown, heart stopping, sick to your stomach phobia. In seven years, Marcus had never taken her blood, and she wasn't sure she'd ever be able to allow Stephan to do so. As the night wore on, she silently hoped that wouldn't be a problem.

Chapter 22

Stephan and Kat entered the Penthouse, weary from their long night. Kat was tucked under one of his arms, her portrait under the other. He happily bore the brunt of her weight as she sagged against him, making him feel every bit the strong protector. Marcus rushed to greet them when they entered.

"Stephan I must speak with you," Marcus said, ignoring Kat completely.

"Well, hello to you too," Kat quipped.

"Oh yeah. Hi Kat… Hi…Um, yeah." Marcus spared her an anxious glance before turning his full attention back on Stephan. "So, Stephan, we need to talk, now."

After Stephan settled Kat onto the couch in the living room and placed her portrait against a bare wall in the room, he and Marcus retired to the library, closing the door behind them.

Stephan took a deep breath and let out a loud, weary sigh as he settled into the claw footed chair across from Marcus. "Talk to me, Marcus. What did you find out?"

Marcus took a deep breath before beginning to relay the information he heard earlier that evening. "I was monitoring the transmission from one of the listening devices and overheard Lucio speaking with one of his guards, a male named Trace. They discussed two humans Trace had brought to the home. Apparently Gage was pleased by the two women. Lucio made comments on how attractive the women were and the guard mentioned he'd had an opportunity to sample their goods, noting that he had been careful not to do any lasting damage. It was sickening."

Stephan's stomach twisted in disgust. "I'm sure it was."

"Gage went on to assure the guard that as long as the women were healed in time for the night of the party, he did not care that Trace had had some fun with them. Later, I overheard Lucio and his mate discussing their party. Apparently his mate, Andrea, is concerned that they would run out of food, but Gage had reassured her by saying that if they ran out of food, they would simply start sooner than planned."

Stephan's mood soured, his dark brows furrowing deep over his eyes. "That sounds very suspect. Do you think Gage Lucio is guilty?"

Marcus nodded. "I think so. They never came right out and used the words hunt club, but from what I could gather, it sounded like that is what they plan on doing the night of the party. It also sounded like Gage has been using his guards to gather the humans for quite some time. At one point, Gage mentioned something about having used one of the humans for his personal pleasure for months."

Stephan scrubbed a hand up his face, brushing back an errant lock of hair. "I am bothered that we still aren't one hundred percent sure, and Nicholai didn't sense any human minds in the house."

"I know, but he did say he could sense fear and malice and smell stale human. Perhaps they found some way to mask what is going on in that house."

Stephan rose to his feet and squared his shoulders. "I cannot simply sit back and allow the murder of innocent humans. I must find out if Lucio is guilty."

Stephan began to pace the room, his long strides eating up the length of the carpet. His lassitude ebbed with each step, his anger becoming an energy that rolled over Marcus. "Didn't Nicholai say the party was in a few days?" A muscle ticked along his jawline.

Marcus gave a curt nod of his head. "Yes, on the 29th."

"If they plan on doing the hunt on the day of the party, that doesn't give us much time. I have to stop this hunt club before any humans are killed."

Stephan's thoughts turned to Katrina. The thought of her being kidnapped and hunted turned his stomach. Rage boiled his blood. "I'm going over there now and find out exactly what is going on."

"Wait, I'll go with you." Marcus pushed from his chair, determined to help his friend.

"No, you stay here."

"Like hell. I really think someone should go with you. Besides, it's getting late. It will be daylight soon."

"I'll be fine. I'm just going over there to try to talk to Lucio, get him to cancel the party. If he won't see reason, I'll leave, and we'll regroup. Plus, I want you to remain here with Kat, make sure she is safe." His tone brooked no argument.

Under Stephan's steely glare, Marcus reluctantly agreed to remain behind. He stood and grasped Stephan's forearms in the way of the warrior.

"Just be careful."

"I will." Stephan released his friend. As he

shrugged into his jacket and turned to leave, Stephan hoped that his assurance would not be in vain.

****

Stephan arrived at Gage's house, his body humming with anger and wrath. His pounding fist shook the door on its hinges as he demanded entry.

"What do you want?" demanded the hulking vampire guard who opened the heavy door.

Stephan squared his shoulders. "I demand to see the master of the house."

"It's late, and he has retired for the evening. Come back tomorrow." The guard started to push the door closed.

Stephan threw a hand against the door, pushing it open as he forced his way over the threshold. "I will see him now. Get him." His voice echoed off the foyer walls.

The guard grabbed Stephan's arm in a bruising grip. "I said come back tomorrow."

As Stephan was pushed toward the still open door, the warrior spun, throwing his weight into the guard, sending him stumbling backwards into the suit of armor at the base of the stairs. His arms moved with blurring speed as he caught the armor with a loud clang, steadying it before it could topple.

"What is going on?" Gage asked as he appeared at the railing on the landing above.

"I need to speak to you," Stephan informed him, working to keep his disdain from showing on his face.

"At this late hour? Dawn is approaching." Gage's eyes narrowed in recognition. "Wait a minute. Don't I know you?"

Stephan nodded curtly. "We were introduced by

193

Nicholai Peterhof."

"Ah yes. Now I remember. Von Haas, right?"

"Correct. I need to speak with you."

"I'm sure whatever it is can wait until tomorrow. It is late. My heartmate and I were about to retire for the day."

"It cannot wait. We must speak now." Stephan moved to the base of the stairs, his hands fisted at his sides.

Stephan watched anger and frustration contorted Gage's face. "What is so important that it cannot wait?"

The Alpha glanced at the large guard coming up behind him. "I don't think you want to discuss this in front of the help. Perhaps there is some place private we could talk."

Gage motioned with his hand. "Come up here. We'll go into my library. But I'll warn you now. I don't have much patience for this so be quick about what you have to say."

While Stephan made his way up the stairs, his ire rose. He smelled the stale stench of humans Nicholai had mentioned. His eyes scanned the home while he followed Gage to the library. Everything visible seemed in order, nothing out of the ordinary. Nothing physical at least, but something didn't feel right. A sense of fear and hatred clung to Stephan's skin. The longer he stayed in the home, the more palpable the sensation became until it clawed at his skin, irritating his already dour mood.

Gage sat behind his desk, his fingers steepled, elbows resting upon the hard wood. He eyed the Alpha warrior cautiously. "Go ahead."

Stephan stood to the side, the position giving him a

clear view of not only Gage, but also the door and windows in the room. Years of training taught him to always keep a vigilant watch on your enemies, especially any opening though which they might ambush you.

"I have reason to believe you are conducting a hunt club." His bluntness did not earn him the reaction he expected.

Gage raised a questioning brow, the only indication he'd just been accused of a heinous crime. "They are forbidden."

"Exactly why I have come. I cannot allow such a disgusting event to take place in my city."

A sanguine laugh escaped Gage's lips, exposing the sharp ends of his teeth. "Your city? I wasn't aware Vegas belonged to you."

"It doesn't matter. I want the humans freed," Stephan demanded. A muscle in his face twitched, the only movement visible on the otherwise still warrior.

Gage leaned back in his chair, crossing one leg over the other. "Why would you even care about such a thing? Not that I'm admitting to having any humans on the premises, but even if I did, they are but cattle. Creatures put upon this earth to sustain us."

The arrogance of this male! Gage sat calmly, not denying nor confirming the hunt club. His lack of denial was as good as a confirmation to Stephan. The male's aloofness only served to fuel Stephan's pique, like lighter fluid fuels a fire, igniting an uncontrollable inferno. His rage burned white-hot.

"Humans are no different from us. They feel. They love. How can you speak so callously about them? They are not beasts to be hunted. "

Stephan's face contorted with fury. Ire flashed in his dark eyes. His power began to coalesce around him, growing until he knew Gage would feel it prickling over his skin.

"Humans are food!" Gage shouted. "A hunt club is an honored tradition among our kind. I see nothing wrong with conducting one."

"So you admit it then, you are planning on doing a hunt club!"

"You dare to come into my home and hurl accusations at me. Throw your power around. If this was old England, I would have your head on a pike! No one, especially a commoner like you, may speak to me in such a way."

The air in the room stilled as Gage drew his own power to him, readying for the altercation Stephan knew was about to come. "Enough of this. What exactly are you accusing me of, von Haas?"

Stephan steeled his features, straightened his spine. He slung his accusations like a mace, with force and purpose. "I believe you have humans hidden somewhere on this property and are planning on having a hunt on Halloween. I also believe you are a sick bastard who gets off on the thrill of a hunt. And I think your heartmate is just as deranged as you."

His anger obviously overcoming his common sense, Gage rounded on Stephan. "Hunting is what vampires do. It's in our very nature. We can pretend we are human, but we aren't. Just like the tiger or lion, hunting is in our blood. To be vampire is to hunt."

As far as Stephan was concerned, Gage had just confessed.

His disgust for Gage grew like a vine that weaved

itself around his subconscious, strangling the last bit of his self-control, allowing his fury to build into a palpable force.

He threw his head back and roared.

Chapter 23

With the roar from von Haas shaking the walls of his library, the sound of his heartmate's voice in his mind diverted Gage's attention. *Are you okay?*

Yes, Andrea, my dear. I am fine.

I can hear you and the male. I'm sending Trace.

I can handle this! I do not need help.

I know you can, but we have guards for a reason.

Ten seconds later, Trace threw open the library door. He arrived in time to witness Stephan's rage rippling from him like a blast wave of a nuclear bomb, knocking down everything in its path, including Gage who landed flat on his back on his expensive oriental rug. Like a thousand knives sticking his body, the vampire's power flowed over him.

"Do you need any help?" Trace asked eyeing von Haas warily when the vampire turned toward the guard.

"Yes," bellowed Gage pointing toward the door. "Get him the hell out of my house! The sun has risen, throw him outside!"

Already braced, Stephan didn't move when Trace rammed into him. Trace wrapped his arms around the male, trapped Stephan's arms to his sides and lifted him off his feet. Stephan struggled as Trace made his way out of the office into the hall, Gage on his heels. The guard's arms tightened around Stephan's middle. Gage heard one rib crack, the sound amazingly satisfying.

Gage felt Stephan summon his strength. After he forced Trace's arms apart, Stephan spun and threw Trace against the wall. His hand shot out to grasp the guard's throat, but his guard ducked, using his agile speed to dart out of reach.

I'm coming.

Damned woman. *No, Andrea! Stay away. Trace and I are handling this.*

His heart seemed to drop to his toes when his mate appeared at the top of the stairs. She stopped as she rounded the corner, her eyes glued to the thrashing bodies in the hall. They were a blur of motion. Her eyes tracked the crimson flying in a wide arc. Her nostrils flared registering the blood before it hit the floor. Connected mind to mind as they were, Gage felt her anger rise. It burned like bile in her throat. Her guard, her friend was losing the fight. She screamed, the piercing sound of which echoed in the foyer.

His heartmate drew Stephan's attention, a fortunate distraction. The vampire turned toward her and his hand hit the now empty wall in front of him. Plaster fell to the floor as his fingers bit into the wall instead of Trace's neck.

The well-trained guard seized the momentary distraction and rushed forward grasping Stephan in a lineman's tackle that sent him crashing down on the floor. Von Haas kicked his legs, catching Trace in the gut, and sent him flying in the opposite direction. The guard landed hard with a grunt of air.

Both males jumped to their feet, settling into identical fighting stances.

Gage moved further down the hall, wanting to get his heartmate to safety. Unfortunately, the males' battle stood between him and his mate. The need to protect his woman and unborn child pushed at him urgently. "Finish him, Trace!" he commanded.

Stephan launched forward, and his fist made contact with the guard's chin, snapping his head back. Trace staggered, but with swift efficiency returned a blow of his own. Stephan's body turned with the impact of the blow to his face. Trace grabbed him once again from behind in a tight bear hug and began backing the two of them down the hallway toward the stairs.

Stephan flung his head back into Trace's nose, breaking it instantly, no doubt causing the body guard to see stars. Trace's hold slackened, and the vampire broke free of his grip. Von Haas kicked out a muscular leg and contacted with Trace's stomach sending him staggering backwards.

The next few seconds unfurled in motion slowed by time in a way only possible during great tragedy.

Gage and Stephan stood side by side watching the guard stumble and collide with Andrea. The pair fell against the banister in a mass of flailing arms and legs. With a loud crack, it gave way beneath their combined weight sending them tumbling down to the floor below. Andrea screamed, her arms thrashing, desperately seeking a purchase that would not be found.

Stephan and Gage both rushed toward the edge of the landing. Gage heard the guard land on his back with a whomp sound, the air knocked from his lungs by the hard impact on the wood floor. His gaze landed on Andrea just as her scream was strangled by a sickening gurgle sound. Both males remained motionless, looking down in horror at the scene below them.

Andrea lay draped, her dress reaching toward the

floor. The sword from the suit of armor below had made a clean slice through her heart; the point could be seen through her chest, its shiny metal now painted with scarlet streaks. She lay impaled on the shiny weapon like an insect suspended on a pin in a collection box, the gossamer fabric of her dress hanging limply like wilted wings. Blood pooled red below her at the knight's feet while her blank eyes stared sightlessly up at them.

Gage felt the ripping sensation with every part of his being, as the sword cut through his heartmate's body. He stood on the landing, frozen. The feeling of instantaneous loss and depravity so great it took his strength, his knees threatened to collapse under his weight. His body swayed as he stood next to von Haas.

Andrea's life flashed before his eyes. Memories of her holding court in England and instructing the peasants blurred into his mate touring Europe during the World War and then the memories changed to her designing the garden for their current home with an exuberant smile on her face. The memories so vivid, each came with its own set of smells and sounds that transported Gage back to those times. Happy times that, thanks to their immortality, he thought would never end.

The sound of Trace's moan pulled Gage from his reverie and back to the present.

He dematerialized down to his mate, and hoisted her off of the sword in one swift motion. Cradling her in his arms, he dropped to his knees. He held her tightly to his chest, brushing one hand down her face. His mind instinctively pushed into hers, needing to feel their connection. He found only a black nothingness, an emptiness that coated his soul in sorrow.

"Andrea…*Andrea*… please no… *no*…" His hand tucked a strand of her hair behind one ear. "Andrea wake up…*please* no… wake up, my dear… please no, *please!*"

Gage begged his heartmate to be well, putting all his love for her behind his pleas, but it was of no use. She would never wake again. Andrea was gone from his world.

The realization tore through his body with a physical pain so great it caused him to collapse over her body. He felt as if his very soul had been ripped from him.

"No! Come back to me!" he roared, so loud the walls of the house shook with his rage, glass shattered. His power surged forward causing the bulbs in the room to explode. Its force knocked Stephan off his feet. Had the bastard not braced himself by throwing his hands behind him the force would have completely leveled him.

Gage glared up at von Haas, allowing his hatred to show in his eyes. Stephan shook his head and had the audacity to look down at him apologetically. "It was an accident. I'm so sorry."

Gage bared his fangs and hissed at the male. "I will make you pay for this! I swear I will see you pay with all you hold dear!"

Two guards bounded up the stairs toward von Haas as two more ran into the foyer. Before they could reach him, Stephan dematerialized out of the house, leaving only a small puff of smoke in the air.

Gage watched his heartmate's killer disappear from his sight. Animosity mixed with anguish, when he looked back down into his heartmate's unseeing eyes, clutching her to his chest. Tears blurred his vision. He lowered his mouth to her hair and began to rock back and forth murmuring, "no, please, no."

But he knew it was too late. He'd known the minute her life extinguished. He felt it throughout his entire body, in each cell. Now not only was his heartmate gone, but so too his child, the child he waited over three hundred years for. His body went numb, all he felt was the anger and rage that filled him. In an instant his entire future was gone, taken by Stephan von Haas.

The guards silently encircled the couple where they sat in a crumpled heap on the floor. They stood stoically, apparently unsure how to be of assistance to their master. Never before had they seen him broken and tortured.

Trace rose slowly. He limped cautiously, pushing through two of the guards to approach Gage. "Can I take her for you, sir?" he whispered.

"No. No one is going to take her! You cannot take her from me!" Gage embraced her tighter, so tight something snapped under the force of his hug.

Chapter 24

Stephan paced back and forth, as he'd been doing since stepping into his library with Marcus.

"You're going to wear a path in the carpet if you keep this up," said Marcus.

"You don't understand. I didn't mean to. I really didn't mean to."

"I know," said Marcus quietly. "I know you wouldn't knowingly hurt a female. It wasn't your fault. It was Gage's. He's the one who tried to get his body guard to kill you."

"I know, but he's not going to see it that way. He's going to want retribution. You should have seen the look in his eyes when he said he would see me pay for her death with everything I hold dear." And nothing was dearer to him than Katrina. Fear for her safety pressed in, making it hard to breathe.

Katrina stood in the kitchen rinsing the dishes from their first meal and loading them into the dishwasher. After eating, Stephan and Marcus had immediately gone to the library behind closed doors. Even her human senses recognized the tension in the penthouse. It hung thick in the air like wet concrete.

As Kat squeezed a Teflon pan into the back of the rack, the doorbell rang. She opened the door to find Nicholai and a very extremely large burly man on the other side.

"Hello," said Kat hesitantly as her gaze shifted between the two men.

Nicholai glided fluidly into the foyer when she stepped to the side to allow them to enter. He bent, kissing her on each cheek. His lips were soft and warm.

"Good evening, Katrina," he greeted, the "R" rolling off his tongue. "Allow me to introduce to you my cousin, Demetri Romanoff."

Nikko stepped aside and made a grand sweep with his arm. Kat watched Demetri turn sideways and step his thickly muscled physique through the door. Built like a professional wrestler, his shirt stretched tight over his massive chest, giving Kat a very good idea of what lay underneath. His mammoth body boasted wide shoulders and biceps the size of Kat's thighs. With his tall frame, he looked like he could be a contender for the Mr. Universe title.

The dark silk shirt he wore tightened further against his shoulders when he extended one of his super-sized hands toward Katrina and took her hand with a gentleness she did not expect. He raised her hand to his lips, laying on a quick kiss.

"It is a pleasure to meet you, Katrina," he said and bent at the waist in a deep bow. "I have heard much about you from my cousin."

Demetri's accent, though much more subtle then his cousin's, allowed Kat to discern he too originated from somewhere in Russia. With his thick body and the way his R's purred from his mouth, he reminded Kat of a tiger. A big, strong, deadly tiger.

"We were summoned by Stephan. He is here, is he not?" Nicholai looked around the room.

"Yes, he's here. He and Marcus are up in the

library. Follow me."

After she closed and locked the door, Kat turned and led the men up the stairs to the library. The two vampires followed her silently, reminding her of just how deadly the breed could be.

Answering her knock on the door, Stephan called out, "Come in."

Marcus opened the library door before she could turn the knob, and she flinched in surprise. He stepped aside so that the men could enter.

"Kitten, you should come in and hear this too. You also need to know what happened last night," Stephan said quietly, the foreboding thick in his voice.

Katrina settled herself on the arm of the wingback chair where Marcus sat. Nicholai parked himself in the other chair as Demetri took up his stance leaning against the bookcase with his arms crossed. From behind his desk, Stephan relayed the events of the previous evening to the assembly. Kat had the feeling he excluded some of the gorier details, probably to keep from upsetting her. And that was a good thing, she decided, because what he did share made her stomach churn.

When Stephan finished the story, Katrina sat motionless, tears sliding down both cheeks, hand over her mouth. "Oh my god," was all she choked out around the lump in her throat. "Oh, Stephan, that is so sad. She and the baby both died?"

Stephan nodded solemnly, looking downtrodden. She could tell how much the situation wounded him and wanted to go to him, comfort him, but looking around the room she decided doing so in front of all his fellow warriors was neither the time nor place. "You know this is not your fault. You didn't mean to hurt the woman."

Demetri straightened, placing his arms by his sides. "But still this is very bad. The female was his heartmate. There will be hell to pay."

"I don't understand." Kat laid her hand in her lap and looked questioningly at Stephan. "What is a heartmate?"

Stephan met her eyes. "When a male finds his heartmate, they are truly two halves of the same soul. They complete each other. They must be together, be connected mentally and physically. If one is lost the other will be lost as well. Sometimes when one dies, the other chooses to meet the sun or have someone kill him. If the heartmate who is left chooses to remain alive, then he will usually become despondent, lose his mind."

"You mean heartmates literally can't live without each other?"

Stephan nodded. "When one finds his heartmate, she becomes his reason for living, Kitten. Without her, he will lose his desire for life. Some will even seek out danger in order to find a way to ease the suffering permanently. As I said, for those who do not die, but are forced to exist without their heartmate to complete them, they go insane from the dismal abyss of depression in which they swim night after long night."

Katrina shifted in her seat, unease creeping up her spine. "So, when Andrea died, Gage blamed you?"

"It would seem so. Yes."

"And you apologized then just dematerialized out of his home?" Kat asked hesitantly.

"Yes." Stephan watched her carefully.

"So," Kat swallow the lump of fear in her throat, "would it be possible for Gage to materialize into the penthouse to get revenge on you?"

Stephan rubbed his chin thoughtfully. "Yes." He nodded his head. "It would be possible."

Demetri raised an eyebrow. "You mean you do not have this place fortified with titanium so it is impenetrable? Do you not have at least one room lined?"

Marcus shook his head. "No. We've had no need to go to such lengths until now."

Demetri tsked. "That is a problem. We'll need to find a way to make this place secure."

"Maybe not," suggested Marcus. "I don't believe Gage knows where Stephan lives. Stephan dematerialized from Gage's home, so no one could have followed them. And I was very careful, made sure I was not followed when I did the surveillance. So I think we are safe here. I don't see how Gage could know our location, unless they followed Nicholai."

Nicholai shook his head. "I do not believe they did. I watched carefully every time I left the house."

Demetri nodded once in acknowledgement of the statement, but a skeptical look remained on his face.

Stephan looked at Kat, his steady gaze unnerved her. "Would you please excuse us, Kitten? We have some other issues to discuss which are strictly for Alpha ears."

"Of course." She stood and hesitated, worrying her lower lip between her teeth as she looked into Stephan's eyes. Trepidation crept up her spine, and she shivered. "Do you really think we are safe?"

Stephan seemed to steel his features before

answering. "You are safe. I would never let anything happen to you."

Katrina could hear the steely resolve in his hard voice and knew she could trust him, believed he would always protect her. With that one declaration, though he did not say the words aloud, she heard how much he loved her. It calmed her like nothing else could.

Chapter 25

Once Katrina quietly closed the door behind her, Nicholai looked at Stephan, "You know there will be retribution. Gage is not the kind of male who will let this go. The anger he feels at her loss will fuel his revenge."

"I know," Stephan acknowledged softly. "We'll have to do whatever we can to make sure he doesn't get a chance to take that revenge."

The four warriors spent the rest of the night discussing possible strategies and trying to guess how Gage might try to get his retribution on Stephan.

Just after dawn, Stephan crawled into bed beside Kat. He looked down on her and contentment filled his soul—the sort of contentment he wanted to last forever. The feel of Kat snuggling next to him stifled the haunting memories of Andrea's death. He gathered her into his arms, and tucked her against his side. As long as she lay safe in his arms, he could face whatever turmoil might come.

"I need you," he said, his voice a low masculine rumble of hunger.

Katrina looked up at Stephan from under her long lashes. She loved this strong, proud man. In his arms she felt protected, secure. The fear from earlier receded replaced by wanton desire and love.

She melted against him, her slight curves fitting

against his firm body. The evidence of his lust pushed against her soft thigh. His hands were on her, seemingly everywhere all at once. His warm, long fingers caressed her skin as he took her mouth in a deep kiss. Her own hands found sinewy muscles when she ran them along his lean physique.

Their kiss continued, hard demanding, filled with desperation.

Stephan moved atop her, his weight pushing her into the mattress. He bent his head and placed a trail of hot kisses down her jaw, then followed the curve of her collar bone, until he found her generous breasts. There, as if starved, he laid a line of hard kisses and gentle bites between the two mounds. Kat held his head to her breasts while he suckled, drawing her deep into his mouth. She arched fisting her hands in his long silky hair; a few strands escaped tickling her sensitive flesh.

He lavished his attention on both breasts. One he teased with his hot mouth, the other his nimble fingers kneaded. His tongue drew one nipple into a hard peak; he rolled the other between his thumb and forefinger until it too hardened for him.

Katrina's writhed under his attention, her body surging with waves of pleasure. Stephan drove her need higher, feeding her pleasure, until she thought she might die from the sensations he gave her. A low keening sound filled her ears, sexy, sensual, as sinuous sensations continued to drive through her.

"I need you," he whispered against one of her taught nipples.

"I need you too. Now. Please," she demanded trying to raise his head back up to meet her own. He lifted his head and looked at her from between her breasts. He laughed, the sound somewhere between a moan and a chuckle.

Her head dropped back onto her pillow as he rose to cover her body with his own. Her legs fell wide welcoming his hips. He slid inside her in one possessive thrust. Her eyes closed, lashes creating two dark crescents on her cheeks. Into his powerful shoulders her fingers dug, seeking an anchor to the earth. They bit into his flesh. Pleasure consumed her with each hard thrust.

She inhaled a sharp breath when he increased the speed of his hips, her body tightening around him. Stephan rose to his knees, grabbing her knees in his large hands, spreading her wide as he continued to drive into her welcoming sex.

His body invaded hers, a thick, hard fullness that brought waves of pleasure so intense she struggled to keep from floating away on a wave of ecstasy. As he moved, everything faded except the passion he built within her. Katrina's eyes locked with Stephan's. His dark eyes drank her in, watching her as she went higher, closer to the precipice of pleasure. It was sexy as hell.

"Come for me," he growled pistoning faster.

Her vision blurred to pinpricks of light, blood thundered in her ears. As commanded, Kat fell over the edge. She convulsed around his shaft, milking him. Her head thrashed back and forth on the pillow, hands fisted in the sheets.

Stephan continued to buck against Kat, unwilling to stop. Not just yet, even though he thought he might go up in flames from her scorching heat surrounding him.

She reached between them and cupped his balls with one hand, gently massaging them. The feel of her grasp tightened his body, sent a surge of pleasure through it that made every muscle harden. She felt so good surrounding him, touching him. As soft as velvet, she was enough to drive any man to his breaking point.

But he wanted more, wanted to be surrounded by her moist heat forever. To have her surround him inside and out. He heard her blood rush through her veins. It called to him, begged him to taste her. His fangs threatened to lengthen, but he pushed them back ruthlessly. He'd not give into the temptation, not until she'd willingly gave him her trust, her blood to take.

Need to pleasure her spurred his hips, and his pace quickened. He pushed deeper into her deliciously hot and tight sex, until his shaft touched her inner most sensitive spot, rubbing against her, driving her need as high as his own. She fit him so perfectly that he knew then she'd been destined to be his.

His face tightened as his own climax built. He looked down, watching her pleasure build through narrowed eyes. A soft mewing sound escaped her throat. Her head back, lips parted. Her fingers flexed against his back, nails drawing blood. It felt lusciously painful, a perfect manifestation of his tumultuous emotions. The combination of sight, sound, and touch drove him over the edge, with her next climax.

He threw back his head and let a roar escape his lips, his face tightening when his own release came. His body collapsed over Katrina, as he pulsed into her. She held him in her arms until he was totally spent.

He fought for breath, inhaling her honeysuckle essence deep into his body. His head rose, his gaze meeting hers. The look on her face mirrored how he felt—completely replete and sated.

Stephan rolled the two of them so Kat rested atop of him. The last shudders left their bodies, leaving only their heavy breathing as evidence of their encounter.

His arms tightened around her. "There's nothing I wouldn't do for you." His deep voice vibrated with a determination which caused her to look up.

"What aren't you telling me?"

"Nothing, *mein schatz*." Did she hear the strain in his voice? He pushed into her mind, needing to know.

Kat wanted to press the matter, but knew that now wasn't the time. Their act was a desperate mating which left her both sated and deliciously sore. She didn't want anything to ruin the moment. Thank the Fates, for he did not wish to ruin this moment either.

She laid her head on his shoulder and drew aimless circles lightly over his chest with her fingers, which brought a genuine smile to curve his lips. A smile that held an edge of male smugness for he could sense her fulfillment.

Tomorrow he could worry about Gage for tonight there would be only her, his Katrina.

Chapter 26

Gage remained as he had for the past two nights, on his knees cradling Andrea's body—her blood long since dry on both her dress and his clothes. He refused to move or allow any of his guards near them. He knew his guards could feel his grief, it hung heavy in the air, causing his stomach to twist into knots.

With sightless eyes, he observed all of his guards come to him. His gaze lowered back to his mate, as they formed a circle around them and began to sing the death chant that had been passed down through generations of vampires. Their voices sounded soft and low, the deep timbre of their song gradually penetrated his mental haze. He blinked. Once. Twice. His gaze rose reluctantly from the beloved woman in his arms to meet the eyes of the guard in front of him.

Gage slowly rose with Andrea draped in his arms. The circle parted so he could carry her lifeless body into the dining room. Prepared by the guards, a plastic sheet draped over the table and one of Andrea's prettiest gowns hung over the back of one chair.

Gage laid her gently on the table barely noting the sound of the plastic sheet crinkling beneath her. He smoothed her matted hair back from her ashen face.

Trace and Alvero walked in on silent feet and handed him two stacks of bowls, each containing an herb which would be rubbed onto Andrea's body. The

215

purpose of which was to help see her into the afterlife. After handing their bowls to Gage, they bowed in unison and backed from the room, leaving him to his painful task.

Tears welled in his eyes, clouding his vision, as he removed her stiff, bloodied clothing so he could wash her body before administering the herbs. A bucket of water sat at the head of the table. His hand plunged deep to grasp the sponge inside. No doubt warm hours ago, the water had probably cooled while the guards chanted around them. The temperature assaulted his skin, and Gage sucked in a deep breath. His first thought was to warm the water, but reality crashed down on him as he realized Andrea would not feel the temperature. She would never again feel anything.

A tear escaped his eye to roll down his face, hitting the water in the bucket.

He wrung the excess water from the sponge. With deferential hands, he washed all traces of blood from her pale skin. His tears fell as he worked, washing over her as much as did the water.

By the time he completed the arduous task, a calm determination had come over him, drying his tears. He put the sponge back into the bucket and turned to the bowls of herbs, looking down at them with a detachment for which he was grateful.

He reverently mixed the herbs with olive oil then, as dictated by tradition, and began with her feet, carefully rubbing on Agrimony and Curry for the protection of her soul. Next he rubbed her legs with Boneset to ward off evil spirits she might encounter on her journey. Then Gage massaged both her hands with Comfrey to ensure safe travel into the next world. His hands dipped into Coltsfoot before he worked them over her arms for peace and tranquility. Finally, he washed her face and neck with Basil for love.

He closed his eyes and took a deep steadying breath, knowing there was one part of the ritual he had yet to perform. He needed to bathe her stomach in Chicory to remove all obstacles in the path to the hereafter.

His eyes tracked down her bare stomach and he laid his hand on the soft skin there. His fingers splayed wide, as if to shield the child cocooned within. Gage quietly hummed the death chant while he rubbed the Chicory in slow, worshipful circles, careful to make sure every inch was covered by the herb, to be sure both Andrea and their child had a clear path to the afterlife.

With the herbal ritual completed, Gage dressed Andrea in her best gown, a pretty white chiffon dress with an empire waist. Once he finished, he smoothed the chiffon folds and gazed down at his mate. She looked like an angel.

He draped his body over her lifeless form, his tears falling onto her face as he lovingly ran one hand over where their unborn child lay cradled. With one final kiss to her cold, still lips, he turned and walked from the room.

Outside four of his guards waited. They entered the dining room reverently and flanked her body, two on each side. In complete silence, they humbly lifted her. When they began walking her outside, Gage moved to her head, gently cradling it in his hands. Together they carried her body outside to the wooden funeral dais which had been prepared for her during Gage's vigil.

Gage assumed the role of officiate and stood in

front of the platform. His guards stood around the stand, forming a circle of grief. They sang the death chant again wishing her peace and a peaceful passage into the next world.

Gage lifted his hands and recited the death prayer saying, "You have left this life, left behind your body, for you do not need it to return to the Fates. May they embrace you back into their fold. Welcome you, protect you on your journey into the Beyond."

After another round of chanting, one by one, each male stepped forward in silence and placed a log under the altar. The final guard, Alvaro, held a lit torch. As he stepped forward, Gage met him, took the torch from the male, and turned toward Andrea for the last time. He said a final silent farewell to his mate and unborn child then lit the logs beneath her. The fire flared to life, consuming her body.

One by one, the others left with their heads bowed until only Gage remained.

Now alone, he allowed his grief to flood his body. The pain took his legs from beneath him, sobs shook his frame. He sunk to his knees in the grass, watching his heartmate return to that from which she had come; dust to dust.

****

Utterly miserable, Gage entered his home and sat at the kitchen table. His clothes, still caked with dried blood, were disheveled and reeked since he had not changed or showered in the three days since the funeral. Words alone could not express how deep his devastating sorrow went. His throat constricted and his eyes became hazy with tears. His stomach knotted causing a gut wrenching pain that made him curl over and heave.

He wept for his Andrea and the death of their future. The moment of her death took with it all his hopes, his dreams, and goals. His future taken by the same phenomenon that took her soul. In a single moment, he'd lost his heartmate, his child, his tomorrow.

Gage rested his head in his hands, elbows on the kitchen table.

"Sir?" Alvero tentatively approached and placed his hand gently on Gage's shoulder.

Gage looked up. He knew his face looked drawn, he'd seen it in a mirror. He probably reminded the guard of a skeleton. Under his tear streaked eyes sat dark circles. His eyes looked sunken into the sockets, his shoulders slumped. He'd barely recognized his reflection.

"Have you eaten anything, sir?" the body guard asked him quietly.

Gage did not reply, simply shook his head back and forth one time before resting it back in his hands.

Alvero sat down across from him at the table. "Sir, I think we should talk," he said motioning for Trace to join them from where he waited in the doorway to the kitchen.

Trace joined the pair, starting to sit in the empty chair to the right of Gage.

Gage's head snapped up. "Don't you sit there. That is *Her* seat." Gage's eyes pinned Trace with the fierceness of a lion.

Trace puts his hands up in surrender and bowed his head.

"Of course, sir." He wisely moved around the table

and sat in the chair to Gage's left. Trace shot Alvero a wayward glance.

"Sir," Trace said cautiously. "What should be done about the ball that was scheduled for tomorrow night?"

"I had completely forgotten about that." Gage heard the defeat in his own voice, and looked from one guard to the other, hoping someone might have an idea. He couldn't make decisions right now.

"Might I make a suggestion?" Alvero offered. Gage nodded his head once, giving permission for the guard to continue.

"Might I suggest you let Trace and I call your guests and tell them the ball and party have been cancelled for this year."

Gage nodded his head once again, unconcerned about what they did. "That's fine. I don't care."

"Very well. Trace and I will take care of the phone calls immediately." Alvero pushed his chair away from the table as if to leave, but before he rose, Trace spoke.

"What about the humans?" asked Trace leaning forward his forearms on the table.

"I don't care," repeated Gage exasperated. "I just don't care anymore."

"Have you eaten tonight?" Alvero asked changing the subject. Gage shook his head. He hadn't been hungry since...

"How about if I go get Red for you, sir. You always enjoy her." Trace offered with a hopeful grin.

"I can't see her," Gage replied shaking his head. "The last time I fed from her it was with Andrea."

"How about if I find someone else for you to feed from?" volunteered Alvero. "You must eat something. You need to keep your strength up."

"Why? If I don't feed I'll die, then I can be with my Andrea again." Gage shot the guard a sharp look. "What's there to live for?"

"Revenge," Trace answered without hesitation.

Gage's eyes snapped to Trace. By the Fates above, the guard was right. His eyes widened as his nostrils flared.

"Yes," said Gage slowly, his voice as hard as stone. "Revenge."

Gage sat up a little straighter. The past few days had been a blur of sorrow and despair. He missed his heartmate, missed her touch, her laugh. Missed the mischievous twinkle in her eye when she teased him.

All that was gone from his life now thanks to that bastard Stephan von Haas. That male had come into his home, accused him of conducting a hunt club, and added injury to insult by killing his mate. He needed to pay for his transgressions, and Gage was just the male to dole out the punishment.

His brows furrowed, lips tightened into a line before he continued. "Bring me a human who is hardy. I want one who is healthy, full of life, who can give me the energy I need to plot my revenge on that sonuvabitch von Haas."

"At once, sir." Alvero nodded and left the room, purpose hurrying his strides, as he went to fetch one of the humans from below.

A slight smile appeared on Trace's face when Gage licked his lips. He could almost taste the revenge. A plan for retribution began to form in his mind. All too soon he would have a plan, a purpose to his life once again.

Chapter 27

Stephan lay in his bed under his red satin sheets. He rolled onto his back, laying one arm across his forehead, his eyes opened wide. Like a scene from a horror movie flickering on the big screen, every time he shut his eyes, he saw the pregnant female fall in slow motion and become impaled upon the sword. It was not just the sights which kept him awake but the sounds of that night, playing over and over again like a stuck record in his head. He hadn't slept in days. The few times he drifted off dreams of what had happened plagued him.

He turned his head and looked at Kat who lay sleeping beside him with her hand tucked under her cheek on her pillow. He gently brushed a golden curl from her face as she nuzzled into the pillow. He looked down and smiled, but the smile faded quickly when the fear crept back in.

He knew Gage's threat to take from him all that was dear was a promise. He couldn't imagine anything more dear to him than the woman lying beside him. She meant everything to him and he worried that Gage would find a way to take her from him. As he watched her chest rise and fall with each breath, anxiety, the likes of which he'd never experienced before, gripped him tighter, like a hand gripping his heart, squeezing until it could not beat anymore.

He rolled toward Katrina and drew her into him. Holding her close, he breathed in her honeysuckle scent, trying to absorb her very essence so he would never lose her.

****

Gage sat in his office, across from Trace and Alvero, plotting a strategy of retribution.

"You know," said Trace, "tit for tat is the best revenge."

Gage raised an inquiring eyebrow at him, encouraging him to continue.

Trace crossed one ankle onto the opposite knee and continued. "We need to find out if von Haas has a heartmate."

Thoughts of the night they met after the ballet flowed through Gage's mind. "When I first met him, he accompanied a female, a human. He seemed rather fond of her. Nicholai Peterhof, might know who the woman is."

Alvero leaned forward, resting his forearms on his thighs. "But if Nicholai knows von Haas, then don't you think he would be reluctant to give up the information?"

"I suppose you are right," Gage agreed. "If we knew where von Haas lived, we could watch the place, take the woman. If Nicholai knows von Haas, perhaps he would know where the bastard lives."

"We could force Peterhof to give us the information," suggested Trace rubbing his hands together as if anticipating the techniques that would be needed to force Nicholai's cooperation.

"I don't like that option, unless it is our last resort. Nicholai was kind to Andrea. I don't want to hurt him."

Gage pinched the bridge of his nose. "Yet still, we need more information on von Haas."

"I looked him up on the internet," offered Alvero. "He owns several businesses, but none of them are here in Vegas. I wonder why he is here."

"That's a good question." Gage tapped his lips with his index finger, thoughtfully. "I wonder...just why is he here?"

Trace shrugged. "Maybe he just came to see the ballet."

"Huh, I don't know...Maybe." Gage looked pensively at the two guards and stroked his hand down his face. "Something seemed familiar about the woman he took to the ballet. I could have sworn I knew her from somewhere. Give me time, maybe I can figure out where I've seen her before."

"Perhaps she is from Vegas. Maybe that's why Stephan is here, to see her." A hopeful expression lit Alvero's face.

"Hmmm." Gage stroked his chin. "I guess that could make sense, if she lives in Vegas he could be here to see her.

"Perhaps I recognize her because I have seen her around town. But where? How do I know her? Maybe I've seen her at a show."

"Oh, yeah." Trace suddenly reached into the pocket with a look of concern on his face. "I'm hesitant to mention this, sir, but the maid found something when she cleaned your room this evening."

"What is it?" Gage snapped, perturbed by the change of subject. He didn't have time for any nonsense. He had more important things to think about like finding the human and exacting revenge.

Trace withdrew his hand from the pocket black pants. "It's two tickets. I think perhaps Andrea planned to surprise you by taking you to a show."

Tears pushed into Gage's eyes, and he quickly blinked them away. Grief had no place within him, revenge and anger were now his emotion of choice. "Tickets to what?" he muttered.

Trace looked down at the tickets in his hand. "To the show Desire, at Reaper's. They're for Friday night."

Gage shook his head. As if he would want to go without his Andrea. "I don't want to go. You can have the tickets, Trace. Why don't you and Alvero go? You two have helped me much during the past days."

Alvero looked at him, brow furrowed over his eyes. "Are you sure? Wouldn't you like to go? Perhaps it could take your mind off of everything for a little while."

"No. Sadly the only thing that show will remind me of is the last time Andrea and I were there." His mind replayed that evening, how Andrea touched him making him feel every bit a desirable male. He smiled remembering how he created a mental cloak to hide them from prying eyes as she whispered in his ear to think of the blonde dancer while she excited him.

Suddenly his eyes went wide with realization. His head snapped up. "I know who she is." His voice, loud with excitement, caused the guards to jump.

"You know who 'who' is?" asked Alvero.

"I know who the woman is...von Haas' woman. I know how to find her. I-I know where the woman works," Gage stammered with enthusiasm. For the first time since losing his heartmate, he felt a moment of happiness.

Chapter 28

Katrina slid into her jacket and walked down the fluorescent lit hallway, the lights glistening off the polished linoleum. As she reached Reaper's side exit door, she thought about Stephan. It had been more than a week since the incident, and he had been very stoic and sullen. He'd not spoken with her again about the accident, she believed in an attempt to ease her concern. However, the lack of dialogue gave Kat's mind the opportunity to contrive her own version of what might be going on in Stephan's head.

She imagined him riddled with guilt over what happened, and she could not ease that remorse, because he would not discuss it. It broke her heart to think of him suffering and not be allowed to console him. The thought of how he must be hurting brought tears to her eyes.

A noble, honorable man, he would not have purposely caused the death of an innocent. Her heart ached to comfort him. He was being strong for her, when it was she who should be strong for him, lifting him up. She rested her hand on the door latch and took a steadying breath, wiping the tears from her eyes with the back of her other hand.

She wanted to be calm and collected when she greeted her chaperone for her ride home. She hoped Stephan would be waiting for her in the alley, but lately the chaperone duty rotated amongst the Alphas, so she wasn't sure exactly who would be waiting for her. She just hoped it wouldn't be Demetri. He scared the hell out of her with his powerful presence and glowering looks.

Outside the rain poured down like a banshee and she wished she'd chosen to wear jeans instead of a skirt and light blouse. As she stepped free of the door an arm wrapped around her waist like an iron trap, pushing the breath from her body. Instinct kicked in, and she thrashed her legs wildly, struggling to free herself to no avail. Self-perseveration sent her skull careening into the attacker's nose.

Pain shot through Katrina's head, but it had the desired effect. She heard the nose break on impact and the assailant dropped her. Kat collapsed in a gasping heap in the alleyway, her hands and knees scraped by the hard asphalt. The punishing drops of rain stung her exposed skin, as she crawled away and fought to regain her breath.

A hand clamp down around her ankle. Its bite flexed her bones and twisted, then pulled her backwards. She grasped at the asphalt, looking for purchase. The pebbles on the hard pavement ground into her hands and legs as she was dragged back. A piece of broken glass sliced deep into her knee. The pain sharpened her senses. As adrenaline rushed through her body, her fight or flight instinct kicked into fight mode.

Kat turned onto her back and kicked the attacker with her free leg. Her heel connected with his broken nose, sending blood spraying across her leg. He tightened his grip on her injured leg, and Kat screamed in agony. She knew he intended to break her bones. She kicked again with the free foot. This time her attacker turned his head so his eye socket took the blow. Her leg, firm from years of dancing, gave a solid blow to his face, and he finally released his grip.

Kat scrambled away from him doing a backward crabwalk into a wall. Suddenly the barrier retreated, faded away from her back. Confused, Katrina looked up taking her eyes from her attacker. The hard rain caused her eyes to narrow and made it difficult to discern the features of the dark figure that stood behind her. Panic coursed through her body. Another attacker! She knew she couldn't take on two.

Then the figure stepped forward into the light provided from the small bulb outside the door to Reapers. Through her squinting eyes, she realized Demetri stood behind her. Relief pulsed through her veins in time with her beating heart.

In one swift motion, too quick for Kat to follow, Demetri scooped her up into his arms and carried her to the H3. He opened the door and tossed her onto the back seat.

"You're injured," he said looking down at her ankle and bleeding leg, his fangs extended.

"Get me out of here." Tears streamed down her face along with the raindrops. She looked him in the eyes, trying to implore him to do as she said. A stoic face met her plea. No emotion, no sympathy.

Kat blinked and her rescuer disappeared, the door to the car closed. Kat looked around, confused. She saw a blur of motion through the rain-soaked windshield, heard the squeal of tires on hot asphalt, then the world became still, silent.

A shadow appeared at the door just before it ripped open. Kat screamed. Demetri's presence filled the car when he climbed into the back beside her.

"Let's go, *now*," pleaded Kat in a shaky voice, still sobbing.

"There's no reason to rush," Demetri informed her. "The male who attacked you is gone. He got into a van while I was putting you in the car. I tried to run after him, but I didn't want to leave you alone in case there were others."

He grabbed her leg.

"What are you doing?" demanded Kat.

"Hold still you're injured." He looked at the bleeding wound on her leg and clamped his hands down on her leg, one on her thigh the other on her calf to pin her leg to the seat.

Kat's panic returned as the large male manhandled her. She struggled to no avail, grabbed the back of the seat trying to maneuver away from him. Her breathing quickened.

"I'm going to close the wound," he announced as his fangs extended.

He bent over her leg and licked at the wound. The healing agent in his saliva sealed the injury before her eyes. Her heart raced, not knowing if he would stop once the wound was healed or if bloodlust would overcome him and he would drink from her. Her breath left her lungs in heavy quick rasps.

Demetri looked at her with hungry eyes, eyes that pinned hers, his dark, penetrating stare pushed into her mind. Kat felt the world sway. Blackness tunneled in and she fell into the dark abyss as she vaguely heard a deep voice say something about hyperventilating and sleep.

****

Stephan sensed the arrival of Demetri and Kat. Apparently Marcus did as well for he joined Stephan in the foyer to greet them. Opening the door wide, Stephan was shocked to find Demetri carrying Kat in his bulky arms. Against his large body, she looked like a child sleeping. Demetri bowed his head in greeting.

"What the hell happened?" Stephan pinned Demetri with a harsh glare.

"Your female will be fine," Demetri replied calmly. "Worry not."

Stephan assessed Kat's injuries. His gaze lit on her multiple bruises and swollen ankle.

"What happened?" he asked again as he captured her ankle to examine the bruising.

"She was attacked. I believe the ankle is only sprained. It will be fine."

"Why is she wet?" asked Marcus looking from Kat to Demetri.

"It's raining," Demetri casually informed them as Marcus took off his shirt and laid it over Katrina's still form.

"Why is she unconscious? Is she hurt badly?" A look of concern furrowed Marcus' brows.

"She is not unconscious. I put her to sleep."

"Why?" Stephan inquired, suspicion raising his voice.

Demetri shrugged his shoulders causing Kat to lift briefly. "Because she was crying, and I don't like listening to a female cry."

Stephan gingerly took the unconscious Kat from Demetri's arms. The Alpha efficiently relayed the story of what happened in the alley.

"By the time I arrived at the club to escort Kat, another male was already there. I brought the Hummer to a stop and realized the male was attacking. It sickened me that he would attack a defenseless female. But your woman did well. She'd already broken his nose when I arrived."

A proud smile crossed Marcus' lips. "That's my Kitty Kat."

"My first priority was Katrina's safety. By the time I loaded her into the car, the male got away. But I got a good look at the van. It was black, no windows on the sides or back."

"Sounds like the same van I saw at the Lucio compound," Marcus remarked.

"That sonuvabitch! Gage tried to kidnap my Katrina," Stephan yelled, causing Kat to stir. Demetri obviously released his command to sleep for her eyelids fluttered open. She looked around at her surroundings, her eyes coming to rest briefly on him. A look of confusion crossed the delicate features of her face when she looked from Marcus to Demetri and finally to Nicholai who had come to join the group in the foyer.

"Where am I?" she asked after she blinked a few times seemingly to clear the sleepy haze from her mind. Her face twisted in pain when she flexed her ankle. It brought tears to her eyes she could not contain. Kat moaned, and Stephan brought her close, holding her tightly to his chest.

"It's all right, *mein schatz*. You are safe now. Demetri brought you back to the penthouse. I'm going to take the pain away. You will be okay." He kept his voice smooth as silk, and Katrina instantly settled in his arms. His lover snuggled against him, and placed her hand around the back of his neck. Stephan looked back at Demetri. "Thank you for returning her to me, my old friend. I am in your debt for all you did tonight."

Demetri waved a dismissive hand. "It was nothing. I can see she is tired. I'll take my leave if there is nothing more you need of me this night."

"Actually I'd like you to stay. I'd like to speak with you some more after I see to Kat. I have more questions.

"Marcus, please get Demetri and Nicholai a drink. I'll be back in a moment."

Stephan took Kat up the stairs, her weight no consequence as he cradled her against his chest. He laid her softly onto the bed. After removing her sodden clothing, he looked upon her battered body noting every scratch, each bruise. "I want to you to take a little of my blood, Kitten. It will speed your healing."

Allowing for no protest, Stephan bit a wound into his wrist and held it to Katrina's lips. Too tired to argue, she reached up, held his wrist to her lips and drew the coppery liquid into her mouth. He pushed into her mind ready to take control should she find the task inordinate. But it was not necessary. As it coated the back of her throat, she tasted him in the thick liquid, and she liked it.

Stephan closed his eyes, savoring the feel of each draw against his skin. A rush of heat coursed through his body. But he swallowed down the lust, for he knew his lover needed to rest and heal.

"That's enough," he said, gently taking his wrist from her mouth. He remained in her mind, needing to know how she felt. As his blood nourished her cells,

Kat's wounds tingled. He looked down and found her watching him as he sat beside her on the bed.

His thigh brushed her ribs when he carefully ran his hands over her body to check for injuries. He started with the scrapes on her palms then ran his hands up her arms, down over her ribs and hips. His fingers lingered while he watched the cut on her thigh begin to close when the healing properties in his blood worked their magic. Finally, his hands trailed gently over her knees and down to her toes.

Satisfied her only serious injury was the ankle, he knelt down beside the bed and closed his eyes in concentration. He felt her watching him as he rubbed his hands together, gathering his healing energy. A soft yellow glow emitted from his hands. Their eyes met when he gathered her injured ankle in his hands, bathing it in the healing light. Kat closed her eyes, and her facial features relaxed as the pain slowly ebbed from her injury.

Feeling confident the ankle had received proper attention, Stephan released her leg. He took her hands in his and sent his healing energy throughout her body.

The warrior left his body, sent his essence into her. Flowing throughout her body, he concentrated on her palms, knees, leg, and ankle. He watched the wounds repair from the inside out, making sure they healed completely before he pulled back into his own body.

Kat looked at him with a tear in her eye. "Thank you. I feel alive, whole again. The pain is gone."

"I'm so sorry this happened." Stephan ran his fingers through her hair brushing it back from her face.

"Me too. But it's okay. I'm fine thanks to you." Kat smiled up at him. Love sparkled in her gray-blue eyes. It humbled him.

"But for me, you wouldn't have been attacked."

"Don't say that. To be with you, I'd suffer any attack."

"You shouldn't have to suffer just to be with me. My world is dark and dangerous. It is no place for a human."

She laced her fingers with his. "But when I'm with you I feel whole, happy. Without you I'd be lost. I'll take a little darkness now and then."

"But…" Kat put a finger on Stephan's lips to silence him.

"Enough talking for tonight," she said as she leaned up and captured his lips with her own.

Her lips, soft and warm, pressed against his. Her tongue darted out, licking against the seam of his lips, begging entrance. He wanted to taste her, wanted to feel her surround him with her warmth, but this was not the time to indulge. She needed to get cleaned up and rest after her ordeal, and he could do no other than see to her needs.

Pulling away from Katrina, Stephan wrapped her in a robe and led her into the bathtub. He filled it with warm water. After helping her into the steamy bathwater, he stepped around the tub and sat behind her.

He lathered a fluffy white wash cloth and washed her body with small circles. Katrina relaxed against the tub as the water washed away the evidence and trauma of the evening.

As Stephan finished washing her legs and reverently rinsed her body, her eyes drooped closed. She fell asleep with the water gently lapped against her tired body. He awakened her when he used a soft towel on her face to wipe the water away. After handing her from the tub, Kat swayed while he toweled the drops of water from her body. Her leaden eyes drooped and neither of them spoke while he worked.

After placing her in their bed, he remained with her until she drifted off to sleep again. Stephan placed a kiss on her forehead and left feeling bereft as he closed the door and headed toward the stairs to join his friends in the living room.

Nicholai motioned for Marcus to stop pacing and sit down in the living room of the penthouse as Demetri carried three glasses of blood and vodka, true Bloody Marys, into the living room.

Nicholai pinned Demetri with his gaze. "Cousin, tell me exactly what happened tonight. I get the feeling you left something out when talking earlier."

The Russian took a long sip of his drink and told his fellow warriors all the details of the fight between Kat and her attacker including how she kicked him not once but twice.

"It amazes me how one so lovely and graceful could be such a fighter. I guess it is true what the proverb says; you cannot judge a book by its cover." Nicholai took a long drink from his glass.

Marcus pressed his friend for more details about the van. After hearing the thorough description, Marcus sighed, his fists clinched in his lap. "I think we have enough proof Gage was behind this. Somehow he found Kat and now he is after her to punish Stephan."

Nicholai nodded in agreement. "I think you are correct. Gage thinks Stephan took his heartmate from him, so he is taking Stephan's woman."

"I agree," Demetri concurred as Stephan joined the group.

"Gage is definitely a threat," said Stephan taking up residence in front of the plasma TV. He crossed his arms over his chest. "I think we need to take him out."

"Those are strong words," cautioned Nicholai, knowing where this conversation was heading.

"I agree with Stephan." Marcus rose from his chair to pace the room. "Gage tried to get Kat tonight. Since that failed, who knows what he'll try next."

"I too think it would make sense for Gage to try something again," agreed Demetri.

Stephan nodded. "I can only guess what he'll try next. He is a male that blames me for the loss of his mate. He tried to take my woman tonight. We can be sure he did not have any honorable intentions toward Katrina."

Marcus stopped his pacing, turning toward his fellow Alphas. "We also believe he was gathering humans for a hunt club. Fates be damned, what if he was going to hunt Kat?"

"Perhaps we do need to take out the threat," Nicholai conceded. He wiped his hand through his hair.

Marcus sat down hard in the leather recliner. "In his grief, Gage is a danger to himself and others, especially other humans. We believe him to be the one behind the hunt club and now he has a personal vendetta against Stephan. He must be stopped." Marcus punched one fist into the opposite palm.

"His house is well guarded," observed Nicholai.

"We should assemble the Council," his cousin suggested. "Together we can easily take care of Gage and his guards."

"I agree," Stephan said, determination furrowing his brows. "Are we in agreement?"

The Alpha leader looked from one vampire to the next, noting each Alpha's agreement by the nods of their heads.

"It is decided then. We shall dispose of Gage Lucio."

Stephan turned to the vampire he sired. "Marcus, call the other Alphas and tell them I request their presence here. For the ones who can't dematerialize here, I'll send my plane after them."

Stephan took a card out of his wallet and handed it to Marcus. "Here is my pilot's number. After you talk to the other Alphas you can call him and let him know which airports he'll need to go to. He can take things from there."

"I'm on it." Marcus stood up to leave, but Stephan halted him by placing a hand on his arm.

"Marcus, I also want you to arrange for Kat to have an extended leave of absence from Reapers. I don't want her going back to work until we get this straightened out." Stephan looked grim, his face drawn.

"Will do. I'll coordinate everything right now."

Marcus left to make the arrangements as Demetri and Nicholai stood to take their leave. Stephan escorted the two to the door.

"Do not worry Stephan," offered Nicholai, knowing his words would not be heeded by the Alpha leader. "We will deal with Gage, then you and Kat will be safe."

"I'm not worried about myself, only Kat. I fear that as long as she is a part of our world she will never truly be safe."

Nicholai bowed his head in silent agreement, knowing no words could reassure Stephan. Then he and his cousin turned in unison and walked out the door.

"Safe travels, my friends," Stephan called out to the pair of them, closing the door behind them.

****

Gage punched his fist through the wall and rounded on his guard. "You're telling me you didn't get the woman?" he bellowed.

Trace looked down at his feet, properly ashamed. "No, I couldn't get her. I was attacked."

"Yeah, by the female," Alvero offered, a grin threatening to crack his lips.

Gage's eyes widened. This was unbelievable!

"You mean to tell me that the mortal female did that to you?" He pointed to Trace's swollen and bloodied face. Trace nodded and his face contorted with pain.

Gage grunted in disgust. "You're pathetic. How could a little human girl get away from you?"

"She surprised me by attacking me. The woman has been taught to fight."

"Even so, you're telling me you couldn't handle her?"

"I had her, until the reinforcements showed up."

"What do you mean? Explain." Gage leapt across the room and pinned Trace to the wall. His hand clamped down hard around the male's throat, and he leaned in close. "And don't lie to me."

"I almost had her," the guard explained, "when the largest vampire I have ever seen suddenly appeared. It was obvious he was her bodyguard. I knew if there was one guard there would be others so I took off."

"Leaving the woman," finished Gage.

Alvero snickered. "I never thought I'd see the day when Trace was bested by a female, especially a human female."

"Stephan was obviously expecting us to try to kidnap the woman," observed Trace. "That's why she was being guarded."

"Perhaps these are why," Alvero said, raising his hand.

Gage looked over at the two metal devices resting in the male's palm. "What are those?"

Alvero dropped the bits of metal on Gage's desk. "I believe they are listening devices."

Gage dropped his hand from his guard and made his way over to his desk to inspect the debris.

"The house is bugged?" asked Trace, rubbing his neck.

"Was bugged," Alvero corrected. "I've had the guards do a sweep of the house. These were the only two devices found, and I destroyed them."

Gage paced the room in agitation. "Our plan for revenge is ruined. No wonder the woman was being guarded. Von Hass knew we were coming. Now that the kidnapping attempt failed, I'm sure he will be even more vigilant in protecting his woman. "

"We need a new plan," suggested Alvero.

Yes they did, thanks to Trace. *Idiotic guard. A waste of flesh really.*

Gage rubbed his chin thoughtfully. "Perhaps in addition to a new plan I also need to get a new leader for my guard, since Trace can't even seem to kidnap one puny woman."

Trace opened his mouth to speak, but Gage shot

him a look that closed his mouth up tight.

"Alvero, you are now the head of the guards. You're first responsibility as leader is to see that Trace is punished for his failure, then report back to me so we can try to conceive of a new plan."

Alvero straightened to his full height, holding his face expressionless. Emotions were not tolerated well by their master, and he had obviously learned that lesson well. Trace had always been Gage's second in command but now Alvero would run the guard. He had better be up to the task.

Gage watched Alvero lead Trace away. A short time later he sat alone in his study and heard the crack of the whip as it bit into Trace's flesh. A wide smile of satisfaction crept onto his face. *Alvero might just work out,* he thought.

Chapter 29

Stephan awoke in the same state he had the previous three evenings—fear knotted his stomach and perspiration created a fine sheen on his brow. His heart pounded within the wall of his torso. His muscular chest heaved heavily up and down as he gasped for air. Like in previous nights, a nightmare inspired his reaction, but this night the dream had been different. Instead of Andrea, he dreamt of Kat, a horrific dream in which he found her mutilated body on the side of a road.

He quickly reached one arm over to gain comfort from the feeling of Katrina beside him. His arm landed on a cool flat sheet. He patted his hand up and discovered an empty pillow. Stephan bolted upright, his eyes wide with fright.

He immediately sent his senses flaring out to locate his love, taking some comfort in the knowledge that since she had drank his blood twice, he would always be able to find her. Immeasurable calm settled over him when he sensed her presence downstairs.

He focused his preternatural hearing toward the kitchen, and heard Kat and Marcus laughing together. With a sigh of relief, he scrubbed both hands down his face and shook off the feeling of dread, sending his dark hair skirting across his bare shoulders.

It was only a dream, he reminded himself as he

dressed quickly to join the pair in the kitchen.

"And what may I ask is so funny?" Stephan strolled into the kitchen, the forced smile on his face did not reach his eyes.

"Oh, nothing," replied Kat, smiling at him. "You really had to be there."

"Care to join us?" Marcus lifted his glass containing blood.

"I think I will." Stephan poured a glass of the precious crimson liquid for himself then joined the twosome at the table, taking a chair between them.

"So, again I'll ask. What was so funny?" Stephan raised his glass to his lips to take a sip of the life-sustaining fluid.

"Oh, we were just talking about past Halloweens," Kat informed him wistfully. "We have always had such fun on Halloween."

"That's true." Marcus nodded his agreement. "Remember the year we went dressed as Cleopatra and Mark Antony?"

"Oh yeah, that was hysterical. You looked so good in that toga, Marcus." Kat took a sip of her coffee.

"Marcus, the Italian, dressed in a toga. I'd liked to have seen that." A smile pulled at one corner of Stephan's mouth when his mind supplied a picture.

"Yeah, it was something to see all right. His legs peeking out from under that white sheet, like two hairy telephone poles," Kat quipped, earning a round of laughter from everyone.

"Hey, I resemble that remark," Marcus chimed in, feigning offense.

"I can't wait to see you in your costume tonight, Marcus." Katrina took a bite of her bagel.

"You're going to be a knockout in yours, Kitty Kat."

"You two have costumes for tonight?" Stephan looked inquiringly at the pair.

Swallowing, Marcus placed his empty cup on the table. "Yes. We bought them a couple of months ago. You have to get them early if you want the good ones."

"Where were you planning on wearing them?" Stephan turned a scrutinizing eye on Marcus.

"We were just trying to decide where to go tonight," offered Kat.

"I don't believe going out is a good idea, *mein schatz*, my treasure. I don't think it is safe." Stephan covered Kat's hand with his, and glared at Marcus who shifted uncomfortably under his attention.

I can't believe you would think taking Kat out is a good idea, Marcus. She could be attacked again. Along with his thoughts, Stephan sent the mental equivalent of a head smack through his mindlink to Marcus.

"We would be going in costume, no one will recognize us." Marcus shrugged. "Besides what are the chances that Gage or any of his men would be going to the same club we choose?"

"Pleeeaaasssee," chimed in Kat, looking up at him with big, childlike eyes. "I love Halloween. It's my favorite holiday, and I want to go out to celebrate it. I don't want to be stuck in the house, afraid. I want to go out and live life."

Stephan could tell she truly didn't want the incident from the previous evening to disrupt their plans. He'd made a similar choice many years ago and knew that you had to live life not hide from it, even if living life meant taking risks rather than playing it safe.

243

He understood the best way to get through something traumatic was to get out and experience life again, but the need to keep her safe warred with his need to please her.

"I don't know," ruminated Stephan, thoughtfully. "I suppose you do have a point, Marcus. Even if we happen upon Lucio, he probably wouldn't recognize us if we were wearing the right kind of costumes. "

Stephan turned his full attention on the beautiful blonde sitting beside him. "Are you sure you feel up to going out tonight, Kat?"

"Oh yes. I'm completely healed and thanks to you, I feel better than ever." Katrina produced her leg to prove her point. Her robe fell away from her thigh, exposing her long smooth skin, when she propped her heal on Stephan's thigh.

Stephan's hand shot out of its own volition, encircling her ankle. After a careful inspection, his gaze followed his fingers as they made their way slowly up her leg and over her knee to climb her thigh. The feel of her creamy skin brought sinful thoughts to his mind.

The sound of Marcus clearing his throat brought Stephan out of his sensual musing. The Alpha pulled the satin material of Katrina's robe over her long leg and gently lowered her foot to the floor. Stephan knew his blood had made her feel good, and he couldn't doubt her conviction or the proof that she'd healed—at least physically.

He nodded his head in agreement.

"Okay," he reluctantly agreed. "As long as we're dressed up, we can go out, but I'll need a costume."

Marcus clapped his hands together and smiled. "Don't worry about that. I have seven years' worth of costumes from when Kat and I have gone out. You can borrow one of mine."

Stephan raised a weary eyebrow in Marcus' direction. "Well, then I guess I have no choice but to agree we can go out."

Kat jumped from her chair and leapt onto his lap. She squealed as she wrapped her arms around his neck in a tight hug. Stephan hugged her back, the male in him satisfied because he'd pleased her.

Marcus rose to his feet, gathered the dishes from the table, and rinsed them in the sink. After putting them in the dishwasher, Marcus turned toward the couple. "Come on, Stephan. Let's go find you a costume."

Stephan stood, gently putting Katrina on her feet before following Marcus into his room while Kat went upstairs to take a shower.

"Here," said Marcus, pulling what looked like a white adult diaper out of his closet.

"What the hell is that?" Stephan gingerly took the cloth between his index finger and thumb. He held the item away from his body as he stretched the loin cloth to its full width between his hands.

"No, look." Marcus brought out a shield. "You can be a gladiator."

Stephan bunched the loin cloth between his hands and sent it hurling across the room to hit his friend squarely in the face. "Absolutely not. There is no way I am wearing a diaper as a costume!"

"No?" teased Marcus, putting the costume back into his closet. "I thought you would have liked being a gladiator."

He sent his young friend a smirk and sat on the

bed. "I don't think so. Next."

Marcus withdrew a white and gold colored toga from the closet and held the garment up for inspection. "You could be Mark Antony," he offered.

Stephan raised both eyebrows and shook his head. "I don't think so. I will not wear a dress. No diapers. No dresses. What else do you have?"

Marcus returned to his closet and shifted through the clothing. "How about this?" he asked pulling out a black cape, hat, and mask. "It's my Zorro costume. You would need to wear a black shirt and pants, but I know you have those. I even have the sword to go with it."

"Ummm, all black, with a mask, and I get to carry a sword," Stephan pondered aloud, stroking a thoughtful hand over his chin. "That will do. The only thing I'm not fond of is the cape, but I'll get by. "

Marcus smiled. "If anyone can pull off a cape, you can my vampiric friend."

Stephan laughed. "Always the flatterer, Marcus."

Hours later, Stephan sat in the living room, waiting for Kat and Marcus to finish dressing. His black silk shirt and pants, hugged his muscular body. He laid his hat and mask on the coffee table along with the sabre, then gazed at the portrait of Kat on the wall. Apprehension about the evening crept in. He did not think going out was a good idea so soon after Kat's attack, but she had wanted to go so badly and he wanted to please her.

He looked up when Marcus entered the room dress as a wolf in a zoot suit. His face and hands covered in fur, he wore a red sports coat, brown pants, black shirt with a white tie, and a matching black Fedora with a red band around it.

"What are you supposed to be?" inquired Stephan.

"I'm the Big Bad Wolf." Marcus swept a hand down his body. "I'm looking for Little Red Riding Hood. Have you seen her?"

"No, I ha—" Stephan's reply was quickly cut off as he spied Kat coming down the stairs. Though dressed as Little Red Riding Hood, there was nothing young or innocent about her. She wore a red mini skirt that flared out from the white tulle crinoline underneath. Tucked into the skirt, a white fluffy shirt with a black corset boosted her full breasts up until Stephan thought they might pop out at any moment. Around her neck was tied a small red hooded cape that hung down to the hem of her short skirt. She wore her hair up in tight spirals which bounced with each step she took. Stephan's gaze drifted from her curls, down her long, shapely legs to the black stilettos with the peek-a-boo toes on her feet. His heart pounded hard in his chest sending desire coursing through his blood.

Marcus turned and Stephan knew the moment his eyes found Kat because the Big Bad Wolf craned his neck toward the ceiling and let out an appreciative "Ah-ooooooooooooo." Stephan hit Marcus on his shoulder, hard enough to cause him to stagger slightly.

"Hey!" Marcus said catching his balance.

"Down Boy. That's my Red Riding Hood. If anyone's going to be her big bad wolf it's going to be me."

"Can I help it if I appreciate a beautiful woman when I see one?"

"Don't make me put a leash on you." Stephan crossed the room and wrapped his arm around Kat's shoulders, giving her a quick peck on her fire engine red lips.

Kat giggled against his lips, kissing him back. "So I guess you approve of my costume," she said grabbing the skirt and doing a quick curtsy.

"Kitten, I will be your big bad wolf any day." He gave her a wily grin and shagged his eyebrows up and down at her.

"You look hot, Red," Marcus commented, as he strolled across the room to join the pair. He handed Stephan his hat, mask, and sword. "I hope you don't mind, but I invited Nicholai and Demetri to meet us at the club."

Shock turned his head to Marcus. "I'm surprised Demetri would come to something like a costume dance."

Marcus chuckled. "I didn't say they were both coming. Nicholai said he would be able to meet us there, but Demetri respectfully declined."

Now it was Stephan's turn to chuckle. "I'm sure he did. I can't imagine Demetri in a costume."

"So are you boys ready to go?" Katina slipped a red, rhinestone covered mask over her eyes.

"I believe we are, Kitty Kat."

"Then let's go." Stephan joined in, extending his arm to escort Kat. Marcus mimicked his stance, and Kat thread her arms through the arms of her escorts.

"Let's go boys. I'm ready to have some fun."

Chapter 30

The trio exited the Mercedes. Stephan handed the keys and a large bill to the valet then tucked Katrina against his side. They headed toward the hottest club on the strip, located in one of the five star hotels. Red looked up in dismay as they reached the line for the club that stretched through the casino and out the front door of the hotel.

"Oh no! We'll never get in." Disappointment dripped from her voice.

Stephan grinned down at her. "Oh, I wouldn't worry about that, Kitten."

The threesome strolled up to the bouncer at the club's entrance, and Stephan glanced at Marcus saying, "Do you want to do the honors or shall I?"

"Be my guest," Marcus acquiesced with a sly grin.

Stephan leaned in whispering in the bouncer's ear and slid some green into his palm. A dazed look overcame his face when Stephan pushed his command into the man's mind. The bouncer aptly unhooked the burgundy velvet rope and stepped aside, ushering the group in with a gallant sweep of his arm, and welcomed them into the club. Kat looked at him with wonder in her eyes.

"What?" He feigned innocence. A knowing smile on her beautiful face rewarded his efforts.

"Oh, nothing," she answered as the trio made their

way into the bar.

They were greeted by Nicholai, who apparently noticed them at the entrance and had made his way through the sea of people. The Alpha wore a Phantom of the Opera costume, the white mask covering half his face, his dark hair greased back. He grabbed the edges of the long cape he wore, tucking it around him, and bowed in greeting toward Kat. She curtsied back, giggling.

"Glad you could make it, Nicholai," said Stephan as Nicholai gave Kat a quick kiss on each cheek. A possessive growl rumbled in his throat.

"So where's Demetri?" smirked Marcus.

"This type of event is not for him." Nicholai smiled. "My cousin is much too stuffy to be caught dead in a place like this."

"Can you imagine Demetri in a costume?" Marcus posed.

"Can you imagine him in the gladiator costume you tried to get me to wear?" Stephan retorted. "Can't you picture him in the loin cloth that looks like a diaper?"

The group laughed boisterously together and headed for the bar.

After ordering a round of drinks, Marcus leaned against the bar. "Demetri in a diaper. What I wouldn't give to see that."

"He definitely wouldn't seem so scary then," murmured Kat.

Nicholai drank his shot in one gulp. "I would give my entire fortune to see Demetri in a loin cloth costume. I am afraid my cousin takes himself much, much too seriously. I do not remember the last time I saw the man laugh or tell a joke. Life was made for love and fun. It is a shame his is devoid of both." Nicholai turned toward Katrina. "Let us not be the same way. Shall we go have some fun and dance?" He offered his hand.

After glancing at Stephan for approval, Kat smiled and placed her hand in Nicholai's, allowing him to lead her to the crowded dance floor.

Stephan watched his date make her way to the dance floor. He and Marcus remained at the bar and ordered a second round of drinks. Knowing Katrina was in safe hands, Stephan took note of the club. It was translucent. Every piece of furniture, the railing, even the bar was made to be see-through. The lighting played through the surfaces giving the place a neon glow when it pulsated in time to the music. The fast beat of the loud music reverberated in his chest and overpowered his sensitive hearing.

"The music is so loud," Stephan said.

"What?" asked Marcus, leaning toward his friend.

"I said the music is loud." Stephan made his voice louder.

"What?" repeated Marcus.

I said the music is so loud. I can barely hear myself think. Stephan used their mindlink to express his thought to Marcus.

Stephan watched Kat and Nicholai gyrate on the crowded dance floor. He cringed each time someone accidentally bumped into Kat.

Marcus pointed to the landing above the bar. *It's quieter and less crowded up in the VIP section. Perhaps we should move up there.*

A perfect suggestion. *Sounds good. As soon as this*

song is over I'll get Nicholai and Kat.

When the song ended, Stephan made his way through the crowd to the couple. "We're moving upstairs. Come on." He gently took Katrina's elbow and guided her toward the stairs, Nicholai hot on their heels.

Upstairs the VIP hostess showed the group to a booth. When he looked at Kat he discovered she was looking around, her mouth gaping wide. Judging by the look on her face, she seemed awed by the splendor. His own eyes, also tracked the room.

Each booth consisted of a semicircular couch with a glass table in front. White fabric beaded with silver sequins throughout draped the walls. Colored lights that changed from blue, to pink, to yellow lit the area. The lights reflected off the white couches and draping giving the illusion that they too changed colors.

The VIP dance floor was smaller than the one downstairs, but not crowded. The lights played off the floor, creating swirling colors of blue, yellow, and pink. He couldn't help but notice the way Kat looked wistfully at the floor.

"Want to dance, Kitty Kat?"

"Love to." Katrina scooted out of the booth behind Marcus.

Throughout the evening, the males took turns dancing with Kat as the hours passed. Stephan had been careful to always cut in during the slower songs, not wanting to miss an opportunity to hold her in his arms. Katrina looked nearly danced out when Stephan approached the dance floor.

"Mind if I cut in?" He tapped Nicholai on his broad shoulder.

"Not at all." Nicholai gracefully handed Kat into

Stephan's waiting arms before leaving the couple alone to join Marcus in the booth.

As Stephan spun with her on the floor he ran one hand down her back and rested it on the small of her back. He pulled her against him, dipping his face to her hair, taking in the honeysuckle smell before resting his chin on her shoulder.

"I love you," he whispered into her ear. And he really did, with his whole heart.

"I love you too," she replied with a sigh.

He heard her heart accelerate, scented her desire as their bodies brushed one another while they danced. He slipped into her mind, allowing her desire to flow into him. He savored the feeling of the contrast of her softness to his hardness. She flowed in his arms like liquid heat, igniting the passion within him.

His hand traveled from her back to cup her chin, and he bent down to capture her mouth. His tongue slid between her parted lips, danced in rhythm to the music. He thoroughly explored the hot cavern of her mouth, tasting her kiss. He'd never get enough of her kiss, of her.

When the music came to a stop, he reluctantly broke the kiss and pulled back to gaze into Kat's eyes. She looked beautiful. Her lips were swollen from their kiss, her eyes slightly closed. She gazed from under her long lashes at him.

A sultry smile came to Katrina's lips. "Do you mind if we sit the next song out? I could really use a drink. I'm hot."

"Yes, you are," he agreed with a husky voice. After seeing her to the booth, he made his way to the bar and ordered her favorite drink. He brought the Long Island

Iced Tea back to the booth, just as the music stopped and the emcee broke in.

"Ladies and gentleman, I have a treat for you tonight. It is time for our annual Comical Costume Contest. We have a real treat for you this year. Our scouts found seven of the funniest costumes in the crowd tonight. Now it's time for you to decide who should win the trophy for the funniest costume.

"One by one the contestants will come out on the stage and strut their stuff. Once you have seen them all we'll bring them back out and you'll vote for the one you like best by cheering. The one getting the loudest cheers will win. Are you ready?" The emcee paused as the crowd responded with clapping and shouting. "Very well let's bring out the first one."

Kat moved forward in the booth to get a better view, her thigh brushed his. Their booth faced the stage, so they had a good view. The group watched the first contestant appear on stage.

A man, dressed in a white T-shirt and jeans, walked out backwards. When he turned around, Stephan could see a stuffed horse's head attached to his groin. The emcee announced, "Ladies I give you Hung Like A Horse."

The crowd erupted with female cat calls and laughter.

"That's original." Marcus took a sip of his bourbon. "Okay, now *that's* funny," he continued, tipping his glass toward the next contestant.

"Next is Shark Attack," the emcee announced. A blonde woman walked across the stage wearing a bikini top and a shark. The costume had been designed to look like the shark was eating her from the bottom up, her chest and head stuck out of its open mouth.

"This damsel is in real distress. She might need mouth to mouth. Any takers?" the emcee asked as the noise from the crowd turned deeply masculine.

"I wouldn't mind giving her a little mouth to mouth," Marcus volunteered. Nicholai lifted his glass in a salute of agreement and downed the rest of his vodka tonic.

"How about mouth to mouth with her?" he asked Marcus sarcastically as the next person walked on stage.

An out of shape, middle-aged man, dressed in a two piece showgirl outfit walked across the stage. A red feather boa and feathered headpiece completed his white and red sequined outfit. "Meet Ooh La La Lola," said the emcee, pausing to allow the man to exit the stage as the crowd applauded. "This next one is a killer. Killer B that is."

Out walked a woman in a large letter B. She held a bloody knife in one hand while blood dripped down her face as well as the B costume.

"We all like pigs in a blanket, but I never knew they could be so cute," said the emcee as a pretty red head with freckles all over her face came out wrapped in a blue blanket that had the heads of cute piglets attached to it.

"Now there is a pig in a blanket I could really sink my teeth into." Marcus smiled an evil grin.

Stephan laughed. "You always have had a thing for redheads."

Kat took a sip of her drink as the emcee announced, "Now this one is for you ladies."

A man dressed up as a medieval knight walked

slowly out onto the stage to a round of feminine cat calls. He wore a chainmail tunic that hung well past his knees. As he reached the center of the stage, he lifted the chainmail to reveal an extremely large penis, the size of a log, sewn onto his groin of the costume. "A Knight to Remember," joked the emcee. Another round of feminine cat calls went out.

Kat laughed so hard she nearly spit her drink all over Stephan. She seemed to be having the time of her life. And he had to admit, he was having a blast this Halloween—thanks to her. Stephan reached over and placed his hand on her knee, giving it a reassuring squeeze.

"And now last but not least, we have Deviled Egg," the emcee announced as a man walked out on the stage. Dressed in an egg shaped costume, with his arms and legs poked out of the fabric, he looked ridiculous. The costume was white with a yellow circle yoke in the stomach area. A pair of big red devil horns attached to the head and a pointed red tail that hung down in the back completed the costume. The man's face stuck through the material just under where the horns attached.

Marcus and Nicholai's laughing stopped abruptly and realization crossed their faces in the same instance. When both men quieted, Stephan sensed the tension rolling between them. The two males turned to look at each other in unison.

"That's..." started Nicholai.

"I know" stated Marcus.

Stephan, we have a problem. That egg is one of Gage's men. Alvero.

Stephan sent his senses flaring out through the

club. He could feel three distinct vampires one of which currently stood on stage. His heart clenched in his chest, threatening to stop its beating as he realized Katrina may be in danger. He berated himself to not being more vigilant and monitoring the club all evening. He should have known there were other vampires in the building. He'd allowed his feelings for Katrina to distract him.

It will not happen again, he vowed to himself

Marcus, we need to get Kat out of here, now, before he sees her or recognizes one of us, Stephan ordered. Marcus' concern passed across the mindlink, flooding Stephan with dread.

I agree. Marcus nodded his head.

Stephan leaned over and whispered into Kat's ear. "We need to leave, sweetheart."

"Why?" Kat looked at him questioningly, the smile fading from her lips.

"That egg is one of Lucio's men. We need to get out of here before he realizes who we are." Stephan pulled the red hood over Kat's blonde locks. Tucked it around her face, relieved her costume had come with a mask. She held the hood closed at her chin with one hand as her other hand found his.

After sliding from the booth and leaving a generous tip, the group made its way toward the exit. Marcus and Stephan flanked Katrina on each side with Nicholai taking up the rear of the group. He glanced several times at the stage as they made their way out of the club to be sure the vampire didn't notice them.

Stephan knew it was a bad idea to go out. He had said as much to Kat and Marcus, but he allowed his emotions for Kat to overrule his common sense. He silently cursed himself for allowing her to be placed in potential danger once again. His mind dreamt up all kinds of scary scenarios which could have happened if Gage's guard had spotted them. For all he knew, other guards might be watching them while they stood waiting for the valet to bring his car around. He scanned the surrounding area looking for anything out of the ordinary.

As he kept a wary eye out for trouble, he realized that as long as Gage was alive his Katrina would never be safe. He would forever be looking over his shoulder. Stephan turned toward Nicholai. "Contact Demetri and ask him to meet us at the penthouse. We need to talk."

Chapter 31

The car ride back to the penthouse had been a silent sprint. Stephan wove in and out of traffic, his only concern getting back to the relative safety of his home. He wanted Kat tucked away safe from the potential eyes of his enemy. As he drove, he kept a wary eye on the rear view mirror the entire ride, watching for any signs that they were being followed.

Stephan ruminated on the close call while he, Nicholai, and Marcus sat in the living room facing each other. No one spoke. Each warrior seemed lost in his own thoughts about the female who stood out on the terrace taking in deep gulps of air. With her arms wrapped around her chest, she stared out over the strip.

Stephan tore his eyes away from his lover. "What did Demetri say when you contacted him, Nicholai?"

"He was with Vlad. They were going to pick up Alex on the way here."

Marcus crossed his leg bringing his ankle to rest on his opposite knee. "So when are the other Alphas due to arrive?"

As if in answer to Marcus' question, the buzzer rang, and Stephan went to usher the new arrivals into the penthouse. He opened the heavy door wide and greeted the three males standing on the other side in the way of warriors, by clasping each one in turn by the forearms. Demetri entered first quietly making his way to the living room to join Nicholai and Marcus.

Alexander Hall was the next to enter. The youngest of the Alphas at barely over one hundred years old, he wore jeans and a T-shirt. After shrugging out of his leather jacket, he ran a hand through his short blond hair. He was unusually silent as he made his way toward the living room.

Vladimir Starikovich followed him through the door and into the living room. Unlike Alexander, Vladimir was a man of few words. While not the biggest man on the team, he was very strong and cunning. Living in Siberia taught him survival skills none of the others had. Skills which had come in handy more than once. He wore his black hair cut in a military crew style and dressed in all black that would, if needed, allow him to slip into a shadow becoming nothing more than darkness.

After greeting his fellow Alphas, Vlad sunk into one of the black leather couches, careful to position himself toward an exit. Stephan watched the six-foot-six Siberian warrior rub his stubbled head, then clasp his hands behind it.

Alex grasped Stephan then Marcus by the forearms and said "It is good to see ya, friends." His southern twang drew the last word out making it sing-songy.

"It's good to see you both," said Marcus, glancing from Alexander to Vladimir.

"Da, I agree," Vlad replied efficiently, as was his way.

"Hey, where's Michael?" asked Alexander taking notice of the only missing Alpha.

Stephan straightened. "My plane was delayed in Savannah due to the weather, so Michael will not be able to join us this evening."

"Michael always was the last to arrive," observed Vlad, his thick Siberian accent making the W's sound like V's.

"That's true," agreed Stephan. "Let me get right to the point."

The Alphas listened while he succinctly relayed the events of the past few days, beginning with the confrontation with Gage and ending with the costume contest. Vlad nodded at Demetri with respect when Stephan relayed how the Alpha had rescued Katrina from being abducted.

Alex smiled knowingly at Stephan when he talked about Kat, probably because his voice went soft when he spoke her name. He couldn't help it. He was in love. And Alex apparently approved.

"So where do we go from here, comrade?" asked Demetri leaning forward to rest his thick forearms on his thighs.

"I'm not sure. Do you have any ideas?" Stephan asked.

Demetri nodded. "I suggest you convert her to make her stronger, less vulnerable."

Alexander gestured at the portrait of vampiric Kat hanging on the wall with a jerk of his thumb. "I thought she was a vampire."

"No. She is mortal," Marcus informed Alex.

Alexander looked perplexed. "But you said she fought one of Gage's guards."

A prideful look adorned Stephan's face. "She did. Marcus has been teaching her how to fight. But she was lucky, caught the male off guard. If Demetri hadn't arrived when he did, I'm afraid things would have turned out much different." Bile rose from his stomach.

"That's why you should convert her," Demetri repeated.

"I don't know. I don't think Kat will go for that," assumed Marcus.

Stephan raised an eyebrow. "Have you spoken with her before about converting?"

"No, but I've known her for a long time. I can't imagine she would be willing to be drained. She has a phobia about such things."

Stephan nodded in agreement. "I've been in her head. I know how much she is frightened of the idea of someone drinking from her. I don't think she will want to do what is necessary to turn."

"Why don't you just force her?" Demetri said with an incredulous voice, as he leaned back against the couch and crossed his arms across his chest. "Why give her a choice in the matter? Simply decide what is best, then take care of your mate. Once it is done, she will learn to accept it."

"First of all, I have more respect for her feelings then to force the conversion on her." Anger furrowed his brows as Stephan explained. "And secondly, I don't know for sure that she is my mate."

"You mean you haven't drunk from her yet?" asked Alex, his eyes wide in astonishment.

Vlad cursed in Russian and scrubbed a thoughtful hand over the scruff of his dark goatee.

"No, I haven't," admitted Stephan, straightening his spine in defiance. "As I said, she has a phobia about anyone drinking from her, and I have respected her wishes by not taking from her vein." Stephan swung a pointed glance toward Marcus when Vlad shook his head in disbelief.

Ever the warrior, Demetri suggested, "If she will not convert, then I suggest we remove the threat and take out Gage."

Stephan looked to Demetri. Now that was a suggestion he would entertain. He nodded his head slowly. "That may be our only option."

****

Kat stood out on the terrace, the cool air chilling her to the bone, and tried to calm her turbulent feelings. The emotions seemed strange, as if they belonged to someone else. She felt anxious, vengeful. A desperate fear crept up her spine, sending tiny shivers throughout her body.

She replayed the previous night's events and the hairs on the back of her neck rose. If Demetri hadn't arrived in time, she would have died at the hands of the guard. She knew she owed Demetri her life, and she had yet to thank him. She silently chastised herself for ever fearing him. She now realized that he was willing to put his own safety at risk to protect her, keep her safe. She owed him a thank you, and she intended to give it to him now before she lost her courage to face him.

Kat squared her shoulders, opened the sliding glass door and stepped into the living room. The presence of power hit her squarely as she entered, practically knocking her back on her heels. As she crossed the room, all eyes turned on her, pinning her under their intense gaze.

"Hello," she said hesitantly, then allowed Stephan to gather her to his side.

"Hello, sweetheart." He gave her waist a squeeze.

"I believe there are some people here who you have not met yet. This is Alexander Hall."

"Hello, Alexander." Katrina extended her hand to the handsome blond.

"Hello, Miss Katrina. It's nice to meet ya." Alex stood and shook her hand with vigor as he gave a broad smile that flashed his perfect white teeth. "And please, call me Alex."

"And this is Vladimir Starikovich," Stephan said when Kat released Alex's hand.

She looked over at the man sitting on the couch. Vlad was leanly muscular; well defined, but not bulky. The black T-shirt and jeans he wore hugged his body showing off his muscles in a way Kat found rather sexy. With his angular face and goatee, he looked like the devil himself as he leaned back in his seat, his long legs stretched out before him crossed at the ankles.

Vlad stood, took her hand, and bowed deeply in courtly greeting over her hand. "Salutations," he said simply, before he sank back down onto the padded black leather.

"Nice to meet you," she murmured, feeling a stir in the air, like something crawling over her skin. It made her uncomfortable.

Kat looked up into her lover's eyes. She'd had every intention of thanking Demetri, but she instinctually knew now was not the time. "I can see you all are talking. I was just passing through on my way upstairs. It's been a long night. I thought I'd go take a bath."

"Of course, Kitten. I'll join you soon." Stephan gave her a quick kiss on her forehead before releasing her.

Demetri watched Kat ascend the staircase and disappear from sight. "There may be another option," he said quietly.

"What would that be?" asked Stephan, hope lightening his voice.

"We could send her away. Keep her somewhere safe."

Stephan rubbed his chin. Before he could respond, Marcus said, "No. No, I won't let you send her away." Fear thickened his voice and it dropped to a menacing tone.

Nicholai raised a hand toward Marcus. "I think we need to hear all options," he said sensibly. "I believe it is called brain-squalling."

A smile took Alex's face. "I think you mean brainstorming."

"Yes, that is what I meant, brainstorming," Nicholai looked back at Stephan.

The warrior nodded his head once, knowing the Alpha's suggestion made sense. "Of course you are right, Nicholai. There's no harm in hearing ideas. Go ahead, Demetri."

"If we were to send her away, it would keep her safe from the threats in our world and give us time to deal with Gage."

Vladimir spoke up. "Demetri makes sense. If she will not convert so she can be strong and safe, then send her away where she *will* be safe."

Stephan murmured, "It is the fact that she has been drawn into our dark world that has made her unsafe." His eyes found the vampire he had sired. "Marcus, can't you see that?"

Marcus lowered his eyes to the ground. Like a

stubborn child, he refused to agree.

"Where could we send her?" asked Demetri.

"I know of a place. I have a friend with a ranch in Utah. I could see if she could go there. Rusty is trustworthy and always looking for help on the ranch," Alex offered.

Marcus straightened in his chair. "That won't work. We can't send her away. She'll miss us and want to come back."

Stephan began to pace as he murmured, "Right back into the dangers of our world."

"That is why her memory will need to be wiped," Demetri reasoned.

Marcus' eyes widened, his hands fisted by his sides. "You mean wipe all her memories of us. That's seven years of memories. It's too dangerous. It could destroy her mind."

"I don't know if I can do that." Stephan raked a hand down his handsome face. Erase her memories. Memories of him. Of their time together.

"If you don't know how, comrade, I can do it for you," offered Demetri, obviously misunderstanding his reluctance.

"No," Stephan bit out between clenched teeth, his jaw muscle twitching. He would never allow anyone else to enter her mind that deeply. He trusted no one but himself to do the deed if it had to be done—not that he wanted to do it. "If it must be done, I'll be the one to do it."

Both Marcus and Demetri were correct, if he didn't erase her memories of them, it wouldn't matter where they sent her, Kat would come right back to their dangerous world.

"Maybe it won't be necessary. Maybe she would be willing to convert," Marcus offered, a hopeful look on his face.

Nicholai clasped a hand down on Stephan's shoulder. "In the words of Emerson, give all to love; obey thy heart." Stephan looked at Nicholai in confusion. "In other words do what you have to do for the one you love, even though it may not be easy." After he nodded his understanding, Nicholai continued, "I am sorry you have such a difficult decision. I hope she will convert for you. I do not envy your tasks."

"I'll talk to her tonight and ask her to convert. If she refuses, then I'll call Alex and he can arrange a safe place for her to go." Stephan desperately hoped her love for him would be strong enough to convince her to convert if for no other reason than to be with him for centuries, but knowing how deeply rooted her phobia was, he tried to resign himself to accept the plan Fate had in store for him—whatever it may be. He glanced in the direction of his bedroom, apprehension twisting his gut.

Chapter 32

Kat stood in the bathroom wrapped in a white, cotton towel and placed her toothbrush back in its holder. The stereo in the bedroom played lightly in the background. Humming softly to the music, she leaned forward against the vanity letting it support her. She struggled with her emotions, tried to sort them out. All evening her feelings had been changing like a kaleidoscope, one moment she experienced fear and trepidation the next she would feel protective, and then worried and sad. It was a confusing mix that somehow did not quite feel like her own. She shook her head, in an attempt to shake the latest feeling of apprehension away.

She walked out into the bedroom and found Stephan sitting on the bed. He patted the mattress next to him.

"Come sit please, Katrina. I need to talk to you."

She sat beside him on the bed, the mattress barely registering her weight.

"I have been wanting to talk to you too, Stephan."

Stephan covered her hand with his. "You first, *schatz*."

"I've been feeling so strange lately. I get these sensations, feelings. They don't seem like my own." Confusion thickened her voice. "I've been feeling conflicted, and then fearful and protective, and now sad."

Stephan's eyes widen slightly. "And love," he added. Kat nodded. "I believe you are probably feeling my emotions. It's from the blood exchange. My blood is now a part of you. It has permeated every cell and what you are feeling are my emotions. I'll forever be a part of you."

"Oh," Kat murmured her eyes down cast. "I didn't know that was possible." Stephan gave her a moment to digest what he had said while he placed his arm around her shoulders.

"It's okay, Kitten. You'll get used to it. Eventually you'll be able to know which feelings are mine and which are yours. Don't let it scare you."

Katrina's mind turned that bit of information over. Knowing how someone else felt, especially the man she loved, might not be such a bad thing. She would never have to wonder if he told her the truth. Most men had a hard time discussing their feelings, at least this way she would always know what Stephan felt whether or not he spoke them aloud. This definitely had advantages Katrina decided.

She looked at him from beneath her long lashes. "You said you wanted to talk to me," she reminded him, when she remembered he'd initiated this conversation.

Stephan took a deep breath before he spoke. "Kat, I love you, and I want us to spend the rest of our lives together…" His voice trailed off as if he waited for her to absorb what he said.

"But…" she prompted.

She watched him swallow, seemingly to gather his courage to continue. "No buts. I love you, and I want to spend the rest of our lives together."

"Oh Stephan!" Kat wrapped her arms around him and gave him a tight squeeze. "I love you too. Of course I want to spend the rest of my life with you!"

He pulled back slightly and looked into her eyes. "I'm relieved to hear you say that."

"You're relieved? But I can feel you are still troubled."

Stephan dropped one arm to the mattress. "Sweetheart, I need to talk to you about something. I can't imagine watching you grow old and die. It would break my heart. When I speak of being together for the rest of our lives, I want that to be centuries. I need to know if you would be willing to convert."

"Convert? You mean like become a vampire?" She worried her lower lip between her teeth.

"Yes." His face remained expressionless. "Yes, I mean become a vampire. Would you be willing to do that?"

She thought for a moment, her mind racing. "Tell me how it is done."

He turned toward her on the bed, and took both her hands into his much larger ones. "The way to convert is for me to take your blood from you as you take mine from me, creating a transfusion of sorts. Slowly the virus that causes vampirism would ease into your blood. It would be absorbed by your body and cause changes in your DNA."

"Will it hurt?"

He squeezed her hands before continuing. "Kat, I won't lie to you. The changes will be painful. It will hurt a lot."

"But you have taken my pain away before?"

"Yes. I would be here with you, taking as much of your pain as I can, but when I have eased your pain in the past, it was because I healed you. As your wounds mended the pain went away. This process is different. I cannot heal you from this. There will be no wounds. Every cell, muscle, even your organs will change from the virus and that I cannot heal. I will shoulder what pain I can, but there will not be much I can do. There will be much pain."

Kat stilled, tension tightening her shoulders. "So once I became a vampire, I would have to drink blood like you and Marcus?"

"Yes, you would. The virus changes our muscles, causing them to grow stronger by creating more muscle fibers. Those muscles require more blood so it enlarges our hearts to pump the extra blood throughout our bodies. Our bodies do not make enough blood on their own to sustain the changes so we must consume the blood our cells and tissues require. The virus will also shrink your stomach to make room for your larger heart. The smaller stomach makes it impossible to eat large quantities of food. Therefore, the blood you consume will also help provide the nourishment you will no longer get from food."

Kat pulled her hands from Stephan and wrung them nervously in her lap. Her heart rate increased, stomach tightened.

"And you would have to drink from me, to convert me?" she asked nervously, her voice but a whisper.

"Yes, that is how it is done."

Kat once again became pensive, her eyes downcast. Stephan stilled beside her, awaiting her decision. Could she become a vampire? Not aging, a plus. Extra strength, also a plus. Allowing him to drink from her? The thought of it turned her stomach. Bile pushed into her throat. Her heart raced, panicked breaths left her body in short bursts.

Decision made, she looked back up at him from under her lashes dark with unshed tears threatening to spill from her eyes. "I'm sorry, I just can't. I can't have anyone drink from me, even you, Stephan. It's too scary." Her tears burned her eyes as the lump formed in her throat. "I want to be with you, but I don't want to be a vampire." The tears began to fall.

"I could give you more time to consider this," he kindly offered. "You don't have to answer tonight."

She loved him dearly, but she didn't need more time. Time wouldn't overcome her fear. They would have a human lifetime; that would have to somehow be enough.

"All the time in the world wouldn't matter. I can't do it. I'm so sorry." Tears streaked down both her cheeks.

"It's all right, Kitten," He gathered her into his arms. After he placed his chin on top of her head, he stroked the long silken strands that flowed down her back. "It's okay, you don't have to convert," he whispered.

Slowly Stephan's eyelids lowered to contain the emotions that suffocated him. If she wouldn't convert, that left him only one choice. He would have to keep her safe the only other way he knew, he would have to send her away. With her memory wiped, it would be easy for her to live away from him, only he would have to suffer. And he loved her enough to willingly suffer any torment to keep her safe.

Katrina pulled back and gently cupped his chin in the palm of her hand. "Look at me, my love," she said gently. "I can feel your sadness. We will be okay. I promise. Who knows, maybe in a few years I'll feel differently."

Stephan opened his eyes slowly, realizing that she would not understand why he felt so distraught. He pushed into her mind to glean her thoughts. Kat's only concern was for him. She wanted to make him happy, wanted to erase the internment of the emotions consuming him. She may not fully understand the reason behind his dark mood, but she was determined to ease his suffering.

As the song, *In the Air Tonight* played sultrily in the background, she began feathering soft kisses in a trail up his neck. By the time she reached his lips, his mouth met hers with a fiery passion. He poured all of his love for her into that kiss. His emotions were too raw. He couldn't be gentle. He needed to be fierce, almost punishing, and Kat reveled in every second of the kiss.

He allowed his emotions to engulf her, consume her, igniting her own fiery passion. His emotions flowed into her until he could not tell where his ended and hers began. They became one and the rest of the world melted away.

One hand slid up her thigh under the towel while the other grabbed the corner and pulled it from her, letting it pool on the floor. Her hands worked his clothing. In their frenzy, together they unbuttoned his shirt so she could slide it off his shoulders before she helped him from his pants.

She slid down his body coming to rest before him

on her knees. His erect shaft jumped when she took it into her hand and leaned forward. Kat licked the length of him, swirling her tongue around his sensitive tip while her hand worked up and down in a tantalizing rhythm. Up and down, in and out. The combination nearly drove him out of his mind. She worked him masterfully, making his body burn each time he plunged into the scalding cavern of heat and fire. She built speed. The combination of suckling and rubbing caused him to throw his head back and growl with need.

His hand fisted in her silky strands, hips worked in time with her hot mouth. She swirled her tongue around his shaft and settled into a fast rhythm of licks, nibbles, and forceful pulls that made him harden further. His stomach tightened with his need as the climax started to build. He pulled from her scorching mouth before he embarrassed himself.

Stephan grabbed her under her arms and raised her to her feet before him. Taking control, he bent and suckled at her breast. Her nipple pebbled against his tongue as he slid one hand slowly along her stomach. He traced the lines of each hip bone before resting his hand at the juncture of her thighs. She opened her legs for him, pushing against his hand as if needing the contact. He found her ready and wet for him. Two fingers glided into her velvet folds and he rubbed tiny circles with his thumb on her sensitive nub. When she began to writhe, his free hand grabbed her buttocks, holding her still for his ministrations. She clung to his strong shoulders. It felt good having her nails digging into his flesh, and he welcomed the pain as an expression of his inner turmoil. He gently nibbled her nipple, causing her to thrash her head from side to side from the pleasure, a small mewing sound escaping her throat.

"Please," she breathed, pleading for more. He willingly gave it to her, wanting to make this evening perfect for her. He brought her over the edge for the first of what he knew would be many times that night. She trembled in his arms when the spasms racked her body.

In the blink of her eye, he had her up on the bed on her hands and knees with him behind her. He sat back on his heels, running his hands roughly along the sides of her body until they rested on each hip. Kat looked over her shoulder at him, her eyes dark with passion.

"Please, take me," she whispered.

He did not need a second invitation. Stephan happily obliged, entering her with one swift thrust that made her arch back toward him. A delicious moan escaped her kiss-swollen lips as he drove into her. Their flesh pounded, the sound drowning out the music playing in the background.

She met him thrust for thrust, their intensity increasing as did the pressure in her. He brought one hand around and began once again rubbing tiny circles on the most sensitive spot between her folds. She straightened, leaning back against him, the angle changing the pressure where they were coupled. He felt another orgasm take her, those velvet folds gripped him like a silken vice.

While she cried out his name, he released her hips and ran both hands up her body until they found her breasts. Slowing the rhythm, he began to knead her breasts in time to his thrusts. He leaned his head and whispered, so his hot breath would ghost over her ear. "You're so beautiful."

He kissed a sultry trail down her neck. When he reached the spot where her shoulder met her neck, his teeth slid down from his gums. His mouth watered as he carefully kissed her pulse, feeling it beat under his lips. His body wanted desperately to taste of her, just a small taste would be enough to know if she was his heartmate. Every instinct in him screamed for him to take her properly and bite into her, but instead he separated their bodies and willed his teeth to retract, for knowing she was his heartmate would not make what waited in their future any easier.

He lay down on his back, and brought her to rest astride him, the sensuous sight taking all other thoughts from his head. Her golden hair enveloped their heads, veiling them from the world. Everything became about her. Every thought, every sensation. Her. She surrounded him until he no longer knew where he stopped and she began.

She braced herself with her hands on his chest as she slid up and down his thick shaft. Each slip brought a new sensation of pleasure racing through his body. Their breath came faster now as he leaned up and captured one of her ample breasts in his mouth. She increased their pace, making him buck beneath her. His hand bit into her hips, and she rode him like a rodeo bronco. Her silken folds tightened around him, indicating she was close to tumbling over the edge once again. She pushed off his chest, arching back when the next orgasm took her. He growled and continued pumping wildly into her, letting her slick muscles milk him into his own release.

Completely sated, Kat slumped over him. They lay together, still joined, trying to catch their breaths. Neither spoke. They simply lay together until Kat fell asleep. Then Stephan gently separated their bodies and rolled her off to his side. He covered them both with the smooth cool sheet as he gazed down on her thinking how much he wished there was another way to keep her safe.

Stephan slid from between the silky covers leaving Kat to her dreams. After dressing, he padded downstairs on soundless feet to discover Marcus sat alone in the dark living room. He slumped down onto the couch across from his fellow Alpha.

"Well," Marcus asked, hope widening his eyes, "how did it go?"

"She won't convert," Stephan replied. The agony washed over his face when the full weight of that simple statement fell heavily on his shoulders.

"How did you present the conversion?" Marcus inquired, alarm raising the tone of his voice.

Stephan efficiently relayed the story of how he had asked Kat to convert. Marcus nodded his head silently when Stephan finished his tale.

"Tell me what you are going to do," he demanded wearily.

"I only see one thing I can do. The only option is to wipe her memory of us and send her away." Stephan sighed, a look of resignation clouded his face as he crossed his arms across his wide chest.

"When are you going to do it?"

"Tomorrow evening." Marcus opened his mouth to protest when Stephan cut him off explaining, "There's no point in waiting. It won't hurt any less if we wait."

Marcus sunk into himself.

What are you thinking, Marcus?

You are in my mind. I don't need to say it.

He didn't. It was all there for Stephan to see. Marcus loved Katrina dearly, cared about her deeply. He couldn't imagine his life without her shining face and bubbly personality to bring him happiness. She was his friend, his confidante, and he loved her in his own way, perhaps not as much as Stephan, but he loved her none the less. The thought of losing her, never seeing her again, ripped out his heart. But he also knew Stephan was right, it would only hurt more the longer they waited.

Stephan pulled from his mind, no longer able to bear his friends feelings which so closely mirrored his own. He watched Marcus in silence. The downtrodden look on his face reflected the one Stephan wore. Both males radiated hurt and sadness as they thought about the inevitable. Stephan knew neither of them wanted to do what was necessary to keep Katrina safe. It was only the knowledge that she would be safe that even allowed Stephan to contemplate such an atrocity.

But Stephan knew they could not be selfish. They had to have the courage to let her go. At least she would be alive, without them, but alive none the less. And her safety had to be put above all else, no matter how much it hurt them to do so.

Stephan looked at Marcus and asked, "Do you have your cell phone on you?"

"Yeah. You need it?" Marcus dug it out of his pocket and tossed it to Stephan.

He flipped open the phone and punched in the memorized number. After a few rings, a familiar voice picked up.

"Hey Alex, it's Stephan…Yeah unfortunately it looks like we're going to need your friend…You're sure it will be safe? …Thank you, that would be great…tomorrow evening. I'll arrange to have her brought to the ranch…And Alex, thanks again."

Marcus said, "So I take it she is going there tomorrow?"

"Yes. Alexander is going to make all the necessary arrangements with his friend for us," Stephan said solemnly snapping the cell phone shut and tossing it back to his friend.

Marcus easily caught the phone and placed it back into his pocket. "I can't believe this is happening so soon."

"I wish it didn't have to happen at all, but it is for her own good," Stephan countered. After swallowing the lump in his throat, he continued, "For tonight, I just want to hold her."

Marcus nodded. "I know what you mean," he agreed.

"I know you do, my friend. You understand better than anyone else how difficult this decision is. I realize this is hurting you as much as it's hurting me."

Marcus nodded his head. "It's killing me."

With nothing more to say, the two warriors went their separate ways to retire for the day, Marcus to his room and Stephan up the stairs. They parted in silence, each consumed by their grief at the loss that was to come.

Back upstairs, Stephan grabbed Kat and brought her against him, squeezing her tightly as he realized this would be their last day together. Kat groaned.

"Stephan," she whispered, pushing back slightly, her hands against his chest. "You're squishing me."

He stiffened slightly when he realized he'd been so rough, and immediately softened his hold. She turned in his arms so she faced away from him, and he engulfed her, drawing her back against his chest. He placed one of his thick thighs over her legs protectively, as she pillowed her head on his outstretched arm. He gently laid his free arm across her chest before burying his nose in her hair, deeply inhaling her honeysuckle scent, trying to take her essence into his soul so she would always be a part of him.

While he lay beside her, he tried to absorb every nuance. He lightly trailed his fingers along her body attempting to memorize each curve, the softness of her skin. He forced himself to remain awake all day so he would not miss one minute of the last few hours with her.

He lamented throughout the day about the decision. Erasing that many memories was not without danger. He would be rearranging her mind and that ran a risk of doing irrevocable damage. He racked his brain trying to come up with another way to keep his love safe.

As he felt dusk approaching, having not come up with another alternative, the time had come. He slipped into her mind while she slept and began the arduous task of changing her memories. Some he erased, others he altered. Finally, he added memories of waking up in a hospital after having been in a coma for years and being excited about starting a new life on a ranch.

The exhausting work completed, he stared down at the woman he loved, knowing her love for him vanished with her memories. He could only hope he had not accidentally done any damage that would take away the core of who she was. Silent tears fell from his eyes to wet her face as he pushed back into her mind once again to command her to sleep until he awakened her.

Chapter 33

Michael Garsoe glanced over as the Alpha leader lowered a sleeping Kat into the passenger seat of his rental car. He took note of her shapely, long legs that peeked out from under her slightly bunched skirt and the blonde hair that flowed around her shoulders in golden waves. Though he usually preferred redheads, he couldn't help but notice Kat looked exceptionally beautiful sitting in the seat beside him.

Michael glanced up at Stephan questioningly. "So what's the cover story?"

Stephan rested a forearm on the door jam and leaned down over Kat, handing a piece of paper to Michael. "I implanted the memory that she had a car accident shortly after she arrived here in Vegas. She will think she's been in a coma for the past seven years because of the accident. You are the psychiatrist who has been helping her to recover.

"You, Doctor Garsoe, know the person who owns the ranch in Utah and you've arranged for her to live there and work so she can make a fresh start. The directions are on the paper I just gave you. Just take Highway 15 out of the city. The ranch isn't too far across the Utah border."

Stephan leaned in the car, clicking Katrina's seatbelt into place.

"Gotcha," said Michael.

"All right." Stephan ran the backs of his fingers down her cheek. "As you drive away I'll release her from her sleep."

Michael nodded in understanding. "As soon as she wakes up I'll start talking to her about the ranch. I'll pretend to be her doctor and keep the cover story. Do you mind telling me why we are doing all this?"

Michael noted the gathering of moisture in the Alpha's eyes. "I'll tell you when you get back. Time is ticking away. You need to be getting on the road."

Stephan shut the door, and Michael brought the engine to life. He eased the rentd SUV out into traffic, watching Stephan in the rearview. The warrior's face wore a painful look as he stood watching the car roll away.

Michael knew the reason he'd been chosen for this assignment was because Kat had never met him, so seeing him now would not jog any memories in her mind. However, knowing that did not make his mood any better.

His flight landed in Vegas less than an hour ago and now instead of checking into a hotel to sleep off his jet lag, he was on the road doing an errand for Stephan that would take several hours. It was all extremely irritating. He rolled his eyes in perturbation.

Katrina stirred, languidly blinking the sleep from her eyes. She turned her head slowly toward the person beside her. The man behind the wheel glanced over at her and smiled.

"Hello, Miss Spencer," he said easily, as if they were old friends. "Did you have a nice nap?" When Kat did not respond he continued. "It should not be too long until we get to the ranch."

"Okay," she replied hesitantly. Kat's eyes closed once again, and she tried to make sense of the jumbled thoughts in her head.

She remembered awakening in the hospital and being told she'd been in a coma for seven years. Despite Dr. Garsoe's assurances, things didn't quite add up. She'd awakened to an implausible story and yet every time she tried to think things through her head would hurt and an overwhelming desire to believe her doctor came over her, pushing all thoughts from her mind. She had some vague recollections of strange memories involving vampires, but she had been reassured by her doctor that they were just hallucinations she experienced during her coma. He told her that it wasn't unusual for people in comas to have strange dreams and perhaps even believe them to be real. It was her doctor who had said that. The man who sat beside her.

She felt desperate, sad, utterly alone. Tears pushed into her eyes. The feelings made no sense, almost as if they were not her own. She shouldn't feel lonely. The only person she knew sat right beside her. And when she thought about the life she was about to begin she felt excited, not sad and yet a tear escaped down her cheek.

Kat slowly opened her eyes and wiped away the lone tear. Gazing forlornly out the window, she tried to come to grips with the fact that she was about to embark on a brand new life, not remembering anything of the past seven years.

As if reading her mind, Dr. Garsoe reached over and patted her hand resting on her knee. "Don't worry if you don't remember all the details, Miss Spencer. It's not unusual for patients such as yourself to forget things after awakening from a coma."

"I know, doctor." Kat bit her lower lip. "I just…It's hard to accept what happened."

He patted her hand once again. "I know. We'll get you to the ranch, and you'll live the life the Fates wanted you to have."

Strange turn of a phrase, she thought as she settled back into the seat. He tried to assure her, but the thought of going to live somewhere she would not know anyone seemed a little daunting.

They rode the rest of the way in comfortable silence, much to her appreciation. With a fluid turn of the steering wheel, they pulled onto a driveway through the weathered fencing that lined both sides of the drive. The tires crunched on the gravel driveway while they traveled up the drive.

Kat watched the split rail fence roll by. She spotted a group of horses grazing and watched as a black and white foal ran along the fence trying his best to keep up with the car. A smile lit her face for the first time that evening.

Kat's gaze shifted to take in the rest of the ranch as they rolled to a stop. It looked immense. She didn't know how many acres, but the fencing went on further than she could see. An impressive two story wooden house sat in front of the Utah mountain range, with a pitched slate roof and square windows through which yellow light poured from the home.

Out came a balding, potbellied man, dressed in jeans and a flannel shirt with a dark beard that outlined the jolly smile on his face. His perfect teeth seemed to shine in the twilight. Reaching the car, he opened the door swiftly and said, "Welcome. I'm Rusty Willis, the owner of this ranch. I'll bet you're Katrina Spencer."

"Yes, that's one of the few things I still remember." She flashed him a weak grin of her own.

"Oh honey, if I could lose some of my memory, I think I'd be happy. I can think of a couple of years I wouldn't mind getting rid of." He laughed, and she exited the car. "You got any luggage?"

The doctor unfolded from the SUV and made his way around to the back before answering the rancher, "Yes. It's in the trunk."

He quickly popped the hatch and handed the bags to the ranch owner. When Rusty took her luggage, Katrina noticed how easily he lifted the heavy bags. It occurred to her that he must have developed great strength working on the ranch all these years.

Maybe working on the ranch would be good for her. She could develop her strength too, although she found herself in surprisingly great shape for someone who had been in a coma for seven years. She must have gotten some physical therapy while she was unconscious.

She watched Rusty head toward the house with a bag in each hand, amazed that all her belongings fit in only two bags. She remembered being told by Dr. Garsoe that her items had been sent to storage when it didn't look like she would be coming out of the coma any time soon. She supposed she should just be glad anything had been saved for seven years.

Kat followed Rusty into the house, and suddenly remembered she'd forgotten to thank Dr. Garsoe. She turned on her heels and waved at the doctor with a hopeful expression on her face. "Bye, Dr. Garsoe.

Thank you, again."

Her doctor glanced at her briefly and entered the vehicle. "Goodbye, Miss Spencer," he said curtly, closing the door behind him.

He tore off down the driveway, the tires spitting gravel in his haste.

Katrina's stomach dropped as she watched the only person she knew leave her sight. She wrapped her arms around her waist in a bracing hug. *All right girl, this is it, the beginning of your new life. Just put one foot in front of the other. You can do this.*

She turned and found Rusty staring down at her from the porch in expectation.

"Come on in, Miss Spencer," Rusty said. The look of pity on his face said he noticed the tears in her eyes.

"Please call me Kat." She hoped her voice sounded surer then she felt and blinked the tears away.

"Very well, Kat. Come on in, and I'll show you to your room. I'm sure you would like to get some sleep. It's late."

"But it's only ten."

"You know the saying, early to bed, early to rise. We go to bed early 'round here because we start at the crack of dawn."

Rusty led her through a sparsely decorated living room. Wood paneling lined the walls. A matching set of red couches sat in an L-shape with identical end tables sitting by each arm. The carpeting, tan to match the walls, had a worn trail that led down the hall.

They made their way down the hall, and Katrina thought to ask, "What time should I set the alarm for?"

"Five a.m. would be good," the ranch owner informed her, opening a door off the hall.

Kat hid her grimace when she entered behind Rusty into a bedroom. If she thought the living room was sparsely decorated, it was nothing compared to the perfunctory bedroom. In the room, two twin beds sat across from each other next to short dressers, each with three drawers. A fan hung from the ceiling, its center globe producing the only light in the room.

Beggars can't be choosers, she reminded herself when tears welled up once more.

She couldn't stop the flood of depression and sorrow that flowed through her. She chastised herself for the self-pity. She should feel grateful for the opportunity, excited for the new adventure she was about to embark on, but instead an overwhelming sadness threatened to consume her, almost as if the emotion wasn't her own.

"So here's the room. I know it's not much, but at the end of a long day all you'll care about is that you have a bed. Not to mention you're welcome to make this room your own. Add any little touches you'd like." Rusty glanced her way, a worried look raising his brows. "Please don't cry, darlin'. I hate to see a woman cry. There is nothing that makes a man feel inept faster than seeing a woman cry."

"Thank you, Mr. Willis." Kat forced a smile. "I'm good."

She wiped the tears from her eyes, unsure why they were there.

"Call me Rusty, hun. Everyone does." He returned her smile after giving her an assessing look. "If there's nothing else you need, I'll leave you to unpack. The bathroom is two doors down on the left. I'll see you in the morning."

"Thank you."

Kat quietly unpacked, donned a nightgown and crawled into bed. Bereavement pushed in on her, when she thought she should be excited. She looked forward to the morning, when she would begin her new life and learn all about ranching. And yet her emotions didn't seem to match her thoughts. She tucked the confusion away to examine later. For now, she needed sleep.

She lay in bed trying to turn her mind off, but found it impossible. As if her body was on a different schedule, it refused to settle. She rolled over onto her back and stared at the fan watching as it rotated above her. A heavy sigh pushed from her lungs. It was going to be a long night.

****

The engine of Michael's rented SUV whined as he sped down the highway. He had been instructed to let Stephan know when Kat had been delivered safely to the ranch so he took out his cell phone and dialed the Alpha's number.

"Is it done?" Stephan asked him curtly.

"Yes. I dropped her off a few minutes ago."

"And was she…" his voice hitched, "okay when you left her?"

"Yeah, safe and sound." The phone went dead.

"Hello… Stephan?" How rude! He slammed the phone down into the console.

Earlier in the evening, he'd been irritated by the inconvenience but now absolute fury at the lack of appreciation from Stephan heated his blood. His ears grew hot when he thought about how Stephan had not asked him about the trip to the ranch or anything about how he was doing. The guy didn't even thank him for going out of his way by heading all the way to Utah, just to do the Alpha leader a favor and that exasperated him the most.

It wasn't his fault weather delayed his flight so he was the only Alpha that Stephan's female friend didn't know. It also wasn't his fault that a mechanical issue kept him from arriving in time to attend the meeting of the Council. And it certainly wasn't his fault that he didn't know that blonde, but yet somehow he ended up being called upon by Stephan to do all the work in relocating her.

Stephan had been curt, barely telling him anything other than get this person to this place. Anger and frustration prickled his skin with heat, and he needed an outlet for the pent up energy.

The thought of going to a casino briefly flickered across his mind, but he swept it away, knowing that in his mood he would most likely make careless mistakes and lose all his money. But he wasn't ready to go back to his hotel room either.

As he drove down Highway 15, he lowered the windows in the vehicle. The wind whistled through the compartment, flowing over him, causing his dark hair to whip around his face. He loved the way the speed felt, the hum of the engine, the vibration of the road coupled with the cool night air. His tension began to ebb.

Michael noted the scenery and struggled to remember why the road seemed so recognizable to him. Memories of a time long ago began to play in his head while he continued down the interstate. Though he'd never been to Vegas before, he definitely remembered having been in Nevada. Then it came to him. Many years ago, before he became an Alpha, he attended a party here.

Pleasant memories brought a fond smile to his face. He knew someone who lived off the highway and that, he decided, was just the diversion he needed for his frustration. An old friend to get reacquainted with, to relive fond memories, would indeed be an excellent diversion, Michael decided, turning off Highway 15 just outside of Vegas.

Fifteen minutes later, he pulled up in front of the large two story house.

Hope they are home, he thought exiting the SUV. A big burly man, sporting a crew cut, met him on the walkway to the front door. Dressed completely in black, the male looked intimidating, even to the Alpha.

"May I help you, sir?" The man crossed his arms over his chest and spread his legs in a defensive stance.

"Yes. I'm here to see Gage Lucio."

Chapter 34

"Excuse me, sir."

At the sound of Alvero's voice, Gage looked up from the book he read. "What is it?"

"You have a caller."

He glanced down at his watch, noting the time. "At this hour? Who is it?"

"He says his name is Michael Garsoe."

Gage put the book down on his desk and materialized at the front door. Gage opened it wide with a smile. "Michael, I'm so glad to see you. It has been almost a century since I last laid eyes on you." Gage stepped back, opening the door wide. "Welcome, welcome. Please come in."

Michael stepped through the doorway with an outstretched arm. Gage shook his proffered hand vigorously, squeezing it tightly.

"The last I heard you were living in Georgia. So what brings you to Nevada?" Gage ushered Michael into the living room and gestured for him to sit on the couch.

Michael sunk into the plush velvet sofa, one arm resting on the back of the couch. "Oh, I just wanted to come and do a little gambling on the Strip and see some old friends,"

Gage grinned. "Nothing like a little jaunt to Vegas to add a little diversity to one's life."

The two males spent the next several minutes catching up on the basic details of their lives. They discussed both Savannah and Vegas in detail, and as they talked Gage heard tension in Michael's voice.

Noticing Michael's tight lipped scowl he commented, "You seem a little uptight tonight."

Michael shrugged his shoulders. "I guess you could say I am a little perturbed today."

"Why?" Gage leaned back in his chair.

"Well no sooner did I get into town, then somebody asked me to do him a favor, and I had to take this woman out into the middle of nowhere."

"Really! Who would ask you to do such a task, especially when you first got into town?"

"Just someone I know named Stephan."

Gage's ears perked up, his mind began to race. Had he heard correctly? Stephan. Could he mean the same Stephan against who Gage sworn revenge? Surely there was only one Stephan that both vampires would know here in Vegas. Gage was suddenly glad he had chosen to receive Michael this evening. Perhaps he could find out some useful information on his enemy. He carefully steadied his face so as not to give away his excitement.

"So what did this Stephan have you do exactly that made you so upset?" Gage asked carefully.

"He had me take this woman out to a ranch and drop her off."

"Really?" Gage raised a questioning brow. "That doesn't sound so bad, spending time with a woman."

"Well, yes, if you like long, leggy blondes."

Could it have been *Her*? Stephan's human? His excitement built.

Michael crossed his arms over his chest. "It was

bad, because it took so damned long."

"Oh? How far away was the ranch?"

"Believe it or not, it was just over the Nevada-Utah border."

"My goodness. That is quite a ways." Thinking quickly Gage added, "Were you able to take the highway, or did you have to take back roads to get there?"

"Luckily, I could take Highway 15 until we got into Utah."

Gage wanted to ask the name of the ranch, but could not figure a way to do it naturally. He bit his tongue and waited for an opportunity to do so. Gage offered Michael a drink, then another. And then one more to loosen his tongue. When he was sure Michael had had one too many, he steered the conversation back to the ranch.

"So Michael, this woman you had to take to the ranch, was she at least pretty?"

"Yeah, actually she was drop dead gorgeous. She had long legs and beautiful blonde hair—a real knock out."

"Did you get any action from her?" Gage wiggled his eyebrows.

"Oh no, no way. My friend made it clear that she was off limits."

An evil grin pulled at Gage's lips, but he sat still, trying to appear only mildly interested as he realized that Stephan had apparently sent his female away.

"Did it take you long to get there?"

"Well over an hour or two?" Michael downed the last of his drink. Ever the good host—a host who wanted his guest drunk—Gage automatically rose to fill his glass to the brim.

"My, that's a long time. Where did you go, the Bucking Bronco Ranch?" Gage guessed hopefully.

Michael shook his head. "No. It was called Rusty Rabbit Ranch or Rusty's Potato Ranch, something like that."

"You mean Rusty's Russet Ranch?" asked Gage, leaning forward in his chair, barely containing his excitement.

"Yeah, yeah, yeah. That's the name of the stupid place," Michael confirmed. His S's slurred from too much alcohol.

"What a waste of your time. That's a long way out there," sympathized Gage, as he topped off Michael's drink yet again.

Gage's foot tapped impatiently while Michael droned on, telling him about the mundane things that had been happening in his life since the last time they'd seen each other. He yammered on to him about buying a townhouse in Savannah, his financial investments and going on a cruise, until Gage thought he might have to physically throw the man out of his house to get him to leave.

Finally Michael leaned forward and said, "So I've been going on and on about myself."

Yes, you have, thought Gage as Michael continued. "Tell me about what has been happening with you. How's Andrea? I haven't seen her yet. Where is she tonight?"

Gage flinched, the muscles in his jaw tightened. He explained that his wife had been injured and died. It was hell speaking of her death, but when he finished, Michael awkwardly offered his sympathies and made a hasty exit, much to Gage's relief.

After watching Michael drive off, he closed the door. Turning his back to the door, he clapped his hands together in glee and a giddy smile lit his face.

"Trace and Alvero," he bellowed.

He could not believe his good fortune and felt like he would explode if he didn't share the information Michael had provided. Michael's inadvertent information gave their plan for revenge new life. When the guards joined him, Gage looked up in silent cogitation.

I promise you, Andrea, I'll avenge your death if it is the last thing I do on this earth before joining you in the Beyond. You have my vow on this, my love.

Chapter 35

She yawned, bone tired after a long day of working the ranch, Katrina hoped she would be able to sleep this night, and avoid the disturbing dreams she'd had the night before about vampires attacking her and being rescued by two handsome men. It had been terrifying. She could feel the fangs sinking into her flesh, ripping chunks from her limbs.

The nightmare had caused her to have a fretful night's sleep and left her exhausted with bags under her eyes. Of course she didn't let that get in the way of doing this day's chores. She had given every ounce of her energy to her tasks, hoping to wear herself out. It worked. Tonight she was exhausted and looking forward to getting a good rest.

She tucked the wool blanket and cotton sheet under her chin and closed her eyes. Depression pushed in on her, even though she was enjoying life on the ranch. She liked the people she worked with. They treated her with respect and kindness. She loved working with the animals and being outdoors. She especially relished learning to ride, so she couldn't understand why she felt so melancholy.

They'd spent many long hours that day riding and as Kat went to turn over in her bed, she felt every minute of the ride. Her back, thighs, calves, even the muscles in her hands ached. She knew as bad as it was tonight, she would be sorer in the morning.

Kat painfully rested one arm on her forehead. She would sleep well tonight—if she could keep her muscles from hurting. A curse burst from her lips, as she realized she'd forgotten to take a pain reliever before going to bed. Just as she contemplated getting up and taking some ibuprofen, she heard the thudding of feet trampling down the hallway like a herd of elephants.

Muscles clench in dissention when she tried to jump off the bed. Slowly she rolled off the bed, and peeked out her door. When she saw Rusty standing there, she jumped sending a shot of pain radiating throughout her muscles.

"Get dressed," he barked. "We got trouble. We need every hand out at the stables."

"What's wrong?"

"A fire!" yelled Rusty over his shoulder, as he ran down the hallway and toward the front door.

Kat quickly drew on a pair of jeans and a sweatshirt, then ran as fast as her legs could carry her. Outside flames leapt into the air, creating an orange-yellow hue that served as the background to the flurry of commotion on the ground. The flames reached at least twenty feet in the air, licking the moon that shone down on the scene below. The scurry of activity reminded Kat of a hornet's nest with angry bees buzzing here and there in synchronized chaos. The ranch hands were busy, each man grabbing two horses from the burning barn to lead them to safety.

She ran toward the stables. The heat scorched her flesh, but she put her arm over her face and ran into the smoldering building.

The smoke stung her eyes, and the intense heat burned her lungs, making it difficult to breathe. She stumbled blindly through the barn, tripping over a saddle that must have fallen to the floor. The packed ground rose to meet her knees, biting into them when she hit. Determination spurring her on, she pushed herself up and moved deeper into the gray-black haze, listening for the sound of the horses whinnying.

She made her way by running her hand along the wall, until she came to a stall holding a terrified mare. She swung opened the stable gate. The mare startled at the motion and reared up on her hind legs. Katrina dodged her flailing legs like an experienced ranch hand, and shimmed along the side of the stall. Coming to the mare's flank, she ushered the mare out with a smack on her rump and the horse ran through the exit into the safety of the yard.

Over the sound of her own coughing, Kat barely heard the small, weak whinny. She got down under the smoke and crawled toward the sound. She found the black and white foal that had raced alongside her car the night she arrived at the ranch. He lay on the ground, gasping for air. Katrina tried to lift him, but her muscles lacked the necessary strength for the task.

"Help! Help!" Her voice, raspy from the smoke, came out more of a squeak than a yell. The heat scorched her lungs, but Katrina forced in more air and tried for a louder voice. "Help! Somebody, down here. Help!"

Suddenly Rusty knelt beside her. Never had she been so relieved to see a familiar flannel shirt.

"I got him." He scooped the foal up into his arms. "Let's go."

With Katrina's hand resting on Rusty's shoulder, they made their way out of the burning building. After they exited, she began gulping at the air like a fish out of water. Her lungs blazed with each breath, protesting the soot and ash that coated them. The tears from her watering eyes no doubt left black streaks down her face while she forced clean air into her lungs.

Cherry red from the heat, her skin hurt as much as her lungs. She gingerly touched one finger to her opposite forearm sending a blast of white-hot pain to her brain.

"Get back. It's going to collapse," Rusty yelled, his voice raspy from the smoke.

She staggered away from the burning wreckage and sat hard on the cool ground, watching as the ranch hands administered first aid to the horses. They worked to corral them safely away from the engulfed stable.

Having no veterinary skills or knowledge of first aid for horses, Katrina knew she would only get in the way if she tried to help. She sat on the dewy ground coughing, trying to catch her breath. With tears streaming down her face, she wiped at her eyes with the back of her arm. Her face and sweatshirt smudged with black, she cried for the horses as much as from her own pain.

The ranchers struggled to attend to the scared and injured animals. The creatures' pitiful cries of pain would echo in her head for years, she was sure. Her stomach pitched from the injuries to the beautiful horses and she had to close her eyes to the sight of burnt, raw flesh. If only she could close her nose to the retched smell.

Suddenly she felt a tug around her waist and was

dragged backwards into the brush. A hand clamped down hard over her mouth when she screamed. She felt a fluttering in her mind just as she began kicking wildly. Her body stilled, no longer hers to control. She could not move, no matter how much her mind screamed to her muscles to respond.

Flung over a broad shoulder, the collar bone of her kidnapper bit into her stomach, as she jostled up and down while they ran through the trees and scrub brush. The ground coursed beneath her. Twigs and branches tore at her clothes and scratched her skin as they flew along. She lay helplessly draped over the man, each movement jarred her already sore muscles and tender skin, each breath burned her smoke-filled lungs.

Their pace slowed and Kat knew a moment of relief until the man callously flung her into the trunk of a car. He slammed the lid, enclosing her in complete darkness.

Terror made her heart race, her breath sawed painfully from her lungs. But, at least, whatever had paralyzed her apparently no longer had her in its grip, for she found she could once again control her faculties.

As they drove along, every bump jarred her sore body. Kat moaned, but fought the pain to reason the situation. Her mind raced. Who had taken her? Why? What did this person want? Why would anyone want to kidnap her?

There were obviously other things in the trunk with her. She felt them bump into her, bruising her tender skin. She groped around, her hand sliding over the rough carpet of the trunk as she tried to discern what the objects were. Might one of them be used as a weapon?

Her hand slid over a rubber object, it was round. A tire she surmised. Next she found what she believed were a set of jumper cables and small mesh bag, none of which would be any real help. Katrina rolled into the fetal position trying to protect her body as best she could from the objects bumping into her. It was an agonizing ride, and Kat was sure she would be glad when it was over...Unless of course something worse waited at the end of the drive.

****

The penthouse seemed empty, deserted. He stared into the closet at the holes where Katrina's clothing used to hang. An ache burned deep in his chest as he stood in his room, and he knew sorrow and regret. It would have been extraordinary to have Katrina as his mate.

Making his way to the kitchen, her honeysuckle fragrance surrounded him. It permeated the whole penthouse, reminded him of her loss every place he went.

Stephan sat at the kitchen table, and stared down on his folded hands. He knew she was safer now, but that thought didn't give him enough solace. Lonely, forlorn, he knew in his heart he'd done the right thing by wiping her memory and sending her away to safety, but he wished things could have been different. He wished someone would wipe his memory clean, so he could be spared the crippling pain of her loss.

He shook away the thought. He wouldn't ask anyone to do that. He didn't want to really forget Kat. He didn't want to lose her completely, the way she lost him.

He put his head in his hands when tears clouded his

vision. One lone tear escaped down his cheek and hit the table with a splash. He wiped off his cheek ruthlessly. He did *not* cry. Fates be damned, how that woman had changed him.

Marcus strolled silently into the room, crossing to take a seat across from him.

Stephan's chest tightened while at the same time his throat constricted. The longer he thought about Kat, the harder he found it to breathe. The weight of her loss sat heavy on his chest. He wanted fiercely to see her once again and struggled with whether or not to go see her.

"Stephan," Marcus said quietly.

The warrior raised his head to look at the younger male wearily. "Yes, Marcus, what do you want?"

"I just wanted to see how you are, check on you." Marcus looked almost as forlorn as he felt. "I miss Kat."

Marcus rested his head in the palm of his hand.

"I do too." Stephan's shoulders slumped, mirroring Marcus' somber demeanor. "But we have discussed this, and we agreed it is best that she is no longer with us. Being a part of our world without being a vampire is dangerous. She is safe at the ranch. We cannot be selfish and put her in danger by keeping her with us."

"Maybe we should go see her," offered Marcus looking hopeful.

"I had the same thought, but wouldn't that make our loss all the more deep?"

"I don't know. I guess it could." After drawing a long pensive breath, Marcus continued. "Sometimes I think seeing her, knowing she is happy, might make it better."

"Yeah," Stephan agreed. "I've thought that too, but I'm not sure I could leave if I were to go and see her. I don't think I could stand to let her go a second time."

When Kat had been with him, each new day felt full of promise. Each night Kat brought a smile to his face. Each evening he'd been kissed by the woman he loved, adored.

After centuries of being alone he'd finally found someone who he wanted to spend the rest of his long life with. Each evening he awoke next to her, watched her eyes flutter awake, and then she'd smiled at him and stroke his face lovingly. It had been the most wonderful experience in all the centuries of his life and surely nothing again would ever be as amazing. Stephan shook the painful memories away, not wanting to remember.

And yet… unable to forget.

Stephan and Marcus stood in unison, and retired to the living room, each lost in his thoughts of Katrina. The phone rang, startling them from their reverie. Being the closest to the phone, Marcus answered it. Stephan watched Marcus hold the phone in his tightly clutched hand. Marcus' pale pallor went ghostly white, his jaw slack. Stephan looked at him with alarm. "What is it?" he demanded.

When Marcus did not answer quickly enough, Stephan used their mindlink to find the information he sought. Alexander had just informed Marcus that Kat was missing.

In a flash, Stephan grabbed the phone away from Marcus, and held it to his ear. "What happened?" he barked into the receiver.

"I received a phone call from Rusty. There was a

fire at the ranch and in all of the commotion, Kat seems to have disappeared." Alex's voice sounded unbelievably calm. But then, were the conversation about anyone else, Stephan supposed his voice would have been as steady. But they did not speak of someone else. It was his Katrina who had disappeared and Stephan's emotions at the news were beyond erratic.

"What do you mean disappeared?" Stephan demanded, his hand cranking down on the receiver.

Alex cleared his throat. "They have checked the ranch and even gone into the surrounding woods on horseback, but she is nowhere to be found. I'm sorry, Stephan, but they couldn't find her anywhere."

Silence hung in the air thick as smoke. Stephan slowly hung up the phone, stunned. His mouth gaped open; worry flooded his system with endorphins.

"What are we going to do?" Marcus brought Stephan's focus back to the penthouse.

"We're going to find her, that's what we are going to do. And I have a good idea where to start."

"Where's that?"

"Gage!" they exclaimed in unison.

Stephan stormed toward the gym with Marcus in tow. He pushed against one of the mirrored walls. It gave way, revealing a weapons room that would make any museum proud. Lined against the walls were numerous guns, knives, swords, and even a cross bow.

"Load up. We're going to go get her."

Marcus obeyed, grabbing the cross bow first. He slung it onto his shoulder and rounded on Stephan. "Wait, there are only two of us and Gage's place is well guarded. We'll need backup."

Stephan slowed but continued to load weapons

onto his body, a knife in his front pocket, a gun in the waistband of his pants. He acknowledged Marcus' statement with a nod and said simply, "Call the Alphas."

Chapter 36

A shiver of unease crept up Katrina's spine when the vehicle slowed to a stop. The trunk opened, and she was dragged out by a hulk of a man. His meaty hands wrapped around her arm in a bruising grip, and he jerked her forward. When she stumbled, he wrenched her arm with enough force she feared he may have pulled it from the socket, but her cry of pain did nothing to ease his grip. He led her into a house, up a set of stairs, and brought her to stop in a bedroom in front of a blond man and another large man dressed entirely in black. The fact she stood alone in a bedroom with three kidnappers, at their mercy, did not escape her notice. Her heart beat wildly in her chest.

"What do you want with me?" she asked with more bravado than she felt.

The blond gripped her chin painfully, forcing her to look at him. "I want you to use your mindlink to contact Stephan and bring him here."

"Who is Stephan?"

"Don't play dumb with me, girl. Playing dumb makes me angry and things get very unpleasant when I get angry."

With a slight nod from the blond, the man dressed in black stepped forward. In a movement too quick for Kat to register, he raised his arm and brought the back of his hand down against her cheek causing her head to whip to the side. As she righted her head, she could feel the sting of the hit and taste the blood on her lips. The pain brought awareness that she had been hit. In her shock, she didn't take the time to examine that it had happened in an instant, so fast she hadn't seen it coming.

"Contact Stephan," the blond repeated through clenched teeth.

"I don't know who you are talking about. You have to believe me. I don't know any Stephan." Kat pleaded for him to see reason, searched his eyes.

"Trace," he said, nodding once toward the big guy.

He reared back, this time slow enough for Kat to register what was to come. Kat winced and struggled against the strong hands around her arms to no avail. Trace stepped forward and hit Kat in her nose, breaking it. As blood tricked down over her lips, he mumbled, "That's for breaking my nose, bitch."

The males' nostrils flared when the coppery perfume of her blood permeated the air. A distinct buzz of excitement filled the room as the men reacted to her injury. Her fear rose to a new level, blocking a little of the pain.

Kat looked over at the blond, tears stinging her eyes. "I don't know any Stephan," she repeated, her voice small with trepidation.

The man in charge smiled an evil grin and nodded again.

"As you wish, Gage." This time Trace's fist landed in her stomach causing a whoosh of air to escape her lungs and she doubled over as much as the goon holding her would allow.

"Since this is going to get messy," Gage motioned

with a wave of his hand toward a spot of blood on the bedroom carpet, "perhaps we should move into the bathroom."

"That would make for easy clean up," agreed the brute holding her.

Katrina struggled against her captors, but they shuffled her into the master bath easily. The man holding her released her and she lost her bearings. A painful crunch sounded when the cold, unforgiving tile bit into her knees. Gage reached down and fisted a handful of her hair, drew her head back, forced her to look up at him.

"Contact Stephan, call him to you. Tell him you are in trouble, and he must come now."

Kat gulped for air—the smoke from the stable and the hit to her solar plexus, a one-two punch that made breathing difficult.

"I told…you. I…don't know…who you are…talking about," Katrina stammered between painful breaths.

"I'm talking about your vampire boyfriend," Gage spit out.

"Vampire?" Kat whispered. "There's no such thing."

Gage's rage contorted his face. He nodded again to Trace who delivered another blow.

A steady turn-taking sequence took place—Gage asked a question, Trace delivered the pain. And time came to a crawl. She thought she heard somewhere that when the human body was injured, the mind shut off and the person went unconscious. She had even heard of people mentally going "somewhere else" when being tortured, but for Kat, such a blessed fate would not be.

Aware of every blow, cut, and break, she longed to slip into unconsciousness. When it didn't come, she began to long instead for death, anything that would allow her to escape the pain her kidnappers inflicted.

During the few moments when the men were not hurting her, she hoped she was having a horrible nightmare that she would wake from sooner rather than later. Her hopes died as each short break was followed by more demands and suffering. She watched through the slits in her swollen eyes as her captors smiled while they inflected their pain.

This can't go on forever, thought Kat as she longed for the respite that never came.

Chapter 37

When Michael entered the weapons room, he realized all the other Alphas had already arrived. No doubt they materialized there while he'd been instructed to drive his rented SUV. Stephan said something about wanting to use his car to rescue the woman. *Whatever.* All Michael knew was that the extra time it took to drive over to the penthouse meant he would be the last one to have his pick of weapons.

He glanced around the room, noting his fellow Alphas arming themselves. They were all adorned in clothing similar to what he wore, a black turtle neck tucked into black cargo pants, and heavy dark combat boots. And those with long hair tied it back in a thong.

They each chose weapons to place on their bodies. Most of the ammo and weapons were coated in titanium, the only metal deadly to vampires. Nicholai favored the titanium knives, while Vladimir preferred nine millimeters, but also took a dagger. Demetri grabbed a titanium-coated sword and slung it over his back after grabbing a .45 which he tucked into his waistband. Alex chambered a titanium round in his semi auto, then grabbed a switchblade to strap on his calf.

Marcus slung the crossbow over his shoulder and turned, eyes locking with Michael's. He watched Michael choose his weapons for the evening.

In the time it took for the Alphas to arrive and choose their weapons, Stephan devised a basic plan to get Katrina back. With his fellow warriors standing around him, he briefed them.

"When we get to the compound, we'll take out the perimeter guards first. Then we'll break into two teams, one going in the front, the other going in through the back of Lucio's place. Once inside…"

Michael's thoughts drifted off as Stephan spoke. He began putting everything together; Lucio's house, his visit, how the girl he took to the ranch fit into Stephan's life. What he had said to Gage played in his mind, and he realized that he was partially responsible for Katrina's kidnapping.

A look of consternation crossed his face briefly, but he quickly steeled his features. If Stephan learned he'd spoken to Gage, Michael was sure the Alpha leader would blame this entire mess on him. In reality, the fault for the woman's kidnapping lay with Stephan. Had Stephan bothered to tell him more information before sending him to deposit Kat at the ranch, he would not have said anything to Gage. *Yes, Stephan is the one responsible for this mess,* Michael thought as he crossed his arms over his chest.

Having discussed the rough attack plan, the Alphas all loaded into the Michael's SUV. Though it claimed to have seating for eight, it was a tight squeeze for the seven large males. "Maybe we should take two vehicles," Michael suggested.

"No," Stephan said. "We need time together to finesse our attack strategy."

Michael cranked down on the steering wheel, his knuckles going white. He had always thought he should be the leader of the Alphas. He didn't need Stephan dictating to him. He turned the key, wishing once, just once, Stephan would take one of his suggestions.

Demetri spoke first as they got underway. "Do you know for sure where Kat is?"

"I believe with every fiber of my being that she is with Gage. But I can find her through my blood," Stephan answered.

When Michael glanced over at Marcus from the driver's seat and raised a questioning brow, Marcus explained, "Kat has drunk from Stephan a couple of times, so he can sense her presence through his blood. He can find her anywhere now."

Michael nodded his understanding.

****

Stephan glanced around the vehicle at his fellow Alphas with pride. He trusted them, cared for them like family. Confident they would have his back as he would have theirs, he listened while Nicholai reminded them that the humans might still be in the house since the hunt had never taken place. Alex and Nicholai agreed that they would look for the humans while the other Alphas took out the remaining guards, leaving Marcus and Stephan to find and free Katrina.

The closer they got to Gage's house, the stronger Stephan could feel Kat's presence. It bolstered his confidence that they would find her once they got into the house. He only hoped they would get there in time.

They parked a half a mile away from Lucio's home and silently ran the short distance to the property. Once at the compound, they found three guards walking the perimeter. They waited, lying prone on the ground, as the guards walked the predictable pattern around the house. When only one guard was visible, Marcus rose to one knee and fired his bow, sending a titanium arrow through the heart of the guard, killing him instantly. The fletching quivered as he fell to the ground. Michael ran over and pulled the dead male back to where the Alphas waited so the other guards would not see the body on their next sweep of the area.

When the second guard rounded the corner of the house, Marcus once again set his crossbow and sent an arrow flying. It too found its mark and the second guard dropped to the ground. This time Nicholai ran up to dispose of the body. Just as he reached the body, footsteps sounded. Apparently the third guard had realized something was amiss and was coming their way at a full run.

Nicholai slid a large knife out of his front pocket and crouched down low against the side of the house. When the guard rounded the corner, the Alpha stood, bringing the blade of the knife up under the third male's chin. He pushed it through the roof of the guard's mouth, lodging it in his brain. With a quick pull of his hand he dislodged the knife, grabbed the male's hair with his empty hand, and used the sharp blade to slice off the male's head.

The guard's body dropped to its knees before flopping over onto the hard ground. Sightless eyes stared in the general direction of the hidden Alphas from the head held in Nicholai's hand. Nicholai looked calmly down at the two bodies lying on the ground.

With perfunctory ease, Nicholai wiped the blade of the knife off on the back of one of the bodies before tucking it back in his pocket. The severed head still in one hand, Nicholai grabbed a body under each arm as if they were footballs and trotted over to rejoin his fellow Alphas.

"I'll do a quick perimeter check," offered Michael.

Before Stephan could agree, the Alpha jumped up and hunched toward the house. Finding the way clear, he motioned for the others to join him along the side of the house. Stephan silently motioned for Nicholai, Alexander, and Michael to move around to the back of the house then pointed to himself, Marcus, Demetri, and Vlad and motioned around the front. Next he counted on his fingers. One. Two. Three. The Alphas separated into two groups rounding their perspective corners in perfect synchronicity.

****

Nicholai tried the back door and finding it locked, gave it a hard shove with his shoulder, bursting through. He stumbled into the kitchen with Alexander close on his heels. Michael however, hung back in the shadows, as if he didn't want to join the melee inside.

"I'll stay out here," he whispered to Alexander and Nicholai. "Cover the back."

Nicholai opened his mouth to protest Michael's offer when they suddenly heard a commotion from the front of the house. He glanced in the direction of the noise then looked back to find Michael gone.

The next second, all hell broke loose. Gage's men scurried from every orifice of the house like ants protecting their nest. Alex and Nicholai pulled their weapons and used them with the speed and grace that only their breed could do.

The first man to enter the kitchen approached Nicholai as he stepped further into the room. With a knife in each hand, Nicholai slashed him quickly across both his stomach and neck simultaneously, causing a spray of blood to arc out coating not only himself, but the guard who approached him from behind. Nicholai spun, taking advantage of the momentary blindness the guard suffered from the blood spraying into his eyes. He brought his knife in one swift motion, up in a diagonal slice, splaying the guard open from waist to heart. He then drove the second knife into the male's exposed heart, causing instant death. The guard dropped to the floor, dead.

Wiping the blood from his face, his gaze found Alex busy with his own attacker. With a guard bearing down, Alexander had time to draw his weapon, but his attacker grasped the gun as well as the hand that held it and pointed the semi auto toward the ceiling. The two men struggled in a test of strength for control of the weapon. Alex brought his free hand over his attacker's, their arms waved back and forth as each struggled for dominance.

Time slowed for Nicholai as he watched the blond Alpha gradually begin to take the upper hand in the conflict. Alex brought the gun down to the guard's chest and fired one titanium bullet clean through his heart, dropping his attacker instantly.

The bullet exited the body, taking a trail of blood splatter with it as it hit the next guard in line. The bullet lodged in the second male's stomach. The second attacker slumped forward, one arm wrapping around his waist, and Alex paused briefly to catch his breath.

The guard saw his advantage in the break, and grasped it like a lion clutching its prey. Heedless of his own pain, the male lunged toward Alex, taking him to the floor, the gun spinning away from them.

Arms and legs slipped in blood as the two males wrestled on the tile floor. Alex came to rest on top of the guard straddling his injured stomach. Squeezing his muscular thighs, he bore down on the bullet wound causing the guard to bellow in pain and writhe beneath him.

Nicholai picked up the gun. "Alex, here." He tossed the gun toward his friend. In one smooth motion, Alex caught the gun and fired a round into the guard's brain, ending the struggle.

"Let's go find the humans." Nicholai pulled Alex to his feet.

Brushing off his pants and shirt, the blond Alpha nodded his agreement to Nikko's suggestion.

"The only place I have not seen in this house is behind that door," he informed Alex, motioning to the white door to their left. "Let's try there first."

****

Demetri bounded first through the front door with Marcus and Stephan quick to follow. Bringing up the rear, Vladimir entered with guns drawn just as three guards came running toward them from the living room.

"Go. You three go," barked Demetri. "I'll hold these guys off. Find your female, Stephan."

Following Stephan and Vladimir up the stairs, Marcus hesitated and looked back over his shoulder. "Are you sure, Demetri?"

Demetri tsked. "Since when have three puny males ever been a challenge for me? Go!"

He rounded on the three burly guards surrounding him at the base of the stairs, removed his sword from its sheath and held it tightly in both hands. Bracing in a

317

fighter's stance, Demetri swung his long sword at the first of the three guards. The male easily jumped back out of the way. As his sword continued its arch, the other two guards followed suit, each one in turn jumping back away from the blade's reach.

Demetri advanced, continuing to swing, trying to push the guards away from the stairs so his fellow warriors could ascend. He needed to keep their attention squarely on him so he swung his sword in long fluid arches, the blade seeking flesh. As Demetri advanced forward, one of the guards circled around behind him and lunged.

Chapter 38

Stephan, Marcus, and Vlad flew up the stairs at a furious pace. Stephan followed the draw of his blood, every cell seemed to pulsate the closer he got to Kat. He knew instinctually where she was and followed the internal vibration leading him.

As Stephan turned to head down the hall to the right, he caught movement out of the corner of his eye. He scanned quickly down the hallway to the left, and realized what was there.

"Down!" Vladimir yelled to Marcus and Stephan who immediately followed the order, diving onto the floor as a hail of bullets rained over their heads, peppering the walls, grating the paneling. Vlad jumped up, his eyes taking in the nuances of the hallway before him. Realizing he needed his hands free, he tucked his guns in his pockets and threw himself at the guard, tackling him down the hall, giving Marcus and Stephan a chance to rise.

As they began to run down the hallway, Trace and Alvero burst out from a doorway, with fists balled.

"Go," yelled Marcus to him. "I've got these guys. Go get Kat."

Marcus' eyes shifted from Stephan to the guard still standing in the hall. With Alvero advancing on his position he quickly raised his crossbow, and shot his last arrow toward the male. The guard pivoted on the ball of one foot, gracefully avoiding the deadly object. Marcus threw down his bow and turned sideways into a fighting stance with his fists in front of him, ready for the fight to come.

Stephan put on a burst of speed. As he ran forward, he stuck out his arm and clotheslined Trace in the throat, taking him to the floor. He barely registered the whump sound that escaped from Trace's mouth as the air was knocked from his lungs before Stephan turned and disappeared into the opening from which the two guards had just emerged.

****

As the guard launched at Demetri from behind, he shifted the hold on his sword and quickly thrust it behind him blindly. He felt the draw on the sword when it sliced through the male. A gurgling sound told him his sword found its mark. He felt the resistance when he withdrew the blade out of the body. The male behind him went down onto his knees, grasping his wound with both hands. Demetri knew it was not a killing blow, but it would at least take the male out of the fight for a few minutes.

He turned his attention to the two guards in front of him. The large Alpha circled around, bringing his back to the front door, thereby assuring that neither of the two guards standing could approach from behind. One of the guards dove forward, grabbing Demetri around the waist, sending him careening back into the door. He raised his sword up above his head and brought the hilt down against the back of the male's head. A crunch sounded when the sword broke through the skull. The Alpha watched the guard collapse to the floor in an unconscious heap.

The guard with the wounded stomach rose to his feet, his body already beginning to heal. He and the uninjured guard charged Demetri together, each grabbing a thick arm.

With a growl that reverberated off the walls, Demetri brought his arms together in a surge of strength. He sent their bodies careening into each other, their heads made a snapping sound when they collided. They stood for a second before Demetri, stunned into immobility. That second was all he needed. With one swipe, he cleanly cut through both the guards' necks, one after the other. Their bodies fell to their knees for a moment before slumping forward to ooze their blood onto the floor at the same time their heads came to a rolling stop beside the door.

The third guard slowly pushed himself up to a standing position. "I'm going to see you pay for their deaths," he threatened.

Demetri beckoned him forward by wiggling his index finger. "Come on if you think you have what it takes to defeat me," he challenged, raising his blood-stained sword.

****

Vlad and the gunman crashed to the floor, and the concussion from the fall sent the automatic weapon flying behind them. They came to rest with Vlad atop the guard. The Alpha could feel something running down his arm and saw red seeping from his shoulder. One of the bullets had caught Vlad in the shoulder as the two men had gone down.

The guard jammed his thumb into the bullet wound, twisting it deep. Vladimir threw his head back, a roar of pain erupting from his lips. The resulting surge of adrenaline coursing through him increased his strength tenfold. He reached down swiftly and removed one of his nine millimeters from its holster. The guard knocked the gun from his hand, sending it crashing against the opposite wall.

As the guard's eyes followed the Nine across the hall, Vlad unsheathed a dagger strapped to his thigh. He gripped the knife with both hands and raised it above the guard, aiming for his heart. The movement brought the guard's attention back onto the figure towering over him, and he covered both of the warrior's hands with his own.

It was a test of strength to see where the blade would land. The bullet still lodged within weakened Vlad's shoulder. The dagger began to turn back toward the Alpha as the struggle continued between the two males. The knife shook from the battle, and Vlad felt himself weakening.

With welcoming relief, Vlad suddenly felt a rush of power as Marcus mentally sent him a surge of strength through their mindlink. Vlad slowly turned the tide, sent the dagger back in the direction of the guard. At the last moment, the guard angled the dagger away from his heart, causing Vlad to strike him in the breastbone, doing little damage.

The guard grunted when the blade sliced him, but both males knew it was an inconsequential wound. The guard pushed Vlad off, heaving him into the wall, which knocked the dagger from his hand. The injured guard jumped to his feet, and grabbed the Alpha by his neck with one hand. Vlad's feet dangled as he was held against the wall by his neck. He struggled, grabbing the guard's meaty forearm with one hand while bringing his other hand up against his elbow. He pushed his hands in opposite directions, breaking the male's bones in two.

Having lost control over his arm, the guard dropped Vlad, who landed gracefully on the balls of his feet. Vlad reached down, grabbed the knife with cat-like reflexes and brought it up swiftly, plunging the dagger into the guard's heart. The guard staggered backwards clutching at the knife in his chest, until he slumped against the wall, taking his final sleep.

Vlad stood for a moment, catching his breath. He looked down the hall and discovered Marcus faced down two burly guards by himself. Fetching the blade from the dead guard's chest, he took off down the hall to assist him. As he made his way past the stairs, he glanced down and witnessed Demetri taking out the third of his assailants. Realizing Demetri needed no help, he quickly turned his attention back to Marcus.

He reached Marcus just as he twisted Trace's head, ripped it from his body, then threw it to the floor with a warrior's yell.

"I got this other one. Go help Stephan," Vlad instructed as he approached. Alvero turned their way.

****

A horrific stench of stale human assaulted his nose when Alexander opened the white door. He descended the stairs cautiously, while Nicholai stood guard at the top, waiting, watching for the enemy. When he reached the bottom, Alex peered around, surprised to not find any guards. He turned back and motioned silently to Nicholai that the situation was not dangerous.

He stepped into the room cautiously, looking around. The cellar was a thing straight out of a nightmare. The air, thick and filled with a dark sense of evil, smelled of stale sweat. There were pallets made of worn blankets on the floor upon which both women and men lay in various states of undress. Some were fully clothed; others dressed only in shirts, while some lay completely naked. They all were caged in cells with rusting metal bars. Bowls with bits of food were left scattered about and each cell housed a spigot for water.

Alex realized that the stench he'd noticed was not just from stale humans as he had first thought, but the smell of death intermingled as well. The potent combination turned his stomach.

"Get Michael," Alex called up to his friend. "We're going to need all of the help we can get."

His roaming gaze took in the sight before him. Human men and women huddled in cells, kept prisoners by thick iron bars. Most sat emaciated in their cells, long forgotten and neglected. With disgust furrowing his light brows, he noted that some of the humans were already gone, dead long enough for parasites to have found their corpses.

"Michael, we need your help. Come here!" He heard Nicholai call out behind, hoping it was his fellow Alpha he heard descending the stairs.

"Where's Michael?" Alexander asked when Nicholai joined him at the foot of the stairs.

"I don't know. I called to him, but he didn't respond."

Alex approached the first cell, attempted to pull it open, and found it locked as he had expected. He turned to Nicholai. "See if you can find a key, or anything we could use to get these cells open."

As Nicholai quickly obliged, Alex turned to the

humans in the cell. "Don't worry," he assured them. "We're going to get you out of there."

Nicholai jogged up behind him. "I can't find anything down here. I'm going to go upstairs and see if I can find any keys on the guards."

Nicholai ascended the stairs as Alex turned his attention once again to the humans in the cell. "It's okay," he encouraged them. "We'll get you out."

One of the men inside the cell nodded and some of the women cried tears of relief. Those that could stand pushed themselves up to wait for their prison to be opened. Most though remained lying or sitting on the cold concrete floor, suffering in silence for it took energy they did not have to whimper.

The sight turned his stomach. No one should be treated this way. No one. Ever.

Alex heard the sound of jingling keys behind him.

"Found them on one of the guards upstairs," Nicholai informed him, trying one of the keys in the lock on the cell.

They worked quickly to determine which keys opened which cell locks. Once all the cells were open, Alex returned to the first one.

"Who can walk?" he asked and several pairs of human eyes rose to meet his.

"I can," volunteered one of the men as he stood slowly unfolding his legs from his seated position.

"I can too," said one of the females using the wall to brace herself when she stood.

"Me too." Yet another woman stood on shaky legs.

Alex turned to the man who had first spoken. "Do you think you could help someone else out of here?"

He nodded and reached down to help the woman

who had been sitting beside him. When she stood, he placed her arm around his shoulder for support. "I can help," he replied, a look of sheer determination on his face.

Alex nodded appreciatively.

"Those of you who are able to walk need to get up and get out." Nicholai's deep voice echoed in the concrete room. "If you can help someone else to get out, please do so." Nicholai opened the second cell wide. "Those of you who can't walk on your own don't worry. We will get you out of here."

Two by two the humans and the vampires worked together to get everyone up and out of the basement prison. They worked steadily, Nicholai and Alexander carried the humans who could not walk under their own strength. On their third trip back down the stairs, they heard movement behind them. Alex looked back over his shoulder. Relief flooded his body when he saw Demetri, breathing heavily and following them down the stairs.

"Nice of you to finally join us," scoffed Alex, a somber smile on his face.

"Yeah, well sorry. I could have gotten here sooner, but I was a little busy."

"We can use all the help we can get. There are still a lot of humans left down here." Alex indicated down the cells with his thumb.

"Where are you taking them?" asked Demetri, heaving an unconscious man over his shoulder.

"Out the back door. We have them sitting on the lawn," answered Nicholai before he continued into one of the cells. "What are we going to do with them after we get them all out?"

Alex shrugged as he walked over to an unconscious woman lying in a cell.

"We'll have to wipe their memories," stated Demetri, grabbing a woman about her waist, hauling her slight form up against his side. "I can make it so they will think they were at some wonderful party in Vegas."

"That would work for the non-injured ones. We can get them cleaned up, you can implant the memory, and then we'll send them on their way." Alex lifted the woman up onto his arms.

"What about the injured ones?" Concern dripped from Nicholai's voice.

"We can implant a memory of an accident and get them to the hospital," Demetri suggested over his shoulder as he muscled the two humans up the stairs.

"Implanting that many memories will be difficult, cousin." Nicholai lifted a frail man into his arms.

Demetri nodded, acknowledging the truth in Nicholai's statement. "We'll take care of it. We always do."

Chapter 39

Stephan stood in the bedroom. His gaze swept the empty room, coming to rest on a closed door in front of him. Stephan burst through the door to the master bath taking in the scene before him. Confusion furrowed his dark brows for he saw no one on the first sweep of the room.

His blood hummed, sent a tingling sensation coursing through his body. Katrina must be nearby. As he turned to leave, he noticed something on the floor behind the tub.

He made his way to the mass, the smell of blood called to him. He instinctually knew what he would find when he looked down on Kat's injured body. His stomach rolled, bile filled the back of his throat as rage coursed through his body.

Her right leg lay bent at a ninety-degree angle from her calve, the bone protruding. Her shirt was red with her blood, soaked to the point of dripping off the side. Her blackened eyes were swollen into tight slits and her nose lay flat against her face. The wounds bled copiously on her arms as the limbs lay uselessly on the tile floor; either broken or dislocated he could not tell which. She winced in pain and moaned, the sound of which fill his ears making his rage grow like a muscle-bound man on steroids.

A furious growl left his lips, resonated off the

walls, and caused her to stir. He went to her with blurring speed. As he reached her, she looked up at him through the tiny slits of her eyes. She flinched. Fear and pain rolled from her, coated him in its sickening film.

Stephan knelt beside her. "*Mein schatz*, what have they done to you?" he asked quietly, his voice but a whisper as he carefully lifted her into his arms.

Katrina's limbs spasmed. Her face, misshapen as it was, contorted in pain. She started to move, then suddenly relaxed against him, as if she instinctually knew safety in his arms. She closed her eyes and leaned against his chest.

"I don't care where we go," she whispered in a raspy voice. "Just get me away from those men."

It was a plea, nothing less. He tasted her fear and pain. It coated his tongue, feeding his need to do something, preferably something that involved pain, fangs, and death. His fangs lengthened as his anger overtook him.

He looked down upon her bruised and broken body, knowing she'd already lost a lot of blood. Her blood still flowed from her numerous wounds. Determination and purpose took his anger, and he realized stopping the blood flow was paramount to her survival.

Stephan leaned down and licked at the wounds on her arm, using the healing properties in his saliva to seal the wounds. The first lick made his world spin. Her blood was unlike anything he ever had before. It tasted like she smelled, like honeysuckle. It warmed him to the core, making his body come alive in a way no blood had ever done before. His vision swam, tilting the room, and his body reacted with every cell screaming,

Mine!

"My heartmate!" he exclaimed, the realization almost causing him to drop her from his lap.

Stephan stilled, stunned at his reaction to tasting Katrina's blood. He'd known he was attracted to her, but until that moment hadn't known she was his everything, his life. His heartmate. The realization changed everything for him.

Her life would forever be linked with his. He would live for her, her love, her body. He would care for her, protect her. She would be his world.

She must survive, he thought as he watched Katrina's eyes close, unconsciousness taking her.

Stephan placed her broken body back on the tile floor, careful to move her as little as possible. He lowered his head and licked her wounds closed, using his preternatural speed to work with haste. He heard Kat's heart flutter, skip a beat. A new desperation gripped him as he realized that he might lose the heartmate he'd waited centuries to find.

After sealing the wounds, he sent his senses into Katrina to assess her injuries. The broken bones and internal bleeding were the worst of her injuries. In addition, she had much bruising and the cuts, though now healing from his ministrations, were still a threat.

He healed the life threatening injuries first, carefully examining each organ for bleeding as he went. He had just started to heal the lesser injuries when Marcus and Alvero crashed through the bedroom door, drawing Stephan's attention from his task. He watched as Vladimir appeared in the doorway just behind the pair.

Gage emerged from behind the bedroom door, just

as Marcus and Alvero entered the room. He slammed the reinforced door shut behind the two males and threw the dead bolts, locking them in and Vlad out. Alvero moved to Gage's left side, as Gage bared his fangs. Stephan rose, left Kat on the tile floor and stood beside Marcus in the bedroom.

"This ends here and now," promised Stephan, his hands fisting at his sides.

Gage growled at the warriors. "I'm going to kill you," Gage snarled. "But before I let you die, you'll watch me kill your female, so you'll know the pain of losing your mate, and beg me for death."

Gage seized Alvero, pushing him toward Marcus. His friend sidestepped the attack and Alvero slammed against the wall face first. He left an impression in the plaster as he pushed away and rounded on Marcus.

Gage summoned his power, and sent it out in a ring of force, knocking down both Stephan and Marcus.

Slowly, Gage reached up and took a samurai sword off the display hooks on the wall. He slid it out of its sheath, discarding the sheath carelessly to the side, and grinned at Stephan. Gage advanced on him with the sword held with both hands in front of his body.

Stephan feigned attacking first to one side and then the other, as his vision locked onto Gage like a laser-guided missile. Stephan pulled back his lips, presenting his fangs in an intimidating show.

Marcus made a move to get between the sword and his sire, but Alvero cut him off. Gage's guard went for Marcus' throat. Anticipating the move, Marcus raised his forearm to block the attack and knocked Alvero's hands away. The guard grabbed Marcus by the shoulders, opened his mouth wide and brought his deadly fangs down into Marcus' neck.

Marcus roared and grabbed Alvero by his shoulders. His fingers bit into the guard's flesh, muscles shook from the effort. The Alpha pulled the male off his neck, but Alvero took a chunk of flesh with him when he flew across the room.

Gage's nose twitched, the scent of the blood and flesh having gotten his attention. Stephan's eyes dilated, and he concentrated on Gage. In one fluid movement, he charged forward, grabbed the sword and wrenched it from Gage's hands.

From the bathroom floor, Katrina's groan pushed from her bruised lips in protest as she tried to move. Gage spun away from Stephan and leapt toward the bathroom. With a single bound, he was on Kat, lifting her tattered body like a shield in front of him.

"Drop the sword, or I'll kill her right now," ordered Gage turning Kat to face him. Stephan stilled his advance, coming to a stop near the two. Kat raised her one good hand and slapped Gage across his face. The slap was not hard enough to do any real damage, but it was contemptuous and demeaning. For Gage, who was obviously used to being in command and respected, it was maddening. Stephan saw the anger climb along his face. Gage trembled, an angry blush reddened his face.

"Now you die, bitch!" he spit out, the disdain dripping from his voice. He shifted his grip as if to break her neck, but the motion gave Stephan just the opening he needed. Stephan reached for Kat, yanking her out of Gage's grasp, and his powerful leg kicked Gage in the chest, sending him flying backwards.

Marcus stepped over Alvero's limp form into the bathroom. Stephan handed Kat to Marcus and advanced on Gage. He scuttled across the floor like an awkward crab, trying to find a place to plant his feet and right himself to standing when Stephan launched himself with the sword held high over his head, the blade pointed toward the male below. The sword met Gage's body in midair.

The sharp blade pierced his abdomen with a slicing sound and came out the other side, sticking into the tile, pinning him to the floor. Gage looked down. He had only a second to register what had happened before Stephan grabbed him with a hand on either side of his head. Stephan pushed with all his might, crushing Gage's skull with a slushy pop.

It was done.

Over.

The bastard was dead.

He would never hurt Katrina again, Stephan assured himself looking down at the messy form below.

"Behind you, Stephan," warned Marcus.

He turned to find Alvero flying through the air in his direction. Thanks to Marcus' warning, Stephan had just enough time to dodge the fangs aimed for his throat, but Alvero still connected with him and the pair fell to the floor. Alvero straddled his chest, the guard's hands around his throat. As his airway began to collapse, Stephan wrapped his hands around the guard's wrists, trying to pry the fingers from around his neck.

His vision started to blur. On silent feet, Marcus stalked up behind Alvero. He plucked the guard off Stephan and threw him against the vanity. Stephan's hand flew to his throat. He rolled to the side just in time to see Marcus plunge his hand into the guard's chest cavity and seize his beating heart. Stephan heard the suction as Marcus withdrew his hand, bringing Alvero's heart with it.

The Alphas watched Alvero's body slide to the floor. With a sigh, Stephan stood slowly, his tired, overused muscles protesting the movement. Marcus gave him an affectionate slap on the back.

"Come on, let's get Kat and get out of here," Marcus said as he and Stephan walked toward the bed where Marcus had deposited Katrina.

Katrina lay very still. Her porcelain skin so pale, Stephan feared she might yet die, but his heart refused to accept the possibility. She could not die when he'd just discovered she was his heartmate. He'd waited centuries for her and he would never find another. He must save her.

He eased on the bed and gathered her into the shelter of his arms. Kat opened her eyes, as much as the swelling would allow. "Who are you?" she asked weakly.

"He is the one who rescued you and saved your life by killing your capturer," Marcus volunteered.

Stephan rose with Kat in his arms. She moaned, the sound both pitiful and sorrowful.

"I hurt," she cried, tears rolling down her cheeks.

"I know, Kitten," Stephan said beside her cheek, his breath drying the tears. "I'm going to make you feel better. Sleep now," he commanded and took control of her mind, sending her into a fretful sleep.

Marcus opened the door to Vlad pacing on the other side. The Siberian's eyes assessed them as they walked down the hall. No one spoke while they made their way downstairs.

The four of them joined the rest of the Alphas who

attended to the humans. Michael joined them in the kitchen just as Demetri and Alex brought up the last of the humans from the basement.

"Nice of you to finally join us, Michael," said Alexander, disapproval making his voice hard while he carried a man out the door to the kitchen.

Michael looked over Katrina. "She looks awful. Why don't I drive you to the hospital, Stephan?"

He could tell Michael was using his mate as a distraction, but there were more important things that needed his attention. He decided to examine Alex's comment later. Stephan looked around at his friends, assessing their injuries. He pinned Michael with an evaluative glare, noting the way he suspiciously shifted his weight and the lack of blood on his person. "Take us to the penthouse. I can heal her there." He turned to look at Marcus and Vlad over his shoulder. "You two join us as well. I'll heal your injuries after I see to Katrina."

"My shoulder is already healing," said Vlad and moved around the couple. "I would prefer to remain here and help with the humans."

Demetri lifted an unconscious human male from where he lay on the kitchen floor. "I will gladly offer some of my blood to Vlad to aid his healing if he wishes to stay."

Vlad gave a slight bow to the warrior in acknowledgement of the gracious offer.

Stephan shrugged his broad shoulders, jostling the woman in his arms. "As you wish. Come Marcus."

A noise of protest escaped Marcus' mouth before Stephan stayed his argument with a fierce glare. "Don't argue with me. I'm hoping that once Kat is healed we will be able to retrieve her memories. Perhaps being with you will help to trigger Kat's memory."

"If you think a familiar face would help, maybe I should join you as well," offered Nicholai, when he strolled into the kitchen.

"It couldn't hurt." Marcus' brow lifted and his lips pulled into a snug line. "Besides you and me, Nicholai is the only other of us that Kat has spent any significant amount of time with."

"Thank you for your offer, Nicholai." Appreciation filled Stephan's heart as they started for the door. "I'd be grateful if you would join us. Michael can drop us off at the penthouse then come back to help the rest of you clean up this mess." He turned his hard stare on Michael. "If that is okay with you."

The Alpha mumbled his response, stomping from the home.

Chapter 40

Stephan carried Kat to his room with Marcus and Nicholai trailing behind him on the stairs. After assuring them they could not be of assistance, he ushered them out of the bedroom and pulled the door closed. Stephan returned to the bed and disrobed the sleeping Kat, letting her clothes drop carelessly to the floor in his haste to bare her flesh to his examination. He carefully analyzed every inch of her body, assessed the extent of her injuries. He noted each external bruise and cut. His gaze narrowed as it glossed over her battered body, each contusion raising his ire. Sitting next to her on the bed, he took a deep steadying breath to calm his anger enough that he could concentrate on sending his healing energy out and into her.

He was meticulous in his ministrations, carefully checking every part of her body. He healed her dislocated arm, sealed her torn spleen, and knitted her broken leg. Next he moved to her face, corrected her nose and took the swelling from her eyes. His hands bathed her body in soft light as they hovered over each plain of her anatomy. He left no place untouched by his healing energy.

After scanning her entire body for a fifth time and finding nothing more he could do, he withdrew from her, swaying slightly from exhaustion. He'd expended much energy during the hours he spent healing his heartmate, and it had taken its toll.

Stephan ran a tired hand through his dark hair and decided he needed a shower and some blood. In that order. After rising from the bed, he grabbed his shirt, pulling it over his head, and grimaced when he realized the material was stiff with blood, Kat's blood. It had soaked into his pants as well, he noticed as he slid out of his pants with an exhausted sigh.

Not wanting to leave his mate alone for one minute longer then was absolutely necessary, Stephan barely allowed his body to get wet from the spray before he soaped himself down and slathered some shampoo on his hair. Next, he ducked under the water to wash the suds from his body then jumped out. With haste, he grabbed a towel and wrapped it around his waist, before he headed back into the bedroom, water droplets still sluicing over the sharp planes of his body.

After donning a pair of sweatpants, Stephan gathered the blood soaked clothes from the floor, both his and Kat's, and headed downstairs for some much needed sustenance. He found Marcus and Nicholai sitting at the kitchen table talking in hushed tones. Marcus rose as Stephan entered, offering his seat.

"No, sit." Stephan opened the refrigerator and withdrew a bag of blood. "How's your neck?"

Marcus rubbed his bandaged wound. "Itchy. Nikko donated to me, so it's healing up quick. But never mind me. How's Kat?" Concern furrowed Marcus' brow.

"She'll be fine…" After joining them at the table, Stephan continued. "…physically, she'll be fine, but mentally…" His voice trailed as his worrisome thoughts consumed him.

"I must restore Kat's memory," Stephan muttered

then downed the entire bag in one long draw.

"I've never heard of a mindwipe ever being reversed before," said Nicholai. "Do you even know how to do it?"

"No," confessed Stephan with a heavy sigh. "But there must be a way. She has to remember me. I will not live without her. *We* cannot live without each other."

Marcus took a long drink of his crimson liquid. "It would be much easier if she would remember us, remember how much she loves you."

"What if her memory cannot be restored?" asked Nicholai sensibly.

"Then I'll have to win her love all over again. One way or another, she is my heartmate, and we will be together." Stephan pinned the Russian warrior with a resolute stare, daring his friend to say otherwise.

"I hope you can restore her memory, 'cause this is *deja vu* all over again." Marcus scrubbed a hand down his face before continuing. "Just like seven years ago, she is in the penthouse after being attacked by vampires, only to discover she is surrounded by more vampires. I can tell you that didn't go over well with her last time. If you can't restore her memory, I doubt it will go any better this time."

Stephan nodded in agreement. He made his way to the fridge for another bag of blood, and consumed it quickly. "No time like the present," he announced, throwing away the now empty bag.

"Now?" asked Marcus. "Right now? But you don't know what the consequences will be."

He knew he'd gotten lucky when he did the extensive memory wipe. That kind of wipe could have caused permanent damage, luckily Kat's mental faculties had remained intact. There was no telling how reversing the process would affect her. It made him nervous as hell, but he had to try.

"There's no reason to wait. The sooner I try, the sooner we'll know the consequences."

"But you are tired. Don't you think you should wait until—" Stephan's raised hand halted Marcus' protest.

"I must at least try, Marcus. Now." His entire being screamed for its heartmate. "I must have my Katrina. I will not wait any longer."

Stephan treaded up the stairs and entered his room on silent feet. He sank onto the bed and took a deep steadying breath to calm his nerves, then sent a mental command for Kat to wake. As her eyes fluttered open, he smiled down at her thinking how lucky he was to have her. He pushed into her mind, determined to remain there so he could monitor her thoughts.

"Where am I?"

"You're safe. You are in my penthouse."

"How did I get here?" She tried to stretch, stopping short when the movement sent pain racing through her body. He'd do another round of healing energy after the memory retrieval.

"We brought you here in Michael's car."

A memory flashed in her mind of her doctor driving her as the handsome man before her held her in the back seat. Stephan smiled, glad she found him handsome.

"Who are you?"

"My name is Stephan."

"Why am I here, Stephan?"

He noted the way she said his name, cold, detached. The warmth and feeling she used to put behind the two syllables now missing.

"Katrina, I want to help you try to remember your past."

Her heart sped up, hope blossomed in her mind for a moment before the doubt settled in. "But I've been trying, I can't remember the past seven years."

"I know. I can help you to remember if you'll let me," he offered wiping a blonde curl away from her forehead. He couldn't keep his fingers out of her silken hair. He had to touch her, needed the physical connection as much as she did.

Kat looked at him with amazement widening her eyes as she tried to prop herself up on one elbow. "I'd like that. When can we start?"

"Right now," informed Stephan and gently pushed her back down onto the bed. "Lay back and close your eyes."

Kat peered warily down at where he touched her. Her eyes widened incredulously when she lifted the sheet to discover she lay naked in a stranger's bed. She clutched the sheet to her chest. Panic took her face. Fear flooded her mind, escape her first thought and her panic flowed into him through their mental connection, making his blood turn to ice as he realized she might try to leave.

"Lay down," ordered Stephan, much harsher than he had intended. His concern for Kat overrode his calm demeanor.

"No, let me out of here." Kat sat up stubbornly, wincing.

"I can't do that."

"Why can't you let me leave?" Her eyes rolled back in her head. Katrina closed her eyes and lay back down on the bed. She was going to faint.

"Calm down, Katrina. You're injuries are still healing. You shouldn't move." Stephan raised his hands in surrender and slid off the bed before continuing. "I won't hurt you, I swear. All I want to do is help you get your memories back."

With more space between her naked body and him, Kat began to calm. Her breathing steadied, and she relaxed into the pillows as she considered him. Her assessing gaze had him pushing deeper into her mind to glean her inner thoughts.

She wasn't sure she could trust the man standing before her. Someone had stripped her of her clothes. She felt vulnerable, exposed. However, she also understood someone must have helped her. She was no longer in the hands of her violent captors. And though she still ached, she knew her injuries were better. While meeting his direct gaze, she decided she probably had the man in front of her to thank for that. If he had helped her, perhaps he could also help her retrieve her memories as he'd said.

Stephan allowed her time to process her situation and after several minutes, Kat finally spoke, "Okay, I believe you. Let's try to get my memories back."

"I'll have to touch your head. Is that okay?"

Kat closed her eyes and nodded. The moment his weight depressed the mattress beside her, her eyes snapped open to pin him with her stare. Sensing her trepidation, he sent a feeling of peace to flow through her, calming her, easing her fear. When Stephan placed his hand on each side of her head, her eyes slowly closed.

Taking a deep breath, he sent his mind further into hers finding the mess he'd created days earlier.

****

Nicholai looked up from where he was sitting in the living room as Stephan descended the stairs. The warrior waited until his friend slumped onto the couch across from him before he spoke. "You look exhausted. How did it go?"

"It didn't go. No matter what I tried, I couldn't get her memories back." The look of despondency on Stephan's face pulled at his strong features.

"I am so sorry. I could try if you like," Nicholai offered and leaned forward resting his thick forearms on his knees.

Stephan considered the offer. When finally he spoke, he sounded reluctant. "Okay, you can try, but be careful."

As Nicholai strode past him, Stephan's hand struck like a cobra, grabbed the Alpha's arm and stilled his feet. "I mean it, Nicholai. Do not hurt her."

Nicholai's steely gaze met Stephan's, his sincerity plainly visible. "Hurting your heartmate is not something I can tolerate. She will not be injured at my efforts, old friend."

Released from Stephan's steel-like grasp, Nicholai took the stairs two at a time. He opened the bedroom door and found Kat sleeping in the large bed. Silently he drew a chair over to the side of the bed, sat down, and placed his hand on her forehead. Without waking her, he slipped into her mind and went to work.

Slowly he became aware of Marcus standing behind him and pulled out of her jumbled mind.

"How did it go?" whispered Marcus hopefully.

Nicholai shook his head, pursing his lips into a tight line. "I could not do anything. I was afraid to get too aggressive in there for fear I would do permanent damage."

Marcus crossed his arms across his wide chest. "Tell me what you tried."

Marcus listened as Nicholai tried to explain how he had attempted to restore Kat's memory. The sound of Nicholai's deep voice must have penetrated her sleep for Kat stirred beneath the sheets.

She turned toward the males. Nicholai smiled down at her with kind eyes. He sent reassuring feelings into her mind knowing that being in a room with two males she didn't know would be upsetting after the trauma she suffered at Gage's hands.

Marcus crossed the room in three long strides and stood at her bedside. "Hi, Kat. I'm Marcus." He introduced himself with a broad smile. "We've known each other for many years, but I know you don't remember me."

Kat gradually nodded her head once in agreement.

"You might not remember me, but I remember you Kitty Kat. Would you like me to tell you about our time together these past years?"

"These past years?" A look of confusion furrowed her golden eyebrows. "I thought I was in a coma for the past seven years. Did I know you before the coma?"

The corners of Marcus' lips turned down into a frown as he realized his mistake. "We have known each other for years. We were great friends. I'd like to tell you all about it, if that's okay with you."

Katrina nodded. "I'd like that, but first do you

think I might be able to get dressed? I'm tired of being naked with all of you men in my room."

"Of course." Marcus went into the walk-in closet and immerged with a white silk nightgown and matching robe.

"How about this?" He handed her the silk ensemble. "Nicholai and I will leave so you can get dressed. I'll be right outside just call when you're ready."

Katrina affected an inquisitive look, and gestured at the gown. "What, Stephan just happens to keep a silky nightie set in his closet in case a guest stays over?"

Marcus smiled. "Is that a hint of jealousy I hear in your voice?"

Katrina look taken aback. "No jealousy, just a question."

"You should not tease her, Marcus," Nicholai chastised, feeling sorry for the woman lying in the bed. She looked so young, so weak. So human.

"I'll tell you all about why there is a night gown in the closet when we talk. Just call when you're ready." Nicholai allowed Marcus to lead him out the door with a hand on his shoulder, and closed the door behind them.

Chapter 41

Kat sat for a moment waiting to see if the door would open. When it didn't, she slipped out from under the sheets and stood carefully on her unsteady legs. The floor swayed and she grabbed the bed for support, waiting until the dizziness passed before she grabbed the nightgown and made her way to the bathroom.

She looked curiously at her reflection in the mirror. Memories of being badly injured while tortured flooded her mind and her knees threatened to give way. She leaned forward, using her straight arms to brace her weight on the counter, when she remembered how they'd broken her leg and nose. Yet the only sign of the injuries still visible was a little bruising and the dried blood on her skin and hair. Her mind wanted to explore how that might be possible, but Katrina ruthlessly pushed the thought away not yet ready to examine it. There were other things that needed her attention, like staying vertical.

Her hand went to her hair, smoothing over the matted strands. It felt stiff and hard under the pads of her fingers. She cringed as she studied her reflection in the mirror and decided a bath was in order.

Kat pushed down the stopper in the tub and ran a bath. Sliding into the water, she savored the feel of steamy water on her body. The warmth soaked into her skin, replacing the ache with a tranquil lassitude. After washing her body and hair, she laid back and closed her eyes, letting the water lap at her skin in a soothing rhythm. Her eyes drifted closed.

Kat startled as she heard a voice whisper in her ear, "Kitten, wake up. You fell asleep in the bath."

Katrina covered herself, as best she could with the wash cloth in her hand and turned to find Stephan kneeling beside the bath.

"Do you always just barge in on a woman when she is taking a bath?"

"No, I can assure you I don't. I came in to make sure you were all right. Marcus grew concerned when you did not call him back into the room to talk." Stephan ran his fingers over her hair. "I was worried about you."

"Get out," she ordered pointing toward the door.

"You don't have to be embarrassed. I've seen it all before," he said easily, as if seeing her in her birthday suit was an everyday occurrence.

He took the wash cloth and rubbed it over her shoulders lovingly. The feel of his caress sent heat pooling down low in her belly. Damned man! He touched her as if he had the right. The audacity!

Wait. What did he say?

She eyed him suspiciously. "What do you mean you've 'seen it before'? Were you the one who undressed me?"

"Yes," he admitted dipping the wash cloth back into the water before running it down her arm and across her exposed chest causing her nipples to pebble as if they were reaching out for him.

A blush crept into her cheeks. Katrina's temper flared. She was tired of being manhandled even if the one doing the handling was incredibly sexy and seemed to have her best interest at heart.

"Get out," she repeated more forcefully and adjusted one arm to cover more of her breasts while she pulled the cloth from his hand. "Get out now!"

She could see Stephan's jaw tighten as he stood, towering over her. "As you wish. I didn't mean to upset you." As he reluctantly obliged her command and turned to leave, he paused, his back still toward Kat. "I put some towels on the vanity for you," he informed her before leaving the bath.

Kat took a deep breath. That man affected her in a way that made her uncomfortable. When he was around she tended to lose all sense of self. All she wanted was to melt into that tall dark stranger, and it scared her. Despite the liberties he took, he demonstrated thoughtfulness and caring that threatened to undo her. She felt drawn to him on a visceral level, like they were destined to be together. And that was just plain ridiculous.

After drying herself off, she wrapped one towel around her lithe body and patted her hair dry with the other towel Stephan left. She found a brush and ran it through her hair. And finally, she brushed her teeth.

Feeling almost human again, she slid into the soft gown, then tucked her arms into the robe, and tied the sash tightly around her waist. After using the facilities, she crawled back into bed and called out to the gentleman who had identified himself as Marcus.

"So you ready to hear about your past?" the handsome man asked, entering the room.

"Yes, but first I have a question."

"Go ahead," he prompted, sitting down beside her .

"Why do I feel so funny when I'm around Stephan?"

"I can answer that by telling you about your past. Are you ready to talk?"

Katrina swallowed hard to gather her courage and nodded her answer.

He told her of their years together. She apparently danced at a club he owned. They were best friends. They lived together for seven years. He explained what her life was like and how both he and Stephan fit into it.

Though he seemed forthcoming, she got the distinct impression he left out specific events and couldn't help but wonder why. But she didn't ask. Instead she remained silent letting him tell their tale.

Coming to the present events, Marcus inquired, "So did you remember any of the things I told you about?"

"No, but it at least explains why I react to Stephan the way I do."

Katrina could not believe all the information Marcus had shared. She had no memory of a large chunk of her life. It was unnerving to know that she was surrounded by people she should know and trust with no memory of them. Marcus had said she loved Stephan, yet as she searched her mind she felt nothing for the man, other than perhaps lust, but nothing more. It seemed so strange, knowing the men in the home knew her so well and she didn't know them at all. At least, not any more. Her only memories were of her foster homes and Dr. Garsoe.

"Wait a minute," Katrina said, confusion raising her voice. "I remember waking up in the hospital. Dr. Garsoe said I had been in a coma for the past seven years. Was that a lie?"

Marcus took a moment before he spoke as if he needed to carefully arrange his thoughts before answering. "Dr. Garsoe is a memory expert. He thought it would be less traumatic for you to think you had been in a coma then to have to tell you that seven years of your life were suddenly gone from your memory."

Well at least that explained why she was in such good shape. She'd wondered how she'd awaken from a seven year coma without any muscle atrophy.

"I still don't quite understand how seven years' worth of memories just suddenly vanished. Was I in an accident or something? Will I ever get the memories back?"

"Perhaps if you look at some pictures, it might jog your memory," Marcus offered.

A lassitude took her body making it heavy. Her lids dipped, vision blurred from fatigue. After the events of the night, the long bath, the even longer story, it was finally catching up to her. Kat stifled a yawn. "Maybe I could look at the pictures tomorrow."

"Was I really so boring?" quipped Marcus with a sexy grin. With his brown hair and matching eyes, any woman would find him attractive, and yet he didn't affect her the way Stephan did. It was a lot to take in. Maybe tomorrow things would make more sense.

"No, you're not boring. I actually really enjoyed talking with you." And she did. "I'm just very tired." Kat gave him a sleepy smile and settled down onto the fluffy pillows, drawing the covers up under her chin.

"Tomorrow, then. Sleep tight, Kitty Kat." Marcus leaned down to give her a quick kiss on her forehead before leaving her to her thoughts.

Chapter 42

The next evening began benignly enough. When Kat awoke it was late afternoon. Surprised she had slept so long, she quickly dressed and slipped downstairs for something to eat. At the foot of the stairs her eyes alighted on the couch to discover Stephan sleeping fretfully.

Marcus mentioned the previous night that Stephan owned the penthouse and that the two of them had been a couple before she lost her memory. She found it endearing and sweet that he chose to give her his bedroom and now slept on the couch—a couch that was clearly too small for his large frame as evidenced by his bare feet hanging off the end. Quietly, she made her way over and adjusted the afghan so his exposed feet would be covered along with his body.

She found herself inexplicably reaching down to brush a stray strand of hair away from his face. Realizing how intimate that seemed, she caught her hand back, holding it to her chest with the other and abruptly left, making her way into the kitchen for some breakfast. She shook her head at the action as she went, thinking that it was too familiar a gesture to do to someone she didn't remember knowing.

Shortly after Stephan and Marcus rose, the penthouse became as busy as Grand Central Station, filled with large bodies of men who Marcus explained were all friends of his and Stephan's.

"Alex, Vladimir, and Demetri are all here to help you get your memories back, Kat," Marcus explained.

"Are you willing to let them try?" Stephan asked. She noted how hopeful he sounded and wished she felt as optimistic.

"I doubt it will work, but yeah, I'm willing to give it a try." Her eyes darted between the men. She doubted the strangers could help her. In truth, they were so large they were a bit scary and made her a little reluctant to be alone with them. However, she pushed her consternation aside, determined to get her memories back no matter what it took.

"I'll go first," offered Alex. "Where should we go?"

Stephan's hands flexed nervously at his sides. "I think the study would be the best place."

In the study, she and Alex arranged two burgundy chairs to face each other. She sat across from the handsome blue-eyed, blond-haired man wondering just what he might try that the others hadn't.

"All right now, darlin'. Just sit back and close your eyes. And hopefully you'll get a big surprise." He winked at her, disarming her instantly with his crooked grin. His southern drawl was like a soothing balm to her soul as he spoke and his affable teasing made her feel very comfortable.

"You might feel me rootin' around your head. Don't worry about it. It shouldn't hurt."

"What do you mean 'rooting around' my head? Are you psychic or something?"

He smiled a big toothy grin. "Something like that. We all are. You ready to give this a try?"

She nodded and closed her eyes, gathering her courage.

He held her hands gently as he worked to retrieve the memories. She felt a flutter in her mind, like tiny gossamer wings beating against her brain. Though unusual, the sensation was not uncomfortable so Katrina sat still and let him try to work his magic.

She had no idea how long he tried, but, after what seemed like hours, when her memories did not return, Alex left and the next man came in.

This man looked scary with his goatee, shaven head, and large frame. His thick Siberian accent reminded Kat of the Russian mafia. The muscular man nearly filled the chair with his girth.

"You ready?" he asked gruffly.

Obviously a man of few words.

She forced a weak smile. "Sure, the sooner the better." Because the sooner they tried the sooner he would leave.

He did not hold her hands, choosing instead to stare deeply into her eyes, his dark, hard gaze boring into her like a drill. The flutter she felt with Alex turned into a dull throb as Vlad tried to unlock her mind, but Katrina gladly bore the small pain in hopes it would work.

Unfortunately, Vladimir had no more luck then the others, and Kat was relieved to see him take his leave when he finished.

A man, who could have easily won a Mr. Olympia contest, entered the study with heavy steps and arms so thick they could not lie fully at his side. When he sat in the wing-backed chair, it moaned under his weight.

Though introduced to him earlier, Kat found

nothing comforting or familiar about this man. His brow furrowed, drawing his eyebrows down menacingly over his eyes, and the perpetual frown on his face made it look hard. They had obviously saved the scariest man for last.

A cold sweat broke out on Katrina's forehead. It seemed all the men were trying to use mental powers to help her regain her memory. She felt their presences in her mind as they worked with her. The thought that the enormous man in front of her now might also invade her mind terrified her.

Without so much as a hello, he grabbed her head with his large hands on each side of her face and brought it forward until their foreheads touched.

"Close your eyes," he barked at her. "I want you to think about the first memory you have after the amnesia and we will work back from there. I want you to think about driving to the ranch."

Katrina's body trembled. She felt the man's power surround her, push into her mind. His mental touch bordered on painful, causing her to shrink from his touch, but Demetri held her fast. Completely at his mercy, she felt wholly trapped with this man. Only her desire to retrieve her memory kept her from screaming out.

When the session ended, Katrina slumped in her chair the moment Demetri's large hands released her head, grateful that the painful session had ended. Relief consumed her, not because her memory was back, but because she was glad to have some space between her and Demetri when he left the library. She remained seated after he left her without saying a word, trying to work up the courage to go down and face the overwhelming men below.

The sound of the stairs creaking under Demetri's massive muscular weight drew Stephan's attention.

"I'll give you this, the female has courage," Demetri said as he descended the stairs. "I could smell her fear while I worked with her, but she stayed with me and tried her best to remember."

"Well, how did it go?" asked Stephan hopefully.

"I'm sorry. I'm afraid it didn't work," Demetri announced to the group, coming to sit beside Nicholai on the black couch.

Alexander crossed his legs at the ankles on the coffee table. "Well, that's it then. We've all tried to help Kat get her memories back."

"All but Michael," accused Vladimir in this thick accent.

Marcus turned a questioning look to Stephan. "Yeah, that's right. Where is Michael anyway?"

"He mentioned something about being in the middle of a building project back in Savannah. He took the first available flight home," Stephan informed the group.

Marcus tsked. "Leave it to Michael to put his own needs first."

"I want to thank you all for trying to help Kat." Stephan met each Alpha's eyes in a show of respect, then leaned his head back against the couch in resignation.

There was no hope now. They'd tried everything they could think of to help Kat. He would just have to accept that her memories were lost forever, and he had only himself to blame.

"With Gage gone, Kat's safe. We could finally be

together for eternity and I've ruined it." Stephan turned his down-trodden face toward Nicholai. "I've taken away any chance we had at being happy. She might never love me again." The thought made his heart clench with a fear that sent a shudder down his spine.

"I'm really sorry," sympathized Marcus. "If I had just let you drink from her the first night you met, you would have known she was your heartmate and things might have been different."

"You were only trying to protect her, and I thank you for that." Stephan laid a consoling hand on Marcus' shoulder before continuing. "I mean it, thank you for protecting her and keeping her safe these past years. I can never tell you how grateful I am that she had you to watch over her. Even if we do not have a future together, I will be forever grateful for the brief time we had."

Nicholai leaned forward, resting his hands on his knees when he spoke. "I hold it true, whate'er befall; I feel it, when I sorrow most; 'Tis better to have loved and lost than never to have loved at all."

"Exactly. I now truly understand what Alfred, Lord Tennyson meant by that." Stephan scrubbed his hand through his dark hair.

For the first time in his long, long life Stephan felt totally helpless. Unable to help Kat retrieve her memories, he was now at great risk of losing her forever. If she could not remember her feelings for him, she might decide to leave him. He could not stomach the thought. A knot formed in his throat as he tried to imagine him letting her go. Again.

It would be impossible, he knew. He'd loved her even before he discovered she was his heartmate. Now that he'd tasted her blood, his need for her drew him to her. He would always be tied to her soul, her body, her blood. She was the other half of him. Without her he could not live, but being without her was exactly what he now faced due to his decision to take her memories of him.

Kat quietly descended the stairs, trying not to draw attention to herself. Of course that only resulted in complete silence. Six pairs of eyes rounded on her as she made her way down. She felt self-conscious in the penthouse with a bunch of strangers who apparently knew her, but she couldn't remember any of them. Oh sure, all the men had been nice enough to help her, even the scary ones, but she still felt awkward around so many people she didn't know, especially when they kept asking her to remember stuff.

"Don't let me interrupt. I was just going into the kitchen for a bite to eat," she volunteered and made her way through the room. She heard the murmuring start up behind her as she entered the kitchen.

After pulling open the door to the fridge, she leaned over and opened the crisper drawer withdrawing an apple. She'd just taken a juicy bite of the Red Delicious when she turned to find Nicholai had joined her. She jumped in surprise. How was it that these large men moved without a sound?

"Can I get you something to eat?" offered Katrina.

"Sure," he replied with a kind smile.

"What would you like?" Katrina opened the refrigerator wide so Nicholai could see the possibilities inside.

He eyed the apple in Kat's hand with desire. "That apple actually looks good. Is there another one?"

Kat reached in, grabbed another Red Delicious, and gave it a toss in Nicholai's direction. He easily plucked it from the air as he moved with her to the kitchen table. Kat's eyes widened when he set a faux leather bound book down onto the table.

"I think you should see this, Katrina." Nicholai tapped the book with one finger.

Nerves tightened her stomach. "What is it?"

"Just a little something I thought you might enjoy."

Kat really liked his thick accent. It made her think of cold Russian nights under warm cozy blankets. *Yummy,* she thought taking a bite of her apple.

"Go ahead open it." He pushed the book across the table so it came to rest in front of Kat.

Kat opened the book gingerly and Nicholai took a generous bite from his apple. Her mouth gaped open when she saw what was contained within.

Chapter 43

Marcus fell onto the couch beside Stephan, and slapped him on the back with a rough hand. His gaze raked Stephan's face steadily. "You look long in the tooth."

"With each breath I take, I smell honeysuckle. It's everywhere. It surrounds me." *Touches every place in my heart.* "She is such a part of me, and yet she doesn't even know me."

"Well you can fix that," suggested Marcus. "Give her time. She fell in love with you once, she'll do it again."

"I don't even know if she has any idea what she does to me." *She completes me and I will love her forever.* "I want to spend the rest of my life by her side, loving her, protecting her, caring for her. Forever."

"I know you will get your chance," assured Marcus. "The two of you were meant to be together. You won her heart once, you'll win it again. I don't doubt that for a minute."

"I wish I had your confidence." Stephan shook his head slowly back and forth. "I hope you are right."

"I know I am. Give her some time, some space. Let her get to know you again. She'll come around, just like she did before. And just think you've already won her once, so you know what to do." A reassuring smile that reached his eyes lit Marcus' face. "Not to mention the worst is over for now. We can breathe again knowing that she is at least out of danger."

Stephan sighed, ringing the back of his neck with one tired hand in an attempt to ease the tension in his muscles. "I can only hope you are right, Marcus," he repeated. "I don't know what I would do if I lost her. I don't think I could live." *It hurts because there is no sparkle in her eye when I reach for her, no love in her voice when she says my name.* "It's killing me to know what we had; what I might have ruined forever."

"Let's look on the bright side," said Marcus, ever the optimist. "She's here in your house. She isn't running in fear of us. She hasn't asked to go back to the ranch. She has been willing to talk to us and listen to what we have to say about the memories. I've been reading her as I'm sure you have too. You know she believes us about her past."

Stephan nodded in acquiesce. "Thank the Fates we have pictures to prove we knew her so she will never have reason to doubt us."

"Exactly, see it's not all bad. Tonight's our last night all of the Alphas will be together. Why don't we try to have a little fun. Have some alcohol, a little food and blood—behind Kat's back of course," Marcus added quickly when Stephan threw him an are-you-kidding-me glance. "And who knows where the night will lead for you and Kat."

Alexander moved behind them. "I have to agree with Marcus. If you just give her time, she'll come around. You'll see." He rested both hands on the back of the couch. "For tonight just have fun. Show her a good time. That's the first step in dating a woman."

"All right," Stephan agreed reluctantly. "Perhaps

you two are right."

Marcus clapped his hands together once and rubbed them heartily. "Sounds like party time. Let's break out the C and C."

"C and C?" asked Alex, straightening.

"Cuisine and cocktails," explained Marcus with a grin.

"Make mine Vodka—straight up," chimed in Vlad, who had been silently listening to the conversation up until then.

Demetri, echoing Vlad's look of elation, said, "Make mine a true Bloody Mary if you would."

"Will do," Marcus replied and turned on the stereo before making his way to the bar.

****

Flipping through the book Nicholai had given her, Kat's perusal of the photos made her frustrated. She couldn't remember being at the places she saw in the pictures, did not remember having worn those costumes before.

In the picture she now looked at she wore a Cleopatra costume and stood next to a man dressed as a mummy. She tapped the mummy costume. "Who's that?" she asked taking another bite from her apple.

"I believe that is Marcus. From what I understand the two of you loved dressing up on Halloween," Nicholai informed her.

"Huh." She huffed, turning her blue-gray eyes to the next picture. This time her face and the face of the person beside her were quite visible. In the picture, she and Marcus stood side by side at the Hoover Dam.

As she flipped through the album she noted how at ease and happy she appeared in all the photographs.

Each smile seemed genuine. She ran her hand over the cellophane covered photos, wishing she could remember something of them, even just one, but none of the memories came to her.

She continued to peruse the album until she came to a picture of her and Stephan sitting in a gondola. "Did I ever go to Italy?" she asked in surprise.

Nicholai swallowed his mouthful of apple and chuckled. "I don't think so. If memory serves me, I believe that is the gondola ride in the Florencia Hotel here in Vegas."

"Ohhh." She ran one finger down the picture of Stephan's face, circling it on his chest. She noticed how instead of looking at the camera like she had been, his head was turned toward her. The look on his face, one of total rapture, made him seem like he was having the time of his life just sitting there next to her.

She breathed a heavy sigh.

"Do you remember anything?" Nicholai asked quietly.

She looked down again at the picture before shaking her head and replying solemnly, "No. Not a thing."

"Well, that is okay." Nicholai shrugged. "It was worth a try. I hoped reviewing some pictures might run your memory."

Kat looked at him with confusion. "You mean *jog* my memory?"

"Yes, yes. Sometimes my English still gets mixed up," he apologized with a shy smile. "So did any of the pictures jog your memory?"

Kat shook her head and took a last bite of her apple.

"I am sorry, Katrina. I hoped the pictures would help."

"I wish I could remember. We seemed so happy." She laid her hand over the picture of her and Stephan as a song whispered into the kitchen from the living room.

After chucking their apple cores into the trash free throw style, Nicholai rested his elbows on the table and steepled his fingers, thoughtfully resting his chin on his index fingers as they touched.

"Let me ask you something Katrina. Do you know how long some people wait to find true love?" Not waiting for her answer his rhetorical question, Nicholai continued, "Some people wait a lifetime and never find it. If you knew the love of your life stood in the next room, would you not go to him?"

Would she? Yes, she decided, she would.

"Love requires bravery, a leap of faith. Will you leap, Katrina?"

Before Kat could respond, Nicholai stood, smiled down at her and extended his hand. "Come, let us go join the party."

Kat took his hand wondering what the evening might bring if she just dared to leap.

Chapter 44

Kat sat in the living room surrounded by beautiful specimens of male virility and she would have had to be dead not to notice. Each man was handsome in his own way from Alex's cowboy looks to Vlad's dark chiseled features. All of them had an air of confidence about them, like they would gladly take on the world and knew they would win. But it was Stephan to whom her gaze kept returning.

Every time he neared, her blood heated with desire. Her heart raced, cheeks flushed with wanton need. Her body knew what it wanted, even if her mind had yet to get on board.

Marcus turned up the stereo and the drinks flowed like the Colorado River through the Grand Canyon. Everyone seemed to be having a great time, even Kat genuinely enjoyed herself.

But her mind kept wandering to Stephan. Nicholai's words ran through her head leaving soft footprints of consideration. If Stephan was her true love, didn't they both deserve for her to give him a chance. She might not remember him, but she could get to know him if she dared take a chance on love.

As the evening wore on, she found herself more and more drawn to Stephan. She appreciated how he and Marcus seemed to be giving her some space—time to think. She could tell by the way his eyes were always on her, that it was a struggle for Stephan to give her room. She treasured the effort, it endeared him to her.

After looking at the photo album, she had resigned herself to the fact that there had been a history between them, and if the smiling faces in the pictures were any indication, it had been a happy history. She didn't doubt any of the stories the men told her. She just wished she could remember. It was like looking at pictures of someone else's life where her head had been Photoshopped in. It seemed surreal.

As she worked the room, she found herself having a good time with all of the men. Kat enjoyed the way they treated her with courtly respect. Talking with Alex and laughing with Marcus helped her relax. Even Vlad and Demetri no longer seemed scary.

One by one the men took turns dancing with Kat. They twirled and dipped her with ease. She never would have guessed these big burly men could be so graceful. Being the only woman in the place, made her feel as desirable as Venus De Milo herself.

As she danced with Demetri, she found a smile tugging at her lips. He moved like a professional, gyrating his hips in time with the fast music. With his old world demeanor, she could imagine him waltzing in a high court of old, easily picturing him in a time long ago. But the sexy way he moved to the modern music amazed and surprised her.

Her gaze however, did not remain on her dance partner for long, but instead her eyes were drawn to Stephan. She couldn't help but glance over at him, taking note of the look in his eyes that made her stomach tighten.

He stood across the room, braced against the wall

with one leg crossed over the other at the ankle and his arms crossed over his thick chest—a chest accented by the black dress shirt he wore tucked into his gray dress slacks. He looked like sin and lust combined into one gorgeous package. The dark possession in his sapphire-blue eyes when he stared at her set every nerve on fire. She felt his gaze roam over her as her body moved in time to the music.

It was clear that the other men had also noticed the possessive way Stephan looked at her, for none of them hesitated to hand her over, when he cut in on them dancing. All of them seemed to bow to his will, as if they did not wish to challenge his authority.

When the music came to an end, the next song to play was much slower. In the blink of her eye, Stephan suddenly stood beside her, his hand proffered. "May I have this dance?"

Demetri backed away as she answered, "I'd like that."

Kat smiled wide, and Stephan took her into his arms. It felt so right, felt good and safe to be with him.

She laid her cheek against his shoulder and breathed in his masculine, woodsy scent. A quiet, contented sigh escaped from her lips and she closed her eyes, allowing the moment to take her. It did not escape her attention that every time a slow song played, Stephan ask her to dance.

While the two of them swayed slowly to the music, Kat contemplated all Nicholai had told her. Though she could not remember her time with Stephan, somewhere deep within her, she felt connected to him. Being held in his strong arms as they had danced together seemed comfortably familiar.

It couldn't be love her thoughts denied, but he was definitely handsome, the most beautiful man in the room, and he'd treated her well. After all, he risked his life to rescue her from the kidnappers. He must be a good man, given how all of his friends had helped not only him, but also her. Obviously they wanted the two of them to be together.

While they rocked slowly in time to the music, Kat decided to accept all that everyone had told her of her past, especially what Marcus had said to her about she and Stephan being in love. She would remain at the penthouse in hopes that something might eventually restore her memories and if not, then more time with Stephan would allow her time to get to know him, even love him. She owed him that.

Owed herself that.

The love coming from Stephan wove a path through her body and wrapped around her heart, warming her from the inside out.

"Kitten," he said, interrupting her thoughts. He waited until she raised her eyes to meet his gaze. She could feel herself falling into his gaze as if mesmerized. Kat closed her eyes slowly and shook away the vertigo. When she opened her eyes again he had stopped moving and looked at her with anticipation.

"Kitten," he repeated softly. "I promise you I will do everything I can to make you happy if you stay. Tell me you will remain with me and give us a chance."

She thought back to the picture of the happy couple riding on the gondola. "Yes, yes I will give us a chance," A look of relief took his gorgeous face.

Abruptly the song playing changed and the mood was broken by the upbeat music. As the tune blared, their attention left one another to focus on Marcus who wrenched his underwear up, making it look like a thong appearing overtop of the kaki waist band of his pants. He began shaking his booty as he sang along to the song, "'cuz she was livin' *la vida loca.*"

Kat laughed at the show. Stephan leaned over and against her ear whispered, "I love the way you laugh." His sexy voice caressed her ear, tickling it with his hot breath when he spoke. Her body reacted instantly. She swallowed the lump in her throat. Her blood warmed from the heat of her desire.

Kat's top teeth tugged at her bottom lip nervously. "I think Marcus has had too much to drink."

"Perhaps just not the right kind of drink. I think he might be a pint too low," Stephan muttered, as he too watched Marcus spasm about.

Kat glanced up at him questioningly, catching him wince as if he realized how strange his comment sounded. Before she could question him about what he had said, he lowered his lips to hers and captured them in a kiss.

She was tentative at first, this was their first kiss— at least that she remembered. His lips were feather light. They skimmed across hers, driving her desire for him higher with the tease.

She relaxed into him and her hands snaked up his arms encircling his neck. Her lips parted in invitation, which he RSVP'd by sweeping his tongue in her mouth. Stephan moaned against her mouth, his passion stirred. Yearning built between them, encasing them in a spell of ecstasy until Katrina felt herself slipping away to ride on a cloud of delight.

The sound of Vlad calling out brought her back

down to earth. They broke their kiss. And when she looked around she realized that Marcus had apparently wiggled a little too hard and backed into the coffee table. Catching the backs of his knees, he crashed down on top of the drinking glasses sitting on the table. It shattered under his weight, slicing through his pants.

"Are you okay?" Alex asked, making his way to Marcus.

"Of course, I am." Marcus brushed the shattered glass off his legs. "I'll be fine."

"You are bleeding," Demetri observed.

"I'll be fine," Marcus repeated, still nestled within the remnants of the table. "Don't worry your pretty little head about it."

Demetri quirked one eyebrow. "I wasn't going to, smartass." He crossed his thick arms over his chest.

With Marcus injured, the mood instantly sobered. The men seemed relatively unconcerned, but the accident was enough to dampen their spirits and no one appeared to be in a partying mood any longer. Stephan seemed clearly put out by the incident as he hauled Marcus up from the mangled table.

Demetri looked down at the mess under Marcus with disdain. "I think that is a sign, it's time for us to call it a night and take our leave."

Vlad quickly agreed and Stephan escorted the group to the door where Kat watched as one by one they all said goodbye, sending each other off with a valediction of "Safe travels."

When it was Nicholai's turn to leave he paused, one hand on the door, and turned to Katrina. "Do me a favor."

She looked up into his serious eyes. "What?"

"Give love a chance. True love is a rare gift, something to be cherished. Don't throw it away."

Katrina moved forward and gave him a hug around his waist. "You know, you really are a romantic at heart."

Nicholai's arms wrapped around her in a steel embrace as he leaned down putting his lips to her ear. "Shhh, don't tell anyone. They all think I'm a badbutt."

Katrina giggled as he drew back. "I think you mean badass," she bantered, amusement sparkling in her eyes.

Nicholai chuckled. "Goodbye, sweet Katrina. Remember what I said."

His long strides took him out the door, leaving her alone with Stephan and Marcus to face the future.

Chapter 45

As they moved into the living room, Stephan watched Katrina try to stifle a yawn. He was not fooled, she was obviously quite tired. He moved closer and slid one arm around her waist. Into her ear he whispered, "Kitten, I can feel how tired you are. Why don't you go up and get some sleep?"

Katrina looked at him. The look on her face said she didn't want the evening to end, but she reluctantly acquiesced. "I guess I am tired."

Stephan nodded and escorted her up the stairs watching her bottom swish back and forth in front of him, swaying in time to the music that still played on the stereo in the living room. As she did her nightly ritual in the bathroom, he took advantage of the time to slip into his own pajamas, waiting patiently for her to finish. She emerged dressed in a shear pink nightgown and Stephan couldn't help but notice how the shade complimented her cheeks. He smiled and drew back the sheet and comforter. "Climb in," he instructed.

After obliging, he tucked the sheets up to Kat's chin, then under the mattress. Music playing downstairs drifted softly into the room while she snuggled into the comfortable sheets.

"Good night, Kitten." He bent down to give her a light kiss on her forehead.

Her honeysuckle smell engulfed him, like an

aphrodisiac making his body instantly hard. Her enticing scent cocooned him in its delicate aroma. He longed to take her in his arms. Only the thought that she no longer knew him, kept him from the bed. He turned on his heels to take his leave, trying to escape before he gave into temptation.

"Wait! Where are you going?" Kat sat up in the bed and grabbed his hand.

"I was going to leave you to your dreams. I need to go down and help Marcus finish cleaning the living room, so I too can go to sleep."

"Oh." The smile fell from her pretty face. Stephan noticed the disappointment in her eyes. Hope filled his heart.

"If you'd like me to stay for a while, I'm sure Marcus could clean up without me."

"I bet Marcus wouldn't mind if you stayed with me for a few minutes. In fact…" She hesitated as if not wanting to appear too brazen. "If you wanted to you could sleep here tonight."

Stephan's face dropped in shock. Kat smiled and patted the empty bed on her other side. "Why don't you lie down? I know you must be tired."

Stephan didn't move, afraid to say or do anything that might ruin the invitation.

"I know we were a couple and this is your room. You shouldn't have to sleep on the couch downstairs when this bed is plenty big enough for the both of us." Kat looked up at him with expectant eyes.

He wanted nothing more than to join her, but he wasn't sure lying beside her was the best idea, especially in his current state of arousal. He didn't know if he could trust himself to keep his hands off her.

Stephan hesitated, his gaze troubled. "Are you sure?"

Katrina nodded her head. He pushed into her mind and discovered she wanted him to lie down beside her and hold her close. She didn't want intercourse, but she needed to feel his strong arms around her to help her feel safe and cherished. He could not help but give her that. He wanted to make her feel safe and loved as much as she wanted to feel it.

He struggled with his decision a moment, then ruthlessly pushed his lust aside and succumbed to the invitation, crawling under the sheets. He lay down beside her, careful not to jostle her as he lay on his back resting his head on his arm. Once he stilled, Kat rolled over and cuddled against his warm body, laying her head on his chest.

"Be careful, Kitten, you're still healing." Stephan brought his arm down, circling around her back. "You didn't overdo tonight with all the dancing, did you?" Concern thickened his voice, giving it a husky quality.

"No. I'm fine. I don't hurt anymore. I think I'm mostly healed," Kat reassured him, snuggling against his chest.

They lay together silently, his fingers running through her soft strands as she ran her fingers along his chest.

"I am so sorry we couldn't restore your memory," he murmured.

"It's okay, Stephan." He winced when she said his name without a hint of love or tenderness. "Who knows maybe one day something will trigger my memories."

As they lay together listening to the song, *In the Air Tonight,* drift softly up the stairs, Stephan caught

Kat under the chin and brought her face to his. Ever so softly he pressed his lips to hers. She responded immediately, rubbing her mouth back and forth, across his. His tongue darted out, licking along the seam of her lips. Her mouth instinctively opened at his teasing. Only then did he taste the sweetness of her kiss. He poured everything he had into that one kiss, his passion, his love. His hands roamed over her back, pulling her gently against the hard evidence of his desire.

The kiss was liquid sex. Her hands roamed over his body until one landed behind his neck and the other in his hair.

His body burned from her touch. It came alive under her hands and lips. Each sensation felt like coming home. This bed, this music, this moment, all felt right. And if her reaction to him was any indication, she felt the same way.

He broke the hold on her lips and began feathering kisses down her neck until he got to the soft spot where her neck met her shoulder. His tongue flicked out to lick her pulse as it beat below her creamy skin. He felt her stiffen in his arms. It stilled him when nothing else could and he looked at her questioningly.

She framed his face in her hands, looking deeply into his sapphire eyes. "Stephan," she breathed, eyes welling with tears.

With that one word he knew. It was the way in which she said his name, with all of the love and passion she used to use when saying those syllables. He gazed at her, his eyes widening as he sat up. His mind raced along with his beating heart.

Did he dare to hope?

"Kat, are your memories back? Do you remember

me, Kitten?"

It took Kat a few moments to form her answer to his question. "Give me…a minute."

Concern had him pushing once more into her mind. Her memories tore across her mind like merciless talons, clawing their way through her mental haze as she struggled to understand them. The memories came out of order, disjointed, a kaleidoscope of colors and images that made her dizzy.

"Yes." The word gushing from her lips like a hiss from a snake. "Oh my God, yes. I remember…everything."

The combination of the familiar music along with his passionate love must have awakened the memory of their life together. Stephan gazed at her and smiled. He grabbed her tightly to his chest and he turned them over.

"Do you remember everything, even what I am?" he asked hesitantly, easing his grip.

Kat thought for a moment, as if trying to understand his question. Finally she nodded against his muscular chest. "Yes, I remember that you are a vampire and an Alpha."

He released the breath he hadn't realized he was holding and squeezed her again tightly against his body as relief flooded his every cell.

"I love you so much, *mein schatz!*" The knowledge that he could finally express his feelings for her without worrying it would push her away eased the tension in his body.

Kat pushed up from his chest, looking at him with eyes that sparkled with her love for him. "Stephan, I love you too. I'll love you for all eternity, *mein* Alpha."

Epilogue

In the last three weeks, Kat had discovered the true bliss of being Stephan's heartmate. Never in her life had she been so happy, so cared for.

So loved.

It was more than just Stephan's ministrations, though what woman wouldn't love having a drop-dead gorgeous hunk of a man indulge her every desire and whim, but it was also being able to share all her happiness with her best friend, Marcus.

She realized she finally understood what it meant to have a family as she came down the stairs and joined Marcus at the kitchen table. "Hi, Kitty Kat," he greeted her. "Or should I call you Mrs. von Haas?"

"Hey yourself." Kat gave him a kiss on the cheek.

Marcus raked her with his gaze. "Man, you were beautiful as a mortal, but you are smoking hot as a vampire. The conversion went well I see. It's good to see you up and about."

Once Stephan had convinced her he'd only wiped her memory to protect her and vowed to never tamper with her head again, Katrina agreed to be converted. The thought of an eternity with Stephan won out over her phobia of him drinking from her. Well that, and the knowledge that his healing assistance would make the process less painful than what she'd already suffered at Gage's hands.

"Thanks." A smile spread across Katrina's face. "It wasn't fun, but I'd go through anything to spend eternity with Stephan."

"Even the wedding?" Marcus teased, knowing darn well she'd loved every minute of their ceremony.

A wedding had been superfluous really because, as it had been explained to Katrina, heartmates stayed together for eternity, but she demanded the official commitment, so they went to one of the numerous wedding chapels in the city for a quickie wedding. After escorting Kat down the aisle in her long white gown, Marcus stood as their witness watching Stephan and Kat exchange their vows before the justice of the peace.

"So what should I call you now? Stephan's like my father since he is my sire so that would make you like my sister because he sired you too, but you are also like my mother since you are his heartmate and wife. So should I call you Mom or Sissy?"

Kat chuckled. "I think Kat will do, thank you very much. But if you keep giving me a hard time, I'll take on my mommy role and take you out to the preverbial woodshed."

"I'm still more than two centuries older than you, Kat. You don't want to get into a contest of powers with me."

Kat put her hands on her hips. "Oh yeah, how do you know what powers I have?"

"You just went through your transition. Stephan hasn't had time to teach you anything yet."

"I have always been able to take you on, Marcus."

"Only because I'd let you win," he joked back.

Stephan came up behind Kat and kissed her on the

neck. "Now, now children. Let's play nice."

"I think I liked her more when she didn't remember us. It's too bad she got her memories back," Marcus quipped, earning a laugh from her heartmate.

"Yeah, yeah." Kat waved a dismissive hand and noticed the set of luggage sitting by the door. "What's with the bags? You're not leaving me are you, Stephan?"

"They're not mine," he declared, shrugging his shoulders.

"They're mine." Marcus rose. "I'm leaving."

"Where are you going?" inquired Stephan, as he slid an arm around Kat's shoulders and tucked her against his side.

"To my home in Savannah."

Alarm crept up her spine. "That's a lot of bags. When will you be back?" Kat did not bother keeping her distress from her voice.

"Not for a while. I'm moving out."

Her heart seemed to sink to her toes and Stephan placed a soothing hand on the back of Kat's neck. He ran the pad of his thumb across her muscles as if to ease the tension gathering there. *It will be okay, Kitten,* he sent over their private mindlink. *Do not fret.*

"I said you were welcome in our home as long as you would like to stay. Kat and I wish you to stay as long as you want to be here."

"I don't want you to go," cried Kat. She ran to Marcus, wrapping her arms around his waist.

Marcus returned the hug, but quickly put her away from him when a growl rumbled in Stephan chest. "Look, Kat, you know what they say. Three's a crowd. I can't stay here forever. You newlyweds need some privacy."

Tears fell from Kat's eyes which Marcus wiped away with the pad of his thumb. "Look Kitty Kat, I'll be around." He took his cell out of his pocket and shook it back and forth. "I'm only a phone call away."

The buzzer rang. Stephan answered it and came back to Marcus. "Your ride is here."

"Well, I guess it's time to go." He gave Kat another quick hug, then gripped Stephan forearms in the grasp of warriors. "I'll be seeing ya." He grabbed his bags and left without looking back.

"Bye," Kat called after him as the door shut behind him. She turned into her lover's waiting arms and allowed him to surround her with his love.

Stephan held Kat allowing her tears to wet his shirt. "Please don't cry, Kitten. We'll see him again."

"I-I know. I just feel like I lost my best friend. Will you promise me we'll see Marcus soon?"

"I promise," Stephan vowed. Kat pulled back, wiping the tears from her eyes.

Knowing she could trust her husband to keep his promises, she smiled. "Do you also promise to teach me how to use my new vampire powers, so I can kick his butt the next time we see him?"

Stephan grinned down at her. "I promise," he repeated. "I have so much to teach you."

She grabbed his hand and led him toward the stairs.

"Where are we going?" he asked.

Katrina looked at him over her shoulder. "You're going to teach me…" She gave him a mischievous look that she knew would get his blood boiling. "…about vampire sex."

A word about the author...

Born in Virginia, Brenda Sparks now resides in the Sunshine State with her incredibly supportive husband and their beloved son.

Balancing her professional commitment to the local school district with her writing is challenging at times, but writing suspenseful paranormal romances is a passion that won't be denied. Her idea of a perfect day is one spent in front of a computer with a hot cup of coffee, her fingers flying over the keys to send her characters off on their latest adventure.

Brenda loves to connect with readers. Please visit her online or stop by her website to say hi:

www.brenda-sparks.com